SHIP OF GOLD

Also by Thomas B. Allen and Norman Polmar

RICKOVER: CONTROVERSY AND GENIUS

SHIP OF GOLD

THOMAS B. ALLEN

and

NORMAN POLMAR

NAVAL INSTITUTE PRESS

Annapolis, Maryland

This book has been brought to publication with the generous assistance of Marguerite and Gerry Lenfest.

Naval Institute Press
291 Wood Road
Annapolis, MD 21402

Originally published by Macmillan Publishing Company in 1987.

First Naval Institute Press paperback edition published in 2014.
ISBN: 978-1-59114-072-6 (paperback)
ISBN: 978-1-61251-527-4 (ebook)

The Library of Congress has cataloged the hardcover edition as follows:
Allen, Thomas B.
Ship of gold.
I. Polmar, Norman. II. Title.
PS3551.L43S55 1987. 813′.54 86-23683

♾ Print editions meet the requirements of ANSI/NISO z39.48-1992 (Permanence of Paper).
Printed in the United States of America.

26 25 24 23 22 21 9 8 7 6 5 4

Cover image: The heavy lift ship *Hughes Glomar Explorer.*

For Scottie and Beverly

SHIP OF GOLD

PROLOGUE

On the night of March 31, 1945, the U.S. submarine *Tigerfish,* rolling on the surface through a low-hanging fog, turned north toward the Formosa Strait. She was about midway between Hong Kong and the southern tip of Formosa when her radar detected a surface ship.

During five weeks on patrol, the *Tigerfish* had not fired a torpedo, and her commanding officer, Commander David Gordon Porter, was hungry for a kill. Porter, a 1933 graduate of the U.S. Naval Academy, had been the commanding officer of the *Tigerfish* ever since she was placed in commission in March of 1944. He had turned thirty-two a few days before the commissioning. Porter had had an outstanding academic and athletic record at the academy, and he was achieving a similarly outstanding war record. Senior officers with whom he had worked all had marked him as a man who would someday wear an admiral's stars.

This was the fourth time Porter had taken the *Tigerfish* out on patrol. The first patrol had been a triumph. When the submarine returned to Guam from that patrol, one of the cooks had carefully painted six small flags on each side of the *Tigerfish*'s conning tower—five with red "meatballs" for merchant ships sunk and one rising-sun flag for the destroyer that the "Tigers" sent to the bottom. In subsequent ceremonies on the *Tigerfish*'s deck, Vice Admiral Charles Lockwood, commander of Pacific Fleet submarines, had pinned the Navy Cross on Porter's chest. Several of his officers and enlisted men, lined up on the narrow deck in their dress whites, received other awards.

On her second patrol, the *Tigerfish* had sunk three merchant ships and a small auxiliary aircraft carrier. These kills had earned Porter a second Navy Cross. On her third patrol, working with two other submarines in a "wolf pack," the *Tigerfish* was credited with only one-third of an oiler. And this, her fourth patrol, was even worse. Nothing. Nothing but frustration and boredom for the submarine's eight officers and seventy-five enlisted men. In Porter, the frustration evolved into hatred—for the war, for the rough weather, for the enemy.

Now, told of the radar contact, he bolted from his cabin, trotted the twelve steps to the control room, and clambered up the steel ladder to the submarine's conning tower.

Staring over the shoulder of the radar operator, Porter peered at the small greenish scope, trying to pick out the luminescent pip of a ship from the background clutter. The radar gave returns from the high seas as the low-lying submarine rolled, making the screen look like a forest, with the target ship a solid dot moving slowly through the trees.

Eighteen-year-old Troy Dodson was the best radar operator on the *Tigerfish*. His young eyes often could find a target on the green pulsating radar screen precious seconds before the two other operators on board would see it.

"Captain," said Dodson, pointing to the glowing dot on the screen, "she's moving fast—about 18,000 yards dead ahead."

After a few seconds at the radar scope, Porter climbed up another ladder to the submarine's open fog-shrouded bridge atop the conning tower and turned his eyes toward the bearing of the invisible target. The *Tigerfish* was dogging the ship, slowly coming into torpedo range.

As the *Tigerfish* closed on the target, the radar detections were fed directly to the TDC—torpedo data computer—located at the back of the conning tower. There a man everyone called "Dakota"—the chief torpedoman and, at forty, the oldest and most experienced man aboard the *Tigerfish*—bent over the primitive computer with his two assistants crowding in. Normally, an officer ran the TDC in attack, but Porter had given the job to Dakota. He was too good to replace at the kill. No one remembered his real name or even the significance of his nickname. Dakota was the sub's expert on "the box," as the TDC was usually called. Information about the target ship, from periscope sightings or radar detection, was fed into the TDC. Its wheels turned and whirred as it sought to estimate a target ship's course and speed and then determine the proper setting for the *Tigerfish*'s torpedoes.

"Jim, let's set up for a stern shot," Porter told his executive officer, Lieutenant James Barrett, by telephone. "If she is a destroyer, I want to be able to make knots or dive away from her if we miss." Below him, in the conning tower, Bennett immediately began preparing for the firing of torpedoes from the *Tigerfish*'s four stern tubes.

"Captain, the TDC has a solution." The TDC's slowly turning dials had stopped. A red light in the shape of the letter *F*—for fire—began to glow.

"Standing by aft. Outer tube doors open," came a report seconds later from the after torpedo room. At the same moment, the TDC transmitted course and depth directions directly to the four torpedoes in the *Tigerfish*'s stern tubes.

The unseen target was still steaming at about sixteen knots through darkness and fog. Her speed and size, as indicated by radar, gave her the appearance of a destroyer. Her course was taking her into the Formosa Strait. The distance separating her from the *Tigerfish* was down to 1,500 yards.

At precisely eleven o'clock, the submarine's stern swung around until it was pointing toward a position several hundred yards ahead of the moving target.

"Shoot!" Porter ordered.

"Fire one," called Barrett. And at two-second intervals, "Fire two . . . fire three . . . fire four."

"Torpedo run time?" asked Porter, his elbow now holding down the press-to-talk key as he steadied his binoculars in the presumed direction of his target.

"One thousand two hundred yards, sir. Two minutes."

There was no response from Porter.

Suddenly, one of the lookouts standing on the platform five feet above Porter called out, "Captain . . . I thought I saw something. Bearing almost dead astern. A flash of white . . . not a light but . . . well, not a light directly, but like something painted white . . . sir."

"Where?"

"Dead astern . . . . There! I thought I just saw it again, sir."

Porter could see nothing.

Below Porter, in the conning tower's eerie red light, Barrett and the others shivered slightly as the cold night air swept down through the bridge's open hatch. Dakota gave thirty-second checks: "one-thirty" and then, thirty seconds later, "Mark."

His last word was never heard on the *Tigerfish*'s open bridge. Less than a mile astern of the ship there was a loud explosion and a muted flash. Seconds later there was another. Then silence.

"Score another one for the ol' cat," screamed one of the sailors in the conning tower. Throughout the *Tigerfish* everyone was cheering and patting one another on the back.

"Jim, let's see if we can pick up a survivor or two for some of the intelligence people back at Guam,'' said Porter as the cheering died down.

The *Tigerfish* turned and slowly headed toward the flash. Soon the submarine was moving through water dotted with debris. Oil gleamed on the water, and a lookout quietly said, ''There they are, sir.''

At first only a couple, and then several, and finally some two dozen figures could be seen moving and bobbing in the water. As the *Tigerfish* nosed toward the men in the water, the Japanese tried to swim away or dive underwater. No one would let the submarine near him.

''Hey, sir, I think a Jap wants to come aboard,'' yelled one of the men on the bow. He cradled a shotgun in his arms. Near him stood two men with Thompson submachine guns.

''Toss him one of those knotted lines and get someone to help him aboard,'' Porter ordered. ''And strip him down. Make sure he hasn't got a grenade wired to him somewhere.''

As the Japanese man reached the side of the *Tigerfish,* the swells smashed him again and again against the hull of the submarine. His hands coated with oil, he could not grasp the knotted rope. Finally, a sailor handed his submachine gun to another, doffed his jacket and shoes, and slid down the rope into the water to help the Japanese aboard.

On the deck, the survivor's trousers, his only clothing, were stripped from his shivering body. No hand grenades or other weapons were found. He wore neither shoes nor shirt. Almost unconscious, he was carried to the forward hatch, pushed down into the forward torpedo room, and ministered to by Mike Paulson, the submarine's pharmacist's mate.

Eight months before, the *Tigerfish* had plowed through the dead and dying of another Japanese ship sunk by an American submarine. The victims then were hundreds of Australian and British prisoners of war who were being taken to POW camps in Japan. They were the men who had survived the building of what would become known as the bridge over the River Kwai. The *Tigerfish* had found only eighteen men still alive. And one of them had died aboard the submarine.

Now, remembering those gaunt bodies, Porter looked down at the Japanese who were still alive and swimming away from the submarine. He jabbed a finger at a cluster of bobbing heads and shouted to the sailors at the bow, ''Kill them. Kill every one of those bastards.'' The sailors on the deck below him looked at each other for a moment, and then a red-haired sailor lifted up his Thompson and began firing. The others had their guns up within seconds. After ten minutes there were no more floating bodies—dead or alive. In the fog-shrouded air the smell of cordite was heavy, and as the sailors on deck walked around, their feet crunched on spent shell casings, which tumbled down between the planks that formed the submarine's outer deck and clanked against the steel pressure hull below.

Mike Paulson did not like Japs, but he knew what the book said about treating prisoners, and so, in his makeshift aid station in the forward torpedo room, he bathed the oil off the little man, swabbed antiseptic on cuts on his face and chest, and found a pair of dungarees and a skivvy shirt for him.

The prisoner was on a bunk above a torpedo reload, still groggy, when Porter appeared.

"There won't be any more, Mike," he said.

Porter looked briefly at the Japanese man, scowled, and seemed about to say something but turned and went aft, toward his cabin, to write a routine report on the sinking.

Secured from general quarters, the *Tigerfish* turned toward the southern edge of her patrol area. When the Japanese survivor regained full consciousness, Lieutenant Edward Haynes, the communications officer, was summoned. Haynes, using his Japanese phrase book, had spent an hour practicing phrases: "What was your ship?" "Where was she coming from?" "Where was she going?" But, in response to the halting first question, the survivor said softly, "I can speak English."

In answer to Haynes' next question—"What was your ship?"—the Japanese said, "The prisoner supply ship *Osaka Maru*."

"My God," Haynes said. "Get the captain."

1

SHORTLY BEFORE NOON ON THURSDAY, July 26, 1979, Captain David G. Porter, U.S. Navy (Retired), emerged from the Farragut West subway station in downtown Washington, one block from the Army and Navy Club. Porter had lunched there, usually alone, every Thursday since he had moved to Washington two months before. Thursday was the day the retired Navy cook at the club produced a curry that took Porter back to his early days aboard ship, a cruiser and then a gunboat on the China station.

Porter paused for a moment at the window of The Map Store near the southeast corner of I and Seventeenth Street, then walked briskly to the curb and waited for the traffic light to change to "Walk." He did not notice the short, stocky man who had followed him from his apartment in Arlington, Virginia, who had been a few steps behind him on the escalator at Farragut West, and who now stood directly behind him. The man, like Porter and several other men in the lunch-hour crowd, wore a light tan suit.

A car—a witness would later describe it as "black or maybe some other dark color with a dirty license plate"—turned onto I Street from Seventeenth Street. The car picked up speed and swerved toward the curb where Porter stood. At the same moment, the man in the light tan suit placed both of his hands against Porter's back and shoved.

The car's bumper hit Porter hard enough to hurl him several feet. He landed face down, his arms at his side. As he tried to lift his head, the car's front right wheel and rear right wheel passed over him. A woman screamed, and, while every eye watched the car speed away, the man in the light tan suit walked quickly back to the subway entrance and disappeared.

The police officially designated Porter a victim of a hit-and-run driver.

From identification papers in Porter's wallet, the police established that Porter was a sixty-seven-year-old retired naval officer and member of the Navy Submarine League whose permanent home was in California. The stubs in his meticulously kept checkbook showed that for the past six months he had paid $210 per month for an efficiency apartment in the high-rise area of Arlington near Crystal City, which was just across the Potomac from Washington. Arlington police were notified, and an officer went to the apartment where Porter had lived alone.

"No local next of kin," the Arlington officer wrote in his report.

After a cursory autopsy to confirm the cause of death that the crushed chest made obvious, Porter's body was no longer of interest to police. It was released to a funeral director who had a contract with the District of Columbia for burying indigents and other people whose bodies were not immediately claimed. Because Porter was obviously no indigent, the funeral director was more zealous than usual in trying to find a next of kin who might pay for a first-class funeral.

Through a friend with the Arlington police, the funeral director had been shown Porter's personal effects from his apartment, which included an Army and Navy Club card, a U.S. Naval Academy Alumni Association card, and a letter from a man who seemed to be another retired naval officer. The funeral director called another friend, one who worked in the death and survivors' benefits office of the Naval Military Personnel Command. Over the years his funeral home had buried many retired naval officers.

By then, Porter's next of kin—a married daughter living in Houston, Texas—had learned of his death through that same Navy office. Responding to the Navy's telegram with a phone call, she said that she had not seen her father in fifteen years. She said she vaguely remembered that he had wished to be cremated and have his ashes consigned to the sea. Within fifteen minutes, the funeral director was on the phone to her. She agreed to a ceremony that would involve the transporting of Porter's ashes to Annapolis, where they would be tastefully scattered into Chesapeake Bay, "almost within sight of the Naval Academy."

The Navy personnel file of David Gordon Porter was closed and stamped "Deceased." It soon would be reopened.

2

Harry Gunnison let the phone ring once, twice, then a third time. He was in no hurry to answer. He was seated at a large table—a slab of teak held up by four long, slender legs—and he was writing a letter to his sister, who had written him a letter again asking for money. "I know you think I make a lot of money in what you call my 'mysterious Washington job'," he had begun. "But let me tell—" And the phone had rung.

After the fourth ring he answered, "Gunnison."

"Let's take a walk," the voice said, then a click and dial tone.

Gunnison looked at his watch, which had hands and Arabic numbers. He was a conservative man who believed in keeping digital displays in computers, where they belonged, and he thought of that fact about himself at the moment he looked at his watch. For a while now he had noticed that he had been indulging in such moments of introspection. He wondered if it had to do with the passage of time—he had turned forty-four a week before—or with a subconscious reaction to the double number of his age, a hangover from a brush with numerology in Vietnam so long ago. Damn. His mind was drifting. Was that part of it, too? Part of getting not old exactly, but older?

All that from looking at his watch. He had twenty-five minutes until his meeting with Jessen.

The strange call was the way Jessen arranged meetings. If Gunnison could not make it, he was to call back instantly. The number would put him through to one of Jessen's gadgets in Langley, and Gunnison would find himself saying something cryptic to a tape recorder. Jessen liked the telephone for messages but not for conversations. So he had two ways of summoning Gunnison. "Let's take a walk" meant a rendezvous in thirty minutes at the Library of Congress. "Let's take a walk *here*" meant that Gunnison would go to the underground garage of the House of Representatives' Longworth Office Building. Precisely thirty minutes after the call, an unmarked, black government car would roll up, Gunnison would get in, and a silent driver would take him across the Potomac and up the George Washington Parkway for the fifteen-minute drive to the headquarters of the Central Intelligence Agency in Langley, Virginia.

The trip to visit Jessen in Langley usually meant a discussion about something relatively sensitive; the rendezvous at the library often turned out to be little more than a brief chat, an exchange of information about someone they both knew. Either way, Gunnison received pay for a full day's work as a CIA contract consultant.

Gunnison switched the phone on his desk to auto-answer and swung around to an open rolltop desk. He dropped the half-finished letter, still on its yellow-lined pad, onto the top of the desk, rolled down the hood, and locked it. He glanced at the two filing cabinets on the other side of the small, sparsely furnished room. Their lock-bars were in place. He walked across the gleaming parquet, opened the oak door, closed it behind him, and locked it with one of six keys on a brass ring he then returned to his pocket. He crossed a room whose walls were lined with shelves stuffed with books, passing through shafts of late-morning light and shadows cast by the bars on the outside of two tall windows.

A car door slammed. Instinctively, he stopped and, standing by the edge of one of the curtained windows, noted another liquor delivery to his neighbor, the staff director of a Senate committee. The house was narrow, but the yard was unusually wide for Capitol Hill, and so the front windows commanded a broad view of the entire block.

Gunnison had noticed that advantage when he had bought the house years ago. He liked being on the alley, away from the corner and the traffic that ceaselessly flowed along Fourth Street. When he bought the house, he had done much of the restoration himself. He liked to think of his efforts as a handsome compromise between the dictates of historical authenticity and a desire for comfortable modern living. The bars on the windows were a commitment to the reality of Capitol Hill, where the haves lived surrounded by the have-nots. The first-floor rooms at the rear of the house—his office and the kitchen—not only had bars but also steel shutters, which could be snapped shut each night at the flick of a switch.

He had been cautious since his early twenties, when, as a Navy enlisted man, he had briefly taken up scuba diving as a sport. Now his only physical recreation was walking, particularly around Capitol Hill, and some pushups and situps in his basement, almost every morning. He weighed twenty more pounds than he had weighed when he had been diving regularly. But he felt that, at one hundred and eighty-five pounds and five-feet-ten, he was almost where he should be on the charts he never looked at. Almost.

He paused in the entrance hall and, as he habitually did, gazed for a moment at a small white jade carving that rested on a pedestal on a black lacquered table. The carving seemed part fish, part dragon. When he looked at the carving, he usually thought about nothing except looking at it. But if there was an icon in Gunnison's life, it was that carving. And, like most icons, it had lost its aura of wonder but retained in its beauty a sense of mystery.

Gunnison stooped to pick up the mail that lay on a hooked rug below the front door's brass mail slot. He scanned the envelopes, put one on a table by the door, dropped four into a wicker wastepaper basket under the table, and kept one in his left hand. He turned around and walked up the steep staircase that ended in a narrow, blindingly bright, white-walled hall, the light from the sun palpably hot on the back of Gunnison's neck. Sighing, he walked around the balustrade, closed the blind on the window at one end of the hall, and turned on the air-conditioning unit jutting from the sill. He opened the door to the right of the balustrade and walked into a room hotter and more radiant than the hall. The opening of the door stirred the air just enough to ripple a mosquito-net canopy that hung from a ring attached to the high ceiling and flowed over a large bed.

He stood in the doorway for a moment, feeling the heat engulf him. "You turned the goddamn air-conditioning off again," he said. He stepped closer. "And it's almost noon."

A small hand emerged from under the net, index finger pointing to a digital clock on the nightstand. "Eleven thirty-four," a soft voice said.

The canopy parted at the side of the bed, and a woman as white as the netting appeared. She held a fold against her for a moment, and in that moment she was blurred, ghostly. He watched as she took that moment and made it hers, made it something to pose within. She turned toward him and placed her hands upon her slim, bare hips in a mocking display of anger. She moved her head slightly, and her black hair swirled, framing her oval face and coming to rest in strands that draped her shoulders. She jutted her lower lip. Then she restored her face to its usual repose and said, "Goddamn it yourself, Harry. I hate *your* air-conditioning. That is a letter for me?"

"Yes. You have good eyes, Chia Min. From your mother."

"Not just good eyes. Good sense. You never take your mail into our bedroom."

"*Our* bedroom but *my* air-conditioning?"

"Yes. Why not?"

"Why not." Gunnison repeated.

She rose from the bed and went into the adjacent bathroom but did not shut the door. He shifted so that he could not see her sitting on the toilet. He had asked her innumerable times to close the door. She had always laughed at his priggish Western reaction to her unabashed oriental habit.

He heard the flush. She emerged brushing her teeth.

"I have to go out," he said.

"I heard the phone. *Your* phone. Not the one that rings here. Business?"

"I guess so. I'll call if it looks like he's going to keep me very long."

She held out her arms, and he went to her. Her mouth was cold and wet. Her back and rump felt unreasonably cool. He lingered for a moment, but duty and Jessen called.

He took a seersucker jacket and a pale blue tie from his closet and went downstairs. He tied the tie while looking in the hall mirror, then loosened it, and unbuttoned the top button of his shirt. No need to wear the costume until he had to. He took another look at the lone envelope he had left on the table. His sister again. He picked up the envelope and tapped it against the edge of the table, then tossed it into the wastepaper basket with the other discards. But a moment later he retrieved it, put it into the inside pocket of his jacket, draped the jacket over his arm, and opened the door to the damp, engulfing heat of Washington in August. He locked the door behind him, crossed the small porch, and took four steps to a low ornamental gate. At the sidewalk he turned left, toward First Street, and then walked up to Independence Avenue, toward the tiered green dome of the Library of Congress. He felt his mind drifting again; it was too hot to concentrate on anything more demanding than walking, and so he drifted into wondering what it was that Jessen wanted him to do.

He liked Jessen more than he had liked anyone else he had worked with or for in the agency for many years. But he had never quite figured Jessen out. Both of them knew enough to recognize the absurdity that often lay unacknowledged within the agency's most elaborate operations. Unlike most officers at his level, however, Jessen did not talk about this greatest of secrets, this priesthood knowledge: Much of what we do is futile. Jessen did not go to the parties in the trim clapboard houses in McLean where the bitter men drifted off into corners, drank too much, and told their funny and tragic stories. Jessen was a loner but not the kind that merely acted that way to gain a reputation as a man of cool hands and cool head. His solitude had been somewhat costly. He had been maintained as a midlevel officer, passed over just enough to keep him edgy for promotion yet not discouraged enough to quit.

And you can't really quit anyway, Gunnison thought. I quit, and here I am, walking to the library, still working for Jessen and the agency, still wondering what makes him tick, still thinking I know him better than anybody else does.

Gunnison crossed to Independence Avenue and continued on First Street, alongside the library. In the library's Neptune fountain, the water flowed as languidly and heavily as the air, and the bronze green sea nymphs looked sweaty. A wisp of hot mist brushed his face as he ascended the steps by the fountain. In the shade at the top of the steps, he stopped to let three formidable matrons spin through the revolving doors. Over their emerging heads, framed in the arch of the entranceway, he could see a black car parked in one of the driveway spaces marked "Reserved."

He recognized the driver. The car was a small limousine, scaled to Jessen's middle-rung status, Senior National Intelligence Officer for Far East Region. The license plate, from the agency's reserved block of Virginia tags, would not appear in motor-vehicle registration files. The driver would be armed and trained in evasive driving.

Jessen was sitting on a marble bench under a mural of the muse of lyric poetry, attended by Passion, Beauty, Mirth, Pathos (eyes raised to heaven), Truth, and Devotion (bowed head). Gunnison, who prided himself on knowing Washington trivia, greeted Jessen by pointing out the attendants of the muse. Jessen smiled, nodded, and, without looking up at the mural, said, "Let's take a walk."

"Christ, Charlie! Don't you ever get tired of this spookery? Why can't we talk here? It's cool and quiet."

"The library is sensitive about agency activities taking place here."

"Activities? What did you have in mind? Kidnapping the poetry consultant? Besides, we—you, the agency—has an office here. I've been in it."

"Research. A research office. Nonoperational. We meet here for *your* convenience, Harry."

"And the reserved parking space?" That was always a consideration on Capitol Hill.

Jessen shrugged and turned toward the archway that led to the lobby and the revolving door. Gunnison followed him through the door, and they began walking slowly down First Street. They turned left along the south side of the library and then west along Independence Avenue.

"One last try, Charlie. We could talk here, you know. Or we could get into your car, which is as obvious as a police cruiser trailing a whore down Fourteenth Street."

"It must be the heat, Harry. You're more bitchy than usual. Chia Min giving you a rough time?" They had walked past the library and turned onto Pennsylvania Avenue.

"Can you arrange to get her deported? I'd like that. Today I'd like that."

"Too bad, Harry. I thought you'd be one of the lucky ones. No midlife crisis. And I thought you took your birthday awfully well the other night."

"Yeah. Thanks for the tie."

"Thanks for wearing it. You know, if you still worked in Langley, you would never wear it there."

"But I'm a consultant now, and so I think I have to stay on your good side, and so I wear it when I see you."

"Something like that. Here?"

Gunnison could not decide whether the single word was a question or a statement.

Jessen opened the door to a neighborhood restaurant-bar, the Hawk and Dove. The black car pulled up to a nearby bus stop and parked next to a no-parking sign.

In the cool gloom they found a booth. Jessen took the bench facing the door. They asked for draft beers, and Jessen told the waitress they would order lunch in a while. When she left, Jessen leaned forward and said, "We have a strange one, Harry. Take a look at this." Jessen reached into his inner coat pocket for a folded piece of paper, which he gave to Gunnison.

Unfolding the paper, Gunnison could see the "secret" markings and the message format that indicated a classified agency communication. Even in the murk of the Hawk and Dove he hesitated to fully unfold it. As a consultant he had no right to handle classified material in a public place. Neither did Jessen. But Jessen sometimes broke a rule, sometimes just to break it.

Gunnison began to read the message. Two words stopped him: *Glomar Explorer.*

The *Glomar.* He had interviewed and proposed men for her crew. He had been one of the principal agency handlers of the ship's ostensible owner, Howard Hughes. And if Hughes, growing madder every day, had insisted on sailing aboard the *Glomar,* Gunnison had been selected—"tasked" in the agency's Orwellian prose—to help decide if Hughes was to come back from the operation alive. As it turned out, neither Hughes nor Gunnison had gone on the *Glomar* when she sailed on her top-secret mission. Gunnison was back in Langley when the stories came in: The hauling up of part of the Soviet submarine. Opening it. Like a sardine can, somebody said. But the sardines were men, corpses. "And we put them over the side, with one of our guys reading from a goddamn Russian Bible. . . ."

He went back to the message. It was from Steve Dysart, the current commanding officer of the *Glomar,* in a back-channel communication relayed through the agency station chief in Tokyo: "Sudden change of plans. *Glomar* taken to Ishiwata-owned shipyard in Kagoshima. Charter owner orders me ashore. Said unneeded except at sea. Suspect ship being rigged for deep-sea grab of wreck not on 5/24/79 list. Request instructions."

Gunnison looked up from the message. "I can figure out a little of this, but I need some background. Any more?" As he spoke he could see Jessen reaching into his pocket again. He played poker that way, too. A card at a time.

"I'll give you the big brief back in the office," Jessen said. "For now, I just want to tell you enough to see if you'll do a little job. Now take a look at this."

He handed Gunnison a Xerox copy of a story from an inside page in the Metro section of *The Washington Post* dated July 27, 1979.

"Recognize the name?" Jessen asked.

"Sure. I remember seeing the story."

"What do you know about Porter?"

"Come on, Charlie. You've got it all on the computers. What do you need me for?"

"Don't be coy, Harry. I want to hear it from the beginning, from you." Jessen held up his fingers for two more beers as the waitress walked past.

"Porter," Gunnison began. "David Porter. A Navy Cross. But a bad court-martial. When I was helping to recruit for the *Glomar,*

I had the Navy run a search for submarine and diving officers who had been court-martialed. The idea was that they would have training, a naval background, and maybe they would want to do something to help the country to make up for whatever it was they had done."

"I remember, Harry. Not a bad idea. And Porter?"

"I didn't even approach him. He was really clean. He had a perfectly fine career before and after his court-martial. He wasn't a potential candidate for me. Anyway, by the time I had got to his name we were pretty well crewed."

"Now, Harry. Let's see how good your memory is about the court-martial."

"Porter was court-martialed because he sank a Japanese ship. That was so incredible that I looked into it. I was curious. I wanted to see what in God's name could make the Navy do that, court-martial a submarine skipper for sinking an enemy ship in wartime."

"And?"

"And it turned out that the reason was that the U.S. government had guaranteed the ship safe passage so she could take medical supplies to Allied prisoners of war. It was toward the end of the war, as I remember. She had delivered the supplies and was returning to Japan, traveling under safe passage when Porter sank her. He said he hadn't got the word."

"You checked the court-martial records?"

"No. I mentioned it to one of the Navy guys I was working with and he remembered there was a piece about it in a Navy journal—the *Proceedings*."

"Right," Jessen said. "You remember right, Harry. There's a record showing you checked a copy of the *Naval Institute Proceedings* that ran that piece out of the agency library."

Gunnison looked up, startled. "What the hell is this, Charlie? You know the answers to all the questions you're asking me." He nodded over Jessen's shoulder. "The waitress. We better order lunch."

Jessen turned and waved her away. "We won't eat here, Harry. It's not my kind of place." He put money for the beers and a tip on the table and stood up. "We'll eat at my desk."

They stepped into the shimmering heat, the small black car pulled up, and they climbed into the backseat. The car was cool.

3

"SORRY ABOUT THE CUTE QUESTIONS back there, Harry," Jessen said. "Somebody snatched those court-martial records. You knew your way around Navy archives . . . and I had to check it. My way. Now we can get down to business."

Jessen leaned back against the gray headrest and picked up the toy-size phone to tell his office that he was heading back to Langley. The car stopped on the approach to the Fourteenth Street bridge. It was not rush hour, but a car had broken down in the right lane, slowing traffic as cars tried to cross the bridge into Virginia and turn onto the George Washington Parkway. Gunnison looked over toward the Jefferson Memorial and the horde of tourists.

He didn't want to look at Jessen. He knew he should have been hurt, offended, insulted. The words sounded vague as they formed and vanished in his mind. Gunnison and Jessen did not talk to each other in vague words, and Gunnison wondered why they had come into his mind. He was not focusing. He thought again of the letter from his sister. That was where the vague words came from. Catherine's letters always oozed with them.

"Thanks for the vote of confidence, Charlie," he said, again talking to Jessen's profile.

"I said I had to do it my way, Harry." Jessen turned and smiled. "You wouldn't want one of our gumshoes to do it for me, would you?"

Gunnison did not answer.

Jessen leaned forward and picked up a worn brown briefcase. Two long straps dangled from it, but the small brass hasp was locked. Jessen pulled a ring of keys from his coat pocket and clicked open the hasp. He riffled through several folders and handed one to Gunnison. "Scan this while you brood," he said. "The more you read now, the quicker you can get out of my office."

The folder contained what appeared to be a draft of a report for the director. The cover sheet, which digested the report, was dated June 27. Gunnison skipped that page and turned to the beginning of the report, a long paragraph labeled "Perspective." That was always the way Jessen started a report, no matter what the agency style manual said.

> On December 20, 1977, at the U.S. Embassy in Tokyo, during a holiday reception, one of the guests, a banking executive named Ishiwata Seno, approached the agency station chief and requested an appointment for the following day.

Gunnison looked up from the report. "This looks a little dry-cleaned. What do you know about Ishiwata that's not in here?"

"It looks dry-cleaned," Jessen said, "because it's short and in English, not like the usual crap they pass around out at Langley. To answer your question, Ishiwata is clean. And he has connections that go back to occupation days. He was a clean young Japanese banker after the war, and he's a clean old Japanese banker now."

"He just walked right up to our man? He knew which assistant to the ambassador to tap?"

"Sure. He knew our man. But that's not so surprising. Those bankers have a very good net."

Gunnison went back to reading the report. Ishiwata presented a formal proposal. He said he had organized a syndicate that was interested in chartering the *Glomar Explorer* for the purpose of locating and salvaging wrecks in and near Japanese home waters. He said that the syndicate included members of the *Soji*. There was a footnote to explain this term. Instead of reading it, Gunnison looked up and asked Jessen, who had just taken another folder from his briefcase.

"Just *read,* Harry," Jessen said, irritably. "For God's sake. It's in English."

"Bullshit. There's more here than meets the eye. The date on the draft is June 27, nearly two months ago. It was prepared for the director but never sent to him. Now it looks like it's being dusted off. What's going down?"

"Keep your mind on what we pay you for, Harry."

"And what is that?"

"You'll find out. As for the *Soji,* if you won't read that footnote, I'll tell you. It's a group of high-finance people. Mostly bankers. Nothing sinister. But they aren't Shriners. They go back to the nineteenth century, when the Japanese started discovering the world. They write poetry and—"

"And have enough to offer the agency twenty-five thousand bucks a day for the *Glomar*."

"They just want to make bucks, Harry. Like everybody else in Japan."

"Bankers," Gunnison said, half to himself. It would be better to call his sister Catherine instead of writing her. He would have to call her tonight. They would talk about bankers.

He went back to reading the report. Ishiwata said he wanted the *Glomar* for one month to conduct a feasibility study, using as his target a Japanese merchantman that had gone down during a storm in the Sea of Japan in 1973. If that operation went well, the group would then charter the *Glomar* for six additional months and would take an option for six more months.

Gunnison knew, slightly, the Tokyo station chief, a man named Riling. He had been on his first major overseas assignment only three months when Ishiwata approached him. Gunnison wondered how significant Ishiwata's timing had been. Riling offered little criticism about Ishiwata's proposal. He noted that Ishiwata declined to name his associates, and he said that the banker had been "guarded and cryptic" about what he expected to salvage from the wrecks.

Only under questioning, Riling said, was Ishiwata willing to reveal the heart of his scheme: Ships that were sunk during and just after the war, he said, contained lead ballast that had gained greatly in value during the decades. So had the coal hauled as cargo or fuel. These commodities, and "whatever durable goods can be cheaply removed," would be the object of the salvage. The ships themselves would not be lifted.

Gunnison started to ask a question, then answered it to himself. The *Glomar Explorer,* he remembered, had been modified since her original mission. That mission was to lift a Soviet missile submarine that had sunk after an internal explosion in April 1968 some 750 miles northwest of Oahu. The *Glomar* had a giant claw that could lift the shattered hulk of the 5,500-ton submarine from a depth of 18,000 feet. The claw slowly—over a period of days—brought a portion of the submarine up and into a "moon pool," a cavernous hangar inside the *Glomar,* where the wreckage was examined, parts and equipment removed and packaged for shipment to the United States, and the remains prepared for a return to the submarine's watery grave.

After the Soviet mission, the *Glomar* was laid up in reserve for several years and then was refitted as a deep-ocean exploration ship, but with her recovery claw intact. She would go to a site where seafloor minerals were likely and would then locate and suck up samples, using a device that resembled a huge vacuum cleaner. Ishiwata apparently intended to modify this device to suck up coal and would also change the lift system to act as an underwater staging for lead and other heavy cargo that would be hauled from the wrecks by robots or small manned submersibles. When the platform was loaded, it would be lifted up to the "moon deck." Structural modifications to the *Glomar* would be minimal for her new role. The giant lifting claw and certain other equipment would be removed.

Riling had passed Ishiwata's proposal along to Langley with a recommendation for approval. Riling's recommendation was endorsed by the ambassador. On his own, Riling had contacted the ship's handlers, an agency-front company in Vallejo, California, which also had endorsed the proposal.

"It looks like it was steamrollered," Gunnison said. Jessen did not answer. He motioned for the report, which Gunnison handed to him. They were nearing Langley's gates, and Gunnison assumed that Jessen wanted to have all classified material in his locked briefcase on the chance that the gate guard might look into the car. Gunnison wondered about Jessen's unusual caution.

The guard simply waved the car through the gate without stopping it. They drove into the building's underground entrance. Jessen signed in Gunnison, who was given a special visitor's pass. They did not speak on the elevator or in the third-floor corridor leading to Jessen's office. Gunnison was using the time to think. He forced himself to focus on the *Glomar* and Ishiwata, not on Catherine and her—no, *their*—troubles.

He was convinced that something in the Ishiwata-*Glomar* affair was ticking away. A routine event had begun to swell into something shapeless, large, and dangerous. No one knew when or how it was going to explode.

Gunnison had enough dealings with agency-front business activities to know that some of them eventually developed a life of their own. They went beyond their mandate as fronts and became enterprises whose managers wanted profits—money that went back to the home office in Langley to supplement appropriated funds. People in the agency did not call it the company merely in jest. Some of its enterprises made money. And, Gunnison thought, so did some of the people who ran them.

They were sitting in Jessen's office, whose two windows overlooking the woods of the CIA compound proclaimed his middle-rung status. Jessen sat easily behind a walnut desk, which, very correctly, did not have any clutter. Gunnison guessed that Jessen was always expecting an unexpected visitor who was going to ask embarrassing questions. He decided not to comment on Jessen's sudden change into a model bureaucrat.

But Gunnison did feel a compulsion to make another comment. Speaking slowly and articulating each syllable, he said, "I guess I can assume that I am being bugged."

Jessen rolled his eyes upward, pressed his hands flat on the desk, and sighed.

"I am making that assumption," Gunnison resumed in his normal voice, "because you only let me in on half of what I presume is a black tale. You showed me a report that was going somewhere, but didn't go there. You and your office have the air of an accident waiting to happen. And . . ." He paused, laughing at Jessen's painful wait for the third revelation. "And, you showed me a piece of paper about a man who is dead. There shouldn't be any connection. But I assume there is."

"I will not comment on the bugging, Harry. I wanted you here because we may have to call some people, and I wanted to be near a safe phone."

Gunnison did not believe him, and he showed it with a shrug and a tilting back of his head. "Porter," he said, addressing the ceiling. "Captain David Porter. You can't call him. So you call me." He lowered his head and leaned toward Jessen's desk. "To find a connection? Is that it?"

"How much of the draft report did you get through?" Jessen asked. He had opened his briefcase and extracted two folders.

"Enough to know that the agency approved Ishiwata's proposal. He made a list of hulks he would be going for—the list Steve Dysart's message refers to, I assume. The list was cleared by various bureaucrats in State and Defense, and then, after everything went with what I think is amazing speed, Ishiwata had the *Glomar* with a mixed crew of Japanese and Americans. Some of the Americans, I assume, are our boys from the old days."

Gunnison waited for a reaction from Jessen. There was none.

"No comment? Well, to go on, the *Glomar* was modified again and set sail in early June. Ishiwata fished some coal out of a wreck in the Sea of Japan, proving his *Glomar* rig worked, and then he made his six-month deal. Around that time, you were assigned to make a report on all this to the director. You wrote a draft and began routinely circulating it. I noticed that the routing list on the report was only partially complete.

"I assume that the report was suddenly withdrawn because you or somebody else discovered that something was going wrong. And so the director didn't get that report. He didn't find out about that something. Now everybody is afraid he *is* going to find out. The buck has been passed to you. And, now you've called on me to help bail you out."

Jessen held up his hand to signal that he wanted to speak. He was being unusually polite, Gunnison thought.

"You know a naval intelligence type named Schwartz? Bernie Schwartz?" Jessen asked.

"Sure. I knew him in Vietnam. Then he was involved in that Israeli commando business. Last I heard he was a commander assigned to the Navy Investigative Service. I saw him a few months ago at drinks with the Navy gang at the Australian Embassy."

"Right. It was the Israeli operation that saved his ass—and got him his commander's stripes."

"You knew that. You were trying me out again."

"Maybe. Maybe not. Now, as you may *not* know, Schwartz has a liaison assignment with the agency. He's kind of a wild man, and the people here usually don't pay much attention to him. Even by the standards around here he's somewhat paranoid."

"That's Bernie," Gunnison said, laughing. "I remember in Vietnam we were always on his ass because when somebody didn't listen to him he'd take his spy stories to the press. I'm surprised he's got that liaison job. I also note you said 'the people here,' implying *you* do pay attention to him."

"Yeah, I do. He knows people. Spent most of his career in Washington. And he married a congressman's daughter. Anyway, Schwartz went into orbit when Porter was killed. It seems that he has made the Navy personnel people send him the notice of every death of an active-duty or retired Navy officer or enlisted man since he came to Suitland. He *has* spotted things down through the years. Like a woman who had been married to three guys who each died within a year of being married to her. Got the FBI on her and she went to jail. But, until now, he never found anything really valuable to *us*."

"And now? What's Schwartz found now?" Gunnison asked. He inched forward on his chair.

"Porter was the commanding officer of a submarine during World War II."

"Yes. I remember. The *Tigerfish*."

"That's right. Well, Schwartz reads the *Proceedings*, too, and he remembered the piece about the sinking of the *Osaka Maru* and the court-martial. He did some sniffing around and called me. Lots of times when he calls me it's just some wild stuff that makes for speculation but not action. This time, though, it was something solid, and I could check it out."

"What was it?" Gunnison asked. He could still sense that he was being led toward a possible trap. The general word in the agency was "fluttering"—you fluttered someone with a lie-detector test or with an incriminating paper to see if he was lying. Gunnison felt that he was being fluttered.

"Christ," Jessen interrupted. "I never ordered lunch. What will you have?"

"Some kind of sandwich on anything *but* white bread, black coffee, and, for God's sake, the end of your story."

Jessen picked up the phone on his desk, touched a button on the console, and ordered two tuna sandwiches on whole wheat bread, two black coffees, and two glasses of milk. He hung up, glanced at a paper from the second folder, and said, "Schwartz told me that he had information that Porter had been killed. I said, 'So what? Why call me?' He said he didn't want to go any further because of possible sensitive information. I asked him what the hell did he mean by that. Well, what it came down to was that Schwartz thought he had stumbled into some big, black CIA operation."

"Had he?" Gunnison asked.

"Not that I know of. He would not talk on the phone. But he did mention your name."

"How did my name come up?"

"Your name was the last one on the Porter court-martial files in Navy archives." Jessen paused, and Gunnison felt the moment of the flutter had come.

The console buzzed twice, and a moment later the door opened. Jessen's secretary brought in a yellow plastic tray bearing their lunch. Jessen paid her and proceeded to dispense lunch to himself and Gunnison.

"Sure my name was in the files," Gunnison said, imagining he was strapped to a polygraph, imagining that he was keeping his voice firm. "Probably nobody since me has looked into it. I checked it out when I was doing the *Glomar* recruiting."

"Right," Jessen said. He leaned forward. "Your name is there. But the file is gone."

Gunnison exploded: "Now it's theft of government records. Don't you trust me? *You.* Not the goddamn agency. *You.*"

"Wait a damn minute," Jessen said, raising a hand like a traffic cop. He made a face as he took his first sip of milk, a tonic for a fledging ulcer. "I don't know who stole what. You aren't accused of anything. When Schwartz mentioned your name, I thought of the *Glomar.* And then I got that message from Dysart. The *Glomar* again. I'm beginning to think that something is going on, some kind of surprise. And I don't want any surprises. That's why I'm sitting on the report for a couple of days. And there's one more thing." He paused for another sip of milk. "Our man in Tokyo has resigned. Riling has a new employer."

"Mr. Ishiwata?"

"You've just made your first good guess, Harry. I'd like a few more. I didn't want a guy in the agency to handle it. Not that I don't trust them, but—"

"But if I fuck up it will be easier on you."

"Something like that," Jessen said, rising and smiling. "Will you take a look?"

"OK. You can start by letting me hitch a ride over to the Navy Yard when we finish what you call lunch. I'd like to find out about those records you think I stole."

"Not think. *Thought.* I trust you, Harry. In my own special way."

4

"LET'S GO TO THE NAVY YARD," Gunnison told the driver, and then he quickly added, "Use the Eighth Street entrance." A Marine sentry would be there, and he would throw a snappy salute to a black government car.

As the car passed through the gate under old Tingey House, there was the Marine and there was the salute. Gunnison, who had been a Navy enlisted man, enjoyed the salute. The car passed Leutz Park, the yard's parade ground, and pulled up before Building 210, one of the many plain grim buildings that recalled the yard's earlier incarnation as the Naval Gun Factory.

Gunnison got out of the car and walked through the first floor of Building 210 to a modified freight elevator that took him to the Navy's operational archives on the fourth floor. He signed the visitors' log, wrote "self" under "Organization" and "research" under "Purpose," and glanced up the list for names he might recognize. Admiral Arleigh Burke, the dean of former chiefs of naval operations, had been in earlier but had been signed out half an hour before. When Gunnison was in the CIA, he had met Burke socially on two or three occasions. He wished he had run into Burke, who was always one to say hello and chat. He was living history. So is this, Gunnison thought. So is this. He flipped through the pages of the research log until he found the name he was looking for. David Porter had signed in ten times between July 1 and July 23, three days before his death.

Gunnison handed the log back to the secretary and asked her to call Michael Calvin, the senior research assistant. They had met when Gunnison had been poring over logs and courts-martial records in his search for *Glomar Explorer* recruits. True to the archivist's unwritten rule, Calvin had not asked Gunnison what he was doing. In the years since the *Glomar* assignment, Gunnison had dropped into the archives often enough to maintain a passing acquaintance with Calvin. Now he appeared out of a maze of shelves and steel file cabinets.

"Cal, I want to talk to you about a man named Porter, a retired captain. He—"

"—came in here several times. Just before his death. I know. You're not the first person I've talked to about Porter."

"Bernie Schwartz? He talked to you, too?"

"I can't say officially, Harry. You know that."

"*Officially,* Cal, Schwartz's name ought to be in the log. Mine always is."

"No need to spar, Harry. Come into my office. Let's talk there."

On one wall of the small, windowless office were three framed copies of plans of eighteenth-century ships of the line. There was a gray metal government-issue desk, a typing chair with a patched green seat, and a pair of gray metal visitors' chairs, one with an arm missing.

A manuscript lay in two stacks on the desk. Gunnison judged that Calvin was one-third through his methodical line-by-line editing of another draft of his book on the evolution of deck guns on ships of the line. Next to a row of yellow sharpened pencils was a silver-framed miniature portrait of a beautiful dark-haired woman. Calvin had painted it just before she died. Gunnison did not remember her as being quite so beautiful.

Cal went over to three green filing cabinets. One had a lock bar. He spun the combination, pulled out the bar, and took several folders from the back of the top drawer.

"This is what Porter was working on," Cal said. "I let him leave it here—for safekeeping." He smiled tightly and, carrying the folders, went to his desk.

"Maybe you'd better start at the beginning, Cal. As usual, you answer questions before they're asked."

"Well, I happen to have a question, Harry. What the hell is this all about?"

"I don't fully know, Cal. All I have are a few pieces. I can't even say that there's an official inquiry beyond Schwartz's questions. I came here from Langley. Schwartz seems to think the agency is somehow involved in Porter's death. I don't believe it is. But somebody may be."

"Schwartz did not deal directly with me at first. He always goes to the top, you know." Cal motioned toward an office down the hall. "He said that he had found out that Porter had been spending a lot of time here in the months before his death. I was the one who had been dealing with him the most—I had taken a liking to him, which, as you know, happens. So Schwartz asked me a lot of questions."

"Such as what?"

"Such as, Did I know what Porter had been working on?"

"And that's it?" Gunnison asked, pointing at the pile of folders.

"Basically, only the raw materials. No conclusions. But I think I know what he was doing. I'll tell you what I told Schwartz. From what I could gather, Porter was trying to clear himself of the charge that was made at his court-martial." Calvin opened the top drawer of his desk and took out a twisted, brown-stained pipe cleaner. He tore off a couple of sheets of toilet paper from a roll in his desk, took his pipe from his pocket, unscrewed it, and began working the cleaner into the mouthpiece.

"It was that disgusting business that made me give it up," Gunnison said. Calvin smiled and began working on the bowl.

"I was told that the court-martial records were stolen. What about that, Cal?"

"That's a bit of an embarrassment, Harry," Calvin said without looking up. "I was making a deal with Porter. Navy Cross and all that. You know. I wanted him to talk for our oral history program. He wanted the original transcript of the court-martial plus the charts the Japanese were using during the war. We have a few boxes of them stored out at Suitland. And, some other stuff, too."

Calvin gathered up the toilet paper, examined the cleaner, decided to throw both into the wastepaper basket under his desk, and began the ritual of assembling, filling, and lighting his pipe, a large black briar. Not until he had produced two billows of smoke did he resume talking.

"So I made a deal. I got the original transcript over here from JAG. The judge advocate general has jurisdiction over those records, you know. Well, I managed to get them over here through a friend in JAG. Plus the charts from the warehouse in Suitland. That made it easier for Porter. He could do his work in one stop.

"He could look up operational stuff here, check the court-martial records, check the Japanese charts against ours, and look over the message traffic—both sides. Then, for an hour or so after people went home, he could speak into a tape recorder for the oral history program." The pipe went out, and Calvin used three matches to get it going again.

"It's getting late, Cal," Gunnison said, "and I'd like to move on this."

"I assume that what happened was that Porter swiped the records," Calvin said.

"So that was how he was going to clear himself? By destroying the records?"

"No, no. Not that, Harry. I think it was simple expediency. He was copying the records, so he could work on them in his apartment, and then he was going to bring back the originals. I'm sure that's what he was going to do."

"But he didn't. And now it's goodbye records."

"Not quite, Harry. My buddy in JAG made a copy, of course. Two, in fact. They didn't have Xeroxes in 1945. Thank God they have them now."

"So the records *do* exist," Gunnison said, sounding exasperated.

"Certainly. One copy in JAG and one"—he nodded toward his filing cabinets—"right here."

"What happened to the originals, the ones you assumed were in Porter's apartment?"

"I don't know. You'll have to ask Schwartz."

"Before I do that, Cal, I'd like to hear everything you can remember about Porter. Especially what is in those folders."

"Porter seemed to be a man who didn't have much time. A heart condition, from what he hinted. He was a very private man. He came here a few months ago, in May, I think. You can check the log. He was methodical about that. About everything, in fact."

"Except about swiping the records."

"I still say . . . Well, never mind. Let me tell you what I think he was doing. First of all, how much do you know about the incident?"

"I read the piece in the *Proceedings*. I remember some details."

"Secondary source," Calvin said with the disdain of an archivist. "The court-martial record is a prime source. It shows what happened. Or what the Navy believed happened."

"Which was, Cal?" Gunnison looked at his watch. He knew that the office would be closing in less than an hour.

Calvin told Gunnison about Porter's fourth and last patrol as commanding officer of the *Tigerfish:* the boring, frustrating days; the excitement when the primitive radar detected a target; the successful attack on the *Osaka Maru;* the taking of the one Japanese crewman aboard the submarine.

"Cal, about his oral-history tapes. Any chance?"

Calvin stood up. Someone was switching off the lights in the huge file area. Gunnison could hear the sounds of an office closing, of people going home. The chief archivist, Dr. Dean Allard, stuck his head into the office. He was pulling on a seersucker jacket. "Still here, Cal? How many times have I told you not to give this miscreant special help?" It was said with a sincere smile. Allard came over to Gunnison and shook his hand. "Good hunting?"

"I'm in good hands, as usual, Dean. Too bad Cal doesn't get overtime."

"It would bankrupt us, Harry." He headed for the door, stopped, and gently ordered, "You'll lock up, Cal?"

"Will do, boss."

"Nice seeing you, Harry," Allard said warmly as he left the office.

As soon as the sounds of the elevator began to rumble in the walls, Cal said to Gunnison, "The tape is pretty much self-serving. The usual stuff you get from someone who was court-martialed. The stuff I think you'll be interested in will be in the transcript."

"I would like to read that transcript, Cal. Tonight."

"We have to close up, Harry. No night readers. Sorry."

As Gunnison started to speak, Calvin held up his hand and smiled. "But I just might be able to do something about that, Harry. Come on. Take a couple of these."

They gathered up the folders on Calvin's desk and went to the Xerox machine in the large, open file area. "Copy of a copy," Calvin said. "Hard to read in spots. But you'll get the story firsthand, and you'll see what Porter was interested in. Little checkmarks in the lefthand corner of certain pages. Those are his checkmarks." He lifted a page and examined it in the greenish glare of the machine. "Just checkmarks. That's all he left."

5

CHIA MIN SQUATTED BY HER STOVE, which sat like a large white box in a corner of the kitchen. She reached into a square opening in the front of the tiled stove and turned on a gas burner. Blue flames encircled the curved bottom of a black wok that fitted into one of two holes on the tiled surface of the stove. Behind the holes were two conventional gas rings. In designing the stove, she had made some concessions to the West.

The kitchen was stark and white, its lower walls white-tiled, its upper walls white stucco. The tan tiled floor suggested the pounded-earth floor Chia Min had known in her childhood home in Taiwan. In the center of the room was a mahogany table bearing bottles, bowls, and a large cutting board, upon which rested a large carp.

Gunnison had called from the Navy Yard to say he was on his way home. He said he was starving, and so she had begun the meal. She had inserted the wok in the stove and begun heating the oil. Now she turned to the table and the fish. She scaled it, shoved a pair of chopsticks down its throat, and pulled out its entrails. She slashed the fish along both sides and took it to the sink, which was porcelain and surrounded by white cabinets. Over the sink was the kitchen's only window, which looked out on the green and brown geometry of her small garden. She flushed the entrails down the disposal, washed the fish, returned to the table, and poured rice wine and soy sauce over the fish.

As she slid the fish into the boiling oil, she heard the three short buzzes that meant Harry was at the front door and that it was he who was turning the key to open the door and enter the house.

"In the kitchen," she shouted toward the door. "Cannot leave the wok."

The door swung open and Gunnison entered carrying a grocery bag. He kissed her cheek and said, "It went well today. Want a beer?" She nodded. He put the two six-packs into the refrigerator, reserving two bottles, which he opened, pouring one into a glass for her. He took a long pull from his own bottle and sat down at the table.

"Hmm. Imported beer," she said, moving back to the table with the browned fish. "You feel rich. You are in a better mood now than this morning."

"I'll tell you about it later." Gunnison tilted his head toward the door to signal that he did not wish to talk in the kitchen. "What did your mother have to say?"

"The usual. 'Come home for a long visit.' I would like that, Harry."

"Yes. You deserve it. It's been a long time, longer than I promised." He finished the beer with a long swig. "Should I make a salad?"

"Yes. Whatever you want." She was back at the stove, adding finely chopped scallions, garlic, and ginger to the oil. She tasted the sauce, then slowly lowered the fish so that it lay, head up, along the sloping side of the wok. With a wooden spoon she dripped the hot oil over the fish. She tasted the sauce again, then sprinkled cayenne powder in it.

From the refrigerator and various shelves Gunnison produced lettuce, two small tomatoes, bean sprouts, and sprigs of parsley. While he worked at the sink, she added cornstarch, vinegar, and sugar to the sauce.

"Just a bit of lemon juice and a touch of oil, Harry," she said. "Not your usual dressing."

"Tremblingly, I obey."

"That's not true, you know."

"What isn't true?"

"I've told you before. The empress did not write that phrase on her proclamations."

"Nothing about the Chinese is true, according to the Chinese."

"That is true, Harry. That is a rare true thought from a round-eye."

They ate quickly and in near silence. They were used to such suspensions of conversation when both knew that the real talk of the day would be in Gunnison's office.

His hands were full—he was carrying another bottle of beer, her brimming glass, and the cardboard box containing the transcript—and so she unlocked the door to his office. The lock had been handmade by an agency-cleared locksmith. Only two keys existed. She usually kept hers in a false bottom of a kitchen drawer. She had taken that key from a pocket of her shorts.

"You shouldn't do that," he said as he walked to a shelf that held a small array of audio equipment. "Somebody could break in, find the key—"

"Never mind the rape. Think of the office."

"You treat security like something eccentric, an obsession. Security is business, Chia Min." He placed a Verdi overture on the turntable, and the room was filled with the sound of menacing brass. He adjusted the air-conditioning at one of the windows. He peered through the slats of the blinds, sweeping the street for any new cars, any faces that seemed out of place. There was now enough noise and music in the room for him to speak. The tone and cadence of his speech changed slightly, just enough for Chia Min to note the difference. She had the sensitive ear of a person who had learned a second language intelligently and thoroughly.

"I've got a lot to tell. But first let's get the decks cleared."

He switched on the playback of the telephone recorder. His preserved voice was his guarded, private voice. He listened to the four messages—the names, without messages, of three old customers; the name, phone number, and request of a new prospect: "James Addison of Kensington Associates. Four—two—seven—eight—one—nine—one. Mr. Elton recommended you. It's about a pipeline security study."

"He's got a lot to learn," Gunnison said, shutting off the machine. "Give him a call tomorrow, on the other phone. Tell him to be more discreet on the phone. Make a date for right after Labor Day."

"Labor Day? You are going away?"

"I may have to travel, for Jessen." He settled down in a leather chair across the room from the desk and table. Chia Min sat in the swivel chair by the desk. She swung the chair back and forth in a small arc, using the toes of her bare feet as a pivot. Gunnison stared at her without realizing that he was staring. Above her white shorts she wore a light blue halter so loosely knotted that the crescents of her small, firm breasts appeared with each rhythmic swing of the chair. He became aware of his staring and looked down at the notebook opened on his lap.

"What do I absolutely have to do in the next week or so?" He tossed her his ring of keys and she swung around and opened his desk. She looked at the yellow pad, then took a diary from an inner drawer and glanced through it. "The Defense Intelliegence Agency reorganization analysis is absolutely due September first. There's no hurry on the Pastore report—but you should call him back." She nodded toward the phone. "That is the third time he's called this week. If I am to call Mr. Addison, shouldn't you call Mr. Elton and get a little background?"

"It has to wait, Chia Min. It has to wait." He took a swig of beer and smiled at her. "You have lovely legs."

"You said we would talk about business. And there is the unfinished business, too. Your sister."

"I will call her tonight . . . Or tomorrow. I have to read her letter."

"There is no need to read it. The letter will be the same as the others, Harry. Money. More money than we have."

"You never liked Catherine."

"That is true. She is a very weak woman."

"She is also the only family I have, Chia Min."

They looked at each other for a moment and, without speaking, agreed to stop the words before they became a torrent, a familiar torrent that could flow between them and leave them standing in the separate worlds from which they had come.

Gunnison and Chia Min had been living together for five years when, planning to leave the agency in 1975, he found himself talking openly, indiscriminately to her. Midway through a sentence about one of his jobs in Vietnam, he had stopped and realized that he was revealing a secret operation, breaking a law. But in that moment he had also realized that she trusted him and had made that trust an element of her love, and he had to trust her or he might lose her. He never knew how that revelation had come to him, but he knew it was true and that it had a mathematical certainty: Trust her or lose her.

At first his trust of Chia Min had concerned the events of his past—sea stories about his work as a young sailor in the Korean War, when he had been peripherally involved in some intelligence operations. Strictly according to the rules, he should not have told her or anyone else about intelligence operations. But there was the desire to tell her about himself, and there was the need to show trust.

He had been recruited into the agency by a CIA officer temporarily assigned to his ship for what the crewmen called a "spook" operation. Gunnison left the Navy in 1954 and went to work for the CIA, which even helped him through George Washington University during the early sixties. Then began several tours with the agency in Vietnam. He had met Chia Min during one of several visits to Taiwan. He had been involved in clandestine PT-boat operations along the coast of North Vietnam to determine the amount of mainland Chinese participation in the war. These operations were sometimes conducted with limited participation by Taiwanese operatives. All of this was freely discussed by Chia Min and Gunnison. After all, Taiwan intelligence—at the CIA's behest—had given her a clean bill of health after Gunnison had reported their relationship to the agency.

There were no secrets between them. He would take precautions—as he did now, talking about business in the one room in the house that was as secure as state-of-the-art electronics could make it. But he did not take precautions in his talking with her. As he spoke to her, he did not monitor himself.

There was therapy for him in this, and they both knew it. He did not naturally wish to bottle up his thoughts and emotions. He was, at his core, a man inclined to talk, a man who wanted to be gregarious. He imagined that he could have been one of those people who become intensely and intimately autobiographical on airplanes. But his natural inclinations had been altered by years of training and experience in the agency and by years of obeying the security regulations that gave him the clearances he had to have to stay in business.

Gunnison quickly told Chia Min what Jessen had told him and what he had learned from Calvin. He opened the rolltop desk, put aside the yellow pad with the half-written letter to his sister, and arranged the pages of the transcript in piles.

"You will not be writing that letter or calling her tonight," Chia Min said. "You will be with those transcripts all night."

He nodded. "You're right, Chia Min. You are always so right." He finished the beer.

She picked up her glass and left the room.

He leafed through the first pile of transcript pages, skimming the charges and the opening statements because he remembered enough of the *Tigerfish* story to know the background. He was looking for checkmarks, which he hoped would point him to the new *Tigerfish* story, the one that might have cost Porter his life.

The first set of checkmarks was in the margins of Porter's own testimony. The marks seemed to be concentrated around questions and answers pertaining to the torpedo run on the *Osaka Maru*. There were no marks in the margins of testimony pertaining to Porter's authorizing the shooting of the men in the water. From his memory of the *Osaka Maru* case, and now from his reading of the court-martial's questions, Gunnison concluded that Porter had really been found guilty of committing an atrocity, not of failing to obey orders. Somehow, in the strange algebra of war, Porter was less guilty of sinking an unarmed enemy ship full of people than he was of ordering his men to shoot people in the water. U.S. naval officers who win the Navy Cross are expected to be heroes, not barbarians.

Porter had been allowed to describe the events leading up to the sinking. He began by setting the scene. The *Tigerfish* and two other submarines had formed a patrol line in the southern approaches to the Formosa Strait, the route taken by those few Japanese cargo ships still sailing, ships trying to bring badly needed food and raw materials, especially oil, from the southeast Asian conquests to the Japanese home islands. For three weeks the *Tigerfish* had spent most of her time wallowing on the surface. Her radar searches found no contacts, except for a couple of fishing craft and a Japanese patrol boat. But high seas prevented either craft from closing in for an attack.

Life aboard the *Tigerfish* had become boring and frustrating. On the evening of March 28, as six of the officers sat in the wardroom, William Haynes, the communications officer, and Locke, the gunnery officer, were doing paperwork. The others were lounging and reading the "message board." All messages received by the submarine—except those classified secret and higher—were routed to all of the officers once a day. After supper the wardroom was a good place to pass the message board around. Only the communications officer and the captain usually read all messages as they were received.

In answer to a question, Porter had described the message board. "It is a large board, about ten inches wide and fifteen inches long. There are two parallel, U-shaped metal bars on the top. Messages are punched with two holes and placed on those bars, in sequence."

"So, Commander Porter," a member of the court-martial, a reserve officer, had said, "you have, in effect, a pile of messages, with the one on the top the most recent and the one on the bottom the least recent."

"Yes, sir," Porter had replied, and Gunnison could almost hear the exasperation in Porter's voice.

Porter had been followed to the witness table by Lieutenant (junior grade) William Haynes, who briskly outlined his duties as communications officer and then was drawn by questions to the evening of March 28. The margins alongside his testimony were flecked with checkmarks.

"Someone was reading the message board. I believe it was Lieutenant Spear. He called across the wardroom table to me. He was pointing to a message on the board."

"And what was that message, Mr. Haynes?"

"It was . . . it was the message about the *Osaka Maru*."

"Yes. I am handing you a copy of a message that is an exhibit at this proceeding. Is that the message you refer to?"

"Yes, sir."

"And will you identify that message for the court?"

Haynes rattled off the numbers and letters that showed the message was sent from the commander of submarines in the Pacific to submarines on patrol in the western Pacific. In answer to questions, Haynes said that the message had been received in plain text and that such unencoded messages were unusual. He was then asked to read the text of the message:

> LET PASS SAFELY THE OSAKA MARU CARRYING PRISONER OF WAR SUPPLIES X SHIP WILL PASS THROUGH YOUR AREA BETWEEN MARCH 26 AND APRIL 3 X SHIP LIGHTED AT NIGHT X MARKED WITH WHITE CROSSES X SIGHTING REPORTS REQUESTED

Haynes was asked about earlier radio traffic regarding the *Osaka Maru*. The message received the night of March 28 was the third in six days. The earlier messages were also introduced as evidence.

"One final question, Mr. Haynes. Was the commanding officer, Commander Porter, in the wardroom at the time you were asked about the message?"

"No, sir. You see, that was it. That was the way it happened. He—Commander Porter—came in just after I talked with Mr. Spear. And, just as I was going to remind the captain of the message—in case he forgot—"

"Forgot? Forgot a message—a message that unusual? Is that what you are saying, Mr. Haynes?"

"It had been a blank patrol, sir. We were all rarin' to go. And the captain came in. And just then the phone in the wardroom buzzed. And that was when he found out—we found out—that radar had a contact. A good contact. And—"

"And, Mr. Haynes, that contact turned out to be the ship that *Tigerfish* then pursued and later attacked?"

"I believe so, sir."

"And that target was in fact the *Osaka Maru*?"

"Yes, sir. The *Osaka Maru*."

Porter had based his defense of the sinking on claims that the *Osaka Maru* had been carrying contraband and had not been following the course described in the earlier messages that the *Tigerfish* had received. The course had been agreed upon months before during meetings in Stockholm. American and Japanese negotiators had not spoken to each other at the meetings. Rather, they had spoken through Swedish diplomats and representatives of the International Red Cross. Because of translation problems, Porter speculated, the Americans did not have clear knowledge of the exact course the *Osaka Maru* would take. He said he also believed that the Japanese used the negotiations as cover for gaining intelligence about American submarine patrols and mine-laying plans.

Gunnison felt sorry for Porter. Blustering, thrashing about, ignoring the pleas of his own defense counsel, Porter had been a poor witness. He'd insisted that he had sunk an enemy ship that was sailing where she was not supposed to sail and was carrying what she was not supposed to be carrying—war supplies and military personnel.

Porter seemed to be trying to justify his sinking of the ship by telling about an earlier *Tigerfish* patrol, when the submarine made a high-speed run to rescue Australian prisoners of war. They had survived the torpedoing of a ship that was taking them from camps in Malaysia to camps in Japan. Porter told of racing on the surface to save the survivors, exposing his own submarine to possible Japanese attack. He tried to explain how he felt about risking the lives of his men to save the lives of strangers.

"There were bodies all over when we got to the scene," he'd testified. "We went very slowly through this sea of bodies, all black and swollen by the sun. We found sixteen of the Australians alive. Sixteen. Another submarine searching with us found about twenty survivors—and a couple of Japs. That's all, maybe thirty-five or so of the couple of hundred Australian POWs on that ship.

"We took them below. All we could do was clean the oil off—sometimes their skin came off on the clothes—and then we would try to get some soup or some medicinal brandy in them. They were so young. Just boys, really. Talking about their families in Australia. Not wanting to die.

"One of them was sitting in the wardroom with me and my exec. He said something about building—pardon my French—about building a 'fuckin bloody bridge'—well, excuse me, but those were his exact words. Those Aussies cursed like chiefs. And he talked about how many of his comrades died, and how sadistic the Japs—the Japanese—were.

"Two days later that boy was dead. My men cried. So did I. We were on the surface. The sea was calm. We sewed his body in canvas. His name was Phelps. David Phelps. We sewed it in canvas, weighed it down with a five-inch shell, and put it in the sea, as gently as we could. One of the Aussies made an Australian flag out of a mattress cover. Painted the design with Mercurochrome and ink. We held that flag over the body, and Mr. Barrett read from a Bible . . .

"Don't you see? That's why we were fighting. That's why I sank the *Osaka Maru*. I had to."

As he neared the end of Porter's testimony, Gunnison began to see that Porter was not a man trying to save his reputation and his career. He was a desperate man trying to show that he had not done anything wrong; a man back from combat telling the men behind the desks that there was a war out there, a war that gave men Navy Crosses if they performed well enough. And to perform that well, he seemed to be saying, a man had to hate. He certainly hated them. The Japs. The *Jap bastards*. He hated calling them the *Japanese,* as the proper people behind the desks did.

The Japanese. Now they want the *Glomar*.

The idea, the connection, came that quickly into Gunnison's mind. The *Glomar*. The *Osaka Maru*. The Japanese.

Gunnison flipped back to the list of witnesses, then leafed through the rest of the transcript. He reached for the small black spiral-bound phone book on his desk and looked up Michael Calvin's home phone number. Gunnison decided he would not call after midnight. He looked at his watch. It was five minutes to twelve. He dialed Calvin.

"Cal. Sorry and so forth. But I'm reading what you gave me today, and I have a question."

"Okay, Harry. A question."

"You sound tired. Cal."

"Not really, Harry. I'm just somewhere else. I'm reading a monograph on the evolution of the lombard into the saker. Guns, Harry. Real guns. What's your problem in the twentieth century?"

"A question. When Porter talked to you did he say anything

about a Japanese being interested in the *Osaka Maru*? A Japanese banker?"

"No. Porter was not that talkative, Harry. The oral history thing looked as if it was going to be a bust, in fact. He didn't want to talk about anything except the court-martial. Nothing about his submarines, nothing about the techniques of submarine warfare. Nothing but the court-martial."

"Did he say why all of a sudden he was showing up at the archives, after all these years? You said you first saw him in May, right?"

"Around then. No. He didn't say much. He said he wanted to set the record straight. That's about all. And he seemed to be in, well, a hurry. I told you he was not in good health. He seemed like a man without much time."

"Well, that turned out to be true. Cal, I wonder about that. I wonder about his getting killed. Did he ever seem threatened, frightened?"

"He wasn't that kind of man, Harry. He was a big man, starred in football or some sport at the academy, I think. And he had that big man's way of acting unafraid. No, I couldn't say he was afraid of anything."

"Cal, one more question. Only one more. I promise."

"Shoot."

"His checkmarks on the transcripts. A lot of them cluster around the testimony that has to do with the location of the *Osaka Maru*. Did he ever settle that? Do you know if he had figured that out?"

"He was very guarded about that. Very guarded. But I got the impression, the last time I saw him, that he was close to finding what he wanted."

"And," Gunnison said, half to himself, "when he was that close, he wound up dead."

Chia Min came in just after dawn. She had awakened several times during the night, each time expecting to find Gunnison in bed next to her. Now she entered the office and found him still sitting at the desk, the transcript pages spread before him.

Gunnison turned to see her approaching with two mugs of coffee. "This is the fourth time. I'm going through the transcript a fourth time. And now I know. I think I know."

"What do you know?"

"I know that Schwartz is not the fool some people think he is.

He was on to something." Gunnison leaned back, took a mug in one hand, and rubbed his eyes with the other. Chia Min sat where she had been sitting hours before. She did not speak. They were both used to that. A conversation between them often consisted of Gunnison speaking and Chia Min nodding. But she did not merely listen, she absorbed.

"Schwartz knew that the captain of the *Tigerfish* had died very recently. What I don't think he knew—and what I now believe—is that Porter would know, or be able to figure out, where the *Osaka Maru* went down.

"Schwartz apparently suspects that Porter was killed. Assuming that, what would be the motive?"

"There are only three motives, Harry. Greed, sex, revenge. But mostly it is greed."

"A lesson learned from your esteemed uncle?"

Chia Min smiled and nodded.

"If there is a connection between Porter's death and the *Tigerfish,*" Gunnison said, "then your three-motive limitation becomes interesting. It's more than thirty years since the *Tigerfish*—and that seems to be a long time for revenge or sex to be a motive. But I wonder."

Gunnison stood, put his coffee mug on the desk, and stretched his arms. He stepped to the window and looked up at the light-streaked sky. "I think I know," he repeated.

"The connection?"

"Yes. I just feel it from the transcript. The connection is the *Osaka Maru*. And the man in the water . . . the only survivor of the *Osaka Maru*."

6

GUNNISON SHOWERED AND SHAVED, ate a poached egg and a slice of seven-grain bread with his third cup of coffee, and, jacket over his arm and briefcase in hand, headed for work along with several thousand other people employed by the United States government. He eased his faded red Porsche away from the curb and crawled toward Pennsylvania Avenue behind a white Renault. Wondering why the French military attaché was leaving for the embassy so early, Gunnison flicked on an all-news radio station. *Somoza resigns and flees to Miami . . . China and the U.S. sign a trade agreement . . . And locally . . .* Gunnison switched to WGMS, "Washington's Good Music Station," and inched onto Pennsylvania Avenue to the accompaniment but not the tempo of the "Firebird" suite.

Gunnison was slowly making his way out Pennsylvania Avenue toward Suitland, Maryland, where several hundred people were also on their way to start another workday in an agglomeration of structures with the nearly anonymous name of the Federal Building Complex. Here were the Bureau of the Census, the U.S. Weather Bureau, the Army Strategic Communications Command, and the Naval Intelligence Support Center—or NISC as the Navy called it, with its penchant for forming acronyms out of anything that could be labeled. In the massive, almost windowless, concrete building that housed the Naval Intelligence Support Center was Bernie Schwartz's current office.

Gunnison had called early that morning. As he had hoped, Schwartz was not yet in, but his yeoman, a pleasant-sounding young woman, said that he was due in about eight-thirty and she would tell him that Gunnison was coming out.

By the time Pennsylvania Avenue crossed the Anacostia River, the outgoing traffic was moving rapidly, and Gunnison decided to stay on the avenue rather than crossing over Kenilworth Avenue to take the Suitland Parkway. He turned off Pennsylvania Avenue onto Silver Hill Road, and then, at an intersection marked by several gas stations and bars, turned briefly onto Suitland Road to use a side gate into the massive government compound. He parked in the general visitors' parking area and walked the few hundred feet to the front entrance of the NISC building. Inside the lobby he waited behind a couple of Westinghouse representatives at the window marked "Visitors." When his turn came, he quickly filled out the form and marked his visit "unclassified," to avoid the lengthy exchange of phone calls with Langley that would follow if he indicated that he wished to discuss classified information.

He was handed a small, red clip-on plastic badge and told to wait until an escort came. He sat on a hard wooden bench across from the sailor who controlled the security doors to the corridors. His visitor's badge noted "escort needed." With some chagrin he watched the two industry reps flash their visitors' badges at the sailor behind the desk and then walk through the security doors unescorted.

His thoughts were interrupted by a tall black woman in a summer Navy uniform, with chevrons of a first-class yeoman on her left sleeve. "Mr. Gunnison?" she asked.

Gunnison smiled and handed her the receipt that had come with his visitor's badge. The slip of paper, a second carbon, was a receipt for himself that she and then Schwartz would have to sign to enable him to enter and leave again. Without further conversation, he followed her through the security doors, up a flight of stairs, and down a long corridor along the front of the building to the doorway of an outer office and waiting room.

Schwartz did not make Gunnison wait. That meant that Schwartz had heard that Gunnison was working on something that might have importance to Schwartz. Otherwise, Gunnison knew, he would have spent the prescribed fifteen minutes of waiting.

"Harry! So good to see you! Sit down." And so it went. The greetings, the sanitized reminiscences about Vietnam, and, finally, down to business.

"So Jessen saw something in what I had to offer," Schwartz said, after Gunnison finished a skeletal account of his meeting with Jessen. Schwartz sat in one of those high-backed leather chairs that tipped back at an alarming angle. He lifted his hands from his clean desk, clasped them behind his head, and leaned back. He swung to put his feet on an open desk drawer. He was very pleased with himself.

"Yes," Gunnison said. "Yes, he was very interested. That's why I'm here."

"My gumshoeing. Your per diem. What would you consultants do without us?"

"We both earn our pay, Bernie."

Schwartz shifted his feet to the floor and swung around, assuming a more industrious-looking position. He made a little tent of his hands. "I suppose," he said, "that you'll be heading off to the D.C. cops."

"I was hoping you'd save me the trouble, Bernie. I'd like to hear what you've found out and what you think is going on."

The hands began to explore the desk. The right hand found a paperclip in a shiny black tray. The right hand placed it in the left hand and began straightening it.

"I've written reports," he said coyly.

"I'd much prefer hearing it in person, Bernie."

The hands found another paperclip to straighten. "OK, Harry. But no notes. I just want you to remember. Agreed?"

"Agreed."

"I have a system set up with the death benefits branch of personnel. I want to see every death, active and retired. And I mean *see*. I worked out a short form they use to make it simple. When I see something like 'angina' or 'carcinoma' on the cause-of-death line, I usually just pass it by. When I see 'cirrhosis' and it's a relatively young guy, I put that in a file according to ship or station. Too many cases of cirrhosis usually means there's too much booze around, and that usually means there's some other kind of trouble. Also, I've found that lots of times a drug death doesn't get reported that way. It may go down on the death certificate as cirrhosis or 'toxic reaction' or 'heart stoppage.' Well, for Christ's sake, that's what death is, right? Heart stoppage. Anyway, when I feel like there's something there, I follow up with a request for the autopsy report. And lots of times there isn't one, and the body is gone.

"Then there are accidents. An accidental death I really zoom in on. You know there was a forensic expert at Harvard who wrote in a medical journal that he figured more than half of all motor-vehicle deaths would warrant a homicide investigation. So—" Schwartz turned his head slightly and, looking sideways at Gunnison, asked, "Am I boring you?" He laughed and picked up his phone to ask his yeoman for some coffee. In less than a minute she appeared with a large wooden tray, which she placed on Schwartz's desk. Arranged on the tray were two blue cloth napkins and a silver coffee set. She poured coffee into the white china cups, which bore the seal of the Navy Investigative Service, and handed one to Gunnison. She poured cream and with dainty tongs placed two sugar cubes in Schwartz's cup. "That will be all, Reed," Schwartz said. He again glanced sidelong at Gunnison. "OK. No more background."

Schwartz's voice changed. He sounded impatient, weary of being misunderstood, harried. All his complaints about life and career were there in that voice.

"I know a guy in D.C. Homicide—ex-Navy. We traded information when I was working on a D.C. drug connection. The stuff was going from Washington to Norfolk and out into the Atlantic Fleet. Anyway, he and I were talking one time, and it happened that he had read that medical article by the Harvard guy. And my friend, Fred, bought the idea. So, when I saw how Porter was killed, something made me call Fred—well, to tell the truth, that something was how quick Porter's daughter got the body cremated. I'll get to that.

"I asked Fred if he would take a closer look at Porter's death. First of all, he said, it was a slick kind of hit-and-run, not the typical case of a panicky teenager who hits somebody and then runs into a telephone pole a couple of blocks away. Fred said he had his suspicions, but there is no percentage in investigating hit-and-runs too hard when there are perfectly obvious gunshot homicides to investigate.

"Anyway, Fred did me a favor. He went to Farragut Square on a Thursday at noon and questioned people—it's an old police technique, a calendar job. You'd be surprised how regular people are. Come back to the same place at the same time, week after week. Fred found a couple of people who had been on the corner when Porter was hit by the car. And one woman said that she thought she had seen someone—'an oriental gentleman,' she said—jostle Porter, knock him off the curb. She said the car came whipping around the corner and hit Porter. And, while everyone was turning toward the accident, the oriental gentlemen turned the other way and, she thinks, went down the subway escalator. Well, what I—"

"Wait a minute, Bernie," Gunnison interrupted, a trace of irritation in his voice. "Is that what makes you think Porter was murdered? Someone seeing an oriental gentleman?"

Schwartz pushed aside his empty coffee cup and began neatly folding the blue napkin. "There is more," he said patiently. "There was a letter. It was in Porter's inside suitcoat pocket."

"A letter? You have it?"

"The goddamn Metropolitan Police had it, put it in a box, and then passed the box along to the Amos and Andy funeral home, and they sent it to his next of kin, a daughter in Texas. I suppose you'll want to go there."

"I hope you'll give me enough help so I won't have to go there. Get all I want here in Suitland."

"I guess I'm saving Uncle Sam a lot of dough. OK. I managed to get her on the phone and I had an investigator down there—a guy from the air station in Corpus Christi—talk to her. We could not get a copy of the letter. She said she had burned it, along with a lot of other things. There didn't seem to be much love lost between her and her old man. Anyway, to get to the point—I can see you're a busy man—she said she had read the letter and she gave our man the gist of it.

"It seems that Porter and his former exec, a retired rear admiral named James Barrett, had kept in touch through the years. She said the letter was the kind that one old friend would write to another. There was some stuff about the court-martial—she said that that was an obsession with Porter. And Barrett asked why he was dredging it up again. Barrett said he had told him all he knew about the ship and the submarine. He said—"

"Excuse me, Bernie. The ship. What was the name of the ship?"

"The ship he was court-martialed over. The *Osaka Maru*. According to his daughter there was no other ship in his life—except for the *Tigerfish*. Well, Barrett said he was worried. He said he was feeling paranoid—that was the word she said he used. Paranoid. He said he had mentioned his feelings to his psychiatrist. He was jittery. Felt he was being watched. He said that Porter should watch out for himself. And he strongly advised him not to go to Japan. She also—"

"Bernie. Wait. Japan? Porter was going to Japan?"

"I told you. He and she were not in contact. She didn't *know* he was going anywhere. She hadn't even known he was in Washington. He lived in California. But Barrett knew he was in Washington and wrote to him there. Barrett said he didn't think Porter should go to Japan." Schwartz, suddenly aware that Gunnison wanted to interrupt, paused.

"And the letter didn't say why Barrett was worried?"

"No. And, if I may anticipate your next interruption—question—I didn't get any more on this. Barrett was a dead end. I had a guy from our San Diego office talk to him. But he wouldn't talk.

There was no way I could push it further. There was no way I could get authorization for a heavier investigation out of San Diego. They had a big drug thing going on. And so it was dropped."

Gunnison went back over the story with Schwartz. Both men understood each other better now, and Gunnison was able to take out his notebook. They talked for another half hour. Then Gunnison closed the notebook and stood up. As he turned to go, he asked, "But why now? After all these years. Why was Porter digging this up?"

Schwartz was leaning back in his high-backed chair again. "I thought you knew. He had seen somewhere—in the *Naval Institute Proceedings,* I guess—that the Navy had declassified a lot of encoded stuff from our submarine operations in World War II. He felt that there was some deep dark secret that the codes had covered up. That's what he told Calvin."

"I wonder why Calvin didn't tell me."

"Motivation doesn't concern those archive types. They don't think like we do, Harry." He smiled and gave Gunnison the half salute he remembered from their days in Vietnam. For a brief moment, there was a bond.

Porter had lived in an apartment in a high-rise warren that spread across three tall, thin, glassy boxes lined up on an Arlington Ridge Road off Shirley Highway. Gunnison found the complex easily enough. Finding the building manager was more difficult. He finally settled for the matronly woman at the desk in the main lobby. Behind her were several long rows of mail boxes. A stiff yellow card stuck out of most of them. There were several cards like it on the desk. They urged all tenants to come to next Saturday's icebreaker at the pool.

"I never got to know him real well," she said. Her white-lettered blue nameplate said "Franny." Her graying hair was short, but she brushed at it with her jeweled hands as if long hair were still there. "But I must admit that he was nearer my age than most people around here." She smiled as she said this, and the smile made Gunnison feel older than he was.

"He invited me to dinner once, and I naturally assumed he meant *going* somewhere. But he meant *in* his apartment. Well, I had a drink—of wine—and then I left. He was apologetic. And we *did* go out. To a nice place near here. Walking distance. A nice enough dinner. But we never, well, dated, again. Just hellos when he came and went. But I was so touched, so shocked, when I saw that he had died. Is that why you're here?"

Gunnison told her he was making a routine check for the Navy, just to settle the death claims. He asked if he could see the apartment.

"I can't show you the apartment. It's occupied. Repainted. The holes filled in."

"Holes? What kind of holes?"

"Little holes. Zillions of them. He had maps up all over. There was hardly anything else in his apartment but piles of papers in boxes. And the maps on the wall. Tacked up all over the place. He said he was writing a history or something."

"Yes, the maps," Gunnison said in his most official voice. "They are government property. There were also some highly valuable papers. Also government property." He took out his notebook and pen. "I want to know about the disposition of the maps and the papers."

"Well, Mr. Gunnison, let me tell you about the porters here. Give them an order and they carry it out. Don't get me wrong. They follow orders. But not an iota more. They packed up the stuff on the floor, and they took down the bed, and emptied the bureau and desk. They did all that. His daughter said we should sell off the furniture and send the check to Navy Relief. We did that. I can show you the receipt." She moved as if to get something from a drawer.

"That won't be necessary. I am only interested in the maps and the papers."

"Anything that was *personal*, like papers, letters, that sort of thing, I personally put aside. I sent them off to her. That is, after the man from the IRS went through them." She laughed and shook a finger under Gunnison's nose. "You government fellows ought to get together. He said it was government property, too. Beat you to it, he did. That's just like the IRS, isn't it?"

Gunnison tried to show no expression. "Very bad interagency coordination. Very bad. I wonder, do you by chance remember his name? Did he leave you a card?"

She was going through the drawer behind the counter. "No card," she said. "I made him show identification, and I made him give me a receipt." She took out a ledger and thumbed the stubs. "Captain Porter died on—"

"On July 26."

"Yes. Here it is. July 28. A Saturday. Working overtime, he

was. His name was Nishihara. Jonathan Nishihara. An oriental gentleman. But an American. I guess the government has to hire all kinds."

That night Gunnison and Jessen took a walk along the Mall and into the cool splendor of the National Gallery of Art, which, like the other magnets along the Mall, was open to the night shift of summer tourists. Gunnison again went over his day, telling in detail what he had reported earlier by phone. They agreed that a check of the IRS was officially necessary but undoubtedly futile.

Jessen and Gunnison were sitting on the marble benches that circled a sparkling black fountain. "I can tell you right now," Jessen said, "the maps and the transcript are in Japan. Along with whoever Nishihara is." He paused for a moment. "I think you should see Ishiwata. We need to extricate ourselves. I've made a reservation for you on a flight that leaves tomorrow."

"That's pretty fast, Charlie. I've got things to do."

"So do they. But you've got a reservation tomorrow." Jessen handed Gunnison an envelope containing the tickets, nodded a quick goodbye, and walked away, his steps clacking on the marble floor.

Gunnison sat for a full minute, watching the water slide over the edge of the smooth rim of the fountain. Then he stood, headed toward the door, stopped, turned around, and hurried partway around the fountain to a stairway and a telephone booth. He had only one thing to do, and it would be better to do it now, without any silent coaching from Chia Min. He gave the operator his credit card number and the number he was calling. While the phone rang, he imagined Catherine coming to the phone, standing by the mirror in the hall, touching her hair, taking a breath, and picking up the phone.

"Hello?"

"You're standing in the hall, right? You didn't pick this up in the kitchen or in Paul's den. Right?"

"I *always,* well, *nearly* always try to answer it in the hall, Harry. You know that. Why do you always make such a . . . a game out of ordinary things?"

They were so different, he thought for the thousandth time. He wondered if he did think of life as a game. Catherine certainly didn't. Never did. Never would. Life had always been a struggle, at best a contest, for Catherine.

"It's just that I imagined I could see you there . . . Never mind.

I wanted to call you. I got your letter. I have to go away. When I get back—"

"When you get back, it will be too late, Harry. I told you in the letter. Paul has only two weeks."

"Is Paul there?"

"No. He's at the bank. He's always at the bank."

Ten years ago, at the wedding, Gunnison remembered, his mother had told every guest she could corner that Catherine had married not Paul Warner who came from Virginia but Paul Warner, a banker from Virginia. *"It's his family's bank, you know,"* his mother had said in her litany of Paul Warner's virtues. Catherine had met him in Boston. She was at Boston University on a scholarship; he was getting the sixties' ticket to success, a Harvard MBA.

"Well, it's just as well. We can talk," Gunnison said, as if he knew what it was that he was going to say. He waited for Catherine to respond. She did not. "I . . . I can't give—loan—you any more, Sis. I can't refinance the house twice. Well, you know how bankers are."

"Not funny, Harry. Not funny at all."

He could hear her begin to cry, and he could picture her sitting now, her left hand holding the phone, her right hand across her forehead, her chin trembling.

"I'm sorry, Catherine," he said, using her name to show he was serious and contrite. She liked to be called sis, but only at certain times. At least he knew that much about her. He searched for words, remembering in that instant another time he had made her cry. She had come into the living room in her white prom gown, swung around in a circle around him and their mother, and he had said, "Well, how about that! You've managed to look pretty for a change!"

"Look. I know it has been tough, real tough on you and the kids—and on Paul. But his family . . . Can't he—"

"I tried to be very specific in that letter, Harry. There is no chance in that direction. No chance. When that loan—Paul's special loan—couldn't be paid on time, the directors told him that he was president in name only. The only thing he has right now is his reputation. They're keeping, well, keeping what happened quiet to protect the bank. His family—it's really just Mother Warner now, and she is too old and ill to be dragged into this—well, there isn't a dime there, Harry. Not a dime."

"Goddamn it, Sis. Why don't you just grab the kids and leave him? This isn't the first time he's pulled this."

"We're *married,* Harry. Maybe you don't understand that." She gained control of her voice and spoke firmly. The crying had stopped. "I am not going to leave Paul over this. It's a matter of loyalty, Harry. Family loyalty."

When Mom died, Catherine's letter had begun, *you said that the family was all just us now. There's just you and me, Harry. I have no one else to turn to.*

"I'm tapped out, Catherine. The house is mortgaged to the hilt. Chia Min and I are living on my income, which goes up and down like a yo-yo. Maybe I can sign a paper, be a cosigner."

"It's no good, Harry. Paul could never get a loan now, not for a long time. The house is the bank's now, you know. They could kick us out tomorrow, I guess. But they're trying to keep this quiet so that Paul can . . . can repay the loan. They gave him time, and—"

"Until the annual meeting," Gunnison interrupted. "Paul's got to put that money back in the till before the meeting or his pals will have to tell the stockholders their president is a crook."

"Damn you, Harry. Damn you. So high and mighty. So quick to judge. Paul is my children's father. He's no crook. He may have used poor judgment, but he's no crook. He stole nothing."

Gunnison had talked to a lawyer. The charge would probably be misappropriation of funds. A small-town banker trying to be a bigtime sharpie. But Catherine was right. He was not a crook.

"I'll think of something, Catherine. I really will. I have to go away, but I'll be back in a few days. I'll think of something. Believe me, Sis. I will."

"I'm counting on you, Harry. The way I always have. And I'll be praying. Just like Mom used to do. Praying that something good will happen to you and me. Have a safe trip, Harry. I love you, Harry."

"I love you, too, Sis. I'll call you as soon as I think of something."

7

GUNNISON WAS ONE OF THE packaged people again, in a giant plane, eating with the little stainless steel knife, fork, and spoon that came in the clear plastic wrapper. He took out the plastic salt and pepper containers from the plastic wrapper, tore off the corrugated ends, and attempted to sprinkle a reasonable amount on the little plastic plates of colorful food. As always, too much salt and too much pepper came out. In disgust he threw the salt and pepper containers to the floor.

A stewardess glided toward him, smiling. He wondered if he was beginning to show the terrorist-hijacker look—the T-H profile. He had long ago read the interagency research reports on that. And now he was acting it out.

He was not himself, he decided, smiling back at the stewardess while trying to explain about the problem of using the salt and pepper containers with tourist class in-flight meals. Since his talk with Jessen, he had tried to do what he had been trained to do, and what he was experienced in doing—keeping his mind and his total being focused on the task at hand, the assignment.

He went over what he had told Jessen: Porter had most likely been murdered. The death was connected to the sinking of the *Osaka Maru*, which was almost certainly the ship that Ishiwata wanted to go after with the *Glomar Explorer*. The man who called himself Nishihara from the IRS had taken material that might have vindicated Porter; possibly the material showed that the *Osaka Maru* was violating the safe-passage agreement. But, after all these years, what did that matter? Honor, Jessen had said. A matter of honor. He had found a quote. Jessen was always able to find a quote. He had taken down from his bookshelf a book about Japan. He had thumbed through it until he had found what he wanted—a saying attributed to a samurai in medieval Japan: "Dishonor is like a scar on a tree, which time, instead of erasing, makes larger."

They had decided that Gunnison would confront Ishiwata with

what was known and tell him that the deal was ended. The embassy had hastily set up the meeting with the explanation that the agency-front company was sending a representative to inquire about the status of the *Glomar* charter. Ishiwata had agreed to the meeting.

Jessen could give Gunnison little on Ishiwata. Now, reading the excerpts from the slim dossier, musing about the man he was to meet, Gunnison dozed off. He awoke suddenly. He thought he had slept for only a moment, but in that moment he had dreamed about water. The dream was one from childhood, a fever dream, his mother had called it. He was a needle floating on a dark, stormy sea. One wrong move and he, the needle, would sink. He remembered the old, terrifying feelings about the dream. And then he remembered that there had been something new, a blur in the sea. He tried to pull the blur from the edge of his consciousness, and for an instant he saw again what he had seen in his dream: naked bodies deep in the dark sea.

He picked up the book he had been reading, the book Jessen had given him, and he searched for the page with the quotation about dishonor.

When the plane landed at New Tokyo International Airport, Gunnison fell in line with the rest of the tourist-class passengers. He was traveling on his own passport, as he usually did. He had not gotten a visa from the Japanese Embassy in Washington because he had not wanted his trip to Japan to become a matter of record at the embassy, notorious for its gossip and leaks. He knew that he could get a temporary visa at the airport, where he presumed that the records would be more ephemeral.

He got in the entry line behind a middle-aged American couple who were arguing about the smoothness of the flight. The woman was particularly attractive; the man was not. The man turned to Gunnison for his opinion, and Gunnison said, "Very, very smooth," to the annoyance of the man and the delight of the woman.

The two Japanese women at the temporary-visa counter put the couple through what to Gunnison was a surprisingly thorough interrogation. He realized he was seeing the first of the airport's visible security screens. The airport, the tightest in the world, had tightened up even more since his last visit. The women scrutinized the couple's passports, asked to see their tickets and baggage claims, recorded the flight they had come in on, the flight on which they intended to leave, asked for the name of the hotel they would be staying at, and, finally, gave them the visas that one of the clerks attached to each passport. The procedure was polite but brisk.

When Gunnison stepped forward and handed over his passport, he was not asked any questions.

"Welcome to Japan, Mr. Gunnison," the older of the two clerks said as she smiled and handed back his passport, which she had opened only to the page that had his name and personal data. She fingered a small white card that had been clipped to a sheaf of papers in front of her. He was certain she had just barely glanced at his photo. "Please follow me, sir." She stood up, spoke a few words in Japanese to the other clerk, opened the countertop to join Gunnison, and led him past the long lines of passengers queued up before the entry booths. She stopped before a booth marked "Airline Personnel Only." There was no line at the booth. The woman spoke briefly to the clerk in the booth, again in Japanese, and he in turn looked up at Gunnison and waved him through with the slightest nod of his head.

Beyond the booth was a stairway leading down to the vast baggage-control area, where passengers were scrambling to snatch their bags from the endless streams of luggage moving along conveyor belts. Other passengers were pushing carts full of bags and boxes toward the long, narrow customs counters.

The woman led Gunnison to the bottom of the stairs and hesitated at a door labeled in Japanese. She turned and looked at Gunnison's suitcase, battered from having been shoved under several hundred airline seats. "You have no other luggage?" she asked.

Gunnison smiled, holding up his travel-scarred carry-on bag.

The woman also smiled, nodded, and opened the door. "I hope you have a pleasant visit to my country, Mr. Gunnison." Through the open door she nodded to the security guard at a desk in the small waiting room. The guard stood and asked, "Mr. Gunnison?"

His yes brought forward a young, muscular man in a chauffeur's gray livery. He spoke to the guard in Japanese and then said to Gunnison, "With the compliments of Mr. Ishiwata. I am to take you to the Imperial Hotel. You have been cleared through immigration and customs formalities."

"I was booked at the Nikkatsu," Gunnison said.

"I am to take you to the Imperial," the chauffeur responded. "We shall go. Now."

The black Lincoln Continental pulled alongside the line of cars waiting at one of the airport's checkpoints and cut in front of the car at the head of the line. Gunnison's driver shouted something to the policeman at the gate. The policeman, whose white belt carried a truncheon and a .45-caliber pistol on a white halyard, angrily approached the Lincoln. The chauffeur reached into his tunic and pushed a laminated card in front of the policeman. The policeman took it, carefully examined it, and, still scowling, waved the first car in line back so the Lincoln could pass through.

The car sped past the symbols of security at the airport, heedless of the posted speed limits. Gunnison carefully noted the symbols: prisoner buses, gray with wire-mesh over their windows; gray armored trucks with water cannon mounted on their roofs; a two-story wooden barracks that stood out from the modern buildings of the airport. The barracks, Gunnison knew, had been hastily put up to house the army of security troops assigned to the airport after terrorists and demonstrators had tried to seize it soon after it had opened.

The Lincoln pulled up to another gate, and after another confrontation between a policeman and the laminated card, the car went through the gate, this one part of a high chain-link fence topped by three strands of barbed wire. They were now on the approach to the high-speed East Kanto Highway to Tokyo. The airport fence continued along both sides of the road.

At the Imperial Hotel, from the doorman to the reception clerk to the bellboy, the deference to the chauffeur was the same. He was obviously known—Gunnison heard him greeted as Kimpei, with respect. He guided Gunnison into a two-room suite of stark elegance. The bellboy opened the drapes in the sitting room, and through the haze the moat-rimmed grounds of the Imperial Palace could be seen.

The bellboy left, and Gunnison turned to the chauffeur. "Kimpei? Your name is Kimpei? I booked a *room,* not a suite, and it was in another hotel. Why am I here? I cannot afford this suite."

"Yes, Kimpei. That is my name. You are a guest of Mr. Ishiwata. Please rest. I will call for you tomorrow morning at nine-thirty to take you to Mr. Ishiwata. You will be ready?"

There were no questions to ask. "I will be ready," Gunnison said, and he showed Kimpei to the door.

Gunnison did not rest. He unlocked his suitcase, took out his notes, and placed them on the table near a low couch. He went into the bedroom, tossed his jacket on the bed, discovered a discreet refrigerator, took out a bottle of Sapporo beer, opened it, and returned to the sitting room. He pulled a chair over to the table and began to read the notes he had made from the files on the *Osaka Maru,* the court-martial, and Ishiwata.

Late that night he replaced the notes in his suitcase, locked it, and slid it under the bed. He then took two straight pins from his shaving kit, bent them carefully, and—on his knees—placed the pins against the sides of the case so that he could later detect any movement of the case.

Gunnison then picked up his jacket, room key, and another pin. After leaving the suite and making certain that the door was locked, he inserted the other pin where the door fitted the jamb, a fraction of an inch below a minute scratch. Any opening of the door would result in movement of the pin; similarly, any effort to feel along the door in the dim light would dislodge it.

Outside the Imperial, he saw that he was being followed, very amateurishly. He walked to a small sushi restaurant a few blocks from the hotel. Whoever had ordered surveillance had used only one man, and he was so obvious that when Gunnison left the restaurant, he was tempted to wave at his shadow. The man was lingering near a line of sidewalk vending machines that offered, in Japanese and English, cigarettes, Coca-Cola, Pepsi, coffee, chewing gum, and Sapporo beer. The man was sipping from a can of Pepsi.

When he returned to his room, Gunnison did not have to feel the door to determine if the pin had been moved. He caught the glint of it lying on the thick carpeting. The suitcase had been taken from under the bed and replaced at a slightly different angle. Both bent pins were lying nearby.

With a sigh of resignation, and another beer from the refrigerator in his hands, Gunnison sat down before a large television set, fiddled with its remote controls, and found himself looking at a Japanese movie that involved scantily clad women who were being stabbed by a madman. He was being pursued by a hero who had a police dog that finished off the stabber by ripping open his throat. Gunnison fell asleep before he could see much of the movie that followed, another blood-red epic whose villain was a mad medieval monk and whose hero was a samurai who used two swords to hack away at the villain's gang.

Twice during the night he awoke suddenly, the wisp of a dream memory in his mind. It was the bodies in the water again.

8

AT PRECISELY 9:30 A.M. Gunnison's phone rang. Kimpei was in the lobby.

They drove in silence through streets just coming alive with the business and pleasures of a Tokyo Sunday. The Imperial Gardens had opened at nine, and the visitors were flowing across the bridges of the moat. Many young couples wore the current fashion, matching costumes of red T-shirt and white slacks or black silk shirt and yellow slacks. Gunnison remarked on it to Kimpei, who muttered, "Next week it will be different, something different. Fashion slaves." Kimpei's emotion surprised Gunnison. He sat back and resumed the silence.

Families pedaled by on ten-speed bikes: smiling father, demure mother, smiling children, all in a row, enjoying the tranquility of half-deserted streets. The cars flashing by were dazzlingly bright in their polished newness. Women in fluttering summer dresses were already assembling under the red-white-blue-and-gold signs that embossed the gilded-plaster entrances to the Mitsukoshi Department Store. The morning was brilliantly sunny, the city and its people elegantly prosperous.

English was everywhere: on the Coca-Cola truck and the laundry truck ("Clean Living" and something in Japanese) that sped along even on a Sunday; on the names of buildings and the names of little shops, and on the banks: Myowa Bank, Taiyo Kobe Bank, Sanwa Bank, Bank of Tokyo, and Mitsui Bank ("Think Money," said a window sign in English). And then a building with no name, in English or Japanese.

The building, on second glance, was two buildings, mated but touching warily. The larger one was tall and white, spare and modern. It surrounded, enfolded, and yet was dominated by, an older, square, gray-stone building. Some of the gray stones, massive and worn, touched the rectangular white stone. But there was no intimacy. Gunnison, who prided himself on his eye for architecture, was fascinated by the deliberate statement in stone: old and new can join, but old must prevail. He had no question where in the Bank of Japan Ishiwata's office would be.

The bank was not open. Its lower windows were sealed with steel shutters, and the huge bronze doors of the older wing were shut. Kimpei stopped in front of the doors. Alighting from the car, he rapidly walked around to open the passenger door for Gunnison and then escorted him up the seven steps to the huge bronze doors. On each door was a pair of lions rampant upon a pyramid made of gold bars.

One of the doors opened just enough to admit Gunnison. The man behind the door, like Kimpei, was tall and thick in the neck and chest. He wore a gray garrison hat, a short-sleeved gray uniform shirt, and gray trousers. On his belt was a Smith and Wesson .38-caliber revolver. Behind him was a shorter man in what Gunnison took to be the standard blue uniform of a bank guard.

At the foot of the lobby stairway stood a third man, shorter than his guardians. He wore a dark, conservatively cut business suit. He approached Gunnison and bowed.

"A pleasant morning to you, Mr. Gunnison," he said. "I am Ishiwata Seno."

"And the same to you, Mr. Ishiwata."

"Please. We will go to my office." He lightly took Gunnison's right arm. "Up these stairs." They walked the six steps of the half flight.

Ishiwata Seno's outer office was Western, old Western, dating to the latter days of the nineteenth century, when banking and much of the West began to shoulder its way into Japan. As the years had passed, the bank had kept in touch with the ways of the West, no matter in what direction other Japanese institutions had gone. Ishiwata Seno's private office was, in fact, modeled after the private office of his friend David Rockefeller—just as much of the computer operations of the Bank of Japan were modeled after those of the Chase Manhattan Bank. Ishiwata and Rockefeller were fellow members of the Trilateral Commission.

Ishiwata motioned Gunnison to what he recognized as an original Eames chair. Ishiwata settled behind a thick slab of a desk, clear except for several sheets of blank paper and a neat array of brushes, stones, and ink holders, the only apparent concession to the Japanese side of his life.

A tense young man came in with a tea tray. Ishiwata curtly dismissed him, poured Gunnison and himself tea with a minimum of ceremony, and, with no further amenities, said to Gunnison, "I understand that you are here to find out what I am doing with the *Glomar*. Your Captain Dysart sent a message to the agency, and now you are here to ask me questions. Well, ask your questions, Mr. Gunnison."

"First, Mr. Ishiwata, not a question but some facts: You said you wanted the *Glomar* for one reason, but now you want her for another reason—a ship that was not on your list. The name of the ship is the *Osaka Maru*."

"I have chartered the *Glomar*, Mr. Gunnison. I have paid the required sum. If perhaps more money is—"

"I did not come here to talk about money, Mr. Ishiwata. I came here to talk about the *Osaka Maru*."

Ishiwata waved his right hand limply, as if to wipe away the subject. With his left hand he smoothed his steel-gray hair. "I have not much time to talk with you, Mr. Gunnison. I have others waiting to see me this Sunday morning and my fellow members . . ."

"Members of the *Soji*?

"Oh yes," Ishiwata said, smiling, "the sinister *Soji*. Like the Trilateral Commission. Plot. Conspiracy. I had given even consultant employees of the CIA more credit than that, Mr. Gunnison. Please do not delay our talk with silly digressions."

Gunnison leaned forward and carefully placed his cup and saucer on Ishiwata's desk so that the cup rattled slightly. "Mr. Ishiwata," Gunnison said, "the death of David Porter is not a digression. It is a matter of grave importance."

"David Porter?" Ishiwata asked.

Gunnison leaned back. "Are you aware, Mr. Ishiwata, of the American expression, Put your cards on the table?"

"Yes, Mr. Gunnison. I am also familiar, quite familiar, with poker. Do you have some cards to play—to put down?" He smiled and pointed to the glistening desktop. "Go right ahead." Gunnison thought that Ishiwata's left hand moved slightly, perhaps to press a button for a recording or to alert the tense young man in the outer office.

"I do not believe it is necessary to tell you about the *Osaka Maru* or the *Tigerfish*, Mr. Ishiwata."

Ishiwata shrugged.

"And I do not believe it is necessary to tell you about the death of Porter. Or his connection with the sinking of the *Osaka Maru*. Or—"

"Please, Mr. Gunnison," Ishiwata interrupted. "You said you had cards."

"The Porter death," Gunnison went on, "makes it impossible for you to continue your chartering of the *Glomar*. As of this moment, your charter is ended."

"These are not cards, Mr. Gunnison. They are a bluff. A man dies, an old man. Some ship is sunk long ago. You know nothing. This ship, the *Osaka Maru*. You expect me to say I never heard of her? Of course I heard of her. Everyone in Japan who knows anything of the Great War knows of the *Osaka Maru*."

"And you want to salvage that ship. You want to use the *Glomar* to raise the *Osaka Maru*."

"Yes. I do not deny that."

"You did not put the *Osaka Maru* on the list of ships you—your so-called syndicate wanted to salvage."

"Correct. I knew that both of our countries are . . . sensitive . . . about the ship."

Ishiwata poured tea into Gunnison's cup. Gunnison picked it up and, as he leaned back in his chair, he felt he had somehow lost whatever advantage he had when he had put the cup on Ishiwata's desk.

"I also knew," Ishiwata continued, "that the name of that ship on the list would set off some reaction, would make some delay. Your State Department perhaps would show interest. As you know, the *Osaka Maru* was mentioned in the peace treaty signed by your country and my country at the end of the Great War. The *Osaka Maru*—"

"Treaty?" Gunnison interrupted. "Which treaty?"

"The peace treaty that Japan signed in September 1951, in San Francisco, Mr. Gunnison. I assumed you knew. The ship is mentioned in a codicil to that treaty. The two governments agreed that the issue of the ship would not be raised again." Ishiwata smiled the smile that was beginning to irritate Gunnison. "Yes. Now I would raise, not the issue, but the ship."

"The history is interesting, Mr. Ishiwata, but it is not part of what I am talking about. A man is dead."

"Men always die."

"I will be frank with you, Mr. Ishiwata," Gunnison began. "I—"

"Frank? I do not believe that being frank is in the little scenario you planned. Isn't that what the agency calls it? A *scenario?* Please,

Mr. Gunnison. Be frank with me. And then I will be frank with you. Put your cards on the table, Mr. Gunnison."

"All right, Mr. Ishiwata. Porter was killed by someone at least in sympathy with you if not in your hire. A man who goes by the name of Nishihara killed him or had him killed. Then he stole, probably to give to you, documents that Porter had assembled on the *Osaka Maru*. With these documents—"

"Instead of merely being shocked at your accusations, Mr. Gunnison, I will say this: You have no proof. This is only the slander of a single man."

"That is true, Mr. Ishiwata. I cannot prove anything. But I don't need to. All I have to do is tell you that we want the *Glomar* back. Immediately. No questions asked. We do not want to do business with you."

"You are perhaps expecting that Commander Schwartz will leak this to the press and embarrass the agency? I hope no one worries about that, Mr. Gunnison."

"If you know about Schwartz, you prove my point. You have been deeply involved in this. Hasn't vengeance—revenge—gone far enough?"

"Revenge? I do not understand," Ishiwata said. Gunnison was surprised by the sudden look of puzzlement on the banker's previously impassive face.

"I know about the men in the water," Gunnison said. "The machine gunning. I know about that. It was—"

"Regrettable. That was the word used in the court-martial, as I recall," Ishiwata said, his face again impassive. "Regrettable." He looked at Gunnison for a long moment. "And that, Mr. Gunnison, that is why you suspect I am interested in the *Osaka Maru*? For vengeance?"

Gunnison repeated the quotation from Jessen about the scarred tree. Ishiwata smiled his irritating smile. "How quaint," he said. "You must excuse me, Mr. Gunnison. Much as I think I know Americans, I find myself becoming more and more surprised by your naiveté. Have you now put down all your cards?"

Gunnison did not answer.

Ishiwata, in pantomime, placed cards before him as he briskly spoke. "First card: I *have* the *Glomar*. Second card: If anyone tries to take her away from me, I will provide the press with information showing that a man from your agency—a former high official named Riling—was deeply involved. Third card: Your sister Catherine is married to a man who has embezzled approximately $100,000 from his family-owned bank in Virginia. Fourth card: To help her, you have borrowed money, at high interest, against your house. Fifth card, and last card, for this is poker: You are for hire. I will hire you."

Ishiwata's left hand moved again, almost imperceptibly, under the desktop, and Gunnison assumed that he had shut off a tape recorder. Ishiwata stood suddenly, walked to a narrow window, pulled back the green drapes, and looked out. Sunlight threw his shadow onto the green carpet. A stooped man, his face dark and lowered in the aura of sun, he turned and faced Gunnison.

"Let us be two men talking alone in a room, Mr. Gunnison. Please do not tell me that you are not for hire. Please do not tell me that you are not interested in solving your problem . . . your sister's problem."

Ishiwata again crossed the room and sat down. The sunlight fell across his desk, and when he polished his gold-rimmed glasses, their lenses created a tiny rainbow that flared for a moment into the air between the men.

"I believe that when you learn *why* I want the *Osaka Maru*, you will be happy to help me." Ishiwata held up his hands. "Please. Before you respond, please let me tell you the true story of the *Osaka Maru*, the story you do not know."

9

"JAPAN LOST THE WAR and lost all possibility of a negotiated settlement on terms favorable to Japan on June 6, 1944," Ishiwata began.

He paused for a moment, and Gunnison interjected, "But June 6 was the Allied invasion of Normandy—almost halfway around the world from Japan."

"Correct," Ishiwata continued. "At the very moment that the Americans were invading Normandy with the first of two million men, more than a hundred thousand other American soldiers and Marines were at sea in the Pacific, moving to assault Saipan Island. It was unarguable evidence of the massive military capabilities of the United States. The massive forces invading Europe would soon be turned against Japan.

"And do you know how we were to counter the assault against Japan? With the *kamikaze,* the 'divine wind.' First airplanes piloted by volunteers that would crash into your ships, then midget submarines that would explode themselves under your ships, and, finally, once you landed on our soil, the old men, the children, and even our women, running against your tanks with explosives strapped to their bodies and against your troops with wooden spears!

"Mr. Gunnison, Japan was a quixotic nation going against the American windmill. While one of your windmill's arms was striking Europe, the other was moving to strike Japan, and still another arm—the most powerful—was developing the atomic bomb, the final arbitrator of war. You were developing atomic bombs and we were sharpening wooden spears!"

Ishiwata suddenly stopped talking. His voice had slowly been increasing in pitch and fervor. Gunnison said nothing.

"Mr. Gunnison, the sharpening of spears was but one of the many, many contrasts that would have showed a rational man—or government—that war against the United States was the hopeless folly of the military mind-set that had engulfed Japan and totally controlled the country from the early 1930s onward.

"Do you realize that after 1936 no government could be formed in Japan without active service officers as the war and navy ministers? The generals even decided who was and who was not acceptable for other government posts—even the minister of finance! That was the low state of our nation."

"And this turned the *Soji* against the government?" Gunnison asked.

"No, not really, for we still conducted the nation's business and decided the major financial issues—as long as there were sufficient funds to buy battleships, aircraft, and arms. But by the late 1930s the military operations in China were totally irresponsible. Our standard of living—even the food available—was declining in order to pay for the Army's operations in China. The Army was, most simply, bankrupting our country. The government was forced to appeal for all privately owned gold, silver, and diamonds.

"The government set up counters in the marketplaces, and the people came and contributed their family treasures and heirlooms. Men and women exchanged their gold rings—their wedding rings—for iron rings. The iron rings became a kind of badge of honor. I do not remember what, if anything, was given in exchange for diamonds and silver. But I remember the gold. I remember that they took gold and gave iron.

"At an early age, Mr. Gunnison, as the youngest of six children that my natural parents brought forth, I was adopted by another family, by a childless gentleman and his wife. Such adoptions were of an old tradition. My new father was a distinguished banker. He gave me a new life, a new name, and the career that I now have. My natural parents were killed during the war, in a train accident not directly related to the conflict. I know little of them and have little to remember them by . . . except this."

Ishiwata extended his right hand toward Gunnison. On the third finger was a plain, dark, iron ring. "It was my mother's. My father, a respected shipping clerk, had given her a gold ring to honor their marriage. The military had taken her gold ring—the only true jewelry she ever owned—and gave her this in its place.

"Thus, Mr. Gunnison, gold has a very special meaning for me."

Unseen by Gunnison, Ishiwata again pressed a hidden button. The young Japanese who immediately entered the room bowed stiffly to Ishiwata. After several curt orders in Japanese, the young man exited with hurried smoothness.

"Mr. Gunnison, I have canceled my other appointments for this morning. In a few moments we will be brought a light meal so that we may continue to talk without further interruption." He paused once more, his face softening as he returned to the past. Ishiwata seemed to pass easily into the past, and his voice took on a softer, more measured pace. It was as if all the words had been repeated in his mind many, many times. It was a story that he knew well, although he may never have told it, all of it, to anyone before meeting Gunnison.

"The assault on Saipan in June 1944 was a shock to the Japanese government and to the few citizens who knew of the catastrophe. The other territory lost to Americans had been mostly captured by Japan in the opening stages of the Pacific war. But Saipan had long been Japanese territory.

"By the time of the battle for Saipan, serious questions were being asked about the direction of the war, even within Tojo's own military staff. The Conduct of War section within the Japanese General Staff was directed by a perceptive and outspoken colonel, Makoto Matsutani. In the spring of 1944, with three other officers, he had prepared a top-secret study that was called 'Measures for the Termination of the Greater East Asia War.'

"He was a brave man, Makoto. He said that there was no hope for Japan to reverse the unfavorable war situation. He urged the Tojo government to begin steps to end the war in the Pacific at the same time Germany collapsed, for after Hitler fell the Allies could direct all of their forces against Japan. And then, after our defeat, they would deal more harshly with us than if we had negotiated a settlement at the end of the European war.

"The Makoto report was a state secret and went only to a few Army, Navy, and civilian leaders. No one raised a direct objection to the clear, concise reasoning of the report, not even Tojo. But within a week of his seeing the report, Tojo had Makoto sent off to a meaningless assignment in China."

"Did the *Soji* see the report?"

"Within a few hours after the report was completed, the *Soji* had it. That one piece of paper, coming from a respected officer of the General Staff, and the fall of Saipan, were the two factors that caused the *Soji* to take action."

"Was the *Soji* legal?" Gunnison asked.

"The *Soji* is not illegal—not in the sense of your Mafia. Rather, it is semisecret and semiofficial, an association of the financial leaders of Japan. The association is named for the fifteenth-century poet who was a genius of the *renga,* the linked verse. The few senior men who control Japan's finances are the inner circle or *Maru*—the members—of the inner *Soji*. Others are candidate-members of the *Soji*, those of the outer circle.

"During the Pacific war, candidate-members included Kaya Okinori, the finance minister of the Tojo government; the chief of the finance section of the Army; the deputy comptroller of the Navy; the deputy director of the War Shipping Allocation Board; and others. Of course, the heads of the major banks were members of the inner circle."

"And you?"

"I was a young man during the war. I had served several years as an employee of the Specie Bank and, because of my interest in maritime trade, was assigned to the War Shipping Allocation Board in 1941. My adoptive father was the head of the inner circle of the *Soji*. Through my revered father's efforts, I was a member of the outer circle, a candidate-member.

"The *Soji* could foresee the devastation that the military government was bringing to Japan. But nothing could dissuade the government, even after Tojo was forced to resign in July 1944. The *Soji* became concerned with the future of Japan after the inevitable Allied victory, after the fall of our society."

Ishiwata had told his story impersonally, almost with the air of a man testifying or lecturing. Now he leaned across the desk and looked intently at Gunnison. "I would have told them all this, you know. All of this. And I would have told them the truth about the *Osaka Maru*." He paused, as if waiting for a response from Gunnison. Ishiwata slumped in his chair, tilting it back. Staring at the high ceiling's garlands of white plaster flowers, he said, "I lied. Yes. I lied on the submarine."

"The man in the water," Gunnison said. "The only survivor."

Still staring at the ceiling, Ishiwata spoke slowly, in a soft voice that seemed to come from a past deeper than the one he had been remembering. "Yes. I lived, as my country had to live. And in the water, that living, that need to live, became my need to live."

Ishiwata's story went back to the moments when he regained consciousness in the forward torpedo room of the *Tigerfish*. He had told the officer who questioned him that his ship was the *Osaka Maru*, a prisoner supply ship. The officer sent for the captain.

Porter entered the compartment and gruffly asked the other officer, "Well, what's the Jap got to say? Can you translate anything?"

"He speaks English, sir," the officer said. "And he says that his ship wasn't a destroyer. It was a freighter, Captain. The *Osaka Maru*."

"He's lying."

"No, sir. I don't believe so, sir. He says that the ship was carrying supplies for prisoners. He said she had safe passage . . ."

"Get these men out of here," said Porter, gesturing to the dozen sailors standing around the Japanese man. Porter turned to the figure on the bunk and said, "Okay, now who the hell are you and what was your ship?"

The answering voice was low and restrained. It contained resignation, but no fear. "I am Mosaka Khoje, purser of the *Osaka Maru*."

"Like hell. What was the *Osaka Maru*? An auxiliary cruiser or something? You were making fifteen or sixteen knots."

"No. We were a merchant ship . . . a freighter. Our ship had been returning from Singapore to Japan under safe passage assured by your government. We were not an auxiliary warship and we carried no guns."

"Haynes," Porter said, turning to the communications officer, "get the unclassified message traffic for the past couple of weeks. Did we have one about some ship with safe passage?" Porter seemed momentarily confused. "Were there Allied POWs aboard your ship—prisoners that you were carrying to Japan?" Now Porter's voice was that of a man afraid.

"No prisoners. We carried supplies for prisoner-of-war camps." Then, perceiving the captain's apprehension, the Japanese added: "We were unarmed, illuminated at night, and plainly marked with white crosses on our sides."

"Captain, there was a whole slew of messages apparently," said Haynes as he came back into the compartment. "We have one from ComSubPac dated the twenty-fourth saying we were to let this *Osaka Maru* pass safely. There are references to several earlier messages. I have Perkins digging them out. I'm not sure we have them all, but apparently ComSubPac had okayed this freighter passing down to Singapore, and Indochina, and Indonesia, and then back up to Japan."

Porter did not reply for a moment. Then, speaking slowly, he said, "Get me those other messages, damn it. Wake Mr. Barrett. Tell him I want a direct course back to where we sunk the ship and then a course plotted to where the debris would have drifted." Grabbing the messages, he ordered a close guard kept on the Japanese—only he or the executive officer were to be allowed to speak to him. Porter, head down, fled the compartment.

"I never saw Captain Porter again," Ishiwata told Gunnison. "I was kept a prisoner on Guam until I was repatriated back to Japan. I asked to testify at his court-martial, but my request was refused. Your Navy did not want the enemy to talk.

"That was the irony, the supreme irony, Mr. Gunnison. I probably would not have told them the truth of the *Osaka Maru*. I was young, afraid. But silence makes wisdom and courage. As I sat in that little cell in Guam and heard the taunting—the 'little rat,' the 'yellow son of a bitch,' and the rest—I decided I would never tell. The secret went down with the *Osaka Maru* and all those men who died." He stopped talking, once more a lecturer awaiting questions.

"Then you were carrying war supplies, just as Porter suspected," Gunnison said. "But—"

"Yes. Yes. Of course. And something else." Ishiwata touched the iron ring on his finger. "Gold," he said. He spoke the word with a hushed reverence.

10

As Ishiwata was about to continue, he looked up, beyond Gunnison's shoulder. The door was opening, silently, and the tense young man reappeared. He carried a large tray, which he placed on the edge of Ishiwata's desk. With swift but ceremonious moves he took from under the tray two fiber mats, which he put down on opposite sides of the desk, first in front of Gunnison, and then Ishiwata. On each mat he precisely aligned a square, compartmented wooden dish, a porcelain teacup, and a porcelain pot of steaming tea. A pair of bamboo chopsticks completed the setting.

The food in the compartmented wooden dishes was identical; the dishes looked like mirror images of each other.

"Fork?" Ishiwata asked, dismissing the man with a nod.

"No, thank you. I usually use chopsticks at home."

"Yes," Ishiwata said, nodding. Throughout the meeting Gunnison had the impression that there was little about him that Ishiwata did not know.

Ishiwata, smiling, said, "I usually eat at my desk. Very American, I am afraid. But it is good fare. *Ika sashimi,* raw squid. *Morokyu,* pieces of cucumber in a *miso* sauce. *Yama imo,* mountain potatoes. They are wrapped in seaweed. Would you, perhaps, like the *morokyu* recipe?"

"For the cucumbers growing in my backyard?" Gunnison asked. "You must have quite a dossier on me, Mr. Ishiwata."

"I make it a practice to know about my potential associates . . . or employees."

"And your enemies?"

"I have no enemies," Ishiwata quickly answered. He was looking directly at Gunnison. "I see that you have raised a skeptical eyebrow. Believe me, Mr. Gunnison, in a culture where vengeance once could kill—routinely kill—enemies and hatred are not taken lightly. I state this very firmly, Mr. Gunnison: I have no enemies."

Throughout the meeting, Gunnison had understood Ishiwata's

every word, every inflection. The words were spoken in crisply perfect English. But, Gunnison now realized, there was an air of translation about Ishiwata's words. Gunnison felt that he was hearing, was understanding, but he was not perceiving. Perhaps, he thought, it was because there was no dialogue going on. He realized that he, the cool and practiced questioner, had been asking few questions, very few. Even knowing this, he could now do no more than ask Ishiwata to tell him about the gold aboard the *Osaka Maru*.

"The *Soji* had overseen the confiscation and use of the gold of Hong Kong, Singapore, and the Dutch East Indies, adding it to Japan's own gold reserves. That gold had remained in vaults during the war, mainly in Tokyo, with little of it flowing out to finance the war. That was paid for in kind—by the labors, privations, and suffering of the Japanese peoples and the labor in the captured territories.

"With the fall of the Marianas, the *Soji* assembled in the provincial capital of Nagoya to create a *renga* and make a decision. One by one, my seniors of the inner circle added delicate phrases to the *renga* that flowed around and around the circle. The *renga* told of a sad day, of dark death—Japan would fall, probably in two years. The conquering armies would tread the land . . . And, they must be denied Japan's gold.

"The gold had to be secreted somewhere to await the day when Japan would again become a member of the family of nations. Our nation would need the gold to recover and become a world leader—for that was the destiny of the Sons of Nippon. So said the *renga*.

"Our problem, of course, was how to carry the gold to a safe hiding place. Airplanes could carry too little gold and were limited in range, unless the gold were flown to Korea or Manchuria. But surely the Chinese would occupy Manchuria, and possibly even Korea, and the gold would be lost. No, the gold would have to be taken to an island in the Philippine archipelago or to the East Indies. There were enough remote locations in those islands, with local groups friendly to the Japanese, that the gold could be kept for a decade or more in secrecy. But that meant carrying it by ship.

"The military leaders would never make submarines available for such a 'defeatist' venture. But members of the *Soji* could easily obtain cargo ships—one of the *Soji*, as deputy transportation minister, controlled all merchant shipping. But cargo ships could never survive the U.S. submarine ring around Japan. Perhaps a convoy . . .

"One of the elder *Sojis* began a *renga* based on a proverb: 'When a fox prowls . . .' Around the circle came the phrases, linked one by one: '. . . a farmer thinks . . .'

" '. . . not of a chicken's death . . .'

" '. . . but of fences . . .'

" 'NO!' I shouted, shocking my seniors in the circle. 'No fences. I will finish the *renga:* "When a fox prowls, the *wise* farmer thinks not of a chicken's death, not of fences, but of ways to trick the fox." '

"At the time I was the circle's youngest member," Ishiwata continued. "My plan was to have the gold's safe passage out of Japan assured by the United States government.

"For several months the United States, through the Swiss legation in Tokyo, had expressed concern over the poor condition of Allied prisoners in Japanese prisoner-of-war camps in captured territory. I suggested that the government should agree to send a relief ship to the prison camps—a ship that would also accomplish the gold transfer. And the ship would be sent out from Japan under America's guarantee of safe passage.

"The plan was swiftly carried out. The military opposed the scheme as 'defeatist.' But the circle persuaded the general staff that a ship carrying supplies for Allied prisoners could also carry arms to beleaguered garrisons and bring important technicians back to the homeland. Although less than two thousand tons of relief supplies were being sent out, the *Soji* circle obtained the use of one of the largest and fastest ships surviving in the Japanese merchant marine, the *Osaka Maru,* a 12,000-ton ship with a speed of almost 17 knots.

"We then began one of the cleverest deceptions of the war. The Swiss officials who watched the *Osaka Maru* loaded at the port of Moji in February 1945 saw crates of relief supplies being loaded; the military officials who watched saw crates of munitions and aircraft parts put aboard; we in the circle knew that crates of gold were also placed aboard.

"The *Osaka Maru* stood out to sea on the morning tide of February 17. It was marked with large white crosses on the sides and top of the ship. I was on board with several assistants. Contacts had been established with 'friends' of Japan in Indonesia. They would take off the gold, and under my direction, it was to have been hidden in an area controlled by pro-Japanese Indonesians.

"The *Osaka Maru* visited Singapore first to unload relief supplies for about 10,000 prisoners in the area. We then sailed south to Indonesia, unloading most of the remaining supplies, although a few cases were withheld for a stopover at Hong Kong en route back to Japan."

"But you didn't unload the gold in Indonesia?" Gunnison asked.

"No, the situation was too chaotic. Part of the agreement with our Indonesian 'friends'—including a young man named Sukarno—was that we would provide several cases of munitions for them to start an anti-Dutch movement after the Japanese evacuated the islands. But it was obvious that if we secreted the gold, it would be found by his informers and used in their revolution against colonial rule. Further, our informants told me of Sukarno's pro-Communist leanings. The situation was too dangerous for the gold.

"I radioed to Japan my description of the situation and advised that the gold must be returned to Japan. The ship's captain, who knew of his true cargo and mission, loaded the ship with tin, rubber, lead, and other materials greatly needed in Japan, and we took on about 1,200 passengers, mostly technicians, government officials, and their families."

"You were violating the terms of the American safe-passage agreement, were you not?" asked Gunnison. There was no hint of malice in his voice, just a desire for clarification.

"Perhaps." Then, after a moment of thought: "It was more a token of protest. The amount of war materials that was carried could perhaps have prolonged the conflict a few minutes, at most.

"My own thoughts were always on the gold. I had been charged by the *Soji.* I had the honor of my adoptive father, of myself, and my own family to uphold. If I could not safely secrete the gold, I must as a matter of honor return it safely to Japan.

"I devised an alternative plan. The captain and I conspired to scuttle the ship in shallow water, to sink her with her cargo. As he did so, he would falsify the markings on his charts so that only he and I would know the precise location of the *Osaka Maru*'s sinking. We would set an explosive charge below the waterline that would appear to inflict the damage from a mine, and we would be able to safely remove all of the crew and passengers into small boats. Then at some future date the gold could be recovered."

"Did the *Soji* approve your plan?"

"I could not put it to them. I had only very simple codes with me that they could understand, such as 'I am returning with the gold,' which the captain could transmit as a message about his first mate's health. More complex messages would certainly be intercepted by our military and arouse their suspicions.

"You must understand that the *Soji* could not allow the *Osaka*

Maru to bring the gold back into Japan. The entire mission to carry supplies to the Allied prisoners had generated much opposition within the military. We could not as easily control the unloading of the ship as we had the loading. The gold had to be secreted outside of the Japanese homeland.

"I had planned to scuttle the *Osaka Maru* in shallow waters north of Formosa. Of course, we were fully lighted at night and had large white crosses painted on our sides. We knew that American submarines were prowling those waters by day and night. Indeed, we intercepted a message from a small convoy just north of us that was being attacked by one of your submarines.

"We thought we had nothing to fear." Ishiwata shook his head slowly. "Nothing to fear. Then, late in the night on March 31, we were struck by a sudden explosion and then another one. My first thought was that the captain had betrayed me and was scuttling the ship prematurely. I ran to the bridge, but I could not reach it. My next thought—rather stupidly, I admit—was to see to the gold. But there was another explosion, and I was thrown from the ship.

"I was in the water. I was cold and covered with oil. I cannot truthfully tell how long I was in the water, but it seemed a very long time. I saw about twenty others floating in life belts and on debris, plus a few floating dead men. One of the dead was Mosaka Khoje—"

"The *Osaka Maru*'s purser," Gunnison interjected.

"I thought it might be easier to explain my presence as a purser after I was brought aboard the submarine than if I were identified as a banker. Remember, I was still thinking that the captain might have betrayed me, that the *Osaka Maru* might have been in a different area than I believed we were. I still thought the ship might be sinking in a place where the gold might have been salvaged."

"And the gold has been in the wreck of the *Osaka Maru* since 1945?"

"Yes. Much to my shame, since I was responsible for it. A matter of honor."

"I see it as more than a matter of honor," Gunnison said. He put his chopsticks on the tray and for an instant thought, with surprising bitterness, about how often he found himself in other people's offices eating from other people's trays. "I see it as a matter of greed."

The two men stared at each other for a long moment. "You tell an interesting story, Mr. Ishiwata. But I want to hear about the man who died much later. I want to know why Porter was murdered."

Ishiwata again pressed the summoning button, and the young man reappeared to take away the trays. "You may leave, Kanzan," Ishiwata said. He looked up at Gunnison, smiled, and said in a conspiratorial whisper, "We will now be alone."

Ishiwata stood and walked to the window, watched the young man leave the building, then turned to Gunnison, motioning him to one of two leather chairs that stood before a niche in the opposite wall. In the niche was a teak stand that bore a gray porcelain vase. In the vase was a single cedar limb that had two small branches. "Earth," Ishiwata said, pointing to the lower branch. "Man," he said, his fingers barely touching the second branch. He bowed Gunnison into the nearer chair and, pointing to the topmost part of the branch, said, "Heaven."

Eyes on the branch, he seated himself, uttered some words of Japanese, then, turning to Gunnison, translated: "Heaven and earth, flowers. The heart of man, the soul of flowers."

Ishiwata seemed to wait for a response. There was none. "We are usually thought of by the West as a gentle people," he said in his lecturing tone. "We are not. Our history is full of violence, of assassinations." He paused, as if reaching for an example at the edge of his knowledge. "Your British ancestors had a king. He was angry, badly angry, toward a great priest. The king said one day that he wished someone would make this great priest go away." Ishiwata looked up, again seeking response.

"Henry the second," Gunnison said. "He looked around one day and said to his court, 'Will no one rid me of this troublesome priest?' Four knights thought that the king meant he wanted the great priest, Thomas à Becket, killed. And they killed him in a cathedral."

"Yes. That is the story."

"Are you trying to tell me that you are not responsible for the death of Porter? Somebody else did it, and so you're not responsible?"

"What I am saying, Gunnison-*san,* is that men were trying to—how is it said—get on my good side? Is that the saying? Yes. Men trying to flatter me, trying to influence the *Soji.*"

"I don't want to argue with you, Mr. Ishiwata. I am here to get the *Glomar* back."

"Yes. The *Glomar*. Your *Glomar*. Another story, Mr. Gunnison."

Ishiwata rose from his chair. "Forgive me, I rarely work on

Sundays. At times I feel like an old man. I must—call it a day? Yes. That is the idiom, isn't it? We will talk more tomorrow. In a more pleasant atmosphere."

"Where is that?"

Ishiwata walked back to the desk and spoke into a concealed intercom. Gunnison detected the name Kimpei as Ishiwata spoke rapidly and authoritatively in Japanese. Then, still standing, he took a large envelope out of the top drawer of his desk and handed it to Gunnison, who had followed Ishiwata back to the desk. "You will read this. I had it prepared on the assumption that you would prefer to see answers on paper instead of from the lips of an old man."

Gunnison began to open the envelope, which was sealed. Ishiwata reached across the desk and touched Gunnison's arm. "You will read it in the car," he said. He began walking toward the door, guiding Gunnison by the light touch on his arm. "Kimpei," he said, "will take you to a place of contemplation. We shall meet tomorrow."

Ishiwata opened the door and placed his other hand on Gunnison's back, as if to propel him out. Gunnison spun around.

"Wait a minute. I am going to my hotel. And I'll take a taxi."

The hand on Gunnison's back tightened, and he felt the pressure radiate through the cloth, as if his arms and shoulders had been gripped. He stepped back from the door, which Ishiwata slammed shut.

Ishiwata looked up, his dark eyes angry. He spoke quickly, carelessly, unmindful of the hissing or the slurring. "You were followed today from your hotel and back. Your room was entered."

"I know."

"You know. You *think* you know. That man is dead. Gold, Gunnison. Gold kills people."

Ishiwata released his hold. He touched his hands to his hair in a brushing gesture that served to calm him. He smiled and in his carefully controlled voice said, "The door of Death is made of gold, that mortal eyes cannot behold." Gunnison did not know the lines.

"William Blake," Ishiwata added. "A poet I greatly admire." He opened the door again, and Gunnison left the office with the feeling that Ishiwata had quoted those lines many times before. The door closed behind him. Kimpei appeared from a side room and escorted him from the building. The day had turned hellishly hot.

11

Kimpei drove fast and fluidly, slicing through the streets and then onto an express highway that Gunnison judged to lead eastward from the city. The car was the Lincoln Continental, big, black, and, according to Gunnison's judgment, armor-plated. The windows had the internal sheen of bulletproof glass. Between Gunnison and Kimpei was a partition of the same kind of glass. Any shots fired directly head-on at the car would be slowed if not stopped by the windshield, Kimpei's body and, finally, the bulletproof partition.

Gunnison sank back against the dark leather. He pushed a button on the fold-down middle arm of the rear seat and Beethoven's "Choral" Symphony resounded. He found the volume knob and softened the music just enough to overcome the whisper of the air conditioner.

He realized there was no point in asking Kimpei where they were heading. There was no point in talking to Kimpei anyway. Gunnison knew the basic, international chauffeur-bodyguard type. He took orders only from the person he guarded. He could not be bribed. He could not be engaged in any conversation more complex than one about the weather or sports. Men like Kimpei were alert and loyal, and they were never curious or informative. Gunnison had learned how well Kimpei adhered to those characteristics on the brief trip from the airport to Tokyo.

On this trip Kimpei had the additional duty of keeping watch on the report. Gunnison realized he would get only one reading of the report and, imprisoned in the car, would have no opportunity to copy it. He began to read.

The report had been prepared by Riling, apparently in the period when he was leaving the agency and going to work for Ishiwata. From the tone of the report, Gunnison judged it had been written for the audience now reading it: an agency representative inquiring about the sudden, unexpected interest in the *Osaka Maru*.

The *Osaka Maru* had gone down in about 3,000 feet of water. Through the years, Ishiwata and other members of the *Soji* had made discreet inquiries about salvage possibilities. But not until 1975, when news broke about the *Glomar Explorer*'s mission of salvaging a Soviet submarine, was there public knowledge of a salvage ship that could reach the *Osaka Maru*.

Ishiwata and the *Soji*, however, did not approach the agency at that time. A paragraph in the report told why.

"The price of gold," Gunnison read, "is the key to any decision to salvage the *Osaka Maru*. The gold in the ship was worth $35 an ounce when she was lost. Until the early 1970s the price remained the same, despite inflation. In August 1971, when President Nixon announced that the United States would no longer redeem foreign-held dollars for American gold, the central bank price was $43 an ounce. In 1976, the price had risen to over $100, and the *Soji* concluded that a strong, continued rise was highly probable."

The report used the price of gold as a backdrop to the *Soji*'s decision to salvage the *Osaka Maru*. At the end of 1978, when Ishiwata approached Riling at the embassy party, the price of gold was over $200. "At that time," Gunnison read, "it was decided that a tentative approach would be appropriate. A scheme to salvage the lead and coal on sunken ships was advanced. The *Soji* believed that premature disclosure about the *Osaka Maru* might delay negotiations. . . . "

The *Glomar* had been chartered and, in tests, had performed up to expectations. And the price of gold had continued to climb. So the decision was made to refit the *Glomar* for deep salvage. "The Americans were to have been informed, but developments made this difficult."

The report also briefly mentioned Dysart's indignation when the *Glomar* was taken to the shipyard for refitting. Around that time, according to the chart accompanying the report, the price of gold had passed $300 per ounce for the first time in history. The report did not say how much gold was aboard the *Osaka Maru*. Nor did it say whether the wreckage had been located. So Gunnison had at least two more questions to ask Ishiwata.

The car was slowing down, and along the sides of the highway Gunnison could see clusters of small, fenced-in houses. There was little traffic on the side streets. Men and women walked at a slower pace. He felt as if he were being taken into another world inside the world of Japan.

The car pulled off the highway and began to crawl up a narrow, winding road. Kimpei turned left onto a dusty lane hardly wide enough for the car. He stopped at a high fence of pencil-thin reeds. He got out of the car and silently reached for the report, which Gunnison had placed back in the envelope. He handed the envelope to Kimpei and stepped out. An almost imperceptible gate opened in the fence. The car door and the gate overlapped slightly, so that, during the moment that Gunnison walked from the car, he was shielded from view of anyone outside the compound. It was not a comforting feeling.

He ducked through the gate, which had been opened by a bent old man with a long, drooping white mustache. He stayed at the gate as Gunnison, led by Kimpei, walked up a curved gravel path to a small wooden house. Near the end of the path was a stepping stone. Instinctively, Gunnison stopped and gazed at the house—its peaked roof, its *shoji* paper windows, its shadowed porch. He vaguely remembered a print that held, in a few slight strokes, the essence of this house.

Kimpei disappeared around the edge of the house. Gunnison stepped forward, and just as his left foot mounted the porch, a smiling, middle-aged woman appeared in the doorway. "Welcome," she said. She pointed the index finger of her right hand to the middle of her dark blue kimono and said, "Fusayo." She bowed and, in a swift motion, knelt and touched Gunnison's shoes. He bent to untie them, but she was quicker. He stepped out of his shoes and into black silk slippers. She stood and motioned him inside.

He entered a room that had no furniture except a low Japanese table and a hibachi. An iron kettle steamed upon the hibachi's charcoal fire. On one wall were three calligraphy scrolls. The *shoji* had been opened on a western wall and the rush curtain rolled up. The window framed a jade green hill, a glimmer of distant sea, and the dark blue sky.

Fusayo poured water from the kettle into a bowl that contained a snowy white towel. She soaked and squeezed the towel and handed it to Gunnison, who grimaced and juggled the hot towel in his hands until it had cooled enough to wipe his face. Fusayo helped him out of his jacket and wiggled a finger as an order for him to remove his tie. Then she helped him into a short, sashed coat of white silk. She motioned him to sit on one of the reed mats that covered the floor.

From an inner room, in silent, mincing step, came two slim young women in kimonos. They stopped before him, paused for a moment, bowed in unison, and then gracefully folded themselves to a mat in a half-kneeling, half-sitting position. They smiled up at him and bowed their elaborately coiffed heads. Their faces bore the whitened skin, red lips, and flaring black lashes of dolls.

Fusayo had seated herself near the wall to the left. "The young lady in the sky blue kimono," she said softly, "is Naoko. She is the geisha of Ishiwata-*san*. The young lady in the peach-color kimono is Takiko." Each woman bowed her head slightly when her name was mentioned.

Gunnison wondered if they could speak English. The thought had hardly formed before Fusayo said, "They will sit and look at you, Gunnison-*san*, as wise as owls, without moving their hands, their heads, or their eyes. They will begin to entertain you merely by a shimmering stillness, as the poet has said of their sweet silence. They will not speak unless they are addressed by you. Both of them, of course, are fluent in your language, and they are well read in English literature." She paused for a scholarly effect. "I, of course, have tutored them in your Mr. Faulkner, Mr. Hemingway, and Mr. Steinbeck, as well as Ishiwata-*san's* favorites, Blake and Pope."

Gunnison's long, dark-browed face rarely showed astonishment. It did now. Behind that look were sudden memories of loud, drunken nights in the Ginza he had known as a young sailor on leave in wicked Sasebo. Memories of whores who called themselves geishas. Of bar girls whose only English words were "champagne cocktail" and "twenty bucks good time" and "okay in mouth sailor for 'five dollah mo.' "

He wanted to animate them with a question. He reached for a question inspired by their inseparable manner. "Are you sisters?" he asked, his voice sounding unexpectedly shy.

"Sisters? No." It was Takiko who spoke, her lips barely moving. "More like daughters of your renowned hostess and our distinguished teacher."

"What has she taught you?"

Takiko rose and went to the doorway from which she and Naoko had entered. She returned carrying a long-necked stringed instrument.

"A *samisen*," Fusayo said. "The *samisen* was invented by a Buddhist, Omi Ishimura. He is buried at the Samisen Temple in

Tokyo. And buried next to him is a cat, to comfort the spirits of all cats whose skins have been used to make the skin of the *samisen.*"

Gunnison was annoyed by the mistress-of-ceremonies droning of Fusayo. But his annoyance drained away quickly.

Almost without sound, a maid brought him a compartmented tray of food arranged in small bowls. She put the tray on the table before him and then handed him a fragile porcelain cup into which she poured warm sake. She withdrew, just to the edge of his sight, reappearing only to refill his cup.

While Takiko drew wispy music from the *samisen,* and while, from somewhere, a drum softly throbbed, Naoko performed the *odori,* a dance of slow and intricate movements of body, feet, arms, and hands. Fusayo sonorously recounted the story that the movements were telling. Then, sensing his disinterest, she fell silent. She realized he needed nothing more than to gaze upon the serene faces and swaying forms before him.

At some unnoticed moment his food tray, hardly touched, was removed, and the maid brought him a cup of tea. And at some other unnoticed moment the day had begun to end. The music and the dance stopped, but the drum faded as if its throb were marching slowly away. To that muffled beat, Fusayo glided about the room, striking a small piece of steel against a block of flint, sending dashes of sparks through the cool twilight.

Fusayo disappeared, the drum died, and Naoko, bowing deeply, returned to the inner room from which she had first appeared. Gunnison was alone with Takiko, who placed her *samisen* on the mat next to her, bowed, and, with a slight motion of her right hand, gestured to the doorway.

Gunnison stood. He felt tall and weighty. He tried to walk softly toward the dimming light framed in the doorway. The door led to a side porch. Takiko glided to his side, knelt, and deftly exchanged his slippers for rope-soled sandals. She gestured to the stones of a path, and he stepped off the porch. He could hear Takiko's faint breathing a few steps behind him as he walked slowly along the path. He had, for the first time in his life, a feeling of the unknown that was linked with wonder rather than fear. The enchantment that had embarrassed him so shortly before—and yet so long before—seemed now to be the emotion of someone else.

He heard the garden before he saw it. Water trickled somewhere ahead. As he and Takiko set off along the path—a seemingly unpatterned array of round and oblong stones—the sound became subtly louder, as if the water itself beckoned him. The concealing shrubs parted just enough to admit them. Now the path was bordered by bamboo, whose cool green strands brushed his face. Ahead he saw the source of the sound. An arc of water flowed from a bamboo sprout into the worn cup of a stone. The stone was gray, yet wear and water had given it an infinite kind of grayness, which Gunnison was surprised to perceive. He felt as if he had never seen stone or glistening or grayness before.

He looked beyond the stone to the garden around him, streaks of green dying in the gloaming of the long summer day. Gunnison had the impression of immensity, of a wildness beyond. He knew that he was merely in a garden. But there was no horizon. Wherever he turned, his eye was caught by a screening shrub, the swoop of a tree branch, a carved stone column.

Takiko sensed Gunnison's search for dimension. "A Japanese garden," she said, "may elude the Western mind. There is no dimension here." Her voice was soft, and it drifted toward him. She walked two or three paces behind him, guiding him, yet allowing him to guide himself.

"The path, we say, is a path of indirection. The path could be straight, like one of your highways." He heard a smile in her voice. "But our path has subtle curves, slight changes in level. If you are unsure of what is ahead, you will think that you are in a mysterious place, a place of enchantment."

Gunnison stopped and turned. He reached out his left hand and enfolded her hand in his.

The path led through a thatched bamboo gate half hidden by a wall of azaleas. Beyond the gate the path gradually ascended, its round stones giving way to narrow slabs, set like stairs. They walked up a grade gentle enough not to tire, steep enough so that they were aware of exertion. The path curved and broadened. They stood, side by side, upon a broad, flat "stopping stone" to behold a great pine whose centuries-old limbs reached out against the darkening sky.

One limb seemed to point to a small, thatched-roof, wooden-sided building. "It is here," Takiko whispered, "that our journey ends. And begins."

She slipped her hand from his and glided past him. She pushed back wooden panels set in grooves around the building, exposing paper-covered latticed windows. Gunnison stepped onto the pebbly track that ended the path. In two strides he was on the porch. He removed his sandals and followed Takiko into the central room. She took a taper from a wooden stand next to the hibachi and lit two black iron lanterns that hung at the farther side of the room. The candles' flames shimmered through blue silk, casting pale shadows on the walls and mat-covered floor.

Silently, she took him by the hand and led him through the front room into the next. At the rear wall of the small room was a conventional Western door, which she opened, disclosing a tiled bath. She disrobed him swiftly and impassively, like a mother with a child, and placed his clothing in a cabinet behind him. He did not turn as he heard the soft sounds of her own clothing leaving her body.

Her hands, warm and soapy, were on his back, his neck, his buttocks, his arms. He began to turn toward her, but she gently pressed her body against his back and began to hum. He felt, rather than heard, the sound that passed through his flesh and bone and sinew. As she hummed, her hands came about his chest and began rhythmically soaping him. Her hands slid down him, to his belly and his swelling member, which she did not touch, and his legs. She stood, still behind him, and pushed down on his shoulders. "Sit," she said, and he found himself perched upon a low, three-legged stool.

Suddenly she was standing before him with a wooden bucket in her hands. Laughing, she dumped the warm water over his head, and with a sponge she playfully sped the water through the suds. She doused him twice again, and then motioned him to the low, round bath, where steaming water whirled. He entered, hardly aware of the heat of the water, entranced as he watched Takiko soap and rinse herself. She slipped into the bath, facing him, and together they explored each other's bodies and the existence she had brought them to. They touched and caressed and gazed upon each other. Once Gunnison tried to speak, but Takiko placed a long-nailed finger against his lips.

Their bodies glowed as she took his hand and led him from the bath. She dried him with a large blue towel and placed a blue robe about his shoulders. She quickly dried herself and dusted with a faintly fragrant powder. She wrapped herself in a yellow robe and, taking his hand, led him back to the small room. Then, taking a long match from a box on a gleaming teak table, she struck it against the side of the box and held it to a black iron lantern on the table.

In the dim yellow light he realized his eyes now were sensitive to shapes and shadows, and he saw her reclining on a sleeping platform next to the table. She reached her arms out to him, and he went to her, trying to move as gently and fluidly as the sense of the night had become in him. It was in that rhythm that they began.

He had not had a thought for hours, he thought now, as he awoke in the dawn that grazed the whiteness of the windows. It could have been the dawn of the world, he thought. Once—only once—before had he felt that same wonder, of exhilaration and new world dawning several hours after making love. That had been with Chia Min, on Taiwan, many, many eons ago.

For a few moments the thoughts came one at a time, distinct, edged, as if the current that normally carried his thoughts still slept. Thoughts of pleasure, of flesh, of a pulsing, of Takiko. He dozed off, faintly aware of Takiko's touch and the reawakening of his body.

Now the mood she imposed was one of vigor, and they became two bodies joined in more familiar strength and power. Kneeling over her, plunging into her, he felt mammoth, a giant entering a child. Now there was a surge of evil in his mind, and, much later, remembering that moment, he believed that she had induced that feeling of evil. In those hours she could induce joy, evil, satiation, frustration. She did all this with twists of her body and grimaces on that doll-like face.

In the mood of strength and power she spoke—sometimes in Japanese, sometimes in another oriental language, sometimes in English. The words he could understand were his name, the words of sex, the words of urging. They began to tumble from her lips as she transformed herself from doll and child to grinning, screaming harlot. Then, the grin changing to a shy smile, she conducted him down from his sense of power and back to gentleness and silence.

She guided him from the bed, repeated the ceremony of the bath—though more briskly than before—and showed him to an anteroom of the bathroom. There he found a toilet, a sink with electric shaver, straight-edged razor, shaving brush, and shaving mug, all seemingly new and unused. His clothes, cleaned and pressed, were on a table by the door. Choosing the razor, he lathered and shaved. He dressed—white boxer shorts, shirt, trousers, socks, slippers, and the sashed jacket. He vaguely wondered when he would see his shoes again. He opened the door to the aroma of coffee.

12

"YOU SHOULD BE VERY, VERY HUNGRY," Takiko said, suddenly laughing as she poured the coffee. "You must excuse me. When I talk of the nights, I laugh and think of joy. But in the days, there are other things I must do—there are eggs and toast to serve—and I do not think joyfully of them. Forgive me. I am sorry."

"You are the most amazing woman I have ever met. This has all been—"

"Like a dream? Yes, Gunnison-*san*, like a dream."

"May I see you again? I don't even know where we are—or who you are—or how—"

"How it all came to be? I am sorry for my interrupting, Gunnison-*san*. But I anticipate your questions and, very immodestly, I anticipate your fondness, your hope of seeing me again." She stood and raised a shade in such a way that light fell across the table but did not glare in his eyes. "You came here a stranger, and if you are to remain a stranger is something I cannot foretell."

"You are . . . employed . . . by Ishiwata?"

"In a way, yes. I have independence—as much as I want. These are not feudal times. But life is good here." She looked at him directly and laughed. "Sometimes *very* good here."

He laughed, caught her changing mood, and began eating. He was famished. Takiko, sensing his hunger, glided out of the room and quickly returned with more scrambled eggs and toast. He felt he was being carefully taken out of the Japanese culture and returned to his own. They sat at a table that could have been in his own home. Everything about him now, except Takiko, seemed Western and somewhat overstated. The reality of the day was eclipsing his memory of the night.

"Where do you live in America, Gunnison-*san?*"

"Washington. And if you want to please me, you will call me Harry."

"Harry," she said, her voice straining slightly to get through the *r*'s.

She sat to his left, just at the edge of his vision, so that he did not have to face her during the unseemly act of eating. Her hands rested on the table, tiny white hands spread as if upon a keyboard. When he patted the hand closest to him, it remained still. He found the stillness disturbing. It was as if she were not fully present.

"And in Washington, Harry, you live with a woman?"

"Yes."

"A beautiful woman?"

"Yes. A lovely woman."

"And she is oriental." It was a statement, not a question.

"She is Chinese. Her family is from Taiwan. How did you know?"

"There was something about your ways, your ways last night, a something that was not typically Western." She said this matter-of-factly. When Gunnison did not respond, she added, "Do you wish to hear more of this?"

"Spare me the details," Gunnison said, laughing to cover a surprising surge of embarrassment.

Takiko poured him more coffee and, leaning near him, asked, "You will be here long?"

As he was about to reply, he sensed that something was going wrong. She had asked one question too many, had moved just a bit too far—from interest to interrogation. He was being worked over. She was good, almost very good. But he had dealt with better.

"No," he said, smiling what he hoped was a sad smile. "I plan to leave today. Unless Mr. Ishiwata has other plans for me."

"You work, then, for Ishiwata-*san*? You will, then, return to Japan?"

"I don't exactly work for him. You might say I am a consultant."

She frowned slightly at the word, and he repeated, "Consultant. Don't worry. Lots of people in America don't know what a consultant does. Yes, I expect to be back. And I expect to see you again."

"It might be difficult to arrange, Harry."

"Don't you mean *expensive*—that kind of difficult? I know something about the arrangements between a geisha and her . . . her—"

"Her special friend. Her patron. Yes, Harry-*san*. Expensive."

"Then Ishiwata is your patron?"

"To a certain extent. But it is Naoko who enjoys a special relationship with him. Perhaps . . . perhaps—"

"Pehaps what, Takiko? Don't be shy."

"Yes. Perhaps it is possible that, because of the nature of the business between you and Ishiwata-*san*, perhaps your fortunes would change?" She lowered her head as she spoke and reached out her right hand, gently brushing Gunnison's thigh.

"Yes," Gunnison said. "Yes. It is possible." He stood and walked to the window. He tugged at the sliding shade, opening the window fully. Takiko joined him at the window. A breeze rippled the paper shade. She adjusted it and then turned to Gunnison. She touched his cheek, and he bent to kiss her lightly. *"Harry,"* she said, almost sharply, to emphasize her words had meaning, great meaning. "I wish you to be rich. How happy it would be for you . . . and your woman. For you to be rich . . . I wonder when I will see you again?"

"I don't know, Takiko. I don't know."

He kissed her and held her. She tightened her arms around him. "I could be part of your new riches," she said, looking up at him and laughing.

"Yes," he said, lifting her and kissing her smile. "Yes, perhaps."

Takiko slipped out of his arms and returned to the table. She began to clear it. "Ishiwata-*san* will be here in a very little while," she said. "It will be better if you have time to . . . compose your thoughts. I shall leave you now. At eleven o'clock you will go to the main house."

Riches. He was being set up for a big offer. A cut of the gold. Ishiwata wanted to hire him, just like Riling. He wondered if Riling had spent a night with Takiko. But, for a moment, a part of him also wondered if there had been more than hired love somewhere in the night he had just spent with Takiko.

Takiko and Naoko met in Naoko's room at the rear of the main house.

"It was good?" Naoko asked, smiling. She took a miniature tape recorder from a secret drawer of her dressing table. The room was westernized, from the blue wall-to-wall carpeting to the off-white wallpaper with posters of rock groups and the four-poster brass bed.

"Yes," Takiko said. Speaking in Japanese, she sounded and

looked demure. She smiled shyly at the question from her elder sister.

"You will now tell me what you learned," Naoko said. She switched on the tape recorder.

"He said he was a consultant." She attempted to translate the word, then said it in English. "He says he does not work for Ishiwata. He says he is a consultant." She said it again in English.

"I want to know more about his words," Naoko said. "It is very important that my people know the exact words. I have told you that many times, little sister."

"Yes, elder sister. I shall remember better in the future."

"Yes, I am sure you will. You are very helpful. Now, was there any mention of money? Any exact amounts? Or of work he will do?"

"No. He is a cautious man about his words."

"He made no mention of what he is to do for Ishiwata-*san?*"

"No. Nothing was said."

Naoko switched off the recorder, removed the tape, and replaced the recorder in the drawer. The tape she carefully wrapped in plastic, deftly folding the edges to make the packet both smooth and watertight so that it could be rapidly secreted in many kinds of hiding places.

"And so," Naoko asked, "he is very good?"

"Yes. Extremely good." Then, detecting a sadness in her sister's question, she said, "But he is not Japanese. He is an American." She was pleased to see her sister smile. Takiko also smiled, inwardly.

The stooped man with the drooping mustache escorted Gunnison back to the main house and took him into a small room off the main doorway. Ishiwata was sitting on a bench in the middle of the room. He wore an elaborately embroidered loose white coat, with white trousers and white silk slippers.

He motioned Gunnison to a bench opposite. Gunnison slipped into the narrow space between the benches and sat not quite across from Ishiwata. Gunnison's knees touched the other bench. He felt awkward, immense, and he knew that this arrangement was calculated.

"You had a pleasant night, Harry?" Ishiwata laughed and slapped Gunnison on the knee.

"Yes. Quite pleasant."

"We are not all business here, Harry. There must always be time for pleasant events."

"Yes. I thank you very much for the hospitality."

"Hospitality?" Ishiwata frowned, then smiled. "Yes. Hospitality. I am sorry. The word. So like *hospital*. My English is far from perfect."

"It will certainly do for the purposes," Gunnison said, allowing a trace of irritation in his voice.

"The purposes? Yes. We must talk about that. I have one question to ask you here. The rest of the discussion will be in the car. The question, Harry, is this: Will you work for me?"

Gunnison had been trained to expect this, but it never had happened. He remembered the training lecture: You must make a decision in a moment if they try to turn you around, the lecturer had said. You must decide whether to reject the offer and maybe lose an opportunity. Or accept—and maybe give the opposition the idea that you accepted too fast. A very delicate moment. You can stall, but only for a short time. It is a very delicate moment.

"I will answer that question when you answer some of mine. They are questions about dead men. There was a man following me, a man who is dead—"

Ishiwata frowned. He put the index finger of his right hand to his lips and looked around the room. "I believe I have your answer, Harry. We can talk about your question in the car."

They left quickly, escorted by the old man, seeing no one else. The car, its motor running, was pulled up close to the wooden gate. Kimpei had the right passenger's door open. He motioned for Gunnison to stand back and allow Ishiwata to enter first. Gunnison followed, saying hello to Kimpei, who did not respond. Kimpei swiftly walked around to the driver's side, got in behind the wheel, and sped the car down the dirt road.

Ishiwata lifted the armrest next to his right arm and pressed a button. The glass partition between him and the driver slid back. Ishiwata spoke rapidly in Japanese, then more slowly in English.

"Mr. Gunnison would like to know about the man who went into Mr. Gunnison's room at the hotel."

Kimpei said something in Japanese.

"Yes," Ishiwata said. "Yes. You may speak about the affair. In English, please. For Mr. Gunnison to hear."

"I killed the man," Kimpei said.

"How?" Gunnison asked.

Kimpei did not answer until Ishiwata spoke two words in Japanese. Then Kimpei said, "I put my hands around his neck. I—" He looked into the rearview mirror at Ishiwata and said a Japanese word.

"Strangled," Ishiwata said. He repeated the Japanese word and then said again, stretching the word as in a language lesson, "*Strangled*. You *strangled* him."

"Yes. Strangled." Kimpei repeated in English.

"And the body?" Gunnison asked. "Where did you get rid of the body?"

There was a rapid conversation between the two in Japanese. Then Ishiwata turned to Gunnison, laughed, and said, "Professional secret." He pressed the button again, and the partition closed.

"There are some things Kimpei doesn't want to tell even me," Ishiwata said, still laughing. "I think he sold the body to some medical school, probably for just a few yen to satisfy himself that he had an 'additional income' . . . so that he can consider himself a man of independent means. That is an important feeling for all of us, isn't it, Harry?"

Gunnison looked out the window. He counted utility poles, and he thought of his talk on the phone with Catherine. He was thinking on two channels, an experience that he understood, somehow enjoyed and yet, simultaneously, dreaded. This experience did not happen that often. But when it did, he understood and felt that experience as well as he understood and felt a piece of music. He could remember past sensations; he could anticipate the sequence of events inside the experience; he could feel the thrill of knowing that he was doubly alive, existing in the now and in the past.

Counting the utility poles. The memory came from an essay on existentialism he had read in college. Two strangers are sitting in a railway car. One man decides to kill the other after counting an arbitrary number of telephone poles flashing past the railway car window.

The talk on the phone with Catherine. Suddenly, unexpectedly, money was appearing. He could help Catherine, do what their mother had told him to do. And no one would be hurt. A Japanese banker would press a button, and that would be all. Money would appear; it would be neither honest money nor dishonest money. It would simply be money that flowed in one direction instead of another.

Gunnison decided he would count three utility poles before he gave his answer.

"I will work for you." *One. Two. Three.* "If you pay me enough." *Four. Five. Six.* "And if you tell me about the death of—"

"Porter," Ishiwata angrily interrupted. "So. I am to tell you of the death of this man. You will have leverage over me. You can blackmail me."

"I don't blackmail people, Ishiwata," Gunnison said. "And I do not work for people who consider killing a boring topic. I want information, Ishiwata. I cannot work for you unless I know."

Ishiwata nodded. "You are a cautious man. You are a man who deposits and withdraws information as I do with money. Yes. Information." He turned and plucked an imaginary thread from the arm of Gunnison's jacket. "Will you stop in Hong Kong for a suiting?"

"That depends."

Ishiwata sighed and spoke slowly. "It is a dangerous game, gold. I can tell you this, Harry. For your own peace of thought? There are some in the *Soji* who do not trust me. One was very untrusting. He tried even to bribe Naoko. I warned him when he did that. One warning is usually enough for a wise man, Harry.

"Then Kimpei told me that this man's servant had been seen entering your hotel. The man who searched your belongings was a servant of my untrusting colleague in the *Soji.* I must confess, Harry, I got angry. I said of this man that I wished he did not bother you or me again. And Kimpei acted upon my rash words. That is all. The man who entered your hotel room exists no more."

"And what of his boss?" asked Gunnison. "Your colleague in the *Soji?*"

"Ah, Harry. Your appetite for information is insatiable. Let me say only that my employees take care of my friends' enemies, and my friends' employees take care of my enemies. My former colleague—no, the English word would be my *late* colleague—also does not exist anymore. That is all."

"A wealthy banker, a member of the revered *Soji* dies, and you say, 'That is all?' "

"But not a banker, Harry. Please. Not a banker. A man of quick, recent money. A man who learned to make money, not to earn it or to earn respect. Someone on the outer part of the *Soji,* not part of the *maru,* the circle. Someone who will be missed by few. A man who had leaned his ladder against a cloud. Let us talk no more of him."

"We *will* talk. You are saying—but you are also *not* saying—that it was this man, this man without a name, who killed Porter. So he knew about the *Osaka Maru?*"

"Yes. He said he wished to work with me. He had ties—connections?—ties in America. He discovered things."

"What things?"

"He discovered that Porter still sought to vindicate his actions in sinking the *Osaka Maru*. Porter was a man obsessed."

"Obsessed by what?" Gunnison asked.

"By the need to know the truth of the *Osaka Maru*'s voyage."

"I wonder, Mr. Ishiwata, if the obsession was not something else."

"I do not understand."

"I think I do," Gunnison said. "I think that Porter had found out about the gold. That was his so-called obsession."

"No. No. That is not true, Harry. He had not *yet* learned of the gold."

"But he might have found out. And so your friend in the *Soji*—"

"Please. Not my friend."

"Colleague? The man in the *Soji* knew that gold was going up, and—"

"Excuse me, Harry. Allow me, please, to continue." Gunnison noticed a glint of perspiration on Ishiwata's brow. He turned up the air conditioning and resumed speaking, more slowly than before. "There was blackmail. My—the man—said Porter would learn of the wealth of the *Osaka Maru* and would try to get it for himself. He . . . killed . . . had Porter killed. And he knew that his death would be blamed on me if he said the proper words."

Gunnison waited a moment before he spoke. "And then," he said, "you killed him and his man."

"Do you have any more questions, Harry?"

"You do know what the price of gold is, don't you?"

"Yes, Harry, I know that. It closed at three hundred and twelve dollars today in London. The gold in the *Osaka Maru* is worth ten times what it was, Harry. Ten times. And it will be worth more. Gold has started to rise to the heavens."

Ishiwata was smiling, calm again. "Do you have any idea how much gold is aboard the *Osaka Maru*, Harry?"

"I have been calculating, Ishiwata. I assumed that you needed a ship as big as the *Osaka Maru* because she would be carrying tons of gold. I guessed at ten tons."

"A ton of gold does not take up much space, Harry. A thin bar of gold weighing a kilogram is about as big as a chocolate bar, one of your Hershey chocolate bars. No, Harry, we did not need a twelve-thousand-ton merchant ship to carry ten tons of gold. We needed the *Osaka Maru* for a much bigger cargo. Seventy-five tons, Harry. *Seventy-five tons*. Soon it will be worth one billion dollars. And within a year it could be worth more than two billion dollars."

They both sank back in the seat, each to contemplate in silence figures beyond ordinary comprehension.

On the outskirts of Tokyo, Ishiwata spoke again to Kimpei. From the tone of his voice it was obvious that he was giving orders. Then he turned to Gunnison and told him that he would be driven directly to the airport. Gunnison's luggage, Ishiwata said, had been taken from the hotel and checked at the airport for safekeeping. He handed Gunnison the luggage claim ticket and informed him that he had a seat in first class aboard a Japan Air Lines flight leaving for Anchorage and New York at 7:30 P.M. He would make a Chicago-Washington connection in Anchorage. The arrangements had the effect of sealing Gunnison in the stockade that was New Tokyo International Airport.

"You will be paid five hundred thousand dollars. You will get fifty thousand dollars now." Ishiwata handed Gunnison a package wrapped in white rice paper and tied with a golden string. "We say, Harry, 'The parting with money is the parting of love.' May that not be so with us." He laughed. "You will get two hundred thousand when the *Glomar Explorer* is in position above the *Osaka Maru*. And you will get the balance when the treasure of the *Osaka Maru* is recovered."

"And what are my duties?"

"They are very simple, but very important, Harry. You are to return to the agency and tell them that there is no connection between me and the dead Captain Porter. You will recommend that the *Glomar* remain in my hands for another thirty days. You will tell the agency that you extracted extra payments from me, that you succeeded in getting the daily fee doubled. The agency will like the increased profits."

"And if I refuse to work for you?"

"You would have refused long before this. You can taste the gold, Harry."

"One million," Gunnison said. He told himself that he was testing Ishiwata, but he also knew he was testing himself.

Ishiwata glared at him. "I do not bargain, Gunnison. I have told you your pay."

"Eight hundred thousand—with three to my sister."

Ishiwata turned his back to Gunnison and curled deeper into the seat. "I will sleep now."

Gunnison watched the city thicken around him. Two boys in identical blue T-shirts waved at him as their car flashed by. Gunnison waved back and smiled. "And I will think now," he said.

13

THE MAIN TERMINAL BUILDING of New Tokyo International Airport sweeps in a large arc that clutches two levels of roadways, one for departures and one for arrivals. Gunnison was dropped off at the main departure entrance. If Ishiwata had accompanied him into the airport—a likely courtesy—the chances were that Ishiwata's presence would have been the cue for surveillance. By letting Gunnison enter the terminal alone, Ishiwata was either entrusting his subject to the tight security of the airport or was handing him over, sight unseen, to a surveillance man. Gunnison decided that this was unlikely, because the man, waiting at some prearranged entrance, would have drawn suspicion to himself and would have run the risk of questioning by the overzealous airport security people.

Thus, as Gunnison entered, he assumed that he was not being followed. To double-check, he walked slowly toward a men's room, stopped at a kiosk to buy a *Nippon Times,* unobtrusively checked the faces of everyone in sight, then went into the men's room. He entered a booth and lowered his pants so that, from appearances, he was an authentic user. He had selected a booth that gave him a view of the entrance door. He peeked along the booth doorframe. Two men, a Japanese and a Caucasian, entered within minutes. Gunnison waited until both had left. Then he timed himself for another ten minutes, which he spent scanning the pages of the *Times.* When he left the men's room, he looked around and did not see any of the faces he had seen before. Satisfied that he was not under surveillance, he walked toward the main corridor. A sudden movement caught his eye.

Two uniformed security men were walking rapidly, not running, toward an elderly man who was standing in front of a flight insurance booth. The man had dropped his pants, revealing his long white drawers. Just as the security men closed in on the man, Gunnison saw the reason for the pants-dropping. The man was merely getting at his moneybelt. Now, having removed a bulky wad of yen, he hoisted up his pants again.

As the security men concentrated on their cautious countryman, Gunnison walked to a cable counter a few yards away. He had hoped that there would not be anyone at his elbow when he sent the message. Alone at the counter, he took a pad, tore off the page so there would not be an imprint on the pad, and wrote:

> TO COUSIN PANG. GOLDEN MOON TRADING COMPANY, TAIPEI, TAIWAN. HAVE BUSINESS DEAL YOU MAY WISH TO JOIN. BIGGEST CLAM CATCH YOU EVER SAW. ARRIVE TAIPEI AS IN OLD DAYS. CP ONE, THURSDAY. YOU BUY TICKET. SHU GEE.

Gunnison had begun composing the cable the instant he left Ishiwata's car. He had searched his memory for those keys that would unlock memories of his dealings with the Taiwanese. Gunnison had been liaison backup on several occasions between the CIA station chief in Saigon and the CIA and Taiwanese intelligence groups on Taiwan. The trips had been to exchange information, to plan incursions into Mainland China—using information gathered by Americans and Vietnamese operating in North Vietnam under CIA aegis—and to evaluate such missions.

As the North Vietnamese regulars overran the South in those hectic days of April 1975, Gunnison had made several rush trips between Saigon and Taipei, using the CIA-operated Air America and other cover airlines to whisk back and forth between Taipei and Saigon in its death throes. Gunnison's principal contact in Taiwan had been General Cheng Ho. He had taken a liking to the brash American who seemed to know so much about the tricks of intelligence-gathering but seemed to know so little about the ways of the people he dealt with.

On those last terrible days of the Saigon-Taipei shuttle, General Cheng had told Gunnison that if he could not be safely evacuated from Saigon when it fell, he should seek out certain individuals of the large Chinese community in the city. These friends of the general would assure Gunnison's safety. The general gave Gunnison a simple contact code that could be used by himself or any of the general's "friends" in commercial telegrams.

Gunnison's carefully worded telegram, which told the general that Gunnison would arrive by Cathay Pacific, gave the flight number and the day of arrival—off by one day. Gunnison hoped the "clam catch" would spark the general's interest. Gunnison had once referred to the massive cost of intelligence operations in "millions of clams," and he had to explain the idiom to Cheng. The general had relished the term and afterwards used it often. Gunnison had signed the message by the nickname Cheng had given him in 1975: Shu Gee, for "young Gunnison."

Gunnison then checked in with the JAL desk for the 7:30 flight to Anchorage. He had about five hours to wait before the flight. He knew that his early arrival would not be unusual. Nervous travelers usually arrived hours ahead of time because they worried about the long distance between the airport and downtown Tokyo. Gunnison spent the next hour in an American-style cafeteria, where he slowly ate a cheeseburger, french fries, and apple pie, followed by three cups of coffee. He was surrounded by Americans, Japanese, and Europeans eating tray-borne meals much like his own. He yearned for *miso* soup or *tonkatsu* pork with fiery hot *karashi* mustard, but he felt that the cafeteria gave him a culinary cover. And, by not having to even think about savoring the food, he had a chance to let his mind shuttle from present to past to future, all the while keeping General Cheng centered in the weave of thought.

Gunnison had first learned of Cheng through an agency dossier that began with Cheng's intelligence career in World War II. As a bright young officer, he served on the staff of General Li Tsong-jen, head of the South-West China Command, Chiang Kai-shek's largest army. Cheng, trusted as a son by Li Tsong-jen, actually was working for Tai Li, head of Chiang's secret police. When Chiang fled from the mainland and set up his Nationalist government on Taiwan, General Li remained behind as acting president, a symbol of the Nationalists' presence on the mainland. Cheng stayed with General Li and continued working for Tai Li—until 1950, when the secret police chief was killed in a mysterious plane crash on Taiwan.

"At this point," the CIA dossier on Cheng said, "his career was at a crossroads. Cheng's enemies on Taiwan saw the death of Cheng's patron as a chance to get Cheng. But apparently Chiang Kai-shek himself intervened. Chiang was said to have trusted Cheng's work and initiative and, when General Li fled from the mainland to America, Cheng accompanied him—at Chiang Kai-shek's personal orders."

Later, in America, Cheng learned English and recruited many influential Americans for Chiang's China Lobby. In 1952 he disappeared from his Washington haunts. He turned up in Taiwan, where Chiang decorated him, promoted him to general, and put him in charge of the American section of the secret police.

When Gunnison made his first visit to Taiwan, he learned that his principal would be Cheng. Gunnison, accustomed to being handled briskly and impersonally by agency case officers, at first bristled against the avuncular ways of General Cheng. "You have much to learn," Cheng said at that first meeting. "Much to learn about your job, about the Republic of China, and about me."

"That sounds like what we call a 'welcome aboard' speech," Gunnison said. "It is made by the captain and is made to tell the new man who is in charge of the ship, in case he didn't know. I appreciate learning, General. But I am not here as a student. I am here as a representative of the United States."

"We will have some tea. Then we will talk. Yes. Welcome aboard, Mr. Gunnison. Welcome aboard," he repeated, pleased with what was for him a new expression.

Gunnison did learn, and the lessons did eventually focus on the ways of General Cheng.

He was tall for a Chinese, and, like most of the Taiwanese officials Gunnison met, had a mandarin air. He was punctilious in the way he conducted meetings in a windowless, dark-paneled room on the top story of a tall, bland building just off Presidential Square. The agency was mostly interested in what was known as the Big Question: Would the People's Republic of China enter the Vietnam War just as she had suddenly surged into the Korean War? That question was high on the agenda of every meeting.

"We told you yes about Korea, and you didn't believe us then," Cheng would say. "Now we tell you no, and you believe us. Curious." Cheng's remark was almost an anthem for the opening of the meetings, which droned on until Cheng formally presented Gunnison with a sealed green folder that contained the latest summary of Taiwan's assessment of the intentions of the People's Republic.

The real meeting would come after the scheduled meeting, when Cheng would enter a black Mercedes staff car with Gunnison and order the Army driver to take them at breakneck speed along North Hsinsheng Road, scattering mopeds, pedestrians, and cars. Their destination was Chilung, Taiwan's port. The car sped through the dark, narrow streets whose buildings yielded history lessons to Cheng and his pupil. One building reminded Cheng of a French occupation, another building of how the Spanish from the Philippines took the city and called it San Salvador. A dilapidated customs house reminded him that Japan twice ruled there. And finally they were at the waterfront (one last profane and historical remark about the Japanese), and there the car would finally slow down, ever so slightly, to careen around warehouses and seemingly head out to sea on a dark, narrow pier. At the end, guarded by soldiers, was a one-story shed. They would get out of the car, pass the shed, and walk up a swaying gangway to the *Golden Moon,* Cheng's junk and second home.

Gunnison had spent many nights aboard the *Golden Moon,* eating simple, memorable meals of rice and fish, served by Cheng's toothless old cook, who tended a charcoal fire in her hole-in-the-deck galley and, as Gunnison and Cheng sipped rice wine in his aft cabin, burned incense sticks to appease the gods of the sea.

Once, just once, Gunnison had been invited to what he believed was Cheng's real home, an apartment off Chiang Kai-shek Avenue. The rooms, Gunnison thought, could have been those of a San Francisco apartment of those days—"modern," with "oriental touches." Cheng was greeted at the door by a smiling, middle-aged woman, whom he respectfully referred to as "aunt." The other male guests were all Chinese and about Gunnison's age, young Army and naval officers, all, he later found, involved in Cheng's intelligence–secret police activities. Each was accompanied by a young woman. Since there was some quasi-professional talk during the evening, Gunnison assumed the women had been "cleared." The twelfth person at the dinner was a tall young woman named Chia Min. She was strikingly attractive, very fair skinned, and about eighteen years old. When the Western-style dinner was served, Chia Min was seated next to him. Gunnison realized at once that they had been paired for the evening.

After dinner, Chia Min and Gunnison left the apartment and walked through Taipei, talking. They had just walked and talked. When—at about 3:00 A.M.—he asked where he should take her home, she told him that the apartment was that of her aunt, who was a distant cousin of General Cheng's. She said she respected the general as an elder and called him by a title that would translate as "uncle." Gunnison left her at the door. A squeeze of her hand was their goodbye.

On his next trip he had called her at the aunt's apartment, but he was given another number to reach her. He never returned to the general's apartment. The general's familiarity with every item in the apartment and his gruff directions to the housekeeper and lone waiter-manservant had convinced Gunnison that it was in fact the general's home. But Chia Min—as they got to know, trust, and love one another—told him that neither she nor her aunt knew the location of the general's first home.

General Cheng's second—or third—home, the beautifully crafted junk *Golden Moon*, was where Gunnison knew he would go after the Cathay Pacific plane landed at Taipei. He was going to the *Golden Moon* for another visit with a man who once had run out of the cabin during a howling night storm and, by Gunnison's shaky flashlight, collected tiny fish tossed onto the deck by the wind. "We must take what the gods bestow upon us," Cheng had said, laughing as he darted his chopsticks from deck to bowl. "No fish is too small for a feast."

At 6:45 P.M., Gunnison entered the departure area and went through the first security checkpoint, where he paid his airport-use tax and submitted his bag for inspection. The gray-uniformed young woman motioned for him to open the bag. She swiftly ran her fingers along the clothing, struck the toilet kit, opened it, examined several items in it, and then fished in the pocket of the bag for file folders and a sealed manila envelope, which she ripped open after a cursory glance at Gunnison. She carefully returned the envelope, closed the bag, and nodded for him to snap it shut.

He walked to the boarding area, found a men's room, and, in a booth, opened the bag, extracted a notebook and some papers, and stuffed them into the left pocket of his coat. The packet of money hung heavy in the right pocket. Still carrying the bag, he went to the gate area, got his boarding pass, and sat in a bucket seat next to a snoring, middle-aged man whom Gunnison took to be an Englishman; he would not remember Gunnison.

The flight was called in Japanese, English, and German. Gunnison joined the hundred-odd passengers shuffling toward the white-walled cave that would lead them to the plane. The Englishman, who had finally awakened, was far behind him. Gunnison was sandwiched between a Japanese man carrying a large basket and a fat American teenage girl bulging out of her jeans and Mexican blouse.

He had checked in early enough to have his pick of first-class seats at the front of the plane. He had chosen an aisle seat. He seated himself there, stowed his bag under the seat in front of him, and took a magazine from the seat pouch. He buckled his seatbelt, leaned back, and thumbed through the magazine. Seemingly absorbed in an article on Sumo wrestling, he waited until he was sure all of the passengers were aboard. The sounds of vibrations in the plane subtly changed, and he sensed that the pilot had begun the countdown for takeoff. He glanced at his watch. Seven minutes before scheduled departure. He would wait three more minutes.

Four minutes until takeoff. One of the hostesses had left the first-class area and was heading back, toward the tourist entrance door. Gunnison unbuckled his safety belt, stood up, and walked rapidly toward the door, reaching it just before the hostess. Her smile never left her face, but she tilted her head quizzically. "Sick," he said. "Too sick." And he bolted through the door. He had timed his move well enough so that he could hear her closing the door, still acting by instinct and procedure. He did not look back.

He ran down the long white cave, stopped at a small counter, saw that no one at that moment was looking toward the boarding entrance, and walked rapidly in a diagonal line toward the neighboring boarding gate, where passengers were queuing up for a Philippines flight. A thought about Cheng's history lessons flashed through Gunnison's mind, and then he was out of the Japan Air Lines area and was walking down a broad passageway to an escalator that led to the general departure area.

He ducked into a place that called itself the Texas Cocktail Bar, sat in the far corner with his eye on the curtained entrance, and ordered a beer. He had two hours before the Cathay Pacific flight.

He was sure that he had a seat, and he assumed that it would be under his old working name, George Walters. Cheng had a good memory for names. The person behind the Cathay ticket counter would not ask for a passport. Nor would the customs people in Taiwan. Gunnison, draining the Japanese beer and signaling for a second, was confident enough to relax. For a few hours at least, *Gunnison* was a name that had boarded a Japan Air Lines plane bound for the United States. He doubted that his absence would result in anything more than a routine message to the JAL manager in Los Angeles. His ticket was paid for; it mattered little to the JAL that he was not aboard. Possibly, just possibly, the agency would hear about it through some low-level informant in JAL, and the information would slowly work its way into the proper agency channels. He would be home before anyone of importance would know that he had diverted himself to Taiwan.

He thought about the battered suitcase under the seat. George Walters would have to buy some clothes in Taiwan. He patted his right-hand coat pocket. George Walters would buy with cash.

14

THE TICKET WAITING FOR GUNNISON at the Cathay Airlines counter was in the name of George Walters and was credited to the Golden Moon Trading Company. When he identified himself as Walters, he was personally ushered through security and to a first-class seat by the chief steward, a tall, slim Eurasian who radiated a resentful knowledge of the ways of power. No one had asked to see Gunnison's passport or any identification.

Gunnison had never learned just how closely the Kuomintang intelligence agency was connected with the airlines that served Taiwan, but he did know that every person entering or leaving Taiwan on a commercial carrier was registered in a special intelligence file. He remembered now, as the plane leveled from takeoff, that Cheng had resisted using computers; he had distrusted any machine that claimed to have a memory.

Gunnison put on a headset, flicked the dial on the armrest to Channel 3—the flight magazine said "Western popular songs"—and fell asleep. He began to dream, then awoke suddenly, his heart pounding. He had dreamed for an instant in startling clarity, and the dream lingered in his waking mind. He could still see the image: a white jade carving of a carp in the instant of transformation into a dragon. The carp still possessed scales and fins, but already the dragon's fiery snout and sinuous tail were beginning to appear.

Gunnison instantly recognized the carving. Cheng owned the original, which dated to the Ming dynasty. Gunnison had a perfect replica, a gift from Cheng. It resided on the table in his front hallway. In the fleeting, quivering dream, the white jade carving had silently exploded into dust. Gunnison had awakened confused and inexplicably frightened: Was it his carving—or Cheng's—that had become dust?

Gunnison looked out on the clouds as they darkened under the coming of night, and he tried to interpret his dream. Chia Min had taught him that. Chia Min. She seemed so far and yet so close now as he felt himself being drawn deeper into a part of her world, a world that he had walked through but had never known. And what did he know about the meaning of the dream? The jade had turned to dust, so violently and so silently. Twin jades. Which had dissolved? It did not matter. The dream was telling him that he and Cheng were linked, and that he must be on guard.

The plane landed in Taipei at the Chiang Kai-shek International Airport. The chief steward, who had made Gunnison his principal charge throughout the flight, took him by the arm and led him out of the plane and into the terminal. The steward took him past the row of passport and security inspection stations to a Bank of Taiwan branch office that jutted from a wall of the arrival concourse. He rang a buzzer four times, a heavy metal door opened, and the steward bowed Gunnison inside.

Gunnison stood in a room of tables piled with stacks of currency. Around the tables, working calculators and abacuses, were a dozen male and female clerks. No one looked up when he entered. To his right, another door opened, and standing in the doorway was Cheng. The general smiled, bowed slightly, and beckoned Gunnison into the smaller room. The steward withdrew without a word.

Cheng motioned Gunnison to a maroon armchair. Exactly opposite was a similar one. Cheng sat silently for a moment, looking directly into Gunnison's eyes, then leaned forward to pour tea for Gunnison and himself. The teapot and two teacups, which bore delicate paintings of flying cranes, were on a low teak table between the chairs. Cheng concentrated on pouring the tea. He removed a knobbed cover from Gunnison's cup, poured seemingly weak tea flecked with greenish leaves, and replaced the cover. He did the same with his cup, even more methodically, Gunnison thought, as if to taunt Gunnison with the slowness and silence of the greeting.

"I am surprised that you still remember me, still recognize me," Cheng said, leaning back in his chair. He left his cup, still covered, on the table. "You Americans do not number the Republic of China among the world's living nations."

"I am glad to be here, General Cheng. I appreciate all that you have done to expedite my arrival. And I have many gifts at home that remind me always of my generous friend in Taiwan."

"Courtesy. We are ever courteous here in Taiwan." Cheng leaned forward, removed the cover from his cup, sipped, replaced the cover, and set the cup back on the table, all in one flowing motion.

He was still smooth, Gunnison thought. Still the man in control.

The man who set up things for you, not so that your way would be easier but so that your way would be his way. Gunnison took the cover from his cup, put it on the table, and picked up the cup, which he kept cradled on his lap. He did not want to mirror Cheng's gestures; he did not want to have his gestures under Cheng's control. Besides, he disliked the Chinese custom of keeping a lid on the teacup. "Keeping the lid on." He had never thought of the tea cover as a metaphor.

"Your message said you had a business proposition, Mr. Gunnison."

"Yes, General. But perhaps I should wait until we are in a more private place. The *Golden Moon*, perhaps?"

Cheng smiled, his eyes disappearing under his lids, his lower lip thrusting forward, his gray teeth hidden. "Yes. The *Golden Moon*. Those days were long ago. Very long ago." He paused for another ceremonial sip of tea. "It is also private *here*. This is, in a matter of speaking, my bank. This room is safe. Very safe." Another sip. "But perhaps you are right. Perhaps the *Golden Moon* would be a more appropriate place to discuss a maritime proposition—it does have to do with clams, doesn't it?"

The general laughed, and Gunnison wondered, as he often wondered, how much Cheng knew and when and how Cheng was going to reveal what he knew. Gunnison felt himself again being taken under control, and again by an old oriental man. Somewhere in his mind he sensed again a shuttling of power, from his will to the unknown will of another kind of mind—and then the power surging back from that will to Gunnison's own mind. An elder of China was very much like an elder of Japan.

"About the clams, Harry," Cheng said, his voice sterner, more personal, and drawing Gunnison from his reverie. "They are not, I assume, for the taking?"

"No, Cheng, not for the taking."

"There will be risks? I do not like risks, Harry. The Chinese do not take risks."

"But you do not ignore fortune."

"Yes. Fortune. Dame fortune. And fortunes." Cheng suddenly rose from his chair and walked to a tall lacquered cabinet. He moved gracefully, betraying no sign of his age, which, from knowledge of Cheng's past, Gunnison put at about seventy. He looked at Cheng now, his back straight, his white hair still full. He took a pair of gold-rimmed glasses from his coat pocket and put them on. His face was smooth, his eyes bright behind the glasses. They caught a glint from the overhead light as Cheng turned toward Gunnison and, smiling his tight smile, held up the book he had taken from a shelf in the cabinet. "Fortune," he said. "Mr. Shakespeare." He tapped a page. "Often, Harry, as you may remember, I go to Mr. Shakespeare as Christians go to the Bible. Or as Chinese—and now Americans—turn to *I-Ching*. I look for an auspicious sign when I am about to start a venture. Or should I say launch a venture?"

"And what does Mr. Shakespeare say?" Gunnison asked. He had a feeling that Cheng relied much more on Cheng than on Shakespeare. But he also knew that there was a side of Cheng that he would never know, the oriental side. As in Chia Min.

"Fortune. Mr. Shakespeare says this about that marvelous word. 'Fortune,' he says, 'brings in some boats that are not steer'd.' And is that not auspicious, Harry? Is that not exactly what it is that you are now engaged in? A boat not steered." He paused. "Yes. It would be appropriate to go to the *Golden Moon*."

The car was still a black Mercedes, but the drive to Chilung was slower and more sedate. On the way to the port, Cheng, as in the old days, recited history along the way. "The buildings have changed, Harry. Rarely can I now point to the old. More and more I, the old one, must point to the new. We started becoming like you, Harry—that theater once was an opera house; now it is a cabaret. You can hire it—and all the young women in it—by the night. The Americanization of Taiwan, they called it. And now, now, Harry, we do not even exist in your country's official world."

Gunnison did little more than respond politely to Cheng's bitter charge that America, by recognizing China, had deserted her friend Taiwan. The car made its way through the dark streets of Chilung and stopped before a long, floodlighted pier. A high wire fence stretched across the pier and disappeared where the edges of the light touched the blackness of the water. The narrow gate of the fence slid open, and a stocky man with close-cropped gray hair stepped forward and flashed a light into the driver's side of the car. Under his open black raincoat Gunnison could see a gunbelt and what looked like the butt of a .45-caliber service pistol. The man grunted at the driver, who got out of the car and opened the right passenger door so that Gunnison preceded Cheng onto the pier. Gunnison squinted in the bright light, which seemed to darken the night rather than illumine the pier. Cheng spoke to the man in the raincoat, who motioned them through the gate. As it closed behind them with a snap, Gunnison heard the car drive off. He turned to see the red taillights vanish around the corner of a warehouse.

Cheng walked next to Gunnison; Raincoat fell in behind, the beam of his flashlight bobbing on the wet wood before them and their shadows.

"No soldiers now. That's changed, too?" Gunnison said. He had suddenly sensed that he was in a forbidden zone, in a place that was somehow illicit. In the old days, he knew that he walked the dock with a general whose armed and uniformed soldiers guarded not only the pier but also the American visitor. Now he felt that the man in the raincoat, and perhaps the general himself, were not official, not legitimate. Cheng did not answer Gunnison's question.

They were at the end of the pier. Another man appeared, apparently out of a shed that, in the darkness, had to be imagined. Cheng spoke to the man in a tone that sounded preemptory. Raincoat's flashlight beam played over the man's feet, legs, and torso—sandals, dark trousers, zippered blue jacket—but did not climb to his face. There was a whirring sound, two dull white lights flashed beyond the pier, and a gangway slapped down. From its other end someone waved a flashlight, whose beam tracked across the planks of the gangway and stopped precisely at the toes of Cheng's highly polished black shoes. He took Gunnison's left elbow and briskly followed the receding light until they stood before the man holding it. Without a word, he led them to a doorway and shined his light on the brass keyplate. Cheng reached into his pocket and took out a key on a long gold chain that glistened in the light. He unlocked the door, propelled Gunnison inside with a sudden, surprising show of strength, and closed the door behind them.

Gunnison heard two clicks—the lock, and then the switch for the overhead bulb that flooded the small stateroom with a burst of glaring white light. Gunnison quickly looked around. The two portholes on either side of the door were blacked out. Gauging the width of the room, he estimated that this could fit *in* the *Golden Moon,* though it did not seem to be *of* the old junk. He rubbed his eyes. His head had started to pulse when they began walking down the pier. It was a kind of headache he had not had for some time. He knew enough about himself to realize that when his head pulsed in that way, deep down where the basics are, his mind sensed danger.

Cheng motioned him to a couch built against the bulkhead farthest from the door. Cheng sat in a metal chair next to a small metal table. It, like the chair, was bolted to the deck. "Welcome back to the *Golden Moon,* Harry," Cheng said. He leaned forward and placed his hands palms down on the table.

"Things have changed, Cheng."

"Yes, Harry. Some things." Cheng lifted his hands and formed them into a prow that pointed at Gunnison. "And you have changed." His voice was harsh, menacing. "You are double-dealing. Perhaps triple-dealing. Not like the old Harry. Not like the all-American boy. The Virginia gentleman." Cheng laughed contemptuously and pointed to the rack on the bulkhead behind Gunnison. "Help yourself."

Gunnison took the sealed bottle of Virginia Gentleman from the rack. He had introduced Cheng to the bourbon, which was distilled and bottled not far from the agency's headquarters in Virginia. Next to the rack was the small leather case he had also given to Cheng. He opened it and took out two silver-edged cups. Etched on one was an approximation of Gunnison's name in Chinese characters; on the other was Cheng's name. Gunnison held up the case and, as long before, Cheng nodded. Gunnison broke the seal on the bottle and filled each cup.

Cheng took his, said, *"Gambei!"* downed the bourbon in a gulp, and held the cup upside down. *"Gambei!"* he repeated. Gunnison imitated the ritual, adding "Bottoms up" to his *"Gambei!"* He liked the feel of fire in his throat and stomach because he could concentrate on the fire and not let his mind wander through Cheng's mental acrobatics of camaraderie and threat, nostalgia and bitterness. He knew that it was impossible to gain an initiative with a Chinese in his own territory, but he had to try. He sensed that his life depended on his trying to take control of the situation.

Gunnison began his carefully rehearsed speech. "Let me tell you about something that we will both be interested in." Then, in what Gunnison would later recall as a most uncharacteristic interruption, Cheng said softly, "Yes, Harry, tell me about your buried treasure—or should I say *sunken* treasure."

For a long moment there was silence, except for the sound of the waves slapping against the *Golden Moon*'s hull. Cheng laughed, fully and honestly. "I hope you still play poker, Harry. You have the best poker face of any American I have ever met. You act as if you are not astonished that I know about your buried—I mean sunken—treasure, about your Japanese treasure ship sunk illegally in wartime by your submarine *Tigerfish.*"

After another moment's silence, as if to break down any barrier that he may have erected between the two, Cheng said, "You know, Harry, I am getting old, I am not certain I recall which of us did better in our few poker games. No, poker was never my game. I played it often, but only with Americans."

"My game is now more like roulette," Gunnison said. He wished he had only thought that remark and had not blurted it out. He smiled, taking the moment to concentrate on every word he was going to say.

"I am here to offer you a deal, Cheng. The best deal you have ever heard." Gunnison held up the hand that still clutched the silver cup. "Wait. I don't want to hear any more of your Fu Manchu crap. You don't have to tell me I'm in your power and all that shit. Sure. You could hold me here, make me squirm. But, come on, Ho"—he used Cheng's given name for the first time—"come on, if I'm double-dealing, what the hell are you doing? I'm no Virginia gentleman anymore. I've quit the agency. And you're no general anymore. You're closer to what I am, Ho. A private person looking for a good investment. And I have it."

"Harry. You still are Harry. Making the big bet with only two pairs. Yes, I know you think you have a deal for me. But let me tell you, Harry. I have one for you. I am aware of your dealings with Ishiwata. I know about the *Glomar Explorer.* If you had not come here of your free will, you would have been taken here. Yes, Harry. A deal. It is simply this: I get the gold of the *Osaka Maru,* and you get a life of luxury—with or without Chia Min—here in Taiwan or any one of several Asian countries where the Taiwanese government would feel you were safe."

"And the split?" asked Gunnison.

"Ah, to know the stakes before the cards are dealt! Tell me, Harry, how much did Ishiwata offer for your services?"

"Exactly five hundred thousand," Gunnison said quickly and, surprising himself, honestly.

"You must understand that I do not really know how much gold is in the *Osaka Maru,* Harry. I am not certain that you know, even if Ishiwata did tell you. Obviously, we are dealing with many, many millions. But, remember Harry, there will be operating costs for my government, and gold is difficult to handle—like poker chips, gold must be cashed in when the game is completed. I believe the term is a 'handling charge.'

"Rather, Harry, let us simply conclude a gentleman's agreement—one between a Virginia gentleman and a Chinese gentleman. Upon the gold reaching Taiwan you will receive exactly five million dollars in currency. That's five million dollars with no taxes to be paid. Most or all will be in American dollars, but we may be forced to include some yen, depending upon the cash on hand at my bank branches at the moment the gold touches our shore. Plus, of course, guaranteed safe passage for you, and a friend if you wish, to any of the countries that we mutually agree are satisfactory for you to reside in. Is that acceptable, Harry?"

"Does one bargain with a friend?"

"No, Harry. And you know better than to ask."

"Then agreed. Five million—*and* a pair of airline tickets," Gunnison held the cup up in a toast to the agreement. But before he sipped, Gunnison said, "Five million—no matter what." Cheng did not speak. "No matter what," Gunnison repeated. He put down his cup. "You realize what I mean by that, don't you, Cheng Ho? You mentioned your government. Come on, Ho. Things can go wrong. You are freelancing. There is no government in this—on my side or on yours."

"I am no traitor, Harry."

"Neither am I. The national interests of the United States are not involved in this matter. My government will not be hurt. I will be betraying no one. It is a business proposition. So please, don't talk to me about governments."

Cheng stood and began pacing back and forth in front of Gunnison. "I am not exactly a freelancer, Harry. There are many channels of intelligence, many kinds of activities in Taiwan. Would it surprise you if I told you that two weeks ago I was in Canton? I am a merchant, a connection between Taiwan and the mainland. I am also something else, something hard to translate. Your plumbers of the Nixon White House? Something like that. I do special jobs. Untraceable. And, as a reward, let us say, I can engage in other activities. There are no pirates anymore, Harry. Not quite. But there are people who deal in what a distinguished ancestor of mine called 'transshipped goods.' "

Gunnison laughed. "Madame Ching," he said. "I remember the tales you told." Gunnison relaxed the grip on his mind; the old cadence of Cheng's voice had returned. Less menacing, more friendly. "She liked to nail people to planks and throw them overboard. Lovely lady."

"You dishonor my ancestor, Harry. She never nailed enemies to her 'beauty bar'—she called it that because, it was written of her, she thought that when they finally accepted the last nails, they looked peaceful, often beautiful. No, never enemies, Harry. Only traitors. Men and women of her own crews who failed to carry out . . . an agreement."

"I will remember that, Ho." Gunnison, motioning Cheng to sit down, reached for the bottle.

"No more for me, Harry. We soon will eat. As in the old days. But now I will tell you of the deal. It can be said quickly, and then the meal will arrive. Here is—"

"Wait. One question. How did you know about the *Osaka Maru* and my meeting with Ishiwata?"

"You will know in the fullness of time, my friend. I promise you that.

"Time," Cheng continued, his voice softening. " 'The time of life is short,' Mr. Shakespeare says. 'To spend that shortness basely were too long.' So we will not talk of that now, Harry. You will learn in the fullness of time. And now, please—perhaps while you sip? No *gambei.* You need a clear head. Perhaps while you sip, you will hear my arrangements.

"Through my association with the government of the true Republic of China—this unrecognized government of mine—I will arrange for a boarding party. There will be, if necessary, unmarked—*untraceable,* I should say—boats or aircraft, whatever I need. There will be enough force, Harry, to seize the *Glomar* with a minimum of bloodshed or perhaps, I hope, no bloodshed, as soon as the gold is recovered.

"You will, of course, be aboard, Harry, and you will give us the help that we may need.

"The ship will be taken to a remote area of Taiwan, a place well known to my honored ancestor, Madame Ching, by the way. The gold will be removed. There will be a certain awkward business in which my government will deny knowing anything about the seizure. Indeed, the term 'pirates' might even be used in the official explanation. The *Glomar* and her crew will be returned, through a third party—perhaps Macao—to the United States. The gold will not be returned. You, the gold, and I will all meet, and you will receive your five million dollars.

"This is the general outline, Harry. There will, of course, be details. You will leave them to me. May I suggest that you remain aboard the *Golden Moon* this evening? Tomorrow you will be flown to Manila on a private flight and you will be put aboard a Philippines Air Lines plane for the United States. If the agency demands to know why you came to Taiwan, I am sure that you will be able to supply a satisfactory answer. Whatever the answer, Harry, it is not to include mention of a meeting with me. Is that clear to you, Harry?"

"Yes. And I assume that there will be a way for me to contact you."

"That will not be necessary, Harry. *I* shall remain in contact with *you.* Just continue doing your job for Ishiwata. The deception should not be difficult."

"I don't think of it as deception, Ho."

"And what is it that you do think of it as, Harry? Transshipment of goods?"

There was a light tap on the door. Cheng rose and opened it to the man in the raincoat, who now was wearing a dirty white jacket over an even dirtier white shirt, open at the throat. He carried a large silver tray that bore two melon shells brimming with a many-colored soup flavored with lotus seeds. "The first course, Harry," Cheng said, smiling and gesturing toward the tray. "It will be a feast fit for the gods of gold."

15

THE AMERICAN AIRLINES RED-EYE FLIGHT from Los Angeles, where he had transferred from the Philippine Air Lines flight, deposited the mortal remains of Harry Gunnison at Washington's Dulles International Airport at 8:35 A.M.

Customs had been handled at the Los Angeles changeover, and so Gunnison, clutching the carry-on bag he had bought in Taipei, could walk directly from the mobile lounge across the plaza, down the escalator, and out to the taxi line. Two days earlier, he assumed, Japan Air Lines had, upon finding a bag but no Mr. Gunnison on the flight, forwarded his well-traveled bag to his home.

The cab ride on the thirteen-mile Dulles access road and then along Route 50 to Washington, along Constitution Avenue, and finally to his Capitol Hill home took over an hour. Gunnison slept during most of the rush-hour ordeal. Mercifully, the airport cab driver did not curse the traffic, at least not loudly, nor play the radio.

As the cab pulled up in front of his house, Gunnison woke, and for an instant he believed that he again had dreamed about the carp-to-dragon transmutation. After paying the cab driver and ringing the door buzzer three times, he inserted his key into the lock, only to have it pulled from his hand as Chia Min yanked open the door. Her normal composure was gone; she embraced him, saying nothing, and laid her head on his chest.

Chia Min was somber as she prepared a breakfast, which they carried into his study. He told her everything about the trip, all that is, except the Sunday night at Ishiwata's retreat. Chia Min then spoke for the first time, to say that on Tuesday there had been a call from Jessen.

"He was quite cordial to me, as he always is. He said whenever I heard from you I was to tell you that you should come out to his place for a walk."

Gunnison questioned her, asking her to repeat every word she could remember from the conversation. Then he dialed Jessen's direct number. Ann Taylor, his secretary, answered by repeating the last four digits he had dialed. "This is Harry, Ann. How are you? Good. Would it be convenient for me to drive out and take a walk today. About 1:00 P.M.? Yes, that's fine. Yes, I'll have my Porsche, same tags."

Gunnison showered, and then he and Chia Min made love. It was a full and cleansing love for both; for her to express her missing him for what seemed much longer than he had actually been away; for him to somehow atone for all of the dishonesty he suddenly felt welling up from some deep and secret place within him.

Shortly before 1:00 P.M., Gunnison pulled his Porsche up to the guardhouse at the main entrance to the CIA complex at Langley. The guard, after glancing at his license plate and his plastic ID card, handed him a day parking card for the lot in front of the main building with the greeting, "Good afternoon, Mr. Gunnison."

Gunnison nodded and turned onto the winding road to the main visitor's parking lot. He walked up the steps and into the large entry area with the CIA seal on the floor. He smiled at the guards barring entrance to the building proper and turned left into the reception area. He filled out the registration form, and the woman behind the counter punched the data into a computer. She quickly received authorization to provide him with the properly colored and marked plastic card that would give him access to specific parts of the building.

He clipped the card to the pocket of his madras jacket, thanked the young woman, and entered the building proper. The attractively decorated halls of the third floor led him to the complex of offices that housed the Asia-Western Pacific specialists and Charles L. Jessen. Ann immediately escorted him into Jessen's office and confirmed that Gunnison still drank his coffee black.

"Sit down, Harry, and tell me all about it," Jessen said as Harry entered. Jessen did not rise but simply leaned back, put down the papers he had been reading, and swiveled his chair to face Gunnison, who sat down on the couch next to Jessen's desk.

"I'll be turning in a report," Gunnison said.

"Forget about the report. I want to hear what you have to say. I'll let you know when I want something in writing on this one."

"It's not simple."

"It never is. That's why we sent you there. What's the problem?"

"He's got the ship. That's the problem. He's also got Riling on his payroll."

"I know that, Harry," Jessen said, his voice irritable.

"I know you know that. But do you know that Riling can help Ishiwata cause trouble?"

"How?"

"By giving Ishiwata enough fuzz about agency operations so that Ishiwata can make it look as if the death of Porter was some agency deal that blew up."

"Bullshit," Jessen said. But his voice, no longer irritable, did not sound convincing. He swung his chair around and pressed his hands against the desktop. "He's waving a wet noodle at us. If anybody killed Porter, he did. And if he did, it's because something about this is goddamn important to him. What is it?"

"Gold. This ship he's after, the *Osaka Maru,* went down with a lot of gold in her."

"How much is a lot?"

"Ishiwata won't say. Just that there's gold. I got him to admit that."

"Tell me more. This is sounding like it has wrinkles."

Gunnison told Jessen Ishiwata's story, from the placing of gold aboard the *Osaka Maru* to the torpedoing and the taking of Ishiwata aboard the *Tigerfish.*

"So it's vengeance, I think," Gunnison concluded. "Vengeance and a chance to get back that gold."

"And he didn't tell you how much?"

"No," Gunnison said, wondering if he had said the word too fast, wondering if he was lying as expertly as he usually did as part of his job. Deception was always a burden for him, but he had been able to handle the burden because he had always told himself that he was lying for good reason, or at least for official purposes. Now, lying to Jessen, he felt as if he were really lying. He rarely if ever lied to friends.

"What *did* he tell you?"

"He told me that another guy in the *Soji* was after the ship and he was the one who killed Porter. The guy was also supposedly tracking me down, and Ishiwata had him and one of his people killed."

"I know, Harry. I know about those guys being killed." Jessen leaned forward. "I'm glad you told me that, Harry. That was one of those geometric facts, you know? The kind that goes like this: I knew that you knew, but you didn't know that I knew. Complicated. But simple, too. You know, I trust you, Harry. But I always have to make sure I am putting my trust in the right place." He paused and, once again speaking in what seemed like his matter-of-fact voice, he said, "Ishiwata is a tough guy. Smart. And cute. He also has an ace up his sleeve."

"And what may that be, Charlie?"

"He—or his banks or his damn *Soji*—has a considerable influence in Japanese industry, especially with Nissan. In fact, he sort of controls them, and because they are one of the three major Japanese auto producers, he has influence on the others as well. Anyway, Ishiwata has convinced a couple of U.S. congressmen—from Detroit and districts where we build cars—that if our government helps him with a certain small favor, he will support continued holdbacks on the number of Japanese cars that are sent to the United States next year."

"How did you hear about that?" Gunnison asked.

"The boss got a call yesterday from State. They knew all about the *Glomar* and the *Osaka Maru*. But they didn't know about Porter. And he didn't mention it to them. They want us to let Ishiwata have the *Glomar* for a while."

"So the signals are changing?"

"Sort of. The boss doesn't have any emotional investment in the *Glomar*. And he's inclined to make a couple of points with State."

"This makes it easy," Gunnison said, suddenly realizing that he was speaking a thought. He tried to cover his surprise and confusion by laughing.

"Makes what easy?" Jessen sounded suspicious, as if he had heard the false notes in Gunnison's laugh.

"My recommendation," Gunnison said. "Your boss made it easy. I was going to recommend that you give Ishiwata another thirty days. Otherwise, there would certainly be some trouble. I thought I was going to have to talk you into it. Actually . . ." He paused. *Damn it. I never use that phony word.* " . . . well, I talked him into doubling the ante. Fifty thousand bucks a day. The agency will get twice as much dough."

"And how about you, Harry?"

"What do you mean, Charlie?"

"I won't ask you how much he offered you," Jessen responded. "My only question is will his offer affect your work with the agency on this project?"

"No," Gunnison replied, with only a moment's hesitation. "Any deal I may make with Ishiwata will have absolutely no effect on my loyalty to the agency."

Jessen looked at him carefully. The answer obviously expected and accepted. "Okay by me, Harry, but the boss might get involved in this, and I'm certain he will want to know how much Ishiwata is paying you. Actually, if it were anyone else but you, I would consider it a conflict of interest. But I trust you Harry. I guess I really trust you."

"So does Ishiwata."

For a moment Jessen did not speak. Gunnison had always wondered how they kept track of everybody here: How often were you bugged? How often were the buggers bugged? And after a while did people forget they were being bugged, the way Nixon had? Was Jessen pausing now because he wasn't sure what was being heard—or was it that he didn't know what he should say next?

"Are you trying to tell me something, Harry?"

"I'm just pointing out that I could keep an eye on things for you and still—"

"And still earn your check from Ishiwata. Sure. I can see that, Harry. I can see that. Be a friend of the agency. Like those guys in Libya."

"Not like them, Charlie. For Christ's sake. There's no national security involved in this. You get me mad sometimes. Sitting there like a goddamn Methodist, making believe everything is black and white." Gunnison wished he still smoked so that he could pause now to light a cigarette. He could only pause, and his pause would be judged. He had spoken too fast, too much.

He began speaking more slowly, with what he hoped was deliberate calm that did not sound deliberate. "Look. I've done my little chore for Ishiwata. Or at least it will seem that way to him. I'll tell him his little back-channel trip through Detroit nearly queered things—until I saved it."

"I don't care if you're making a little on this, Harry. But it is a delicate matter. Or could be. That guy is tight with some big names in this town. Harry, he didn't need us—" Jessen's hands swept out, one pointing to a window, another to the wall. "And he didn't need you. Don't you see, Harry? He's using people just to use them. He's got enough money—and enough influence—to keep the *Glomar* as long as he wants her. Maybe this guy trusts you, Harry. But for God's sake don't trust him." Jessen smiled, stood, and reached out his hand.

"Now I've got to kick you out and get to some other chores. My guess is that the *Glomar* charter is extended. I can finally finish that report on *Glomar* for the director. I don't think we have to worry about Porter haunting us. So it looks like you can go back to Ishiwata and be a hero." Jessen came out from behind his desk and walked to the door, where Gunnison stood. "I'm not really a Methodist, Harry. You know usually where the right side is on things. So do I. It's never black and white. Okay?"

"Okay."

"Now. Why don't you and Chia Min come over Sunday night? We'll do some ribs on the grill. You bring beer and dessert. By then I should be able to tell you we have a green light on this thing. Actually, by then maybe you and I will take a walk and discuss your role. I'll have Joan call Chia Min. Okay?"

They were lying in bed, the mosquito-net canopy quivering to the cool air washing through the bedroom. A compromise during lovemaking: the air-conditioning—and the canopy. He had bought the canopy in Taipei at her request. It seemed so long ago. She was talking now, softly, as she did when she wanted his full attention. She could speak so low, so softly that there was no way to listen to her without listening to her alone. Now amid her words he could hear the whirring sounds of the air-conditioning. He got out of bed and padded to the wall switch.

"A spiraling, Harry, a spiraling of . . ."

As he got back into bed, he looked at the clock's glowing dial: 5:35.

"A spiraling, Chia Min? I'm sorry. I didn't hear you. A spiraling of what?"

"I see a spiraling of deceit, Harry. Higher and higher to a place where the turning must stop."

"It's late, Chia Min. Or early." His voice sounded loud and weary.

"Not too early to talk. You must make choices, Harry. A choice. The spiraling must stop."

"It seemed simple until I talked to you." He turned and touched her hair. He lay back, his eyes on the level of her eye. She was staring straight up, and he could see only the faint line of her profile in the gauzy light.

"Ishiwata wanted me to get the *Glomar* for another month, wanted me to fix things. Well, he's fixed them himself, but *I* can claim the credit. I can go to him and tell him it's all fixed. As soon as the *Glomar* is over the wreck, I—we—get two hundred thousand dollars."

"And then?" she asked, turning her face toward him, erasing the profile. She had raised her voice. "And then," she continued, "will you betray the Japanese man, this Ishiwata? Or will you betray General Cheng? Someone. You must betray someone."

"I will betray no one. That is such an oriental word, Chia Min. Betray. Ishiwata is no fool. He was using me as one of the channels to get what he wanted. I am no fool. Five hundred thousand dollars—and no trouble. Or five million dollars and a lifetime—a short one—filled with trouble."

"Or both," Chia Min said. She moved quickly, sliding over him, out of the bed, and into the bathroom. She did not shut the door. When she finished, she flung a blue robe around herself and walked out of the bedroom, silently closing the door behind her.

As they often did, they resumed in the kitchen an argument that had begun in the bedroom. She was standing at the sink, her back to him.

"You said *both*. Your last word was *both*," he said. "You mean take the money from Ishiwata. Take the money when he thinks he is going to get his gold. And then go to Cheng, continue with Cheng. *Both*. No spiraling to that, is there?" He walked to the sink and put his arm around her shoulder. He could feel her tighten.

She turned around and looked up at him, her face the mask it always became when she was feeling deep emotion. "Nothing is wrong except you say things that don't make sense."

"Like what?" He sat on the stool and picked up an apple from a wooden bowl on the counter. He tossed the apple into the air twice. The third time it fell to the tan tile floor. Chia Min picked it up, looked for a bruise, washed it, and returned it to the bowl. "Like what?" he repeated.

"Money. You have made it mean so much—Catherine. It is always lately Catherine. Money for Catherine and that person she is married to."

"It's true that I must help Catherine," Gunnison said, his voice echoing the emphasis Chia Min had put on his sister's name. "I suppose you resent Catherine."

"Resent? I do not believe so, Harry." She sighed, picked up the apple, and handed it back to him. "I do not resent. I see Catherine as another burden, something you must carry. Perhaps something that gives you a reason—what looks like a good reason—to make this deal, this betrayal."

"No," Gunnison said sharply. "Not betrayal. Not that."

"And why is that, Harry? Why is this not betrayal of your country?"

"Because my country doesn't *care* about this. This is not a matter of national security or national interest."

"So, Harry, what you mean is it is not quite treason."

"No, Chia Min. This is a matter of money. I have a chance to get enough money to help Catherine—the down payment, the fifty thousand, will go to her right away—and enough money to keep us alive and well for a long, long time."

"That money—the alive-and-well money—would be the money from General Cheng?"

"Yes. I want to give Catherine as much as she needs. But, compared to Ishiwata's money, the money from Cheng is a fortune. Yes, alive-and-well money."

"And you plan to invest your money, the money that you keep for you and me, with that man named Gleason, the man who helped Wilson."

"You sound displeased, Chia Min. I just want to put the money in Gleason's hands. He'll open an account for us in Bermuda. It's cash, hard to handle. Taxes. You don't understand?"

"I understand, Harry. I suppose Wilson was very wise. But not so wise that you don't know where his money is. And if you know, the agency knows. I do not understand that, Harry."

Edwin P. Wilson had been a high-ranking officer in the agency, a specialist in clandestine activities. Around the time he quit the agency, he turned up as a consultant to an exporter of terrorism, the Libyan dictator Muammar al-Qaddafi. Through a mutual friend of Wilson's at the agency, Gunnison had been directed to Patrick Ignatius Gleason, a Washington lawyer who specialized in handling cash. Gunnison had learned the details of Wilson's cash transactions and had found out how he had set up shadowy corporations and bank accounts in Bermuda and Switzerland.

"What don't you understand, Chia Min?"

"You are not Wilson."

"Yes, Chia Min. I know that. I know that I am not hurting anybody. I'm just doing business. But it is business that must be secret business."

"I am not a child. Or someone who uses 'oriental' words, Harry.

I know that the money has to be hidden. I am talking *business*. This Gleason. I suppose you trust him." Her voice trailed off in what Gunnison recognized as a familiar signal of displeasure with one of his decisions.

"Okay, Chia Min. What are you *really* trying to say?"

"May I suggest that you already know a banker in Taiwan?"

"Cheng? General Cheng? You must be kidding, Chia Min."

"Not kidding, Harry. Being realistic. He is to give you a lot of money. You have his word—but only that. If he were forced to put that money through some kind of channel, onto some kind of paper . . ."

"I see what you mean. Yes. You do talk business. I'll hold off on talking to Gleason. We'll just keep the down payment locked up here for a while. You can buy groceries with it." He laughed and went to the sink. This time her body did not tighten when he put his arm around her waist.

"Many groceries," she said, turning her face up to his.

"This is going to be a nice Sunday after all," Gunnison said.

That night, after the barbecued ribs, and after Joan, Chia Min, and the three Jessen children had gone into the sprawling McLean house, Jessen and Gunnison sat back on the Sears lawn furniture. It was nearly ten, but there was still the faintest light in the western summer sky.

"Well, Harry. It's a go. They've even got the Navy in it now. The Navy's going to help him find that goddamn wreck. They're calling it an exercise. Classified test of some new bottom-sounding sonar. That guy knows where the strings are and how to pull them."

"So do the people in Detroit, Charlie."

"Yeah. But watch him, you hear?"

"I'll watch him."

"Or he'll watch you—oops, there's the high sign from Joan—the kids are in bed and we'd better go in or she and Chia Min will divorce us." Jessen looked up suddenly, started to say he was sorry, but decided what the hell, and walked silently toward the sliding glass door with Gunnison. Since Gunnison had returned to the States with Chia Min, there had been hints that he would do better with the organization if he were to marry Chia Min. It was, as Jessen once had told Gunnison, "a matter of image, not security." Methodists, Gunnison thought again. A bunch of Methodists.

16

THE OPERATION WAS DESIGNATED SPEARMINT, a not particularly opaque code name. An elaborate and highly classified "memorandum of understanding" was drawn up between the Navy and the CIA, with a digest of its contents going through routine channels to State. The first activity involved what the memorandum called a training mission. This was assigned to the nuclear submarine *Redfin*, which took on the mission when she set out from Pearl Harbor on her next Pacific patrol.

Using the AN/BQS-32 search sonar and the new cable-controlled MNV (mine neutralization vehicle) Mark 3, the *Redfin* easily located and photographed the sunken hulk of the *Osaka Maru*. One of the crewmen, who was taking a correspondence course in Japanese from the Navy's language school, was even able to read her name on her stern. (He was summoned to the captain's cabin and firmly told to forget what he had seen. The mission was very highly classified.)

The *Redfin* had reached the spot with help of charts provided by Ishiwata.

The charts had been delivered by a Japanese man who appeared on Gunnison's doorstep two days after his Sunday evening conversation with Jessen. The man bowed low to Chia Min when she opened the door. Very respectfully, he asked for Gunnison-*san*.

Chia Min hesitated to ask him into the house, but the almost immediate appearance of Gunnison saved her that decision. The visitor was then invited into the hallway. He glanced curiously at the jade object on the table. With apologies, he briefly examined a small photo he had of Gunnison, and, after returning it to his pocket, asked Gunnison to place his signature on a three-by-five card he produced. Gunnison signed, and the man took the card. The man bowed again, and thanked Gunnison for identifying himself. The man then gave Gunnison a long, rolled package.

"You are Nishihara," Gunnison said, his voice hovering between statement and question. The man did not answer. He smiled up at Gunnison. "Nishihara. So you are not dead." The man smiled again.

Gunnison led him up to the office, followed him through the door, and locked it.

"We are safe here. Safe to talk," Gunnison said, pointing to a chair across from the rolltop desk. Gunnison sat in the swivel chair in front of the desk and spun toward the man. "And, so, talk."

"You may call me Nishihara, if you like," the man said, dismissing the idea with a swing of his right hand. There was a choppiness to the gesture, and in it Gunnison perceived control and strength. "There is not much to talk about, Gunnison-*san*," he said. "I am a delivery person."

"And you are delivering the charts you stole from Porter's apartment as well as Mr. Ishiwata's maps?"

The man shrugged.

"The woman who runs the apartment house can identify you."

"I do not believe that is probable, Gunnison-*san*." The man slumped in the chair and spoke in a sing-song. "I can be a very little, very stupid Jap if that is the role I must play." He sat up straight and spoke more gruffly. "So. Today the role is delivery person. You are to give these to your Mr. Jessen or to what person is best to give it to in Operation Spearmint. These are Japanese charts, with translations in the margins."

He took the top from a long blue plastic tube and removed one of the charts. He went to the bookshelves, took down several books, idly reading their titles. He crouched on the floor near his chair and spread out the chart, holding it down with the books. Gunnison crouched on the other side of the chart.

"This is not an original," he said.

"Charts. Not works of art, Gunnison-*san*. Ishiwata-*san* has the originals, of course."

"You—or somebody—took Porter's stuff and transferred them to an old Japanese chart."

"We will talk about what is here, Gunnison-*san*." The man pointed to the chart. His nails were glossy and squarely trimmed. "You will tell anyone who asks that these came to you by special messenger from Ishiwata-*san*. You will say that you were told that he had found charts similar to those used by the captain of the *Osaka Maru*. Ishiwata-*san* remembered the degrees of error used by the captain to show a false course so the ship would not be found when it was scuttled." He stumbled over the last word. He spoke as if he had memorized what he had been told to say. Gunnison wondered how much he understood.

"There are other charts," Nishihara said. "One shows the planned route of the *Osaka Maru,* as was agreed. Another chart shows the actual track the *Osaka Maru* followed. Another—"

"So Porter was right. The ship did go off course."

"Porter. Porter. I know no Porter," Nishihara said. He did not like being interrupted. "These other charts"—he nodded his head toward the tube—"will help to explain this one. It is here"—his glistening fingertip touched a thin red cross—"that the ship was . . . was . . ."

"Scuttled?" Gunnison asked. "You know the word 'scuttled'?"

Nishihara swung his hand angrily, as if he were striking a blow. "The ship. The going down of the ship into the sea." He glared at Gunnison and jabbed his fingers at the chart. "This . . . This you will take to the people who search."

"And then I am to become the delivery person, Nishihara?"

His eyes did not leave Gunnison's face. Gunnison had the ridiculous image of two Sumo wrestlers circling each other. He stood up and returned to his chair by the desk.

Nishihara remained crouching by the chart, arms on his knees, shoulders hunched, a coil of strength. Still glaring at Gunnison, he said, "Delivery is sometimes a dangerous business, Gunnison-*san*. I was told you were professional." He swiveled his head, quickly surveying the room. "There are a dozen ways I could kill you in this room. You do not know who I am."

"I know who you are. You're a thug, a messenger."

Nishihara, in one fluid move, leaped toward Gunnison's chair, spun it around, and his arms and chest became a vice pinning Gunnison to the chair. Just as suddenly, he relaxed his grip.

Gunnison stood, his chest spiked with pain, and swung his right hand toward Nishihara's throat. Nishihara parried with a chop of his left hand across Gunnison's arm. Then he thrust the heels of his palms at Gunnison's chest and shoved him back into the chair.

"I am being kind and instructive, Gunnison-*san,*" he said. "I want you to know who I am. I am not a thug. I am someone who is paid to do such things as kill. I am not authorized to kill you. Or you would now be dead."

"You were to deliver the charts," Gunnison said. "Give them

to me." He reached out his right hand, and pain shot along his arm. He tightened his jaw. His hand was trembling.

Nishihara leaned down, picked up the books and replaced them on the shelves. The chart began to curl. He rolled it, returned it to the tube, and, bowing slightly, handed it to Gunnison. "Ishiwata-*san* instructed me to give you a name—a password, he said—so that you would know you were dealing with an agent from him."

"All right. All right," Gunnison said impatiently. He had not doubted that Nishihara was from Ishiwata. "What is the password?"

"Ishiwata-*san* said for you to 'remember Takiko.' " He repeated the name.

Gunnison nodded.

"Good," Nishihara said. He handed Gunnison a card with a Washington phone number on it, nothing more. "When you want to reach me, call this number. Let it ring five times. Hang up, dial again, and let it ring one time. I will be here within fifteen minutes."

Gunnison unlocked the office door and followed Nishihara to the hallway. When Gunnison opened the outer door, he saw a car parked directly across the street. The Japanese driver turned his head and looked directly at Gunnison. Nishihara got into the car next to the driver. The car was a black Maxima, made by Nissan.

Gunnison decided not to call Jessen in advance. It would be better to be a bit mysterious; it would make the charts worth some chips. He drove to Langley and convinced Jessen's secretary that he should be admitted, refusing to check the long blue tube he was carrying at the outer office. He waited nearly an hour until Jessen emerged from a meeting. He passed the hour making up imaginary conversations with General Cheng.

He handed over the tube without saying how he had got the charts. Jessen did not ask.

"I want something for these," Gunnison said.

"Try me," Jessen said.

"I want to be aboard when they go for the *Osaka Maru.*"

"Ishiwata really holds the cards on that. But I don't see any problems. Might be a good idea to have you aboard anyway. If anybody asks, I'll say I didn't know. Fair enough?"

"Fair enough," Gunnison said. He hoped he paused just enough before adding, "I assume that the best way out to her will be from Taipei?"

"Your old stamping grounds. I suppose so. I'll send a message to Dysart. Like a class reunion."

*

Three weeks later—on a cool September day—Jessen summoned Gunnison for a walk. They walked west on Independence Avenue in the afternoon of a lingering Washington summer. But in the Botanic Garden greenhouses, at the bottom of Capitol Hill, the chrysanthemums already were bringing forth the colors of fall. They sat on a bench just inside the entrance and talked of football until the rear guard of a New Jersey orchid-growers society had filed past.

"Dysart sent us word yesterday," Jessen said. "He figures that they'll have the *Glomar* over the wreck in two days."

"How does it look?"

"Dysart says not bad. The *Redfin* sonar produced some nice images, and they have video tapes. The *Osaka Maru* is lying at a forty-five-degree angle. Her masts won't interfere with a lift. They rigged the *Glomar* at that Japanese shipyard so that the claws will grab the wreck and pull it against the *Glomar* hull. Then the divers will go through hatches in the *Glomar* and hack their way into the hull of the *Osaka Maru*. Dysart makes it sound simple."

"But you sound dubious," Gunnison said.

"I'm still dubious about the whole damn deal. Just a feeling. I can't get out of my mind that Ishiwata was mixed up in murder to get what's in that wreck." Jessen put his hand on Gunnison's shoulder. "Maybe I'm not doing you a favor saying you should go aboard." He stood up and looked down at Gunnison. "I just might show up, you know. Might just arrange to make an inspection trip about that time."

"Don't worry about me," Gunnison said. "Ishiwata and I trust each other."

17

GUNNISON WAS GLAD CHIA MIN was not there when he arrived home, straight from his meeting with Jessen. She was away on one of her afternoons studying the Chinese porcelain collection at the Freer Gallery. She always went alone; her Freer afternoons were her personal time. Well, right now he needed his personal time.

During his walk up Capitol Hill from the Botanic Garden greenhouses, Gunnison had decided what he must do. Now, standing in the hallway of his home, he felt his stomach tighten. He was feeling the impact of his decision. It hurt him. *Hurt,* he was surprised to realize, was the word for it. He had decided to close out his life, beginning here in the hall. And it hurt.

He looked at the white jade carving of the carp becoming a dragon. No. He could not take that. He could not take much more than a couple of suitcases. The carving could not go with him. He turned out of the hall and walked into the narrow, book-shelved room that led to the locked oak door of his office.

He stopped before one of the shelves and leaned closer to read some of the titles. He had never got around to organizing the books. Spy novels stood next to reference works. A history of the Korean War was between a book on chess and a book about Asian folklore. He reached for a book—*A Thousand Days.* Catherine had given him that because she knew he liked to read about the Kennedy years. He flipped it open and read, "To My Big Brother, In Memory of the JFK We Both Loved. Love, Sis." He held the book for a moment and then put it back on the shelf. *No books. I don't have to take any books. I'll be able to buy all the books I want.*

He unlocked his office door and sat at his rolltop desk. *This ought to be easier. Just throw away. Don't think.* He opened the big side drawers and took out a handful of files. Unanswered letters. Bills. The car's title. Stationery. A file folder marked "Must File."

He carried the papers to a tall wastepaper basket that sat inside a metal frame that held a shredder. Gunnison began feeding the papers into the slot and switched on the motor. Paper, cut to the agency's specification of three-sixteenths of an inch wide, began cascading into the basket. Once in a while Gunnison held a paper aside and put it on his desk.

When he had cleaned out the papers from his desk, he unlocked the filing cabinets and began sorting through the files. He lingered now and then over a few files, but soon his pace quickened. He went through the files faster and faster. He fed papers into the shredder until the basket was filled. Then he carried the basket out of the office and into the den, where he threw the tangle of strips into the fireplace. He did this several times, until the fireplace was full. Then he got some grocery bags from the kitchen, filled them at the shredder, and stacked them by the fireplace. Late tonight, when the smoke would be seen by few eyes, he would burn everything. That would be the last task.

Gunnison had nearly finished the files when he heard the front door being unlocked. Carrying a bag overspilling with strips, he met Chia Min in the hall. He leaned down and kissed her on the forehead.

"You are finally cleaning up your files," she said, with just a hint of a question in her voice.

"More than that, Chia Min. Life. I am cleaning up my life. We must talk."

He took her into the shambles of his office, turned off the shredder, fussed with the sound system, and, to the accompaniment of Beethoven's Eighth Symphony, told her that he had met with Jessen and would be leaving for Taiwan tomorrow.

"This is the end," he said, pointing to the piles of paper and the shredder. "We must leave Washington and never come back."

"Can't we turn that down?" Chia Min asked. She sounded irritable. Gunnison knew that she did not like his tendency to make quick, independent decisions and move fast. This, he knew, was happening too quickly for her.

"No," he said, as softly as he could. "No. I can't turn it down. I no longer trust even this room." He looked around it, remembering how Nishihara's eyes had done the same.

"We will have to move fast, Chia Min. Very fast."

"Move?" she said. Now she looked around, and he could imagine what was going through her mind: an inventory of an ordinary move, a moving of things from one place to another.

"We must *go—flee*," he said. "We can take nothing. Do you understand?"

"My bed. My kitchen."

"There will be a new bed. A new kitchen. A new life."

"This is the price, then. For what you are getting."

"Yes, Chia Min. The price is that we must leave and never come back." He knelt in front of her chair and rested his head in her lap.

"A tightness of muscles," she said, kneading the back of his neck with her supple fingers.

"I must leave tomorrow," he said. "I can never come back. You must leave two days later. You can never come back. We must not make it look as if we are not coming back. I am going on a trip. The agency knows that. Jessen is sending me. So I can take a suitcase—two suitcases. Even that may be dangerous. You can take nothing. You must simply walk out the door, lock it, and do something natural—like going to the Freer."

Her fingers stopped massaging for a moment, then they began moving rhythmically again.

"The house. All our things . . ."

"They *are* things. They can be replaced. You will drive to National Airport, leave the car in a long-term parking lot, and take a plane to San Francisco. Do not use your real name. Pay in cash. Tonight give me your credit cards to destroy. When you get to the airport in San Francisco, go to Cathay Airlines. I will have arrangements made. We will meet in Taiwan. You understand?"

"Yes," she said. "I understand." She stopped massaging his neck. "The house, this valuable house, this will go to Catherine. And all that is in it."

He lifted his head from her lap. "Yes."

"You are burning these papers?" she asked. He nodded.

"There will be things I will burn," she said. "Many things. Dresses and all my beautiful things. They are too small for Catherine. And my other things, my books and my letters. These will be burned. She will have nothing of mine. Nothing."

"I feel much better from your touch," Gunnison said, rubbing his neck. "And now, I must finish up in here."

Gunnison stood up and returned to his desk. She went out, and he locked the door behind her. He knew that the click of the lock would bother her. But he had to do it. The lock was not to keep her out of the room but to keep her out of his thoughts as he planned what had to be done.

He was suddenly sad, not because he was closing out his life but because there really was so little to do; it was so devastatingly easy.

After all the papers had been shredded, he wrote checks to pay the utilities and the charge accounts. He did not want to leave as a deadbeat. Chia Min would mail out the checks from San Francisco.

Finally, Catherine.

He had put aside a large manila envelope. He had been filling it with papers that he thought she would need, for the house, the car. To this he now added a check made out for all but ten dollars in his checking account.

Then he wrote the letter to Catherine:

> This is a little like that day after Dad's funeral, when we figured out how to pay his bills and, as the lawyers say, wind up his affairs.
>
> I'm not being morbid. Just realistic. It is like closing out an estate. I'm selling the house to you by turning over the quit-claim deed enclosed. It's legal enough to give you ownership, but to be on the safe side, use a good lawyer.
>
> There may be some people asking for me. Show them this letter. It does not tell you where I am going, and it is proof that you don't know where I am.
>
> You may never hear from me again. I love you and I wish there was some other way to do this. All I can do is pay some dues. The dues will appear in your lives as soon as possible. I cannot tell you how the dues will arrive or how much they will be. But enough will come to relieve you of the burden you and Paul now bear. And there is the house. I'm enclosing the keys. Please get here as soon as you can. And try to get tenants in here. Otherwise, word will get around that the place is vacant and the burglary brigade will have a field day.
>
> I have to leave this town, this country, Catherine, to make a new life.
>
> I don't believe I'm doing anything wrong. I am not doing anything against the national interest.
>
> The dues you will receive from me will be from money I have earned.
>
> I have earned what I will be sending you, Catherine, and you have earned the right to have everything I can

give you. You have been a loving sister, and I will miss you. Love from Chia Min, and love to Paul.

He signed the letter, "Your real and loving brother, Harry." The "real" came from their childhood. He and Catherine had been adopted. They were not related by blood. "But you're really my brother, aren't you?" she had asked him when she had found out. He had put his arms around her and hugged her, and he had said, "That's pretty real, isn't it? I'm real and I'm your brother."

And that had settled it, he thought, looking at the thick brown envelope on his barren desk. It was all settled now. It was all real.

18

THE FOLLOWING MORNING, as Gunnison sat back in his first-class seat en route to Los Angeles and watched the Chantilly countryside slip below the L-1011, the president of the United States sat about twenty-five miles away and read through his once-a-month listing of the Central Intelligence Agency's "family jewels." First compiled in 1973 by James R. Schlesinger when he was director of central intelligence, the family jewels report was a compilation of sensitive intelligence activities and projects. It was a simple list of seemingly innocuous code names plus two- or three-word explanations. For example, *Arab Ashes (Israeli nuclear concerns)* was the entire entry for a long-term CIA operation that involved providing Israel with information about nuclear-weapons developments by various Middle East nations. The president had seen many of the jewels listed before.

The president rapidly scanned the listing. It had changed little from the previous month's list. He liked it that way. The president believed in overt, aboveboard dealings. Tell a person or country exactly what kind of poker you were playing and deal the cards fairly. Of course, it was okay to keep your cards close to the chest, and so intelligence *collection* was fine. But when it came to *action,* play the cards straight for all to see—and the White House, not the CIA, would direct the action. Thus, in his administration, every significant intelligence activity had to have a go-ahead directly from the White House.

Near the end of the list the president read, *Operation Spearmint (Glomar Explorer).*

"What's this one here, son?" he asked the young CIA liaison officer, who was standing a respectful distance back from the president's massive desk.

"Which event is that, sir?"

The president turned the list so the young agent could look

across the desk. He tapped the entry with a pencil. "This one, young man—this Operation Spearmint."

"That's an event involving the salvage ship *Glomar Explorer*, sir."

"Now, I can see that for myself, son. But what is the ship *doing?*"

"I'm sorry, Mr. President. I cannot go beyond the briefing paper with that event."

The president looked up. The CIA officer was on his first trip alone to the White House. The family jewels listing was simply a ritual, brought over once a month from Langley. Someone had once suggested that it be delivered by messenger to the White House, but all directors of central intelligence since Schlesinger had preferred that an officer personally hand it to the president and then bring it back to Langley, never letting the copy out of his sight. Xerox machines had long ago lessened the CIA's trust of the White House staff.

"Well, here's the phone. Call Langley and get someone over here who knows and have him tell me."

"I'm not authorized to make such a call, Mr. President."

The only other persons in the room were the president's private secretary and his national security adviser, Keith Saunders. The president turned to Saunders and said, "Damn it, Keith, this is exactly what I mean."

The president turned to the man from the CIA.

"You are about to see me get mad. Really mad. After what we've gone through with the CIA the past few weeks this youngster—nothing personal, son—this young man tells me that I cannot know what the hell this Operation Mint, or Spearmint, is."

Then, turning to his secretary, the president directed, "Now I want the director himself here at 3:00 P.M. today. I don't give a damn, pardon me, Helene, where he is. I want him in this office at 3:00 P.M. today, and I want to know exactly what's going on. And, Keith, have Bob Martin check this one out. It's about one of our ships, and so I want to know what the Navy knows about this and whether they're involved or if the CIA is doing this—whatever the hell *this* is—all on their own."

By 3:00 P.M. the president was a full hour behind schedule for the day. A large number of people had gathered in the reception area by that time. Not only was the director of central intelligence waiting, along with Jessen and two aides, but the director of naval intelligence and an aide, the deputy secretary of treasury for international affairs and an aide, a deputy assistant secretary of state and an aide, two medium-level representatives from the Department of Defense, and an assistant director and his aide from the Office of Management and Budget. The more senior men sat, their acolytes hovering near them.

The only talk was in near-whisper conversations confined to the seniors and their aides. No one from Defense, for example, talked to anyone from State. The director of naval intelligence spoke about the Redskins with the young lieutenant commander who held the director's gold-braided hat and a rolled-up chart. The director of central intelligence removed his reading glasses, returned a black-covered briefing book to one of his aides, then looked Jessen in the eye (a habit he had learned from a self-help book long, long ago), and said, "Let me handle him. I know him." The man from State heard this and nudged his aide, repeated the remark in a whisper, and both he and his aide smiled. They had been through bigger White House flaps than this one, and they had a connoisseur's understanding of how a flap would end. The CIA was in trouble again.

At 4:10, the director of central intelligence and, by surprisingly specific direction, Jessen were summoned into the Oval Office. The president was at his desk, looking over a sheaf of papers. Seated in front of the desk, their chairs arranged in an arc, were, to the president's left, Keith Saunders and Bob Martin, a deputy counselor to the president who was also a rear admiral in the naval reserve and, to the president's right, the president's secretary. As Jessen entered, behind the director, he had the feeling he was walking into a drumhead court-martial.

The president looked up and nodded to the director. He did not indicate for him or Jessen to be seated. "Okay. It's been a hectic day. So I am only going to say this once. Operation Spearmint is off. Finished. Ended." He paused, for he was a courteous man and he had seen on the director's face the beginning of what looked like a response. But the director chose not to respond.

The president tapped the sheaf of papers with the sharp point of a yellow pencil. Under that pencil was the result of Martin's frenzied search for information on Operation Spearmint.

Martin had begun with some old friends in the Navy plus a private defense analyst who was very well connected to Navy sources. He learned quickly from them about the Soviet sensitivity toward any use of the *Glomar*. He also found out about the CIA-Navy "memorandum of understanding," which had involved a transfer of funds in a way that long ago had been condemned by the Office of Management and Budget. Someone at OMB had suggested that Treasury would certainly be interested in anything that involved the "discovery" of a large amount of gold.

Martin told what he knew to Treasury's assistant secretary for international monetary affairs. Only one year from retirement, the career bureaucrat went off like a rocket (which is what his subordinates called him behind his back when he responded to real and imagined crises). He told Martin he would have an official reaction in two hours—and he did. What the assistant secretary discovered was that rumors about the gold hunt had already begun to circulate in the gold markets of London and Zurich. "I took the initiative to check with friends in State," he told Martin. "You will be hearing from a colleague there. He is, so to speak, my opposite number. I briefed him, cautiously."

Martin knew then that he had hit pay dirt in his own hunt. The Treasury bureaucrat had correctly sensed that the call from the White House had been made to get negative responses, not support. What on paper would have looked like an objective request for information was, in the tone of Martin's voice, a request for ammunition to shoot down another bureaucrat's project. The Rocket had come through. Martin made a note to see to it that, after a decent interval, the Rocket received a nice, personal note from the president and that the date of his subsequent retirement was noted on the White House calendar.

Martin, in pre–White House days a West Coast public relations executive, had done his homework and done it well. And, knowing how the president liked material presented, he had written a clear, concise, and useful document, which supported a position he knew the president would want to take.

Still tapping the papers, the president spoke with the authority of the men who had supplied the information before him. Although he had received the papers only twenty minutes earlier, he had scanned them, had asked Martin a few pertinent questions, and he could now intelligently discuss the issues with anyone but an expert on the subject.

"I have here," he said to the director, "a list of potential problems that's longer than the wine list at Dave Chasen's."

He looked down at the papers, then up at the director. "I can call in all those people out there and have them tell you what they think about this operation." He paused. "Or I can just tell you what I've got here. What do you want?"

"I . . . I would like to hear *your* assessment, Mr. President," the director said, his eyes focusing briefly on Martin.

"Okay," the president said. Turning the sheets of paper carefully and deliberately one at a time, he said, "Assuming that the Japanese merchant ship was loaded with gold, we have opposition to the gold being brought up by the International Gold Commission and by the Union of South Africa. The Russians object to any activity by the *Glomar Explorer* unless they have an observer on board. Well, screw them.

"The Japanese government will object because what is involved is the reopening of the touchy question of gold taken from the British and Dutch during World War II. That damn ship"—he glanced at the paper—"the *Osaka Maru* ship is even mentioned in the treaty that ended the war. The Chinese will object because they claim the wreck is in their waters. I say *will* because, thank God, nothing really has happened. And I want it kept that way.

"Next, our Treasury Department. The people there agree with the international gold people—and I find out that State is being blackmailed by some Japanese car dealer . . . and . . ."

Exasperated, the president put the papers down and looked at the man standing at the director's shoulder. "You Jessen?" he asked.

"I am, sir." Charles E. Jessen took a step forward.

"I understand from one of these papers that you are the man in charge—the man responsible. Now I want you to listen and listen very carefully. This operation is called off, effective now. I want you to personally fly out to the *Glomar* and tell the captain that the operation is off." The president emphasized this last statement with a gesture of his hand across his throat. "That's all, gentlemen. Thank you."

As the director and Jessen turned to walk out, the president called after them, "And I mean in person. No more of your communications screw-ups like you had in the *Pueblo* and the *Liberty*."

There was no response as the men filed out. But once clear of the White House, away from the others and walking alone with the director, Jessen said slowly and carefully, "I am sorry, sir. But perhaps we should have said something about the *Pueblo* and *Liberty* being Navy communication screw-ups, not ours, and . . ."

"Please, Jessen, no more today. Just take care of it. Do whatever The Man says. I've got problems of my own. Just do whatever he says."

Inside the limousine the director said nothing. He stared out the window as the car raced down Seventeenth Street, to the Mall area, across the Memorial Bridge, and down onto the George Washington expressway toward Langley. Twenty-six minutes after leaving the White House, as the car pulled into the underground entrance of the CIA building, the director turned to Jessen: "Charlie, I've got a lot of other things on my mind these days. I'm sorry you're put on the spot with this. Do what you have to do to turn the project off. Obviously, cost is irrelevant. And one more thing, that consultant who worked on this deal . . ."

"Gunnison, sir."

"Yeah, Gunnison. He's out. Pull all of his clearances. I don't want him to touch anything belonging to the agency or even the government."

Jessen spoke rapidly, knowing that the director did not want to hear one more word on the subject. "Sir, it might not be that easy."

The director waved away the driver, who had come around to open the door. They remained seated in back of the car. "What do you mean, Charlie? Fire the son of a bitch. That's pretty easy."

"He's on his way to Taiwan. He was to be aboard the *Glomar* when she made the snatch."

"Charlie, goddamn it, I don't want details."

"I realize that. I just want to make clear that to stop the project and to fire Gunnison I have to go to Taiwan."

"Fine. Go to Taiwan. Turn him off there. And then go to the ship." The director moved forward in his seat, and the driver opened the door. "It's pretty simple, Charlie. For God's sake."

"Not that simple, sir. I think we should talk."

The director frowned and nodded. The driver opened the door, and the director and Jessen stepped out of the car and walked the few steps to the elevator that would lift them to the director's third-floor office.

"No calls," he said to his secretary as he led Jessen into the office. They sat on a couch under a Maine seascape painted by the director's wife. Jessen looked up at it for a moment. Fog, the faint image of a sail, and beyond it the even fainter seam of sky and sea.

"Your wife paint, Charlie?"

"She's a potter, sir."

"Oh, yes," he said, somewhat embarrassed. He looked toward a tall gray vase that stood empty next to four matched, morocco-bound books on a shelf behind his desk. "And a damn good one." He smiled mechanically at Jessen.

"All right, Charlie. What's the news that you didn't bother to put down on paper so that goddamn bastard Martin could find it?"

Jessen, in a series of brisk, barren sentences, told what the agency knew about Ishiwata and the *Soji*.

"Jesus! Thank God Martin didn't find out about all of that," the director said. He looked at Jessen and shook his head. "God. I can see there's more."

"Yes, sir. It's Gunnison, sir. He is doing a little freelancing."

"And you knew it?"

"Yes. He is a friend, too."

"We'll get to that later, Charlie. I want to deal with the stuff The Man put on my plate. We shut down the operation. Then we worry about loose ends. How well do you really know this guy Gunnison?"

"Very well. I can get his file . . . "

"No need to get any more people into this. Keep the file clerks out of it. I'll stand by your assessment. You trust him?"

"I trust him . . . as much as I would trust anyone in this business."

"Including me?" the director asked. Again, the mechanical smile.

"Including you—and including me," Jessen responded without hesitation.

"Okay, Charlie. Maybe you should get our assets in Taiwan mildly interested in Mr. Gunnison. While you're there, take a look. I don't want any surprises on this. And neither does The Man."

"I've already asked for a very quiet check on Gunnison's contact in Taiwan. And I'm doing a little discreet checking on my own."

"Keep it discreet, Charlie. And no matter what, you do what I told you in the car. You fire him. As of now, he has no clearances, no government contracts, and he doesn't get any more—ever."

"Yes, sir."

The director got up from the couch a moment before Jessen rose and walked to the door. As he put his hand on the knob, the director said, "And, Charlie. If you have to, you can persuade him as much as you want. You can go the limit on him, Charlie. If you have to."

"There's no national security involved—"

"When the president gets on my ass, Charlie, that *is* national security."

*

Jessen's personal inquiry into the affairs of Harry Gunnison would involve the questioning of only one person. That night, telling Joan that he would be gone for most of the evening, he left his home in McLean and drove his own car to Capitol Hill. He found a parking space across the street from Gunnison's house. He was about to open the car door when he saw Chia Min pass under a street light on the opposite side of the street. She was walking in his direction. Without knowing why, he decided to follow her. He quietly got out, closed the car door, and walked toward the corner.

He had not tailed anyone in a long time, he thought to himself as he watched her get almost to the corner and cross the street, perhaps a hundred yards ahead of him. Her walk, he observed, seemed almost catlike. She did not seem to hurry, but she moved rapidly. Up Fourth Street he followed her the two blocks to Pennsylvania Avenue. She entered an all-night pharmacy on the corner and, after a few seconds, he took the risk and followed her in. Through the glass door he could see that the checkout counter was free. He moved to it as soon as he was through the door, keeping his back to the rest of the store.

At the counter he looked over the racks of candies and mints. The young girl behind the counter, her face blank and bored, chewed gum and almost perceptibly counted the seconds until her shift ended, whenever that was.

While he was examining the candy, Jessen glanced sideways and saw Chia Min at the wall to his left, standing in one of three open telephone stalls. He could clearly see her hand as she stabbed at the buttons. She held the receiver in her right hand as her long, slender fingers depressed the buttons. Assuming he had spotted her as she started to hit the buttons, he counted seven digits—a local number. Squinting, he thought he saw her listen more than speak, but he could not be sure. No matter what she said or heard, it was quick. A message drop. He glanced at his watch for the exact time.

He waited until she left the store. He then purchased two rolls of mints from the bored salesclerk, and went into the phone stall and jotted down the phone's number.

Fifteen minutes later he pushed the doorbell of Gunnison's house. He had the odd feeling that nothing had happened between the time he had parked his car and now.

The peephole opened. He smiled, and Chia Min opened the bolted door. He noticed that she had put on tiny gold slippers.

"That's all right, I know where to hang it," he said as she started to take his windbreaker. Although Washington Indian summers were usually hot, a fall breeze stirred the air. More like late in October than September, he thought. He knew that he would give Chia Min an anxious moment when he opened the hall closet and hung his jacket next to her blue cape, which still held the aura of the night air.

"Chill in the air tonight," he said, wondering what her response would be.

"I could feel it when I opened the door," she said, smiling up at him.

She led him into the kitchen, where, she said, she had been about to mix some dough to rise overnight. He noticed that the kitchen showed no signs of activity. She poured them both a glass of wine from a bottle that was half full. The bottle was a German Mosel—with the unlikely brand name of Dr. Zen Zen. Although both Gunnison and Chia Min were oriental in their culinary tastes, both preferred German beers and German wines and rarely touched the hard stuff. Strange, Jessen thought. But then most of the pros in the intelligence business were strange.

Then, as he thanked Chia Min, Jessen suddenly realized that he had placed Chia Min in the "intelligence business." He wondered why—for just an instant. He had never thought of her that way before.

"You want to know about Harry?"

"That's the way of it, Chia Min. I wish that I could say that I was here to see you. But Joan and Harry wouldn't understand."

She smiled and bowed her head. "Nothing like that from you, Charlie. Good old steady Charlie."

"You sound as if you wish I weren't."

"Sometimes, Charlie. Sometimes." She squeezed his free hand in both of hers, then withdrew and picked up her own glass. With her other hand she stroked the hairs on the back of his hand.

He was not surprised by her coquettish response. She had often playfully flirted with him in the past. But rarely had they been alone for even ten minutes. Never before had they been alone like this. Now he sensed in her behavior more than a flirtation. She was putting on an act, a diversion. He moved his right hand from beneath hers, ostensibly to refill his glass. The wine was good—and he again wondered why he had thought of Chia Min in the intelligence business.

"Chia Min, much as I might like to be otherwise, I must be serious. It's about Harry."

"Trouble?" she asked sharply.

He wondered if he would have sensed an added dimension to her anxiety if he hadn't seen her making the phone drop. Was she anxious because she was telling something to someone—or because she had just got information from someone and she had not heard of any trouble?

"A little trouble," Jessen said, leaning back. "Have you got some coffee?" The tête-à-tête act was over, and they both knew it.

She began making coffee in an automatic maker. She had not made any coffee since Gunnison left that morning. Jessen remembered that she drank only tea, a special kind of jasmine. He would get her some in Taiwan.

"I'll tell you as much as I"—he started to say *can*—"as I know." He was glad her back was turned. "Harry seems to have been anxious to go to Taiwan." He paused, trying to read a reaction. Now he wished her back was not turned. "I didn't ask him about it. I trust him. But sometimes I worry about him. Worry. And trust." He paused again, and Chia Min turned from the counter. She punctuated the word with a nod that Jessen thought was too prompt.

"He knows you trust him," she said. "He always plays it straight, as far as I know."

"What do you know, Chia Min?"

"I know very little, Charlie. I am a woman. Harry never tells me much about his work."

"I'm not sure of that, Chia Min. Surely something involving your own homeland. Surely he would discuss that with you."

She returned to the chair opposite him and refilled her wineglass. The bottle was empty now. She touched his hand again, this time in a way that seemed to him friendly and genuine. "There *is* something going on, Charlie. But it has nothing to do with his work. I am sure of that."

"What can you tell me, Chia Min? Just me. No one else. Nothing official. Nothing to be written down."

"All right. It's my mother. She wants to come to America. She also wants to liquidate her property and her valuables in Taiwan. Quietly, without notice. She wants to convert the money she gets to American dollars. And she wants to get those dollars into the United States without losing any of them to anybody." She looked up at Jessen and smiled. He felt the phony act starting again.

"Like not losing them to the Internal Revenue or the United States Customs?" He laughed. "Okay, Chia Min. That's all I wanted to know. Harry is really doing something private. And I hope I'm invited to the banquet when your mother arrives."

"It will be some time," Chia Min said quickly. "Not right away."

After a cup of coffee and some chatter about Harry's annoyingly secret ways, Jessen gave Chia Min a cousinly kiss goodnight on her cheek and drove home.

From his secure phone at home he called the duty officer at the agency and asked for an overnight check on the taps at the Chinese-American Friendship Association. When the United States had recognized the People's Republic of China and had dropped recognition of the Taiwanese, an arrangement had been worked out between Taiwan and the United States. Although no official relationship could be maintained between the United States and Taiwan, both parties set up "friendship organizations," supposedly manned by private citizens. As a matter of routine, through the National Security Agency, the CIA maintained a telephone tap on the Friendship Association office in Washington, the headquarters for Taiwanese activities in the United States.

"Anything special you want to have checked?" the duty officer asked, filling out a request form.

"Yes. I want to know if a call was made to the association at 8:46 tonight from a District pay phone. If such a call was placed, I'd also like to know whether there is any pattern of such calls. The booth phone number is 655-8291. The association may also have made calls to that number."

"I'll get the paperwork started. Classification?"

"Secret. And urgent."

"Everything is urgent, Charlie. Everything."

"It's the way of the world, Phil. The way of the world. Goodnight."

At eleven o'clock the following morning, a tap analyst brought Jessen a one-page report. Chia Min's call had been to the association. Jessen had before him a digest of that call and similar ones. The digest indicated a series of calls between a concerned daughter and a helpful bureaucrat regarding the issuing of a visa to the concerned daughter's mother in Taiwan. At the end of the digest, however, was a *Comment:* "Mild cryptoanalysis of conversation indicates a two-person commercial code. Association conducts similar conversations with other nationals, some of whom are commercial agents, others intelligence agents. This caller could be either."

At the bottom of the form, under *Further Action,* Jessen wrote,

"None." He asked his secretary to make arrangements for a commercial flight to Taiwan under his working name.

He had hesitated sending a message to the *Glomar Explorer* the day before, wanting first to review Gunnison's file and see Chia Min. Now he dictated an urgent message to Dysart, captain of the ship. It said: "Suspend all operations. En route. Arrive 26 September Taipei. To *Glomar* 27 September. Do not—repeat—do not recover target." Then, to add emphasis, he added, "For Director." For a fleeting moment he had toyed with using the president's code name.

Jessen went back to the thick folders on the *Glomar* operation stacked on his desk. They were already charged out to his office, as he was head of the project, and thus he did not have to go to the "clerks," which he would have had to have done for Gunnison's files. Still, the folders on the *Glomar* contained much of Gunnison, written in his clear language—clear, Jessen realized, because Gunnison used short words and wrote bluntly. Jessen, who was quite active in Dartmouth alumni activities in Washington (and had just recruited a recent graduate), smiled at his musing about Gunnison's writing style. Gunnison, Jessen realized, sometimes showed off his relatively humble background—orphan adopted by an elderly couple, Navy enlisted man, night-school graduate of George Washington University while he worked for the agency. Jessen could think of at least three high-ranking agency officials who had tougher backgrounds than Gunnison's, but they never advertised their rags-to-Langley sagas.

He brushed aside the odd thoughts about Harry and now, by hunch not reason, reread the recent memos from Gunnison. There seemed some kind of balance of extremes—on the one hand, Gunnison and Ishiwata demanding the *Glomar* be used; on the other hand, the president saying that the Chinese, Russians, South Africans, and the American government demanded that the operation cease. He imagined the balance, a tug of war with the *Osaka Maru* being pulled one way, then the other. Why did he see it as extremes? And then he saw why. The governments did not want the gold disturbed, for many reasons. Ishiwata and Gunnison wanted the gold. It was as simple as that. Ishiwata and Gunnison wanted the gold.

19

TAN CHIH-KENG LOOKED DOWN at the heavily congested Pearl River from his tenth-story window in the white building that housed the headquarters of the South Sea Fleet. The building, relatively modern compared to the rest of the ramshackle city, was one of the few benefits of the Japanese occupation of Canton from 1938 to 1945.

As the "responsible person" for the South Sea Fleet, Tan had under his command the smallest of China's three fleets but had responsibility for what was the most critical border, that with the People's Democratic Republic of Vietnam. The Hanoi government had won control of the entire coastal region of the southeast Asian peninsula—largely with Chinese assistance—and then the fascists in Hanoi had turned on the long-suffering Chinese. Now, as the situation along the Vietnam-Chinese border was heating up again, came the report of the *Glomar Explorer*'s activities at the other end of his area command.

With an inward sigh, Tan turned from the peaceful congestion of the Pearl River to face the men seated in his office. Another sigh was warranted, he lamented, for his principal deputy was away at Yulin, the main base of the South Sea Fleet, on Hainan island. Thus, 54he must make the key decisions himself.

"Comrade Tan," spoke up his staff political officer, Tuan Techang. "It is evident that we must demonstrate the efficiency and dedication of our men by immediately carrying out this new assignment of the party."

A thought came to Tan: Could he measure frustration in his life by the number of inward sighs per day or—today—perhaps per hour? Tuan's statement was to be expected. But he could not put Tuan in his place—that of a political hack—because Liu Taosheng, the chief political officer of the Navy, was also present. Finally, after an embarrassing delay in responding to Tuan, the fleet commander declared, "Of course. We shall carry out our responsibilities to the fullest." He estimated that seven-eighths of Tuan's utterances consisted of drivel.

"Are you certain that you are able to, Tan?" The speaker was Liu.

For the first time during the meeting, Tan glowered.

"I do not mean to imply that the esteemed South Sea Fleet is unable to meet its operational commitments," Liu continued. "I wish only to say that with the current problems on the Vietnamese border, and the limited capabilities of your fleet, it might be better—shall we say more efficient?—to have Zheng's fleet conduct the surveillance of the *Glomar Explorer* and be ready to act if necessary."

"The *Glomar* spying activities are within the operational area of the South Sea Fleet," Tan responded. "The South Sea Fleet will undertake the required surveillance and whatever action is necessary—or directed—from naval headquarters. We would ask of our honored colleague Zheng only that our aircraft be able to refuel at Chaoyang if absolutely necessary." Then, turning to the others in the room, Tan said, "Thank you comrades," hoping to end the frustrating session.

As the others quickly walked out—with Tuan, the last, casting an obvious I-told-you-so look toward the political deputy of the Navy—Tan looked at Liu, who stayed behind. "You wanted the remainder of our meeting with just the two of us present?"

"Yes, Tan," the political deputy said. "But first let me say I do not like your attitude on this matter or the others that we have discussed for the past two days. No, not at all."

"Comrade, I mean no disrespect. But while naval headquarters and the Eastern and Northern Fleets play political games with Russia, Korea, Japan, the United States, and even Taiwan, arguing over who can come how close to whose ship, I am in a periodic shooting war with our late allies, the Vietnamese. Still, every time I ask for men, equipment, or spare parts—let alone for more ships or aircraft—I am told that the important theaters are to the east and the north."

"Then why not give up jurisdiction over this *Glomar Explorer* matter?"

"Because if I did so, it would be used as further 'evidence' that the South Sea Fleet does not need additional resources. Do you see my dilemma? Please, Liu, you and I have never been good friends. But speaking now as professional officers, don't you see that this is the better course to steer?" No sooner had Tan completed his statement than he realized his inability to make an impression upon the Navy's deputy for political matters.

"Very well, Comrade Tan. You may carry forth. But you will be under critical observation on this matter. Further, while we do not wish to interfere with the peaceful uses of the sea, the *Glomar* operation is undoubtedly a joint American Navy–CIA adventure, a national enterprise. And thus it may be necessary for our government to respond in our own national interest. If the Americans are indeed attempting to raise the *Osaka Maru,* the People's Republic cannot permit the treasure to escape its rightful owners. It is just payment for the rape of our nation by the Japanese."

"I agree completely," Tan responded. Although the Navy's deputy for political matters was still standing, Tan eased himself down into his chair. He expected Liu to give a political-historical lecture.

But Liu asked a question unencumbered by rhetoric: "What is the disposition of the American ship, based on this morning's reconnaissance flight?" Tan unrolled the daily situation chart, which had been almost hidden by the mountain of papers on his desk.

Liu studied the chart for a few moments. Liu's many years of service in the Army had made him comfortable with maps and even nautical charts. Liu had been in the Red Army for many years, as had most senior Chinese naval officers into the 1970s, when they were assigned to naval duties in the massive shakeup of the defense establishment. "I see that the American operation continues within our zone of defense interests."

"Yes, Liu. I believe that since the *Glomar* is technically a unit of the U.S. Navy—or at least was at one point—we would have some justification for even boarding the ship to make certain that the operation does not constitute a military threat to the People's Republic."

"What forces do you currently have assigned to watch the ship?"

"Twice daily I am flying a search plane over the area, generally taking photographs once a day."

"Have the photographs revealed anything?"

Tan was tempted to say that they would have revealed much more had he been provided with the sufficient number of modern telephoto lenses he had requested long ago, but instead he decided to say, "Nothing significant.

"Indeed," he continued, "the only really significant aspect of the *Glomar* operation has been that the ship arrived within two miles of the exact spot where she is now working. That means truly excellent search and navigation capabilities in view of the depth of water in which the *Osaka Maru* is sunk."

"What about surface forces?"

"I have two patrol boats in my northern sector that have been told what is known about the situation and are standing by."

"Nothing larger?"

"No. With the Vietnamese situation, the only unit that I have north of Hainan Island is a single destroyer, plus some ships undergoing overhaul at the Yulin base."

"Very well," the political officer said, looking up from the chart. "In the name of naval headquarters, I want the destroyer to immediately put out for the *Glomar Explorer,* and I want the American ship kept under direct observation until further notice. We must know at once when the ship of gold is raised near the surface. Indeed, to be prepared, I wish you to embark as many troops as the ship can accommodate—perhaps fifty?"

"I think that would be a problem if the ship is to remain at sea for more than a week or two. Perhaps thirty troops?"

"Yes. Whatever you think appropriate. But I do not want a landing craft or anything else in the area or the troops visible during daylight hours to indicate their presence. Now, what is the latest information on the Russian spy ship in the area?"

Three days later, almost one thousand miles northeast of the white building on the Pearl River at Canton, other naval officers were also discussing the Soviet spy ship observing the *Glomar Explorer*. At the Soviet port of Vladivostok, Admiral Emil Nikolayevich Spiridonov, commander-in-chief of the Soviet Pacific Fleet, lacked Tan's view of the outside world. Although Vladivostok, on Golden Horn Bay, has been compared to Naples for scenic beauty, Spiridonov's command center was far below ground, in what was described as a "survival structure," shared with the alternative headquarters of the Far Eastern Military District.

"In conclusion, Comrade Admiral, the report from the surveillance ship *Primorye* clearly indicates that the Americans have located a ship hulk on the ocean floor, and the *Glomar Explorer* is now moored directly over it and the lift may have already begun." The officer, Captain Third/Rank Ivanov, an assistant staff intelligence officer, closed the folder and stood silently. No one else in the room said anything.

The air-conditioning equipment hummed loudly. In the corners of the room, moisture seeped through the cinderblock. The main walls, except for the one bearing the room's two doors, were covered mostly with a fiberboard material. Multicolored maps of the immediate Vladivostok and Petropavlovsk areas and overall charts of the western Pacific were pinned to the boards.

"Do we know for certain that the American ship is over a sunken surface ship or could it be a submarine?" the fleet commander asked.

"The *Primorye* has used mainly passive sonar in the monitoring operation, sir. However, she did undertake an initial bottom profile search with active sonar as soon as she arrived on the scene. The captain reported that the hulk appears to be a ship significantly larger than a submarine," the intelligence officer responded.

"And we still have no indication about the identification of the target of the American efforts."

"No, sir. None at all."

"Very well. Thank you, Ivanov." The admiral rose and motioned for the several officers standing in front of his desk to move over to the nearby worktable. A large chart of the South China Sea was spread over the table. Numerous notations and arrows were drawn on the chart. "Well, Yaroslav Maksimovich?" the admiral said as his chief of staff leaned over the table. "Now that you have left the 'coastal forces' and come to the real Navy, how do you like the real world?"

Spiridonov's reference to coastal forces was an on-going joke in the Pacific Fleet. Vice Admiral Yaroslav Maksimovich Kudel'kin had previously been deputy commander of the Baltic Fleet and before that commander of the Caspian Flotilla, both with very small operational areas compared to the broad Pacific–Indian Ocean regions that had been his responsibility since he arrived at Vladivostok in 1976.

"I have charged our Comrade Kudel'kin with coordinating this project with a special staff," Spiridonov continued. "The main fleet operations staff is already fully engaged with the Iranian and Afghanistan problems and with our normal workup period this time of year in the Pacific."

Spiridonov pointed to each of the markings on the chart, as if reviewing the situation more for himself than for the assembled officers. "Now, then. First, we know an American nuclear submarine carried out a seafloor reconnaissance of this area, possibly in cooperation with a British naval survey ship.

"Second, the *Glomar Explorer* arrives in the area. A notice to mariners plus the usual CIA-sponsored phony press articles said she was to be engaged in seafloor mining." There was a low chuckle from two or three of the officers in the room.

"Next, a Japanese warship appears to be heading for the area. Since we know the *Glomar Explorer* has many Japanese in her crew, this appears to be a joint Japanese-American intelligence activity." Then, almost as an aside, "And that, my friends, may be the most unusual and the most significant aspect of all these happenings.

"Then a Chinese warship appears on the scene. Our satellite surveillance showed that she embarked troops before departing Haikang. Are the troops to be placed aboard the *Glomar Explorer?* Probably. But to defend her or to capture her?

"Finally, we are told that an American nuclear submarine may again be in the vicinity.

"What else is relevant?" No one volunteered an answer. "Then we can say that, despite all of this knowledge, we are completely in the dark as to what the Americans and Japanese—and possibly the Chinese—are up to." He paused. "Yes, Ivanov?"

"Sir. Could the Japanese-American effort be to *place* something on the ocean floor, not to raise something?"

"An interesting speculation. Could you elaborate for us?"

All eyes in the room turned to the blond, wavy-haired intelligence officer.

"I would only put forward a few possible options, sir. Perhaps a multiwarhead mine that could prevent passage of our ships through the Taiwan Straits, although such a weapon would be better placed farther north in the channel."

The discussion—and speculation—continued for several hours. Often—too often in the fleet commander's opinion—there was silence. Finally, after the session had gone on for almost six hours—through dinner and several carafes of tea—Admiral Spiridonov, leaning back in the swivel chair behind his massive desk, spoke in a low, resigned voice. "Kudel'kin. Meet as often as you deem necessary with your special project staff. Keep me advised at least daily—preferably twice daily. At this time I believe we should increase our subsurface surveillance." Picking up and opening a folder, he added, "I wish the submarine *Petroverdets* to break off her current exercise and undertake a detailed underwater surveillance of the *Glomar Explorer* operation.

"Also, Comrade Kudel'kin, I wish your appraisal as to the adequacy of our satellite coverage of the area. I believe the situation may be of sufficient importance to ask Moscow for increased coverage if we deem it necessary. At some stage we will be asked by Moscow exactly what is happening, and at this time I am not certain how I would answer that question."

Standing, in a manner to signify the end of the long meeting, Spiridonov said to no one in particular, "Ah, a fine way to start a new command. What next, I wonder?"

Of the many men in the Far East who met to discuss the activities of the *Glomar Explorer*, only those assembled in Tokyo had almost full knowledge of the operation. They were men attending a series of meetings of Japan's National Defense Council, the highest level advisory group on national security matters available to the prime minister. The activities of the *Glomar Explorer* under Ishiwata's charter had galvanized the Japanese government to action, and the prime minister had called the first defense council meeting in twenty-seven months.

The members of the council included the prime minister, foreign minister, finance minister, director general of the Japanese Self-Defense Agency—the official name for the armed forces—and the director general of the Economic Planning Agency. The nature of the crisis also drew to the meeting the director general of the Japanese intelligence agency and the head of the Maritime Self-Defense Force and his operations chief. In an unprecedented move, the prime minister directed that the principals would meet regularly until the crisis was resolved. "The *Osaka Maru*," he said "could reopen the entire Pacific War issue of the disposition of gold and other valuables taken to Japan for safekeeping during the effort to establish the Greater East Asia Co-Prosperity Sphere." He paused and slowly added, "We do not wish to have that problem raised, as we do not want the *Osaka Maru* raised." He smiled at his pun.

It was the first council meeting to be held in the new foreign ministry building in the Kasumigaseki district, southwest of the Imperial Palace. Some of the men were shocked to hear the prime minister use the wartime "co-prosperity sphere" terminology. All realized the gravity of the situation, now being emphasized by terms not heard in government circles for three decades.

Each meeting began with a briefing by Atachi Fukuda, the director-general of the Cabinet Research Bureau, the euphemism for Japan's national intelligence agency. Atachi provided the latest information available. Initially he also informed the meeting about the Gunnison-Ishiwata dealings, but then he extended his briefing to include the progress of the *Glomar Explorer* and the subsequent involvement of other nations in the situation.

At the urging of the prime minister, Atachi continued to stress the potential complications of the raising of *Osaka Maru,* as well as the problems that would be produced by the sudden appearance of so much gold on the market. "Please recall, gentlemen, that the case of the ship was so significant to Japan that on April 6, 1949, there was a resolution by the House of Counselors at the fifth session of the Diet waiving Japan's claims against the United States for sinking the ship. From a legal viewpoint, of course, that would include the cargo—Mr. Ishiwata's gold.

"Now, for a Japanese national of high standing to become involved in an attempt to raise the ship could be most embarrassing to Japan, especially with a view toward the delicate economic negotiations now being conducted. Remember, the waiver of claims to the ship was considered a precondition to a peace treaty ending the war."

"But I am still confused by this Gunnison individual," the prime minister said. It was the third meeting of the council. "How could the American CIA entrust such a mission, dealing with our esteemed Ishiwata, to a—how did your sources put it—'consultant' and not a regular agent?"

"Our sources indicated that Mr. Gunnison was sent because of his past work with the CIA as a regular agent and his involvement in many naval activities in this part of the world. After he carried Mr. Ishiwata's requests to Washington, control of the operation was assumed by regular CIA officers, headed by a Mr. Charles Jessen."

"And your sources are quite reliable?" asked the prime minister. Only he and the intelligence chief knew the identity of those sources.

"Extremely," replied the director-general of intelligence. Looking at the nine other men around the table, he smiled inwardly with the knowledge that at least five had enjoyed the pleasures of evenings with the sisters who entertained Mr. Ishiwata's guests. As several of the men pushed back their chairs and rose to take more tea and small sandwiches from the sideboard, the director-general, whose university major had been differential calculus, wondered how many times five could go into two, and the number of combinations that were possible.

When the meeting resumed, the finance minister explained the potential impact on the international gold market if the *Osaka Maru*'s cargo were to surface. The foreign minister then explained the political implications. Britain and Holland had never withdrawn their formal inquiries concerning gold taken from the banks of Hong Kong, Singapore, and Batavia.

"And we are helpless to stop this catastrophe that Mr. Ishiwata is about to bring down on us?" interrupted the prime minister.

"Sir. He is a private citizen. He may have stepped over the line in contacting the American CIA. However, we have used many private citizens before to help the government and have unofficially sanctioned their dealing with the American government, especially their Defense Department," the director-general politely added.

"Yes. But this is different. He is working against the interests of the state, and in direct opposition to the wishes of this government. Is there no action we can take?"

"No, sir. Not on this matter. However, the municipal police are investigating a murder that is believed to have been performed by Mr. Ishiwata's chauffeur, Kimpei. The problem, it seems, is that the corpse was sold and has been partially destroyed in tests by medical students at Tokyo University's school of medicine."

"Does the police commissioner feel we can obtain evidence linking Mr. Ishiwata to this?"

"Perhaps, Mr. Prime Minister. It will depend upon the willingness of the students to testify. Unfortunately, the police commissioner fears that, once they are identified, Mr. Ishiwata will buy them off."

"If we may regress to the subject of the *Osaka Maru,* has there been any further contact between Mr. Ishiwata and Mr. Gunnison since the first payment of money?"

"No, sir."

"Has this Mr. Gunnison completed his assignment, then, for Mr. Ishiwata? For the CIA?"

"That, Mr. Prime Minister, is the only part of the issue that confuses us. Mr. Gunnison has left Washington to fly to Taiwan. We believe that his first visit there after meeting Ishiwata was to take care of separate business. I believe the American expression is 'freelance' business. At least that is what he told his superior at the CIA." This small indiscretion caused some of the nine men sitting around the table to look up at the director-general of intelligence. It had been a calculated slip, intended to remind them that he had superb sources of information abroad as well as inside Japan.

"However, his trip to Taiwan included at least one visit with General Cheng Ho. Cheng is a banker. He is also a former deputy chief of Nationalist Chinese intelligence and continues to function in the espionage role."

"I know of him," the finance minister remarked. "A banker of dubious ethics. His banking activity is in part a front."

"He is a full-time banking executive, although it is a highly specialized banking enterprise," the director-general continued. "But he periodically becomes involved in intelligence operations when the Taipei government requires a man of his many and special talents and contacts. Indeed, we are told that Cheng is not paid for his government work but merely is allowed to carry out his overseas banking efforts with a minumum of government interference."

"A cheap way to pay one's spies," the naval chief piped up. "Ah, no offense intended," he added quickly, bowing slightly from his seated position in the direction of the director-general.

Everyone in the room knew of Cheng. Some had met him at various times in their careers, some as early as World War II when Japan invaded China and Cheng was a young Army officer fighting against them. He had been captured by Japanese forces in Shanghai—some said he allowed himself to be captured in order to pass an important message to a senior Chinese intelligence officer already in Japanese hands—and had then escaped. To have been held by the Kempeitai—the Japanese military police—and to have survived an "examination" without revealing any secrets and then to have escaped was unprecedented.

Since the war, the story had been embellished many times, but Cheng's achievements as a young Army officer were impressive even if not exaggerated. (Some of the tales said that Cheng had escaped from the Kempeitai *that time* by successfully impersonating a Japanese officer, an incredible bit of audacity and luck.)

For a time after the war, Cheng had served in Japan on the staff of General Hsu Yung-chang, who represented China at the surrender ceremonies aboard the battleship *Missouri* in Tokyo Bay. In later years, some of the Japanese seated around the table had at times worked with Cheng and at times against him, depending upon the politics and the funds involved.

"And do you believe Cheng could be involved with the CIA on the *Glomar* in some way?"

"No." The director-general hesitated a moment. "Let me say that our sources within the Ishiwata establishment indicate that Mr. Gunnison expressed the belief that he would personally come into a great fortune. I think perhaps Mr. Gunnison—and *not* the CIA—may be dealing with Cheng."

"Then Mr. Gunnison may be double-dealing with Mr. Ishiwata?" the prime minister asked. "Should we so advise Mr. Ishiwata? Perhaps we can use this knowledge to get him to stop the operation."

"I would doubt that, sir. As I stated earlier, there are some indications that the U.S. government may halt the operation—just indications, based on some very recent information from Washington. However, Mr. Ishiwata is now en route to the *Glomar Explorer*, I believe to make certain that the gold is raised and to be there when it is."

"Is our escort ship on the scene, Admiral?"

"Almost, sir. The frigate will arrive tomorrow morning with orders to observe and under no conditions to take any action."

After a moment's hesitation, the prime minister said, "We will do whatever is necessary to stop the recovery of the gold. Even if it means we stop the *Soji* . . . Even if it means taking actions to physically stop the *Glomar Explorer*."

20

JESSEN WAS MET AT THE Chiang Kai-shek International Airport in Taipei by the agency's resident chief in Taiwan, a tall man with the slight stoop of a scholar. His name was Edward Cosgrove, and he was on his last tour of duty before retirement, a time that made some men very cautious and others very careless. Jessen wondered which it would be for Cosgrove. His principal talent was fluency in four Chinese dialects. But perhaps his most important asset was Mrs. Cosgrove, who was Taiwanese and a general staff officer's former mistress.

Cosgrove flashed some credentials at the customs officer and, shouting in Chinese to several men and women in uniform, opened a path for Jessen through the noisy crowd that pressed against the customs counters and baggage bays. Cosgrove shouldered open a side door and plunged into a new mob of travelers and their flocks saying hello and goodbye.

Beyond the lobby, Cosgrove grabbed Jessen by the arm, and they carved their way to the outer doors of the departure wing.

A vintage blue Buick pulled up, and the two Americans got in the back. Jessen, recognizing the driver, said, "Hello, Hu." The thick neck and shaved head in the front seat did not move. Hu claimed not to know a word of English, but no American he worked with believed him. Hu had defected from a Red Army garrison near Canton by diving into the sea and swimming toward Hong Kong. A British patrol boat picked him up, and he soon went to work for the British, and possibly the Soviets, in Hong Kong. Later, he worked for the Americans in Hong Kong, which was where Jessen had met him.

Jessen closed the sliding window behind the driver and said to Cosgrove, "I thought he was still in Hong Kong."

"Drifted in when we were making the quick change after we broke off with Taiwan. We lost the State Department types and got a lot of grief from the Taiwanese. We're making do with whatever bodies we can get. He's not bad for jobs around our 'friendship office.' And the Taiwanese more or less trust him."

"That could be a bad sign," Jessen said. "I don't like to trust anybody they trust. Unless we have outside bona fides on him."

"Not to worry. We don't give Hu much to do. But we need Chinese tails, and he's pretty good. Not terrific, though. Gunnison shook him yesterday."

"Gunnison could shake anybody he wanted to shake." Jessen looked out the window to give himself a moment to decide how much he should say to Cosgrove. Before Jessen left Washington he had sent a message to Cosgrove telling him that the *Glomar* operation was to be scrapped but that Gunnison was not to be told. Now he searched his memory for any previous contact between Cosgrove and Gunnison, any encounter that might have bonded them so that Cosgrove would have tipped off Gunnison. All Jessen could remember was that Cosgrove was not fond of consultants in general, especially consultants who had formerly worked for the agency and now potentially had loyalty to customers other than Langley.

He knew that Cosgrove was waiting for him to start the conversation. But he looked out the window for a few more moments, as if lost in thought, as befitted a boss visiting a subordinate. Taipei was spreading outward, gouging the green countryside. Taipei always depressed him. It was such an ordinary city, such a gray place. Buildings that looked like factories. He turned to Cosgrove and said, "Just wondering out loud. Why would Gunnison want to shake Hu? What's Gunnison got to worry about?"

"Well, it pays to be cautious. It pays to throw off a strange tail. And maybe he didn't want *us* to know who he was going to see."

"What do you mean by that?" Jessen asked sharply.

"Just a rumor. Something Hu turned up," Cosgrove said, nodding toward the head in front of the glass. "I hadn't put a big tag on the story. But it now looks as if Gunnison was here in August. News to you?"

Jessen, watching the back of Hu's head, thought he saw it move slightly at the word *Gunnison*. Jessen glanced toward the sliding window. "This our car?"

"Ostensibly, it's a livery, owned by Hu. We can't register—"

"Okay. I get it. Tell me, now, how has the weather been?"

Cosgrove and Jessen did little talking until Cosgrove, in a burst of Chinese, directed Hu to turn off the freeway from the airport and drop them at the National Palace Museum.

"I told him to pick us up in an hour," Cosgrove said as they left the car. "This is a grand place to talk. Want my seventy-five-cent tour?"

"Business is business, Ed. But I think I can spare a few minutes, especially to see the jade. That's what I remember most from the last time here."

"You have a cool, green memory, Charlie. Funny about the jade. That's where Hu lost Gunnison. That is to say, that is where Hu *says* he lost Gunnison."

They were walking rapidly past an exhibit of scroll paintings. Cosgrove slowed down and turned toward the jade galleries.

"Did Gunnison meet anybody?"

"Who knows? No pun intended. All we have is Hu's word, and that isn't much. I need some good people, Charlie. As I've said in report after report—"

"You've made your point," Jessen said, looking around the gallery.

Cosgrove did not finish his sentence. He led Jessen to a large case at the other side of the gallery. "Hu said he lost him right about here." Cosgrove crouched before the lowest shelf in the case. He removed his gold-rimmed glasses and peered at one of the jade carvings, his nose flattened against the glass. A guard took a step toward him and said something in Chinese. Cosgrove spat something back, and the guard retreated.

"Here it is," Cosgrove said, pointing with his glasses to a carving about six inches tall. "Recognize it?"

"No," Jessen said. He looked more closely. "Wait . . . I have seen it—recently."

Cosgrove smiled and straightened up. "I've never had the pleasure of being in Mr. Gunnison's house," he said, "but—"

"That's it," Jessen said, staring at the carving. "At Gunnison's. In the hallway, I think. But how did you know?"

"A guess. What you are looking at is magnificent, one of the museum's prize possessions. But it's not an original. It's old and it's valuable. But it's not an original. It's a copy.

"Take a closer look," Cosgrove urged, and Jessen crouched down. "See the veining of the jade? How it accents the scales and fin? There's a very good twelfth-century drawing of the original piece. No such veining. That's how an expert found out that this one's a fake."

Jessen stood up. "Interesting. But what the hell does this have to do with Gunnison?"

"You remember General Cheng, don't you?"

"That old pirate? Sure. How could I forget that son of a bitch?" Jessen had an instant recollection of a Chinese officer who was ushered into his office in Seoul during the Korean War. The officer was Cheng, and he told Jessen he could rescue five American fliers who had been shot down over North Korea. Cheng said he knew that the Air Force would not pay to get them back but that the CIA would. He wanted $2,000 for each one—payable in gold to Cheng personally. Jessen paid. They never met again, but Cheng arranged the deliveries, as he called them, and the fliers were safely returned.

"Yes," Jessen said. "I know Cheng. So what?"

"The museum once had the original of this piece," Cosgrove said, as if he had not heard the question. "But Cheng somehow got it out of here. The story goes that the museum knows he stole it but does not know how. Very Chinese. Cheng liked it so much he had the best jade carver in Taiwan make him some copies. No one knows how many. They are exquisite." He nodded toward the door. "Shall we press on?"

"Let's take a walk and start the business," Jessen said, leading the way out of the gallery and toward the main hall.

"This *is* business, Charlie. Just keep listening. Cheng saved the museum's face by getting his best replica back in the case, no questions asked. Because he was a big shot in Chiang Kai-shek's Investigating Bureau—the secret police—no one dared ask any questions. But the story became one of those you hear again and again. Then the story got an embellishment. It was said that Cheng was giving other copies to special friends. And, being Chinese, the story had an odd point to it."

"You can be kind of Chinese yourself sometimes, Ed," Jessen said. "I would very much like to hear the point." He quickened his stride. They were near the entrance now.

Cosgrove touched Jessen's sleeve and stopped. Jessen kept walking, propelled by momentum, annoyance, and a sense of authority. But Cosgrove tugged again and pointed. Hu was standing near a postcard rack in the entrance lobby and was talking to the guard from the jade room.

"One of those little Chinese coincidences," Cosgrove said, motioning Jessen to a bench behind a pillar and out of sight from Hu. "I've long since given up on trying to separate the coincidences from the conspiracies. The carving could be a coincidence."

"You said you were getting to the point," Jessen said, leaning forward to see beyond the pillar. Hu had gone; the guard was still there.

"Just this, Charlie. Cheng supposedly gives copies of the carving only to certain people—certain friends. It shows a carp changing into a dragon. Well, that's what it's supposed to signify. It's supposed to mean that Cheng expects the person who gets the carving will change."

"Everybody changes."

"Not as much as that carp does."

"I'd swear that Gunnison has had that thing for years."

"Cheng is a man of great patience. According to Hu—"

"Who you don't trust. What's the value of anything from Hu?"

"Well, Charlie, *I* work here. I make judgments. I speak the language."

The ultimate putdown, Jessen thought. The ones who can speak the language always act superior toward the ones who can't. He and Gunnison used to talk about that. They had both singled out Cosgrove as a prime offender.

"And," Cosgrove continued, "I am *not* giving Hu that much. But, according to Hu, someone who could be Gunnison slipped into Taiwan in August and met with Cheng on his boat, an old pirate junk."

Jessen suddenly felt tired. He started to ask a question but then just nodded to Cosgrove to go on.

"All I can tell you is that a name on an airline's passenger manifest did not check out with our list of arriving and departing Caucasians. Some round-eye was slipped in, apparently from Tokyo."

"Who gives you the list? The Investigating Bureau?"

"Yes. And it's one of those things they don't fool around with. No percentage. It's an easy way for them to give us something. I don't believe they screw around with the list. Too easy for us to cross-check some names on it. I think the list is bona fide."

"What was the name of the guy who slipped in?"

"George Walters. Recognize it?"

Jessen hesitated, as if trying to recall something from what was known as one of the best memories in a business renowned for good memories.

"Gunnison's working name," Cosgrove said, pausing to add, "in case you've forgotten. I checked it. Of course, it could be a coincidence."

They stood up and headed for the entrance. "There's a good

restaurant here, just across the driveway," Cosgrove said. "We can have tea there while we wait for Hu."

"He's got a radio in that car," Jessen said. "Can you reach him through a phone?"

"Yes, I think so. He won't be far."

"Okay. Tell him to come here and pick *you* up as soon as possible." Jessen looked at his watch. "I have a date to meet Gunnison for a late lunch. We're both at the President?"

"President," Cosgrove said. In deference to the lack of the definite article in Chinese, people who knew the language did not call the hotel *the* President. Cosgrove could see the glimmer of annoyance on Jessen's face, but he would not lower his standards just because—

"President," Jessen repeated. "Adjoining rooms?"

"Yes."

"No bugs? No taps?"

"Not unless you want them, Charlie. It might take a little time to—"

"I *don't* want them. I can handle this one, thanks. No bugs, no taps."

Cosgrove nodded and opened the door of the restaurant, allowing Jessen to precede him. A plump waitress, who wore her hair in the queue of a maiden, smiled and spoke to Cosgrove in Chinese. She led them to a table near a telephone booth.

"I've ordered tea," Cosgrove said. "I'll phone for Hu. And a cab for you?"

Jessen was drumming the fingers of his left hand on the white tablecloth. "I would have preferred a beer," he said, holding up his drumming hand when Cosgrove offered to change the order. "Never mind. Yes. I want a cab to the hotel. I don't want Gunnison to see me getting out of Hu's car. I'm sure Gunnison has some grand place picked out for lunch. But to make it simple, tell Hu that if Gunnison goes anywhere it will be after lunch and without me. Tell Hu to get on Gunnison's tail again. And tell him not to lose him this time."

Cosgrove started for the phone booth. "On second thought," Jessen said, "tell her I want a beer."

Jessen had read somewhere that the best way for a man to end an affair was to take the woman to a fine hotel, order the most expensive meal in the house, and, over the first round of drinks, begin to break the news. He had hoped to do something like that with Gunnison. But here they were in the hotel's teahouse, eating very humble noodles and dumplings and sipping tea. The dumplings were doughy. Jessen and Gunnison had gone past the hearty hellos in the lobby and had chatted about nothing in particular.

"This town is one of the best places in the world for food," Gunnison was saying. "Every kind of Chinese cuisine here. Canton, Sichuan, Hunan. And we stay in the hotel eating goddamn noodles. If you weren't the boss—"

"Well, Harry, that's about it, isn't it?" Jessen said. "I *am* the boss." He smiled very weakly. "The first time we talked about this job, we didn't even eat, remember?"

"Sure. The Hawk and Dove. But we had a couple of beers."

"Right." Jessen signed to the waiter and ordered two bottles of Snowflake beer. "Now, Harry. What have you been up to?"

"I got here yesterday. Late yesterday. I pretty much stuck to my room. I was dead tired from the trip."

"You were tailed yesterday, Harry."

"Really? Couldn't have been very exciting for him. One of the bureau's boys, I suppose."

"No, Harry. One of ours."

The waiter arrived and made a small ceremony out of pouring the beer. Neither man spoke until the waiter bowed and turned from the table. "Why the tail?" Gunnison asked. "What's his name—Cosgrove, isn't it? Cosgrove using me for a training exercise or something?" Gunnison laughed.

"Let's forget about that right now, Harry. There's something much more important." Jessen had not touched the cold glass of beer. Now he wrapped both hands around the glass and said, "The *Glomar* deal is off, Harry."

Gunnison picked up his glass, took a sip, and said, "That's impossible, Charlie. Impossible. It's like calling off a building just before they put the roof on it."

"I'm afraid it's very, very possible and very, very definite, Harry," Jessen said. He told Gunnison about the scene in the Oval Office, but he did not tell about his orders to fire him. Maybe that could be changed. It was a separate issue.

"I still say impossible, Charlie."

Jessen took his first sip, put down the glass, and rolled it between his hands. He was surprised that Gunnison had shown so little reaction. But something was smoldering.

"Let's be professional about this, Harry," Jessen said. "When the president says shut something down, it gets shut down."

Gunnison leaned forward and stared directly at Jessen. "I *am* being professional, Charlie. For God's sake. Some things don't get shut down, no matter who says what. You know that damn well. Presidents come and go, and some things keep going on."

"I'm surprised, Harry. Really surprised. I had thought you'd see what I was saying—understand what I was saying—and say, 'Okay. No big loss.' "

"I can't say that, Charlie."

"So you had a side deal going with Ishiwata. Sorry about that, Harry. It can't be helped. Look. You got a job from us, a paycheck from us. You tried to get some more from him. And the deal didn't work. The building didn't get a roof on it."

"That's what you're going to tell Ishiwata? That the United States has decided to just tell him to go fuck himself? That he spent a lot of money—built the building—but they say no roof? Bullshit. There's something more to this, isn't there? Uncle Sam is going to try to hold up Ishiwata. That's it, right?"

Gunnison was beginning to react. He was speaking more quickly than normal. And the tone of his voice had changed. There was a beseeching quality. Jessen had never heard that tone from Gunnison before, and the realization was saddening. But it was Jessen who had said that this was to be a professional conversation, and feeling sad about a friend—a friend who happened to be working for you—was not professional. Jessen's own voice changed, hardening into what he thought of as his command tone.

"The United States government has made a decision to take back the *Glomar Explorer.* That's my job. I'm flying out to the ship tomorrow and taking control. In the national interest, the *Glomar* is being withdrawn from charter."

"Bullshit! That's bullshit! Some kind of a goddamn deal is going on. That goddamn White House is working a deal."

"This isn't helping, Harry. There is no deal. Ishiwata is a big boy. The contract for the charter has a clause covering exactly this. If Ishiwata doesn't like it, there are lawyers."

"And if *I* don't like it?"

"It does not matter one iota whether you like it or not. My orders are from the president of the United States. They have nothing to do with what you want or don't want."

Gunnison had finished his beer and was toying with a teacup. He put the cup down and wiped his hands on the big white napkin.

Then he wiped the faint sheen of sweat on his temples. He lowered his voice to say, "Okay. Sorry for the outburst." He picked up the teacup, saw that it was empty, poured a few swallows of tea, and tipped the cup to his lips.

"Okay." He wiped his mouth. "Let's talk about the practical side of this. First, I'd like to go with you tomorrow when you go out. It might help if I'm there. Ishiwata trusts me. I think I can help."

"I figured that, Harry. You're still on the payroll. I figured that you would go out with me. Ishiwata is aboard, right?"

"I talked to Dysart by radio telephone this morning," Gunnison said. "Ishiwata had just arrived with his bodyguard. Apparently, Ishiwata flew out to the *Glomar,* directly from Japan in a flying boat. Really impressive."

"Did you speak to him or just Dysart?"

"Just Dysart."

"And I assume you've looked into a helicopter already?"

"I've got one on standby, tomorrow from Kaohsiung."

"Fine. Let's plan to leave Taipei by seven-thirty tomorrow morning. We should be able to get out to the ship by early afternoon."

"Okay. I'll call as soon as we're through here. Any other orders?"

"Come on, Harry. Not orders," Jessen said. The tension had eased, but he sensed that Gunnison was acting, that somewhere within him he was still shocked, still wishing that he could continue his deal with Ishiwata.

Jessen insisted on picking up the check. They got into the elevator together. Gunnison held up his five fingers and the operator nodded, saying, "Yes. Fifth." He turned to Jessen, who said, "Fifth."

"Keeping an eye on me, Charlie?"

"Thank Cosgrove. I don't even like the President's Hotel." Jessen stressed the *the.*

At the fifth floor they got out, side by side, and walked to their rooms. "I'm going to take a long nap," he said. "Maybe we can have dinner tonight in one of your four-star restaurants?"

"I told Chia Min that I would visit her mother," Gunnison said. "Maybe tomorrow night, when we get back."

"You won't have my sparkling company tomorrow night, Harry. I'm staying aboard the *Glomar* until she gets clear—probably a day or two. I'm supposed to make a daily report for the director. Besides, by tomorrow you should be on your way home. It should be a quick round trip to the *Glomar* for you."

"Right. Well, I suggest that we leave the hotel by six-fifteen. I'll line up the car."

"Thanks, Harry. And if you get back early tonight, call me. Maybe we can have a nightcap."

"Don't wait for me, Charlie. Chia Min's mother will probably keep me up all night."

Jessen had his key in the door. He turned to Gunnison. "I always thought she didn't speak English."

"Chia Min's brother does. And he'll be there," Gunnison responded without hesitation.

"Well, don't let him keep you up too late. Big day tomorrow." Somewhere in the back of his mind, he remembered Harry once saying that Chia Min was an only child. Harry must be slipping. Jessen thought about going into Gunnison's room right now and making him explain his connection with Cheng. But Jessen dismissed the idea, deciding to keep focused on *Glomar,* his highest priority. He could handle Gunnison's extracurricular deals later. Harry's deals would make the firing easier for both of them.

Gunnison had unlocked his door and was entering his room. Jessen stuck his head out of his room and said, "Be careful, Harry."

Gunnison stopped, one hand on the knob, the other holding the key. He looked directly at Jessen. "Always, Charlie. Always."

21

ROOM SERVICE IN PRESIDENT'S HOTEL was provided by a corps of "hall boys," each a slim, smiling, quick-moving young man who knew a few phrases in English and in Japanese. On each floor of the hotel, near the elevator bank, was a hall-boys' room. In it were irons and ironing boards, a cooler for beer and soft drinks, a hot plate and kettle for tea and instant coffee, cups and glasses, carafes and teapots, laundry bags and dry-cleaning bags, and all the paraphernalia needed to respond to a guest's needs.

The door of the room was windowed. In front of the door was a glass counter displaying small pink bars of soap, jars of enigmatic Chinese lotions, tubes of shaving cream, and such odd bits of merchandise as little furry wind-up toy animals and plastic statues of Buddha and Jesus. On the top of the counter was a bell for a guest to strike to summon a hall boy from the inner room. But, no matter the hour, rarely did a guest have to hit the bell, for always there was a hall boy, either lounging behind the counter or smoking in the inner room, sitting on a wooden chair tipped against the wall and watching through the window of the door.

No one could use an elevator without walking past the hall boys. No one could open a door in the long hallway on either side of the hall boys' room without being registered in the peripheral vision of the hall boys. No one could walk up or down the stairway at either end of the hall without making a noise that would turn a hall boy's head. No one could blind a hall boy with a bribe because hall boys were bright enough to know that the Investigating Bureau often used round-eyes to try to bribe hall boys. The Investigating Bureau, which preferred to deal with trustworthy hall boys, never had to bribe.

The hall boy on the fifth floor, as requested, called Hu as soon as the two Americans went into their rooms. About fifteen minutes later, the hall boy called Hu again. Hu was sitting on a bench in the lobby, with several cab drivers, near the bank of house phones.

When the third phone from the left rang, he got up from the bench. The drivers who had been flanking him on the bench looked at each other and smiled. Hu's true occupation was fairly well known to such Investigating Bureau informants as cab drivers and hotel workers.

The hall boy called to say that the American Gunnison had ordered a beer, and when it was brought to him he looked as if he was about to leave. He was hanging up the phone when the hall boy entered. His tan raincoat was on the bed.

"Enough," Hu said. "Watch the door, cautiously. He is an aware man. When the door opens, call this number. Let the phone ring once."

Hu hung up and walked over to the desk where a graduate of the hall boys, now an assistant manager, was checking in a busload of Philippine tourists. Hu found a vantage point from which, without being obvious, he could see both the elevator and a door leading to a stairwell. He leaned against the desk, to the annoyance of the assistant manager, who frowned but prudently said nothing. A few minutes later one of the house phones rang once. He did not react until the stairwell door opened.

Gunnison bought a *Newsweek* from the newsstand near the elevator bank, waited until an elavator disgorged a load of passengers, and, mingling with them, headed for the outer doors of the lobby. Hu slipped through a side door that opened to the driveway curving up to the main entrance of the hotel. Hu assumed that Gunnison, as before, would stand in the driveway and wait for a car to pick him up.

Hu got into his car, which was parked at a taxi stand, and slowly coursed the driveway so that he did not have to pass Gunnison. Hu drove one block down Teh-hwei Street to an intersection from which he could see the hotel entrance and the tall man in the tan raincoat.

Five minutes later a black Mercedes pulled into the driveway and Gunnison got into it. The Mercedes slowed at the end of the driveway. Hu saw that the car's turn indicator showed it would pass him and head north on Chunshan Road. He pulled his car out of the intersection before the Mercedes turned, so that for a few blocks the Mercedes was actually following him. Gradually, he let the Mercedes gain on him and pass him. He lagged behind the big black car and wrote its license number in a notebook lying open next to him on the passenger's seat.

The Mercedes turned onto the freeway, toward the airport,

but, gathering speed, it passed the airport exit and crossed the Keelung River. The day's drizzle had turned to rain, borne on the eastern winds that often brought typhoons at this time of the year. Sheets of rain pounded the car, and Hu gripped the steering wheel, leaning forward to catch a glimpse of road at the moment when the wipers managed to sweep back an arc of rain. Two red dots appeared ahead.

"That does it," Gunnison said, tapping the Mercedes driver on the shoulder. "The car behind us speeded up when we did. I think he's following us." The driver nodded.

"What's your name, driver?" Gunnison asked. He felt it would be a good idea to know this driver in the next few minutes.

"Shan," the driver said, smiling in the rearview mirror. "It means mountain. General Cheng gave me name." All Gunnison could see was that Shan was broad across the shoulders. He assumed the rest of the mountain.

"Okay, Shan. Turn quickly off the next exit. Understand?"

"Yes. We have fun with him. Okay?"

The car sped up, and Gunnison was thrown back against the seat. He turned to see what looked like a solid wall of rain pierced by two rapidly diminishing pinpoints of light.

"Not so goddamn fast, Shan. We don't want to lose him. I'd like to know who he is."

Shan hit the brakes. The car skidded to the right, but Shan smoothly steered into the skid and swung the car onto an exit ramp. He pumped the brake and slowed to a stop. He turned and grinned at Gunnison, pointing through the rear window.

Gunnison could make out the form of a car backing up at the exit. The car's lights swung through the rain and became pinpoints of light again. Shan started up.

"Pull into the next side road, Shan," Gunnison said.

"No worry. Shan knows what to do."

Shan pulled over to the right side of the road, his eyes on the rearview mirror. He rolled down his window and reached for something under his seat. The rain whipped in. Gunnison slumped down in the seat and eased open the right rear door in case he wanted to bolt from the car. The rain whipped in through the slot of the door. He pulled up the collar of his raincoat.

Shan had parked at the sloping shore of a lake. The pelting rain churned the water. The other car pulled alongside slowly. Shan shouted at the driver, who leaned toward the passenger's side of his car and began to roll down that window. Hu shouted back to

Shan. Then he shifted his eyes and saw what Shan had poked through his own open window. Still leaning toward the window, Hu jammmed the accelerator and the car lurched forward. But Shan needed only to shift the 9-millimeter Makarov automatic pistol slightly.

The sounds of the two shots were muffled by the rain. The first shot clipped the top of the Buick's window and entered Hu's right temple. The second shattered the window. Gunnison was not able to see where that one hit, but he knew that somewhere in that large head there were two bullets. Gunnison had seen just enough of the man to recognize him as the one who had followed him into the museum the day before. He had casually mentioned it to the man Cheng had sent to him with instructions for tonight's meeting.

Now he was dead or dying in a car rolling down a dark and empty road. Shan slammed the Mercedes into reverse, made a U-turn, and sped back toward the freeway. Through the rear window, Gunnison thought he saw the blue Buick veer off the road and skid on its roof into the lake. The car disappeared in the rain and darkness.

"Did you know him?" Gunnison asked, surprised at the even sound of his voice. He suddenly remembered the last time he had heard gunfire. Saigon, in the final days.

"Enemy. Good he is dead," Shan said.

"Who did he work for?"

"Americans. Most of time, Americans."

"The Americans on Tunghwa Street?" Gunnison's voice was softer now. The American Institute's friendship office was on Tunghwa Street.

"Yes. American spies on Tunghwa Street. CIA spies. CIA is General Cheng's enemy."

Shan spoke a few words in Chinese, then translated them, as if to himself: "General Cheng says, 'One time friends, another time enemies.' Now enemy time."

"What about me, Shan?" Gunnison smiled at the eyes that narrowed in the rearview mirror, lit by the reflection of the instrument panel's lights.

"General Cheng says you are friend . . . now. Please to lock your door. No good to fall out."

The Mercedes was back on the freeway and heading toward the highway to Chilung.

*

Gunnison stepped out of the car at the entrance to the dock, into the rain now falling in steady sheets. Shan expertly cupped his right hand under Gunnison's left elbow and, just slightly tightening the grip, fell in step with Gunnison. Shan was as tall as Gunnison, with the build of a light-heavyweight boxer, the rolling gait of an athlete, and the confident air of a well-trained military officer. He wore sharply creased khaki trousers and a dark blue zippered windbreaker. His hair was close-cropped, and his brown, ankle-high laced shoes were highly polished. Gunnison leaned into the rain and held his right hand over his head as a shield. Shan swung his free arm in time with his stride. He obviously had long served in the Taiwanese Army or, perhaps, Marines.

The dock itself looked military again. This time, guards were visible along the dimly lit pier leading to the *Golden Moon*. They were not in military uniform, but they might as well have been, for all wore khaki trousers and dark-blue zippered windbreakers. All wore blue beach hats, which offered little protection from the rain. Gunnison got a good look at three of them. They were carrying Israeli-made Uzi submachine guns, only partially concealed under the windbreakers.

Two more guards, seemingly clones of those along the pier, stood on the deck of the *Golden Moon*. The only visible sign of their weapons was the bulge under their zipped-up blue jackets. Gunnison crossed the gangplank to the deck of the junk.

He immediately noticed that the junk was different. The deck had been sanded or holystoned and almost shone in the darkness. The deckhouse aft was larger and, he thought, higher. And, forward, abaft the foremast, were two small deck structures, like hatch combings but larger. There was a small, commercial radar can attached to the main mast, and there were cables running to the short mizzen mast. He assumed, but in the rain could not see, that whip antennas or wire aerials were attached to the mast. Shan guided him down a hatch opening.

Once below decks, Shan stamped the rain from his boots and Gunnison did the same. The interior of the junk was lighted in red—battle lighting, Gunnison thought as Shan pushed him to a massive teak door and knocked twice. In the moment before the door opened, Gunnison realized that during his several times aboard the junk, he had never been forward below decks. Always he had been aft, in the main cabin—which now seemed to have been enlarged—or below decks aft, in the galley and some of the storerooms when Cheng would rummage around for the odd bottle of German hock or other wine he knew was hidden away somewhere.

The teak door swung open to reveal a large compartment brightly lighted by fluorescent ceiling fixtures. Gunnison could see little of the room itself beyond the guard standing there. He was a giant of a man, in a black turtleneck sweater and khaki trousers. He wore a shoulder holster, and Gunnison could see the butt of a 9-millimeter Makarov pistol, the same weapon that Shan had used to kill their tail. Gunnison was certain that there were eight 9-millimeter rounds in the magazine, and this clone would not hesitate to use the pistol if the general ordered it.

A single word of Chinese was spoken behind the guard, and he immediately stepped aside. Shan followed Gunnison into the room. He heard the teak door shut and bolted behind them.

Cheng was standing at a map table at the far end of the cabin. The room, or compartment—for Gunnison now was thinking he was on a combat craft—had no windows or portholes. Along one side were at least three radio transceivers, a radar console, and what Gunnison thought was a covered sonar console. His two-second scan of the room was interrupted by Cheng: "Over here."

Gunnison turned and walked over to Cheng, who was standing beside a chart table.

"Is everything all right?" Cheng asked. "You look pale."

"No, Ho. Everything is not all right. Far from it."

Suddenly, the expression on Cheng's face hardened. He spoke sharply. "Aboard the *Golden Moon* you will address me as General Cheng or simply General. Is that clear?"

Before Gunnison could answer, Cheng began to walk past him toward the door, which was opened instantly by the sweater-clad clone. "Come, we speak in my cabin," ordered Cheng.

Gunnison clenched his fists and followed Cheng. As soon as they were through the doorway, the clone in the black turtleneck closed and locked the massive teak door, slipped on a blue zipup jacket he had grabbed from a hook outside the compartment, and fell into file behind Gunnison and Cheng. Shan seemed to have disappeared.

Walking aft, at a half-stoop because of the low overhead, Gunnison felt and heard the craft's twin tubo-charged diesel engines cough into life. Their vibration quickly settled down into a very low throb as Gunnison felt the *Golden Moon* begin to move. The passageway along the starboard side of the junk was narrow. Twice

Cheng and Gunnison and the clone had to press themselves back against the wall as seamen rushed by them. Most wore turtleneck sweaters, khaki trousers, and boat shoes, unlike the combat boots of the gun-toting clones.

Just before the three men climbed up the short ladder to the next half-deck, Gunnison saw stacked behind the ladder several drums of 20-millimeter ammunition. These circular magazines, each holding sixty rounds, were familiar to Gunnison. The 20-millimeter rapid-fire cannon that used them had been the main armament of the black-painted PT-boats the CIA and the Navy had used for clandestine operations off the North Vietnamese coast.

Obviously, Cheng's junk carried more firepower than the pair of antique cannon decorating the main deck; the *Golden Moon* was a small combat craft. After climbing the two short ladders at the stern, the three men arrived at Cheng's cabin on the main deck. The clones opened the door to the cabin, and Gunnison followed Cheng into the dimly lit room. The door closed behind Gunnison. The furniture was familiar. But, somehow, Gunnison realized that the room was smaller. He surmised that the addition he thought had been made to the deckhouse had encroached upon the cabin space.

Chang went to the table in the center of the room, picked up a telephone Gunnison knew had not been in the room during his visit three weeks before, and spoke a few short, crisp orders. When Cheng turned back in his direction, Gunnison stepped toward a chair. "May I sit down, General?" Gunnison asked, trying to sound jocular. He had a feeling that his attempt at familiarity did not get across the chasm between the two men. He decided to sound angry: "Listen, Ho. I'm not one of your goddamn part-time soldiers. Bad things have happened. Bad things. Big problems."

"You can speak full English sentences to me, Harry," Cheng said, looking up. He had been writing with a small gold fountain pen on a long sheet of yellow paper. He screwed the cap on the pen and placed it in the breast pocket of his black tunic before he resumed speaking. "What are the bad things and the big problems?"

"That man your man Shan killed worked for the CIA—and Shan knew it."

Cheng shrugged. "He also worked for the Investigating Bureau. He worked for anyone foolish enough to hire him. Shan never liked him. The killing of that man was your bad thing?"

"He—and his death—will be linked to me. There will be questions asked," Gunnison said, waiting for a response. There was none. He continued, trying to keep his voice normal. "But, yes, there is something worse, something more difficult to deal with. The United States has decided to stop the *Glomar* from raising the *Osaka Maru*. I have just come from a meeting with Jessen. He is here to stop the operation. He is under direct orders from the president."

"I am not surprised, Harry. Gold does strange things to people. I suppose all that gold frightened your president."

"I am sure it was something like that, something you can fix," Gunnison said, pausing deliberately before he added, "General."

"You can be annoyingly patronizing, Harry. Now, I suppose your next question is, What will we do?"

"Yes," Gunnison said. A slightly built crewman in the ubiquitous black turtleneck had appeared. The door to the cabin apparently was unlocked. The crewman brought a bottle of *maotai,* a fiery liquor distilled from sorghum.

Cheng picked up the bottle and poured the clear liquid into two small cups. *"Gambei,"* he said, and tilted his head back to drain the cup. *"Gambei,"* Gunnison repeated and drained his cup. The *maotai* burned its way down his throat and into his stomach.

Cheng went to a book rack at the end of the cabin, just out of the light that illuminated the table and the tall, opaque bottle of *maotai.* Gunnison could not see what it was.

"Harry, I am going to explain to you why I am not perplexed by your news." Thumbing through the book, as if to instantly refresh his memory, Cheng explained, "In the days of her prime, the *Golden Moon,* under one of her many names, had sailed from Chilung and attacked small merchant ships in the Formosa Strait, off Hong Kong or Canton or Shanghai.

"She pounced on a good one in—1952, I think it was—yes, 1952. She was a British steamer, on a passage from Hong Kong to Chilung. She was about ten miles off Taiwan when the *Golden Moon,* then the *Ill Wind,* that would be the translation. The *Ill Wind,* a terrible name for a ship, but in a tradition. . . ."

Gunnison felt he was once again a bright adolescent dealing with his mentor. He knew Cheng expected him to ask, Why did she have such a name?

"Tradition. There is a tradition that there is a Goddess of Disenchantment—that is the conventional translation for Westerners—and that she presides over the realm of the ill-fated. Pirates and hunters of gold are in that realm, my friend. There is a famous poem about the ill-fated."

Cheng poured another cup of *maotai* and handed it to Gunnison. Cheng did not take another cup of his own. But he said, "*Gambei*," and Gunnison repeated the word and drank the *maotai* in one gulp. He held the cup upside down before his host in the traditional manner.

"*Ill Wind*," Cheng said. "*Ill Wind*. I must remember that this is the name of a ship that is gone but still is here, still is where we are." He poured Gunnison another cup, and this time neither said *Gambei* as Gunnison drained the cup.

"The captain of the *Ill Wind*," Cheng said, "by tradition had nailed upon his mainmast a poem from the goddess. I will read it to you: 'They brought on themselves spring grief and autumn anguish. Wasted their beauty, fair as flowers, and the moon.'

"And, so, Harry, we come to the autumn anguish. Strange, yet fateful, it was also in September that the *Ill Wind* stopped the British steamer. As the boarding party sought to come aboard, the lookout sighted a mainland Chinese warship. The captain of the *Ill Wind* knew that if he boarded the steamer and took off the rich cargo he knew she carried, his ship would be easily caught.

"Still," Cheng continued, "the *Ill Wind* was brought alongside the freighter, her men stormed aboard, easily subdued the small crew, and moved the cargo to the *Ill Wind*. She broke away from the British steamer with the Chinese gunboat perhaps five thousand yards away. Just then a storm arose. The fall season is notorious in the Strait for sudden storms. The *Ill Wind* was holed several times by Chinese gunfire, but the old diesel engine and sails permitted her to escape into the storm."

"Cheng—I mean, *General*. I've heard almost the same story about *another* ancestor of yours more than a hundred years before."

"But that, Harry, is the very point. The audacity of my ancestors has always provided rewards. That is why we must go after the gold. With audacity we shall triumph."

"Come on, Cheng, you're dealing with the U.S. Government and the American Navy. There's a full-time surveillance watch on the *Glomar*. There have to be foreign ships all over the place."

"Yes, Harry, and there is an American submarine watching the foreign ships. It will not be watching a junk, nor will it be able to detect or take action against helicopters."

"So that's how you plan to do it. But Jesus, Cheng"—this time the General's look forced Gunnison to correct himself. "Look, General, Jessen is flying out to the *Glomar* tomorrow and telling them to stop the lift. To let the damn *Osaka Maru* fall back to the ocean floor. That's the end of it. Nothing else can lift that tub at those depths, and no diver can reach it."

"But the gold will be brought aboard the *Glomar*. *You* will see to that, Harry."

"No, damn it, I can't. Jessen will order the captain, an agency man named Dysart, to simply halt the lift and let the hulk fall back to the ocean floor."

This time Cheng refilled both cups. Gunnison knew he could not refuse to drink *maotai* with Cheng. But he also knew that his tolerance for the potent liquor was rapidly being approached. "*Gambei*" said Cheng, draining his cup and holding it in the inverted position. Gunnison did the same.

The effects, he could feel, were reducing his powers of concentration.

"Look, Cheng, er, General Cheng, there's no way—no way—I . . . I can get Jessen to not close down the operation, not close down . . ."

"Harry, Harry, we will delay Jessen and you will go talk to this Captain Dysart. You are still an official of the CIA."

"No. Jessen, he's expecting Jessen, Jessen." Gunnison could feel the words slurring off his tongue.

"Of course, but we will delay Jessen."

"And if he's delayed he'll call the ship and tell them he is . . . delayed."

"Then we will delay him so that he cannot call."

There was another *Gambei*, at least one more, Gunnison knew. But later he would think that there was more than *maotai* in his cup. And his arguments were refuted, quietly and simply by the general, who was drinking with him, cup for cup.

Then there were others in the room. Men sitting quietly, their eyes on Gunnison as he explained over and over that he could not save the ship of gold. The president himself had directed the operation to be stopped. Gunnison tried again and again to make the point.

Finally, Gunnison could remember only that at last he had given in, accepting as his own Cheng's belief that the lost gold belonged to those who could take it.

Then there was Jessen. Talk about Jessen. Cheng kept saying simply that Jessen would not arrive.

Cheng finally spoke a few words to one of his lieutenants, who leaned forward and said in good English to Gunnison, "The delaying of Mr. Jessen will be a minor matter."

Gunnison recalled no more. He had a sensation, but somehow not a real memory, of flying—flying off the *Golden Moon,* up toward the sky and the stars. It was as if he were Jacob, having fought with an angel—no, a fallen angel, Cheng the devil—and was then borne up the ladder to the heavens.

Shortly after Gunnison was lifted aloft to the dark heavens in a helicopter, Cheng emerged on the open deck of the *Golden Moon,* walked aft, and looked over the stern counter. Several feet below him, seamen suspended by ropes had removed the large oak board into which had been deeply branded the name *Golden Moon.* The area where the oak board was removed was carefully painted and protected from the spray by a tarp. Then, with blue-light illumination casting huge shadows on the wood, the sailors carefully screwed into the stern counter tarnished-bronze letters that spelled out *Good Wind,* and beneath that in smaller letters, *Hong Kong.*

As dawn broke, the sailors visible on deck wore dungarees and T-shirts. Two of them wore bras stuffed with rags, loose blouses, skirts, and wigs.

22

GUNNISON WOKE UP WITH THE HEADACHE of a hangover and with a cold, senseless memory of being aloft, of flying through the air. He knew his mind well enough to know that he had not dreamed that memory. It was real, as real as this awakening, and just as hard to sort out.

He had always prided himself on his ability to know immediately where he was when he awoke. On this day—*on this morning*—he did not know where he was, and he felt no fear, which he knew as part of himself, but panic, which he rarely had felt.

He began by trusting his eyes rather than his memory. He was lying in his shorts and T-shirt, under a thick, dark brown blanket on a narrow, metal-framed bed. The bed was against a pale blue wall. He sat up and reached out his left arm. His hand touched a bed like the one he was in; the blanket on the other bed was tucked in tightly with the edge of a white sheet showing from under the blanket. There was no pillow on that bed, and, as Gunnison discovered when he painfully turned his head, there was no pillow on his bed.

Between the beds was a nightstand, and on it was a battered brass lamp with a pink shade too large for it. The lamp was on. Opposite the door was a dresser, and next to it, in a corner, a sink and a towel rack.

. . . Something was coming from the darkness he had flown through and from the darkness of his mind. *Jessen.* They had been talking about Jessen . . .

The door to the room opened and Chia Min walked in.

"Good morning, Harry," she said.

He moved quickly, too quickly, to get out of bed. Standing, he felt his body slump back. He fell against the bed, half sitting up.

She crossed the room and sat next to him. She gently pushed him back to the bed. As he started to speak, she put a cool finger against his lips.

She went back to the door and locked it. She took off her shoes. She removed her jeans, her white blouse, her black bra and black bikini panties. She slipped under the brown blanket. Without any conscious effort, he began to harden as she knelt over him, her hands alternately fondling him and then moving across his chest. And then lowered her body upon him. She was in charge. She held him down, and he sensed that he was not to move. Only she was to move, always in the same slow tempo, never with the frenzy he had so often known.

At what was for him the final moment, just before she stopped and arched back, at that moment, he knew that she was somebody else and had been somebody else for a long time.

She dressed quickly and sat on the other bed. He noticed her shoes as she laced them; she was wearing tennis shoes. She had worn them only the few times she had played tennis. He had tried to teach her. She was awful. And now she was wearing them, she said, because she was soon to be flown to the *Golden Moon* on the same helicopter that had carried Gunnison from the junk through the night sky to Kaohsiung. Just to have packed them, he realized, she had to have known so much. He thought of her in their bedroom, selecting what she could take and what she would never see again. She had taken a pair of tennis shoes.

"In the fullness of time," Gunnison said. "That was what Cheng said. I would know in the fullness of time." He turned to Chia Min. "And you. You said that, too."

"Yes," Chia Min said. "A favorite expression of General Cheng, my uncle."

"He's holding you. Using you as a hostage," Gunnison said, leaning forward to hold her head in his hands. She did not move.

"Harry, oh, Harry, oh, Harry," she said. She reached up to touch his hands, and she began to speak as a schoolchild might speak; her words coming like the words of a recitation, words uttered reluctantly, painfully.

"Remember how we met? That was chance, Harry. Good fortune. And my falling in love with you. Also good fortune. When this happened—" She had been speaking slowly, like a schoolgirl. Now her words came more quickly so that the recitation would be over and the hall would empty and the day would end. "When this happened, General Cheng saw an opportunity, for me and for you, Harry, for us. And for our homeland. He asked me to let him know what you were doing. And I did, Harry. But I never did anything that would harm you. Believe me, Harry."

"Sure, Chia Min," Gunnison said, his voice tired and drained of harshness. "Sure. I believe you. Go ahead. There must be more."

She had ended her recitation. But now, in a firmer, slower voice, she said, "Yes, Harry, much more. Let me tell you. When you decided that you would betray the agency to get so much money, when you decided that, you did it on your own. That was not my doing, Harry."

"Yes. Not your doing. But when I said I was going to Cheng, you saw the golden opportunity come again. A chance to feed him more information, a chance to be valuable again."

"Yes. And I saw something you did not see, Harry. Or something that you chose not to see." She waited for him to speak, but he did not. He was looking down at a worn green carpet. "I might never have been able to get out of the United States. The agency would have held me. You had gone. From that moment I had nothing, no protection. You could have been betraying me, Harry, the way you were betraying the agency, betraying Ishiwata, betraying Jessen."

"Cheng!" Gunnison exclaimed. "Cheng told you all this, fed you this—"

There was a knock at the door. Chia Min stood and unlocked it. A small man entered. Behind him, just beyond the doorway, were two taller, huskier men.

The small man seemed to hunch himself even smaller. He seemed to be saying with his smiling face that he did not ordinarily wake guests this way. Gunnison pulled the blanket around himself and stood. The two men in the doorway were about six feet tall and muscular. Both obviously wore shoulder holsters under their windbreakers. Blue windbreakers. His memory was coming back.

As the smaller man, bowing and gesturing, began to speak in Chinese to Chia Min, Gunnison interrupted him.

"I've got to get to a phone," he said, "I've got to talk to Jessen." He turned to Chia Min. "No more betraying." He could feel his head clearing. "No more betraying."

"I must go, Harry," she said, standing before him, looking up at him as she always did when they argued over something trivial. He tried not to look down at her. But he could not keep his eyes from her.

"We will be together again, Harry."

"In the fullness of time?"

"Please, Harry. There are duties . . . Duties that must be performed."

"I can imagine what they must be, with a boat full of sailors."

She slapped him hard, first with the front of her hand and then the back.

"I go aboard the *Golden Moon* because my uncle trusts me nowhere else. I am not a prisoner but a guarantee. A hostage, you called me. He knows I will not betray him only if I am at his side. He knows, Harry, that I love you, and he wants to use my love for his protection."

"And what do I do?"

"This man is Yang, who is General Cheng's deputy. He will tell you."

She said something to the small man and took a step toward the door. She turned and said, "We will see each other again, Harry. A new life, you said. There will be a new life."

She left through a door she did not close. The small man remained where he had stood. He waited for a few moments, as if listening for something. Then he said to Gunnison, "My name is Yang. I work for General Cheng. You stay now."

A few minutes later the man came back, made motions for Gunnison to get dressed, and stepped outside, closing the door behind him. Gunnison dressed hurriedly. As he approached the door, it opened. Gunnison wondered how long he—and Chia Min—had been watched. She couldn't have known, he told himself. She couldn't have known.

Yang led him down a hall. The two other men walked behind. At the end of the hall was a small, deserted lobby. Worn green velvet shades were drawn across the windows flanking the outer door of what Gunnison assumed was a hotel or minor-league safe house.

Yang pointed to a door in the lobby. On it was one of the few Chinese writing characters Gunnison knew, the square symbol for *man*. Gunnison opened the door and went in. The stench enveloped him. He urinated into a stained stone trough that ran the length of one brown wall. He stood back from the permanent puddle under the trough.

He went back into the lobby and made washing motions over his hands and face and pointed down the hall, toward his room. Yang shook his head.

"Mr. Gunnison wants to wash his face and shave," Gunnison

said, raising his voice and again pointing to his room. Yang shook his head.

Gunnison realized he had underestimated Yang. He was in command. Yang tilted his head toward Gunnison and spoke two words in Chinese. The two guards moved swiftly and flanked Gunnison, their arms touching his arms, with just enough pressure for him to feel pinned.

"We go now," Yang said.

"Where am I?" Gunnison asked. "Where are you taking me?"

"You are near Kaohsiung. The general wishes you to be on the *Glomar Explorer* at a proper time. We go now."

Yang turned and Gunnison followed, with the two guards behind him. They walked down a corridor that led away from his room. Halfway down this corridor Yang opened a door at the top of a dark stairwell. He pulled a string on a bare overhead bulb. They descended in the dim light to what looked like the door of what had been a walk-in refrigerator. One of the guards yanked the handle. As the door swung open, a caged bulb lit in the high ceiling. The room smelled of sweat and urine, not meat.

There was a cot in one corner, a slop bucket in another corner. Next to the cot was a low table. A guard put a grease-stained cardboard box on the table. The box contained a small tin of tea, the standard Chinese white porcelain tea cup, with top, and a tall thermos bottle that Gunnison recognized as the kind Chinese use for keeping tea water hot. Two white cranes flew against the bright red sky painted on the bottle.

"Food later. Now, tea," Yang said. He led the two guards out, and the door slammed behind them.

The food—a bowl of rice with bits of fish, shredded ginger, and slivers of red pepper—came hours later. Gunnison had lost track of time, and he thought that may have been the reason for his transfer to a cell without windows.

When he finished his food and used the slop bucket, he heard a click and the light vanished. In the solid darkness he forced himself to sleep. Once he was awakened by the sound of the door opening. He lay still while someone entered in the darkness to remove the food tray and slop bucket.

He tried to will himself to sleep. After a while he was not aware of sleep or wakefulness. He did not dream, and he tried not to think. But he could not rid himself of the wordless thoughts that formed in his mind as the faces of Jessen and Chia Min.

He awakened blinking at the light. Above him stood Yang and the same two guards. They took him up the stairs and down the corridor to the lobby. He motioned toward the room marked by *man*. Yang smiled and nodded.

When Gunnison came out, he took a step toward the corridor leading to what had been his room.

"This way," Yang said. "We go now."

"Why am I a prisoner?" Gunnison asked. He stroked his chin, and estimated from the stubble that he had been kept in the basement for at least twenty-four hours.

"Not prisoner. Special guest," Yang said. One of the guards opened the outer door. "We go now."

They all stood for a moment on the portico, waiting for a car to pull up. Gunnison took a deep breath of the cool air. It was dawn, a gray dawn with rain falling lightly.

Gunnison and one of the guards got into the backseat of a car. It was a dark blue Chevrolet with a small line of Chinese characters stenciled on the front door. Staff car, Gunnison thought. Yang got into the passenger's seat in front; the other guard became the driver.

Gunnison rolled down the window. He breathed in the cool morning air and fought to get his mind working. He started with his memory of yesterday . . . Lunch with Jessen. *Jessen*. The name flared in his mind. *Jessen. Something was happening to Jessen.* They had had lunch on Saturday. Yesterday. No. Not yesterday. . . . Then he had left the hotel, and his car had been followed . . . Step by step, he reached back to his talk with Cheng aboard the *Golden Moon*.

Yang and the two guards had all lit cigarettes. Gunnison felt as if he was going to throw up. He pulled his head away from the window to ask Yang, "What day is this, Yang?"

"Day?"

"Yes. Is this Monday? Monday morning?"

"Yes, Mr. Gunnison. This is Monday, Monday morning." Yang laughed, pulled a pack of Marlboros out of his pocket, and offered Gunnison a cigarette. Gunnison waved the pack away and again put his head to the open window. Yang laughed again.

23

STEVE DYSART, CAPTAIN OF THE *Glomar Explorer*, was a betting man. His skill and luck as a baccarat player were legendary in casinos throughout the world. He did not like sucker bets. But he had not been able to resist the offer of his executive officer, Jack Mooney, who gave ten-to-one odds that the flying boat carrying Ishiwata to the ship would not be able to land in a sea-state three.

Dysart knew that the plane could land in a whitecapped sea. He had looked up the plane's specifications when he had got the message with the precise details of how Ishiwata would arrive. The *Shin Meiwa* flying boat, the largest seaplane in the world, was powered by four 3,000-horsepower turbojets, had a wingspan of 109 feet, and, according to the handbook, was built exclusively for the Japanese defense forces. Dysart had wondered how Ishiwata rated the use of one.

Dysart heard the plane just before he saw it—from somewhere in the darkening sky the high whine of the engines. She broke through the gray, not like a bird but like the great machine she was, a mechanical monster, the whorls of her four propellers glinting like eyes. She slipped easily from air to sea, one moment a thing of the sky, the next moment a strange winged boat roaring toward the *Glomar*.

Dysart's best boatswain was the coxswain of the motor launch, which set out from the *Glomar* as soon as the flying boat touched the sea. Frank Blair, a former Coast Guard officer, was in command of the launch. He stood off from the port wing of the plane; a sudden high wave could have crushed the launch against the underside of the wing. The pilot was wise about small boats. As Blair smartly swung parallel to the plane's fuselage, the pilot played the engines so that the prop wash countered the chop of the sea.

Blair pulled alongside the port hatch of the seaplane, and, when the hatch opened, he threw a quick salute to the man in the hatchway. Taketomo, assigned by Ishiwata as leader of the Japanese aboard the *Glomar,* had insisted on being on the launch as an escort. He sprang forward, and, one foot on the gunwale, the other on a hemp fender chafing the side of the plane, he lightly touched the arm of Ishiwata Seno as he emerged from the hatchway.

Dysart was impressed by the agility of the man, whom he knew to be at least in his late sixties and perhaps older. Ishiwata stepped nimbly into the launch, nodded to Blair, and sat next to Taketomo on a seat forward of the coxswain.

Dysart, his binoculars on Ishiwata, missed the disembarking of the big man who followed Ishiwata. Then, at the left edge of the binoculars' field, a black shape appeared and disappeared. Dysart swung the binoculars slightly and saw the back of a man sitting on the starboard seat, his arms draped over two large suitcases. Dysart made a mental note to have the chief steward, at the first appropriate moment, search the luggage for arms and photograph any interesting contents.

The hull of the *Glomar,* stabilized in the billowing sea, stood steady against the bobbing launch. Ishiwata, with no hesitation, jumped across the foot of water between the launch and the gangway platform of the *Glomar*. The bigger man did hesitate, and he stumbled onto the platform. The launch came alongside the forward boatfalls to be hoisted aboard.

Dysart stood at the head of the gangway, his gaze swiveling from the people coming up the ladder. His captain's mind would not fully rest until he knew that the motor launch was safely griped and secured. He could not take his eyes off this operation no matter who was coming aboard. He was smiling when Taketomo presented Ishiwata to him, but the smile was for his crew and the safe securing of the launch. Dysart was a captain, not a diplomat.

Dysart was not introduced to the big man, Kimpei. Two Japanese appeared at the head of the gangway, spoke rapidly to Kimpei, and then vanished with him and the luggage.

Dysart escorted Ishiwata to the guest quarters, a VIP cabin adjacent to the captain's cabin (and once planned as the cabin Howard Hughes would occupy). With a great flourish of polite words and phrases, Ishiwata disappeared.

The next morning—Sunday the twenty-seventh—Dysart was back at the rail, watching for a new visitor. He glanced at his watch. Ishiwata had come aboard the day before. He had spent almost every waking minute with Taketomo, a somewhat mysterious veteran of the Maritime Self-Defense Force—the Japanese Navy—who claimed to be nothing more than an officer on Ishiwata's Yokohoma-based yacht. Taketomo was in charge of the thirty-six Japanese members of the crew, but all orders came from Dysart, either directly or through Mooney, who insisted on calling Taketomo simply "Tomo." Taketomo accepted this with a smile that, Dysart noticed, got thinner as the days wore on.

Dysart had rather pointedly insisted that Ishiwata join him for breakfast. Dysart knew, peering again at the gray, that there was trouble ahead. There had to be. Something to do with Jessen's orders.

But where was Jessen?

Dysart forced himself not to look through the gray sky toward shore, some ninety miles off the starboard bow. He knew that he would hear of Jessen's arrival first from Roth, the communications officer. Roth would send word as soon as the ship's radar picked up Jessen's helicopter.

It was a long time, Dysart thought, since a captain conned his ship by using his senses and the senses of his crew. He once calculated that he had three computers for every man on board. His ship was more electronic than human. He looked down from the low bridge to the equipment-cluttered main deck of his ship. She rode easily in the swells, held within twenty-five feet of a specific position by an automatic positioning system. Sonar reflections from the ocean floor, star sightings, and satellite data were poured into a computer that regulated the "thrusters"—five small propellers in the ship's hull. Their spurts of power kept the ship stationary.

Dysart had great confidence in his unique ship, odd-looking as she might be. She had what appeared to be a huge oil derrick amidships. Flanking this were two steel-girder towers. Each of the three structures was about as tall as a twelve-story building. The derricklike rig housed controls and heavy machinery for operating the recovery claws.

When a lift began, the towers were lowered beneath the keel to support the claw, which could lift seven thousand tons. For the Osaka Maru hoist, special floatation bags had been provided in the Japanese shipyard. The bags, attached to the hulk with the help of a submersible carried on *Glomar,* permitted the modified claws to lift many times their designed capacity. As the object grasped by the claws was brought to a point just beneath the ship, the still-lowered towers supported not only the claws but also the object.

(If the object was less than two hundred feet long and seventy-four feet wide, the object could be brought into the ship's center well—the "moon pool." This was accomplished by opening huge, horizontally sliding doors in the bottom of the ship. As soon as the doors were slid closed again, pumps would begin emptying the moon pool of its sixteen thousand tons of seawater. Technicians could then minutely examine the object in the moon pool, transformed into a kind of dry dock.)

The *Osaka Maru* was far too large to be brought into the moon pool. But it was being raised to a position under the *Glomar* where divers could pass through the flooded moon pool, enter the hulk suspended below, and easily remove the cargo. That was the plan.

So far, the recovery operation had gone perfectly. The *Osaka Maru* was now suspended just four hundred feet beneath the *Glomar*. But, as usual, Dysart thought, there was more to the operation than the mechanics. Where was Jessen? He had sent a message, via Langley, saying that operations were to be "suspended until arrival." Well, that was the case, all right. The goddamn tub was suspended.

Dysart assumed that whatever was going on had to do with the appearance of foreign ships in the area. Back in 1974, when the *Glomar* was recovering the Russian submarine, Soviet spy ships—AGIs in naval parlance—in the area periodically looked over the *Glomar*. But now, radar, and at times even binoculars, revealed that the Soviet AGI dogging the *Glomar* was not the only foreign ship keeping her under observation. There was a Chinese destroyer, a frigate from the Japanese Maritime Self-Defense Force, and at times two small patrol craft from Taiwan. Periodically, aircraft from all three countries, as well as at least one unidentified plane, had flown low over the *Glomar*. The mainland Chinese flights were the most frequent, generally twice a day. The *Glomar*'s thrusters kept her almost motionless as the *Osaka Maru* swung gently below, trapped in the gigantic clawlike lifting devices. A sitting duck. Dysart calculated his armament in the weapons locker in his cabin: a few shotguns and maybe a dozen handguns, mostly .45's . . .

First had come the message from Jessen. Then two hours later came the message saying Ishiwata was flying out to the *Glomar*. Something had gone wrong. And Ishiwata himself did not seem to know what it was. Immediately after Ishiwata arrived aboard, he had begun methodically questioning Taketomo. Dysart had learned of Ishiwata's confusion through crude translations of the conversations in Ishiwata's cabin. Roth had remembered that the agency had prudently bugged what was to have been Howard Hughes' cabin. And Roth knew enough Japanese to give Dysart an idea about what was being discussed.

"Captain." Dysart turned to see Roth. "Two things, sir. First, our pal in the cabin is about to leave, and he just told Tomo maybe you'll let some information slip at breakfast."

"Fat chance. I don't know a goddamn thing myself. What else?"

"A message," Roth said, handing Dysart a metal clipboard. "It's from Gunnison, sir. A clear-language radio-telephone message. Funny he didn't use code."

Dysart initialed the message and handed the clipboard back. "Strange," Dysart said. "Says he's coming aboard tomorrow morning. No mention of Jessen, though, and I thought they were together on Taiwan. In fact, I'm certain they were supposed to come out together."

"Maybe they are together, and good ol' Gunnison just thought it wasn't important enough to mention his boss," Roth said.

"I guess so. Let's get the other guest cabin set up for Jessen. If you don't mind, I'll have Gunnison shack up with you in the Pullman bunk in your cabin."

Dysart dismissed Roth and turned back to the rail. As he did, he saw Mooney, his exec, coming up the ladder.

"Jack," Dysart said, "it's time for that breakfast that Ishiwata is honoring me with. Have one of the stewards ask him to join me in my cabin. You, too. I assume I don't have to ask his man Kimpei."

"Aye, aye, Captain. I think his man will just camp outside your door while he's in there. He just seems to hover around Ishiwata. I don't know when he eats or craps."

"Is he armed?"

"We found two revolvers in his gear, which one of our people just happened to have moved and checked out. But if you're his size, you don't need any."

"There's Ishiwata on deck by the A-frame," Dysart said, pointing down. "I guess he's getting hungry. I'll just go down and take him to my cabin myself. And Jack, if you want to get some of that hundred bucks of yours back, I'll give you three to one that Ishiwata never sees his gold."

"No way, Captain. On this operation all bets are off."

Dysart never forgot who he worked for, and he understood the special problems of a ship flying the agency's invisible flag. He was used to serving an extra master now and then—the Navy, oil companies, Howard Hughes, Ishiwata—but he had only one real master, the director of central intelligence at Langley.

Dysart had been told to follow a charter master's orders unless he heard otherwise or unless his judgment dictated otherwise. The director himself had told Dysart that. So Dysart had followed orders and had taken the *Glomar* into the shipyard at Kagoshima. But then Ishiwata had come aboard and had ordered Dysart off his own ship. Dysart had argued politely at first and then had gone off—only under protest and only because he wanted to get a safe message to Langley via the Tokyo station chief.

Dysart and Ishiwata had finally come to terms. Ishiwata was smooth and powerful. He had convinced Dysart that the agency had given Ishiwata full backing. And, when Dysart was to take the ship out of Kagoshima and to head for the Strait, he had queried Langley and had been told that no less than the U.S. Navy would be aiding in the search for the *Osaka Maru*.

So Dysart had relaxed. It would be a good yarn, the snatching of the ship of gold. He knew about the gold. Everyone on board did. No one knew how much. But they knew that there was supposed to be gold. And who could tell? Maybe there was gold down there. And maybe there was not. An interesting bet.

"Please," Dysart said, indicating the chair to his right for Ishiwata. Jack Mooney sat to Dysart's left around the small table in the reception area of Dysart's cabin. Smiling and chatting about ship prints, Ishiwata promised to send Dysart artists' proofs of several Japanese ship etchings that had been struck in very limited editions. Ishiwata began asking more semitechnical questions about the ship and her capabilities as soon as the conversation about the ship prints was interrupted by two stewards, who cleared away the fruit cups that had brimmed with sliced fresh fruit Ishiwata had brought with him. Now the stewards were serving mushroom-and-cheese omelettes and a choice of bacon or sausage.

If Ishiwata was concerned about trouble with the mission, he did not show it. He did not mention Jessen. Neither did Dysart.

Ishiwata, who obviously had been reading technical manuals sent to him by Taketomo, began asking Dysart about the hoist of the *Osaka Maru*. The captain described how the small research submersible *Albert*—"We call it 'Fat Albert' because it looks like a comic character"—had been sent down to examine the wreck.

"The *Albert* holds an operator and two observers," he continued. "It can also lift some material in its small claws. From what the *Albert* saw, the *Osaka Maru* can be lifted snug against *Glomar*'s bottom. Then, with the doors to our moon pool open—"

"Excuse me, Captain. I believe I understand. You have been, then, successful thus far?" Ishiwata asked. He had finished his omelette. Dysart noted that each time a steward served Ishiwata, he had carefully thanked the steward—not in a condescending manner, but politely and directly.

"And you have been successful?" Ishiwata repeated.

"Well, yes," Dysart replied. "We have got her off the bottom."

"So I understand," Ishiwata said. "But she hangs there, Captain, clutched in a great claw. The claw does not move, Captain. Why have you stopped the operation?"

Ishiwata's voice rose, and he repeated one sharp word, "Why?"

The sparring was over. Dysart hesitated, wondering what to answer. As he began a long, technical explanation, the phone on the bulkhead behind his chair buzzed loudly. Tilting his chair backward, Dysart picked up the receiver and said, "Captain here." He listened for a moment and then excused himself. "Jack, see that someone looks after Mr. Ishiwata. Gentlemen, I must check something out."

"What's all this?" asked Dysart as he climbed into one of the six metal cubicles on the *Glomar*'s deck. They resembled vans without wheels, and they were in fact called vans. They formed the nerve center for the ship, a sort of modular control center. Two of the vans contained the controls and related equipment for the claws; two housed what older crewmen called radio shacks. One handled coded communications and monitored the ship's radar; the other was the sonar control. It was this last one that Dysart entered.

As soon as his eyes became accustomed to the dim light, the three CIA technicians and the Japanese sonarmen directed Dysart to one of the several consoles. The horizontal lines that were slowly traversing the screen had a slight bump.

"It's a submarine, sir," the senior sonarman said. "We 'painted' her about ten minutes ago. This is a tape. We picked her up on our half-hour sweep with active sonar. What's particularly disturbing is that we didn't get her on the passive sonar until after we got her active."

"Then she's a modern, quiet boat?"

"The propeller-turn count indicates an older Soviet nuclear-propelled sub," the leading CIA technician said.

"But she's too quiet, Captain," the Japanese technician added. Dysart looked at him in surprise. A quick learner.

"Right," the American agreed. His career had been about evenly divided between the Navy's classified seafloor sonar projects and the agency. "I think we missed her on passive sonar because she was going slow—might have had her pumps shut off and was using natural convection to move the reactor coolant fluids. Anyway, Captain, she's out there and fairly close, about 30,000 yards."

Dysart moved to the wall phone, turned the channel selector to COMM, and pressed the ringer.

"Roth? Dysart here. Break out the codes. I'm going to have a message for Langley in a few minutes."

24

JESSEN HAD ASKED FOR A wake-up call at 6:00 A.M. on Sunday, the twenty-seventh. He was to fly out to the *Glomar Explorer* and personally direct Dysart to send the *Osaka Maru* back to her watery grave—with the gold intact. Not fully trusting the hotel or the hall boys, he had backed this up with a request of Cosgrove that he call at 6:30. So, when the phone at his bedside rang in the dark, and when he heard Cosgrove's voice, Jessen assumed it was 6:30 and he sprang fully awake. But it was not 6:30. It was a little past 4:00 A.M., and Cosgrove was saying, "You know who I am. We have a slight problem. The kind Judge Crater had. I am in the lobby. Assume that everybody is listening and watching."

Jessen had laid out his ship-boarding costume the night before. He had worn the costume only a few weeks before—light blue denims, kelly green flannel shirt, worn, graying sneakers. Joan had approved of everything except the sneakers. They had spent the weekend on Chesapeake Bay in a sailboat owned and crewed by a friend from the agency and his wife. Now over the costume he pulled a heavy woolen sweater that Joan had packed in his suitcase. She had figured that he would not be home for his birthday, his forty-eighth. But he might make it after all, he thought. He might be able to clean this up and be home in three days.

There was a tag still attached to the sweater. He put on his clear-framed glasses and, though he knew he did not have the time, he idly read the tag. "Greetings from Ireland," it said. "The woman of Ireland who knitted your sweater has signed her name on the other side of this tag. She has also 'signed' your sweater with the special pattern that marks it as a sweater worn by the fishermen of her village." Then, filling his pockets from the stuff scattered on the bureau, and slapping his pocket for the hotel key just as he closed the door behind him, he remembered what Joan had said about that tag. "They told me at the shop," she had said, "that the special pattern was a way of identifying a fisherman's body when it washed ashore. Irish fishermen usually don't know how to swim. I'm glad you do."

Jessen, turning from the door, smiled. Joan. She could appear in his mind so unexpectedly, so vividly.

He decided to use the stairway, not so much to avoid the hall boys but to get the kinks out of his legs. It would be a long day. Cosgrove seemed surprised to see him come through the stairwell door. Or perhaps Cosgrove was surprised to see him in his sailing outfit. Cosgrove, who dressed with the authority and confidence of an American foreign-service official, was wearing a double-breasted dark wool overcoat and a narrow-brimmed light gray fedora. A white silk scarf concealed what Jessen assumed to be a white shirt and tightly knotted striped tie. The stripes would be either blue and white or blue and gray. Jessen stifled an impulse to apologize for his costume.

Cosgrove was standing near a stern red couch in the center of the lobby, a firmly rolled black umbrella in his left hand. He motioned Jessen to sit down, and then, tugging at his sharply creased gray trousers, he perched on the couch and half turned toward Jessen. "Good morning, Charlie. Sorry for the early wake-up. I've got to talk to you."

"Okay," Jessen said. "Who is the Judge Crater? Gunnison?"

"It looks that way. I got a call an hour ago from a fairly reliable type in the Garrison Command—you know, the security police here. I guess he was *told* to call me. But he acted as if he were informing. He said that the local police in a town on the road to Chilung found a car upside down in a lake. They pulled a body out. Shot twice in the head. Close up. It was Hu, the man I had tailing Gunnison."

"You've checked Gunnison's room?"

"I checked with the hall boys. Didn't want to cause too big a fuss. They say he never came back yesterday."

"He told me he was going to visit Chia Min's mother. But I didn't quite believe him."

Cosgrove, in deference to Jessen's rank and friendship with Gunnison, did not ask why. But the unasked question hung in the air between them for a moment, and Jessen added, "It was the way he was acting. I just had a feeling he wasn't going to pay a courtesy call on an old lady."

"Where did she—does she—live?"

"I assume in Taipei somewhere. We can look her up. But it can wait. How did you know Hu was still tailing Gunnison when he caught it?"

"He had written a license number down. Gunnison had left the hotel in a black Mercedes. We knew that from a hall boy who said he was in the lobby and saw Gunnison get into the car. The license number is for a black Mercedes. And . . ." Cosgrove hesitated.

"And the car belongs to Cheng?"

"To a trading company on Hwai Nin Street. Cheng controls the company." Cosgrove nodded toward a sleepy hall boy who was silently approaching them on slippered feet. "We shouldn't be talking here."

Cosgrove looked up from the sofa and spoke sharply to the hall boy, who replied softly and handed him a sealed blue envelope, faintly scented. Scrawled across the envelope in pencil was "Mr. Charleston, Room 509." Cosgrove handed the envelope to Jessen, who opened it, gingerly took out a single sheet of paper, and, tilting his head toward a dim light near the sofa, read, "Cannot make 7:30 flight. Will meet you for 10 o'clock flight at airport. Helicopter at Kaohsiung on 2-day charter, will wait. Sorry. Will explain in person. Walter."

Holding the paper by the thumb and index finger of his right hand, Jessen passed it to Cosgrove, who held it in the same way and read it. "Sounds awfully phony, Charlie."

"Yeah," Jessen said, removing his glasses and rubbing his eyes. "For one thing Gunnison's work name is *Walters*."

"What do you make of it? Somebody holding him?"

"As you said, Ed, we can't talk here."

Cosgrove stood up and plucked a hair off the sleeve of his coat that had touched the sofa. Jessen followed him through the lobby, past a Chinese who had just materialized near the darkened souvenir stand. They passed for a brief moment through the cold, drizzly morning to the warmth of the car, an elderly Lincoln that had once belonged to the American ambassador to the Republic of China.

They did not speak during the ride to the squat building on Tunghwa Street that housed the Chinese-American Friendship Office. The American Institute on Hsinyi Road was the unofficial and unrecognized substitute for the American Embassy. The institute handled much of what the consular section of the embassy had handled: trade and visa matters, the problems of lost or baffled

American tourists. The Chinese-American Friendship Office had two missions—the open one of spreading propaganda through its library, films, and cultural activities, and the closed mission of supporting an American intelligence network.

The car stopped at the wrought-iron gate of the building, which had been erected in 1895 by the Japanese, who were then occupying the island. Its steep, overhanging tile roof seemed to press the dark shape of the building deeper into the ground. The windows on the first floor were shuttered. A greenish fluorescent light glowed behind a window on the third floor, in the inverted v of the roof. As the car stopped, lights flickered on behind the venetian blinds at two windows on the second floor.

Just inside the gate was a dimly lit kiosk. A Garrison Command guard in a dripping, olive green poncho stuck his head out of the kiosk. The drizzle had turned to stinging rain, which made a faint, hollow sound as it pelted the guard's GI-style helmet. He extended a white-gloved hand for Cosgrove's laminated identification card. The guard made an elaborate ceremony of checking Cosgrove's card and registered Jessen, who handed the guard a Virginia driver's license in the name of Frederick W. Charleston. Throughout the ritual, Cosgrove, with one hand holding the black umbrella and the other gesticulating, railed at the guard in three dialects.

"There's what we laughingly call a safe room on the second floor," Cosgrove said. He checked them in with the lobby guard, an American, who had been dozing, his head cradled in his arms on the table in front of him. He wrote something in a ledger and next to it Cosgrove signed his name and wrote "F. Charleston, guest."

The safe room consisted of walls, ceiling, and floor nested inside a preexisting room. Cosgrove unlocked the outer door, then pressed the digits of a combination lock on the inner steel door. He switched on the lights and locked the steel door behind them.

"Welcome to the 'spy nest,' which is what our reluctant hosts call it," he said. He walked to a narrow counter along the far wall and plugged in a hotplate. From a carafe he poured water into a kettle on the hotplate. "We'll have tea in a minute."

"Did they complain about this?" Jessen asked, looking around the room.

"They are getting tacky about us, Charlie. That guard at the gate. Endless forms. Almost weekly attempts to penetrate this room under various silly guises." He sighed. "And soon, I am happy to say, it will all belong to—who, Charlie? Cassell? Payton?"

"We're thinking of Hosmer. Rebecca Hosmer."

"A woman. How novel. Well, Taiwan's not much of a spot anymore, is it?"

"The business, Ed," Jessen said, exasperated. "Can we get to the business? It's kind of early for chitchat."

"Sorry. I've told you all I know for sure. I haven't pressed too hard on this because, theoretically and officially, we were not involved with Hu. Or with the car and passenger he was tailing. I don't want to get the locals excited. They know something is up, of course. But—"

"But they don't know *what* is up? I'm not sure about that. Cheng is obviously aware that Gunnison is being run on some operation. We don't know what Gunnison has been telling Cheng. But we do know—check that; *I* know—that Gunnison isn't supposed to be dealing with Cheng, officially, theoretically, or anything else. As of this moment, Ed . . ." Jessen paused, trying to make his sadness sound like weariness. "As of this moment, Gunnison is to be treated as a nonemployee, a nonconsultant."

"As opposition?"

"No. Not that bad. There is no real national security interest in this thing." While Cosgrove fussed over making the tea, Jessen brought him up to date on Operation Spearmint.

"And so, Ed," he concluded, "no matter what the hell Gunnison may be up to, I can't let this get me off track. My job is to close this thing down. The Man told me to do that, and that is my main mission." He took a sip of tea, held the thick, white mug up, and said, "Fine. Very fine, Ed."

"Thanks, Charlie. It does hit well, doesn't it?" He sipped and stood before a huge wall map that centered on the island of Taiwan. Touching a manicured right index finger on the northern edge of Taiwan, he said, "Here, here in Taipei, we have just about all of our assets, Charlie." He moved his finger down the mountainous spine of the island to the port of Kaohsiung. "And here, in Kaohsiung, we have nothing."

He turned away from the map and gently put his mug on the long, polished table. Cosgrove folded his arms and looked down the table at Jessen. "Two things, Charlie. One, I recommend that you hold off doing anything until we find out what happened to Hu and what the hell Gunnison is up to. The note, for instance. I can confirm your suspicions as soon as Groves comes in. Technician, jack-of-all-trades. We can have him check to see if Gunnison's prints are on the note, and—"

"And it would mean a query to Langley to get the dope on his prints. No soap, Ed. I don't want to query Langley about anything. As far as the director knows, I am here, I am about to close down the operation, and there are no problems. I want him to keep thinking that: No problems. So no communications with Langley on this."

"I see your point, Charlie. But there is you to consider. You're my responsibility. I'm supposed to give you backup and keep you happy and safe."

"I'm safe enough," Jessen said, his right hand sweeping the air in front of him.

"I said I had two things, Charlie. The second item is that I batten things down here and go with you to Kaohsiung. You'll need a reliable interpreter the moment you land, if not the moment you get in the puddle-jumper that takes you to Kaohsiung."

"Thanks for the suggestions, Ed," Jessen said, peeling off his woolen sweater. "Hot as hell in here." He carefully folded the sweater, put it on the table in front of him, and leaned his elbows on it. "But I have got to do what I came out here to do. I'd appreciate a lift to the domestic airport—at Sungshan, right? But then I would like you to get about your business. Find out what Gunnison is up to—or was up to. That note . . . I'll go alone to the *Glomar*."

"On the ten o'clock flight?" Cosgrove asked. He looked at his watch. "You've plently of time for breakfast and the seven-thirty flight."

"I know. But I'm willing to go along with the note. We can get paranoid so easily in this business. Maybe Gunnison succumbed to a piece of ass and was too drunk to write. Maybe there is a lousy—but innocent—explanation."

"You still trust him, Charlie? You just said you canned him a minute ago."

"Trust is a funny word. I don't trust his judgment anymore, I suppose. But I still trust him. As a man, as a friend. How about some more tea?"

Cosgrove filled both of their cups and sat down across the table from Jessen.

"Look, Ed. I know how all of us like to get things on each other. I probably wouldn't tell you this if you weren't a short-timer. But I am pretty sure I know what Gunnison is doing. It has to do with helping Chia Min's mother. And it may not be entirely legal."

"Family business? Come on, Charlie. If you can talk frankly, so can I. I don't trust *your* judgment about Gunnison. He doesn't get the green paycheck like the rest of us. He quit, like Wilson. Gunnison hung on to make dough as a consultant. Like Wilson."

"He's not Wilson, goddamn it!" Jessen slammed the mug down, and drops of tea sprinkled across his white sweater. "Wilson left the agency and went to work for Qaddafi." Cosgrove walked over to the counter and returned with a paper napkin. He began trying to wipe the tea stains off the sweater. "Thanks," Jessen said, lowering his voice. "Sorry. But it's not the same, Ed. Wilson was working for a dictator, a killer. Harry Gunnison is working for himself."

Cosgrove, back at the counter, unplugged the hotplate, wiped down the white Formica top, and, without turning to Jessen, said, "Maybe that's worse, Charlie. Let's go to breakfast." He turned, smiling. "And talk about the Redskins."

Cosgrove left word with the lobby watchman that he and Mr. Charleston were going down Tunghwa Street to an all-night restaurant, An Lo Yuan. One of the specialities of the house was fried kale in oyster sauce. Cosgrove convinced the chef to add scrambled eggs to the dish. Cosgrove also managed to have the waiter find instant coffee.

They did talk about the Redskins, as genuine, statistics-laden fans. It was not so with some others in the agency. Just as many officers under Schlesinger had become birdwatchers, many officers under the new director had become Redskin fans. Some, according to the gossip in Langley, had even pressed analysts into service as football handicappers who provided knowledgeable chatter for Friday morning conferences with the director.

Jessen began to fidget over his second cup of coffee, and Cosgrove realized that the Redskins had ceased to be a useful distraction.

"I'd like to go back to the shop and flip through files," Jessen said abruptly.

"On Cheng? There's not much that's fresh."

"Just to pass the time, Ed."

"So you're going to wait till the ten o'clock flight?"

Jessen nodded.

"I repeat my recommendation," Cosgrove said, signaling for the check. "Let me go with you."

"I repeat my answer. No, thank you. I feel even more compelled to leave you here to deal with whatever is going on. If I need to know anything, you can reach me through Dysart. But I should be back here in two days—en route *home,* don't worry—and I'll have a chance to fill you in. Believe me, by that time I will know much more about Gunnison. And then I will officially fire him as a consultant. So don't worry about my judgment."

"Sorry about that, Charlie."

"No need to apologize, Ed. Now, as soon as I finish this breakfast of champions, let's head back to the shop. And later I would appreciate a lift to Shunghan airport."

There was a note in a President Hotel envelope, on President Hotel stationery, waiting for Mr. Charleston at the China Airlines check-in counter. The clerk who handed the note to Jessen told him that Mr. Walters had changed their reservations to the ten o-clock flight and had then canceled his own reservation. "Smoking or nonsmoking?" the clerk asked.

"Nonsmoking," Jessen said, though he knew most passengers would be smoking no matter where they sat.

Cosgrove had insisted on staying with Jessen in the passenger lounge, a room filled with people, baggage, noise, and the smoke from the tobacco and other burning substances of a dozen nations. Jessen would have preferred to have been left at the curb to walk around outside. But Cosgrove had waved off the car and escorted him into the terminal. Jessen would also have preferred not having Cosgrove there hovering over the note, which, like the "Mr. Charleston" on the envelope, was typed.

"Go on without me," the note said. "Tied up on family business. Will get to site by own arrangements. Estimate will arrive by 1600. Walters."

"Well, at least they got the name right this time," Cosgrove said.

"I like this one better, Ed," Jessen said, taking the note from Cosgrove and pocketing it. " 'Family business.' I told you that Gunnison was probably working on something for Chia Min's mother."

Cosgrove looked as if he were about to say something. He shook Jessen's hand and said, "Goodbye, Charlie, see you in a couple of days." He paused. "Give Gunnison my regards."

As Cosgrove plunged through the crowd, Jessen edged to the ticket counter and got his boarding pass for flight 105 to Kaohsiung. At least the numbers were readable. 1-0-5, he read. The rest meant nothing to him.

He found a vacant spot on the ledge of the terminal's curving windows that looked out on the runways. He had often wanted to learn Chinese . . . or Vietnamese . . . or Japanese . . . But always the press of service had eclipsed the few chances he had had for real language study. A word here and a phrase there. That was all he could muster. The rest of his energies had to go into the operation, the running of the locals he could never really understand. . . .

He thought he heard the word *Kaohsiung*, and he knew he heard the numbers 1-0-5. He pushed into a ragged line behind an elderly man and woman, followed by a younger man carrying what smelled like a sack of ginger. In the amplifying cylinder of the plane, the murmur of voices in the line became a deluge of sound. People scrambled for seats and, disregarding signs in two languages, began lighting up. The plane soon was as smoky as the lounge had been. Jessen's head was pounding, and the fried kale seemed to be reassembling itself in his stomach. He found a seat on the aisle, plugged his ears with the set of earphones he had been handed when he received his boarding pass, and turned down the volume so that he heard only the faintest hint of the strange clink and clatter of Chinese music. He tried to concentrate on nothing. Self-hypnosis can turn off the world, a therapist at a party had once told him. But she had never been on a China Airlines plane bouncing down a runway on a rainy morning, with her nostrils full of tobacco smoke and her stomach full of fried kale and eggs. He tried to concentrate on where he was going. He was more familiar with that kind of concentration.

The plane would fly the length of Taiwan in less than an hour and land him in Kaohsiung. He had been there only once, more than a decade before. Although it was an important international port and an industrial metropolis, Kaohsiung was usually of little interest to the agency. During the Vietnam War the agency had maintained a presence there, but, as interest and assets dwindled in Taiwan, the agency had concentrated its resources in Taipei. He was going, he realized, to a place where he would be entirely on his own.

As he thought of that place, an image in his mind took him back to an industrial tour conducted by an enthusiastic factory-owner who parted his hair in the middle and, as he sat behind his desk, actually hid his hands in the cuffs of his tunic, like a mandarin. The man, named Koo, had taken him to electronics factories, a concrete plant, and finally to a wig factory. And that was what he remembered now: a young, delicately beautiful Chinese woman, her black-haired head bent over the felt head of a mannequin bolted to the workbench. The young woman had a blue comb in her right hand, a blue brush in her left hand, and she was combing the long, blond hair pinned to the mannequin's head.

Jessen dozed off. He awoke, perhaps twenty minutes later, with a second memory blurred, part of a dream. He held for a moment an image of the harbor. Most of the ships were gray. But there were three white ships moored in a row, hull to hull. Lashed to their masts were wavering bamboo staffs on which fluttered banners of yellow and red and blue. The colors were so rare in that gray harbor that his memory had held them. He wondered if he would get a chance to see them today. He had asked his guide what they meant. "Good luck," the interpreter had said. "They are banners of good luck."

The plane set down roughly. As it taxied toward the humped silhouette of the terminal, Jessen leaned over his neighbors and looked out at the small airport. Still raining. Still gray.

He struggled into the sweater, trying, unsuccessfully, not to thump the passenger on his right. He mumbled an apology and got a smiling bow of the head in return. He looked down at the front of the sweater and frowned; the tea stains were still there. Joan would know how to get rid of them.

He squeezed himself into the aisle and shuffled forward, carrying his zippered shaving kit under his arm. He carried no luggage, mostly because he knew that a suitcase, no matter how small, was never worth its contents on a helicopter or for a single night on a ship.

In the Kaohsiung passenger lounge he spotted a man with a cardboard sign that said "China Sky Helicopter. Mr. Charleston." Jessen walked rapidly toward the man, waved his hand, and started to speak. The man, short and swarthy, shook his head, saying, "No English." He was a native Taiwanese, Jessen judged, a descendant of the aborigines who once ruled the island. Jessen followed the man through a side door to a red Datsun pickup truck.

Jessen had hardly slammed the passenger's door before the truck roared off. It skidded around the plane Jessen had just left, cut across one of the runways, and sped to the other side of the field. There, in a jumble of oil drums, piles of lumber, and the bent, rusting skeleton of a small aircraft's wing, was the Quonset hut that was the headquarters of China Sky Helicopter.

The hut was cluttered with wooden crates and aluminum containers. Jessen assumed that most of China Sky's business was freight, and he resigned himself to an unupholstered ride. He stepped around an oily tarpaulin that covered strange shapes stacked almost to the ceiling.

There were two men behind a chest-high counter. Their hair was crewcut, and each wore a crisply pressed khaki shirt and a white, ascot-knotted scarf around his neck. One of them said something to the driver, who went outside, returned with the cardboard sign, handed it to the man who had spoken to him, and went out again. Jessen heard the truck start up and roar away.

The man with the sign said something to the other man then disappeared through a metal door that led to what looked to Jessen like a storage room.

"He will be pilot," said the second man. Jessen had offered an American Express card, but the man said, "Prepaid. All prepaid." He pushed a ruled piece of looseleaf paper across the counter. Along the top of the paper were two lines of Chinese characters handwritten in red. About halfway down the page, hand-lettered with what looked like the same smeary ink from a cheap ballpoint pen, was Jessen's working name and the date. Using his own pen, Jessen signed below the name.

He passed the paper back to the man and pocketed the credit card and his pen. The man opened a thick looseleaf binder on a table behind the counter, clicked the rings open, inserted the paper, and clicked the rings shut. A performance, Jessen thought. He's going through the motions. That looseleaf is too accessible to be a real record of manifests. There must be another set of books. China Sky does more smuggling than legitimate chartering, I'll bet. Gunnison knows how to pick them.

"How's the weather out there today?" Jessen asked.

"You will go soon," the man replied.

"How do you find out about the weather?" Jessen asked."I don't see any radios or weather charts."

"No problem," the man said. He motioned Jessen through the metal door. They walked the length of the Quonset, past more wooden crates and more objects covered by tarpaulins. The man opened an outer door and pointed toward a Bell-13 helicopter about fifty feet from the hut. The rotor blades dropped like wilted petals. "Go," the man said. "You go."

Jessen heard the door slam behind him as he trotted toward the helicopter, head down through the light rain. The door on the passenger's side hung open. He put his left foot on the step just as the rotor blades began slowly turning.

"Good morning," he said to the pilot, who had put on a blue windbreaker and a black visored cap. The pilot shrugged.

"No English?" Jessen asked.

The pilot shrugged again. Jessen strapped himself into the seat and looked out the cockpit bubble to the gray beyond.

The helicopter shuddered, the engine's throbs fused into a loud and steady hum, and they were airborne, skimming over the brown fields that edged the airport, rising over the sprawl of roads radiating from the harbor. There was one touch of beauty below, and, seeing it, Jessen remembered that he had wanted to go there when he had been in Kaohsiung so long before.

Just for an instant he had seen it, the patch of blue that was the surface of Cheng Ching Lake. They had already gone too high for him to see the lake's zigzag bridge, which warded off the evil spirits who can travel only in straight lines.

Jessen had forgotten the name of the lake, but he had remembered the story. And as he remembered, he suddenly felt that something was wrong, dangerously wrong. The pilot had no chart. He had not used his radio.

Jessen touched the pilot on his right shoulder. "Back," Jessen said. "Back," pointing toward the receding land.

The pilot did not speak or turn his head.

Jessen grabbed the pilot's shoulders and shook him. His shoulder was surprisingly thin. Jessen dug his fingers into cloth, then into flesh. The helicopter trembled slightly as the pilot removed his right hand from the control stick.

He reached into the holster strapped under his seat and pulled out a 9-millimeter Makarov automatic. Jessen let go of the shoulder and lunged for the gun. The pilot wheeled the helicopter sharply to starboard. Jessen flung out both hands, one toward the gun, the other toward the control stick.

The pilot struck Jessen's left hand away and grabbed the stick. Jessen's right hand encircled the pilot's wrist. The pilot twisted the gun barrel toward Jessen's chest. Jessen slipped a finger behind the trigger. The pilot twisted the gun again, breaking Jessen's finger and burrowing the gun's muzzle into the thick white wool of Jessen's sweater.

He fired twice. Then, as Jessen fell back, the pilot aimed the gun and fired a third time, shooting Jessen in the forehead, over his left eye.

The pilot replaced the gun in its holster, looked at his watch, and headed due west for ten more minutes. Then he unbuckled

Jessen's seatbelt, opened the passenger door, and tilted the helicopter sharply to starboard. He shoved out Jessen's body, which fell through the gray sky to the dark sea five hundred feet below. He pawed through Jessen's shaving kit and threw all of the contents out of the cockpit. The new leather bag he stuffed under his own seat. He then turned the helicopter back toward Kaohsiung.

At about that same time, in the Quonset hut of China Sky Helicopters, the sheet of paper that Jessen had signed was removed from the notebook, crumpled, placed in a small heating stove and, with the Mr. Charleston sign, burned.

25

DYSART'S MESSAGE TO THE HEADQUARTERS of the Central Intelligence Agency in Langley, Virginia, expressed his concern on four matters: first, the failure of Charles Jessen to arrive aboard the *Glomar Explorer* as scheduled on the twenty-seventh; second, the precarious position of his ship, with the hulk of the *Osaka Maru* suspended some 400 feet below the *Glomar;* third, the continued proximity of Chinese and Japanese naval units as well as a Soviet intelligence-collection ship; and, fourth, the appearance of a submarine, tentatively identified as a Soviet nuclear submarine, less than twenty miles from the ship. He then requested confirmation that Jessen was still en route, his estimated time of arrival on the ship, and, if Jessen was to be further delayed, permission either to bring the *Osaka Maru* up to the *Glomar* and secure the hulk or to cut it loose.

After the message was encrypted, it was transmitted to the U.S. Naval Communications Station at San Miguel in the Philippines. Eighteen minutes later, the San Miguel facility had pulled from the ether the series of digits that represented the message, which was then automatically recorded on magnetic tape for retransmission. The message was put "on hold" for several minutes while the main transmitter was handling a lengthy message from the Commander U.S. Seventh Fleet to the Pacific Command headquarters at Pearl Harbor.

During the transmission of that message, atmospheric disturbances, caused by a solar flare on the sun, began reducing the quality of the message. The communications watch officer at San Miguel then directed that the *Glomar* message and several others awaiting onward routing be sent to the U.S. Naval Communications Station at Exmouth, near Northwest Cape, Australia, for retransmission to Langley. Dysart's message remained at San Miguel for almost an hour. It was then retransmitted to the Australian station; it arrived in the midst of a watch change. This caused more delays, as did waiting for a link to be established to Pearl Harbor, from where the message was retransmitted to Langley. After computer decoding, it was placed on the desk of the CIA watch officer a few minutes before five on the morning of Sunday, September 27.

About twenty minutes earlier, a related message had been received at the Navy Command Center, the nerve center of the U.S. Navy. Located on the fourth floor of the Pentagon, between the C and E corridors, just around the corner from the offices of the chief of naval operations and the secretary of the navy, the center—also called Flag Plot—was the place where "plots" were kept on the locations of all U.S. and significant foreign ships on the world's oceans.

To some extent, the Flag Plot is an anachronism, for the chief of naval operations, the senior admiral of the U.S. Navy, has no day-to-day operational control over naval forces. Rather, the Joint Chiefs of Staff, as a "corporate body," and the secretary of defense direct the nation's military operations through area commanders—generals or admirals who control all military forces in their areas. The chief of naval operations, or CNO in Navy jargon, is a member of the Joint Chiefs of Staff and at times is ordered by them or the secretary of defense to direct specific operations.

On Sunday, September 27, the CNO's responsibilities included the "Spearmint Protective Requirement." Since the ill-fated *Pueblo* affair, when the North Koreans captured a U.S. naval intelligence-collection ship some dozen miles off the Korean coast, whenever an intelligence operation was under way in a forward area a senior military commander was assigned responsibility for backup security for the operation. Although under charter, the *Glomar* was still considered a national asset and was therefore kept under security watch. Her backup security—with the responsibility for keeping track of foreign forces in the area and providing immediate protective measures—was the office of the chief of naval operations.

Within the Navy Command Center, the Navy captains who alternated as the watch officers were kept aware of the *Glomar*'s activity and the foreign ships and aircraft in her vicinity. There was no particular concern about the Chinese, Japanese, and Soviet surveillance of the operation. It was to be expected in the area. After all, a Soviet ship had periodically kept watch on the *Glomar* while she was secretly lifting the Soviet missile submarine.

The center also kept track of the U.S. military forces in the Far East that were available to go to the ship's rescue if she were in danger. In general, these were fighter aircraft on Okinawa or in the Philippines or aboard U.S. carriers in the region. The center had to know the immediate status of these aircraft, and if they were dispatched for other missions or were not available because of maintenance problems or other reasons, the center was responsible for designating other aircraft.

By early Sunday afternoon, there were plots being kept that indicated the relative position of the several Chinese, Japanese, and Soviet surface ships in the area of the *Glomar.* In addition, the twice-daily flights of Chinese reconnaissance aircraft were being plotted. The Naval Intelligence Center in Suitland, Maryland, was providing estimates of Soviet satellite passes over the ship, based on trajectories predicted by the North American Aerospace Defense Command, which keeps track of all objects in space.

Thus, the potential threats to the *Glomar* operation were being tracked on a real-time basis. At 4:00 P.M. in Washington a message arrived at Flag Plot by teleprinter from the Naval Ocean Surveillance Center at Pearl Harbor. The center was the central monitoring point for the Caesar/SOSUS "web," the seafloor acoustic system in the Pacific. The SOSUS (*So*und *Su*rveillance *S*ystem) listening devices were anchored in lines that acted as invisible barriers in the Atlantic and Pacific oceans, as well as in some smaller seas. Submarines passing through these barriers were detected and their movements recorded. The acoustic data received from the SOSUS arrays was partially processed at several overseas locations and then transmitted to fleet intelligence centers, with the one near Pearl Harbor coordinating efforts in the Pacific.

The message arriving at Flag Plot was based on sounds picked up minutes before by the monitoring station in Japan. It had alerted two other Pacific stations. The sounds were triangulated and flashed to Pearl Harbor, where they were correlated with the data bank of taped submarine noises.

A nuclear submarine produces noise during its movement through the water; distinctive sounds of fluids circulating in the reactor plant, auxiliary machinery, and the gears that reduce the steam turbine output to the propeller shaft. Because different types of submarines have different noise "signatures," some individual submarines are identifiable.

The Naval Ocean Surveillance Center at Pearl Harbor received the sounds picked up by the three SOSUS stations, relayed by communication satellites, on Sunday morning Washington time. It took four minutes for the computer bank at Pearl Harbor to correlate the sounds against the tape files of acoustic signatures of foreign submarines known to be in the Pacific Ocean.

Two minutes later, the duty officer at the center was advised that a modified Soviet *Victor*-class submarine was within 100 miles of the *Glomar*. At his direction, another computer check was run to determine whether the designated submarine was one of the two Soviet submarines of that type in the Pacific known to have nuclear weapons on board, either antisubmarine homing torpedoes or the SS-N-15 rocket weapon.

Five minutes later, the Pearl Harbor computer indicated that the submarine was the *Petroverdets,* currently based at Vladivostok following an overhaul and modernization at the Komsomolsk shipyard on the Amur River. The submarine, under Captain First Rank Georgi Ivanovich Svjatov, had been on a limited exercise, simulating an attack on a mock Japanese convoy, when it broke away from the exercise and steamed south toward the southern entrance to the Formosa Strait. The SOSUS network determined that the Soviet submarine was about twenty miles from the *Glomar Explorer.*

The Pearl Harbor watch officer activated a preselected code message that was flashed, via satellite, to Flag Plot. In a matter of seconds, the Naval Communications Station at Annapolis, Maryland, pulled in the message and—because of its priority—automatically retransmitted the message via both radio and land lines to Flag Plot.

Thus, at 4:18 on the afternoon of Sunday, September 27, an urgent message began arriving in Flag Plot. The message was prefixed with the words PINETREE, PINETREE, PINETREE. The code word PINETREE was the alert that a foreign "platform" carrying nuclear weapons was closing on a major U.S. warship or sensitive project, in this case the *Glomar Explorer.*

As often happens in bureaucratic jargon, the origins of a term are forgotten, and no one in the center that morning knew that PINE had originated from the term *P*ositive *I*ntelligence of *N*uclear *E*xchange, with *tree* being added in a long-discarded scheme of padding highly secret intelligence terms with a second word.

The Flag Plot's senior watch officer immediately called the chief of naval operations at his quarters in old Tingey House, adjacent to the Eighth Street entrance of the Washington Navy Yard. Simultaneously, the watch officer's assistant, a commander, alerted the National Military Command Center at the Pentagon. He then called the Pentagon's underground garage. There, the Navy's duty driver, a Marine lance corporal, put down his *Navy Times,* stubbed out his cigarette, looked briefly in a mirror as he adjusted his tie and the collar of his khaki shirt, and headed toward the duty car.

Moments later he was speeding across the Fourteenth Street Bridge, toward the Southwest Freeway and the CNO's home. The watch officer then called the watch officer at the Central Intelligence Agency.

John Peck, the CIA watch officer that Sunday afternoon, was tired and frustrated. As a ritual in the ordeal of a separation from his wife, he had spent the night—and the first few hours of the morning—drinking. Earlier they had talked for several hours at the apartment of the friend she was staying with. He had got about three hours of sleep before taking the watch.

Dysart's message from the *Glomar Explorer* and the call on the secure telephone from the Navy Flag Plot arrived within five minutes of each other. Peck immediately realized the significance of their timing and began to track down Jessen, via Cosgrove on Taiwan, and Larry Perkins, Jessen's deputy, the backup CIA program manager for Operation Spearmint.

Peck reached Perkins at home and spoke in cautious doubletalk. Then came the answering message from Cosgrove: "Can trace him as far as Kaohsiung. Effecting further trace." Peck quickly made a decision to buck this one higher. But the deputy director of central intelligence and the deputy director for operations were not in the Washington area. Reluctantly, Peck called the director's limousine, which was parked outside the Robert F. Kennedy Stadium.

In a minute, the chauffeur was out of the car and heading for the VIP boxes on the north side of the stadium. As he trotted down the aisle toward the boxes, the crowd roared. The Redskins had just made an interception against the Dallas Cowboys.

"Go, go, go," screamed twelve-year-old Mike Levine from the press box of the stadium. "Dad, Dad, we're gonna win!"

Mike's father, Nate Levine, an assistant national editor of *The Washington Post*, had got the press-box seats from a friend in the sports department as a present for his son. Levine himself could not have been less interested in the Redskins. Rather, he had amused himself by watching the spectators across the field with his binoculars. In one of the VIP boxes he had spotted the director of central intelligence, his wife, and several friends, among them the brilliant and very young man who everyone knew would be the next secretary of the navy, and his attractive young wife.

As Levine watched, someone in a black coat and cap—probably a chauffeur—approached a man in a dark suit standing near the box, his back to the VIPs. A moment later the man moved the few yards to where the director was seated, leaned across a couple of people, and motioned to the director. Levine, watching the pantomime conversation, decided by the director's expression that he was probably making apologies to his wife and friends. He departed in a brisk walk, escorted by the two men.

A few moments later, another spectator in the box turned and whispered something to a man who then departed at a trot. Quietly, while Mike's attention was glued to the action on the field, Levine withdrew to a desk in the outer area of the press box and picked up a telephone.

"National desk," Levine said to the operator at the *Post*. "Bob? Nate Levine here. Look, is there anything on the wire or on the desk on some national or international crisis?"

"No, Nate, the desk is clean. Nothing exciting happening here except the game."

"Bob, something *is* happening. I can feel it. The head of CIA just left the game, and you know what a fan he is. How about having somebody call around? Have the city desk check if it was something personal. Where are his kids? And I want you to run a couple of checks—State and Defense—to see if anything is happening."

"Come on, Nate. So he had to take a piss and leave the game for a couple of minutes. I bet he's back in his seat when you turn around."

"Bob, do what I ask. Okay?"

Levine just barely heard the "*Shit!*" before the phone clicked off. Walking back to the press-box window, he realized how foolish he would feel if indeed the director was back in his seat. But when he again pointed his binoculars at the VIP box, two other seats were empty—as was the seat of the director of central intelligence.

Damn, Levine thought to himself, the national desk had good people. Why was Bob Stets on the desk that day? Probably Bob was simply overtaken with Sunday, Redskin Sunday, lethargy.

He tried to think of someone the national desk would not think to call. Two names came to mind: John Peck, an extremely capable young CIA officer, and Bob Martin at the White House. Peck recently had been separated or divorced; Levine tried to remember who had kept the townhouse in the breakup. The northern Virginia telephone directory revealed Peck's number, but a call brought no answer. A call to his own home—with assurances to his wife that Mike was not stuffing himself with hot dogs and peanuts—brought Bob Martin's unlisted Virginia telephone number. Martin was at home; no, he didn't mind being called on Sunday. He was simply wading through the Sunday *Post, New York Times,* and *Los Angeles Times.*

Levine told what he had seen and asked what was happening.

"Nate, let me check around on this. I don't know of anything. Let me make a couple of calls and I'll ring you back at the stadium," Martin said. Levine knew Martin would play it straight—probably straighter than he himself would if the circumstances were reversed.

Martin now joined the several other people in Washington and northern Virginia, most of them unknown to one another, making calls about the *Glomar Explorer.* A call to the White House and then to national security adviser Keith Saunders brought Martin no information. Martin's relationship with the CIA was not good, but as a retired rear admiral, he still had several Navy contacts. And most world crises affected the Navy. He began calling Navy offices where he knew people. The fifth call hit the jackpot.

"We're just getting the information now," said the voice of a onetime shipmate who had been called into his Pentagon office on another problem. "Flag Plot had an alert a short time ago about a Soviet sub near the *Glomar Explorer.* I really don't want to say more over this open line. And there's a CIA guy missing or in trouble. Why don't you call Flag Plot? But *don't* call me for details on this one."

Less than two minutes later, Martin was speaking to the duty captain in Flag Plot, telling him that he wanted a briefing officer at the White House in thirty minutes. Next he called back Saunders. In cryptic terms, Martin explained that there was a "situation" and that perhaps Saunders should ring the agency for information.

Forty minutes later, Saunders joined Martin in Martin's third-floor White House office. With them were representatives from the Navy and the CIA. Their information on the subject, or, more accurately, lack of information, coupled with the PINETREE alert and Dysart's message, led Saunders to call the vice president and recommend that the White House crisis committee stand by.

With the excuse that he would try to round up a couple of stenographers and a mess steward—"I think we'll be here a while"—Martin went into an empty office and called Levine at the stadium press box. Martin wanted some of the director's problems to get into print.

"There *is* something going on, Nate," he said. "So I'm doing what I said I would do. I'm calling you."

"Well, what the hell is going on?" Levine asked, keeping his voice down.

"Let me give you a suggestion," Martin answered, lowering his voice. "Get your expert on gold to tell you what the impact of over a billion dollars in gold would have on the gold market."

"Jesus! Can't you tell me more?"

"Not now. Just check on the gold market. That's all."

The Redskins had lost, 24 to 12, and Kennedy Stadium had long since been emptied when the men began entering the room that President John F. Kennedy had labeled the Situation Room. The room, in the basement of the West Wing of the White House, had a low ceiling and dark walls. As the meeting began, the dim light suddenly brightened. The players, speaking in muffled tones, assembled quietly: Keith Saunders, the secretary of state, the under secretary of defense for policy, the chief of naval operations, the chairman of the Joint Chiefs of Staff, and, sitting away from the conference table, Bob Martin. A few minutes after all had been seated, the vice president and the director of central intelligence walked in. Except for Martin, no aides were present.

At each place around the massive table was a folder containing essentially all of the known information of the day's events in the South China Seas. It was a thin folder.

After giving each attendee a brief opportunity to thumb through the folder, the vice president turned to Admiral John Watson, the chief of naval operations, sitting to his left. The CNO was wearing slacks and a sport jacket, the typical dress of the men around the table.

"All right, Admiral," the vice president began, "let's take it from the top. My understanding from Keith is that the president personally directed that this operation be stopped." Halfway through the statement, Watson realized the significance of the vice president's entrance with the director of central intelligence. It was a distraction play.

"The president actually used the word *kaput*, I am told," the vice president continued. "Now there seems to have been some communication delays or snafus, both in getting the word to the *Glomar Explorer* and in our learning of her current situation . . ."

The admiral was sucking air, trying to keep control of himself and not interrupt. From the corner of his eye he saw Saunders motioning him to just let it pass.

"Uh, Mr. Vice President." Saunders interrupted. "Let me make it clear that this is—or was—a CIA operation, with the Navy only providing support. If I may, I believe the two critical issues appear to be what happened to Mr. Jessen, the CIA officer sent out to stop the operation, and the current status of the operation." Then, seemingly to take control of the session, Saunders turned to the director and said, "Can we throw some light on these questions?"

"As I said walking down here, Mr. Vice President," the director of central intelligence said, "The communications snafus—or slowdowns might be a better term—were within the Navy system."

"But that's not the point," the vice president responded. He had picked up the cue from Saunders. "The questions are why is this CIA operation not shut down and, now, what's happened to your man—this Jessen?"

Every eye in the room was on the director. He glanced down at the looseleaf notebook he had carried into the Situation Room. He started to open it but instead simply picked it up and turned it face down on the table.

"All right, Mr. Vice President. The frank and honest truth is that we just don't know a goddamn thing about what's happening right now. All we definitely know is that Jessen got as far as Taipei, checked into his hotel, made arrangements through our station there to go out to the *Glomar*, left Taipei at least, apparently got into a helicopter, and then disappeared."

"Apparently?"

"Yes, Mr. Vice President. It was a small firm that we've used in the past that flies the helicopters. But they're claiming Jessen never arrived at their office, although we know he reached Kaohsiung. That is a port in southern Taiwan."

"Thank you for the geography lesson. But let's get to the issue. You mean to tell me—to tell us—that we don't know the whereabouts of a senior officer of the government on a mission directly for the president?"

"We are, sir, looking into this matter. Our man in Taipei—"

"Of course you're looking into it. Fine. What resources do you have on Taiwan that can be used to carry out the president's order?

Let's get this straight once and for all. The reason that man, Jessen, was on Taiwan was to carry out the president's order. Now what I want to know is what are *you* and *your* agency doing to carry out what the president told you to do? Told you *in person,*" the vice president quickly added. He hesitated as he thumbed through some notes. "Oh, yes, this Gunnison. Is it true that we now have associated him with the murder of one of our own people in Taiwan?"

The director's look of resignation turned to shock and then surprise. He wondered how the White House already knew about the dead driver. Obviously, he thought, another agency leak. *Someone else out to get me.*

"Mr. Vice President," he said after his own moment of hesitation, "I can assure you we will use all available facilities to ensure that the president's orders are carried out immediately and that the operation is halted. I assure you that we will have a complete report as soon as possible."

Sitting quietly behind Saunders, about six feet from the director, Bob Martin made another check on the pad he held in his hand. He enjoyed keeping track of the number of times the director used the term "I assure you" or some variation.

"I am getting concerned, gentlemen, about the concentration of foreign military forces in the area." The new voice being heard was that of the under secretary of defense. "Admiral, are you satisfied with the security provisions we have for the *Glomar?*"

"Yes, sir," the chief of naval operations spoke out. "I have been in contact this morning with the commander-in-chief of the Pacific Command, and we have sufficient standby tactical aircraft in the region to provide air cover to the ship within a very few minutes. And I have ordered one of our nuclear attack submarines in the region, the *Queenfish,* to shift her patrol area so that she could rapidly be on the scene if required."

There was a slight interruption as a secretary entered the room and handed the vice president a note. "It's nothing, gentlemen," he said. He whispered a few words to the secretary; the audible words, "pick up" and "wife," reassured the others in the room that it was a domestic issue. Bob Martin took advantage of the few seconds to scribble a note to Saunders and lean over to hand it to him.

As soon as the vice president's attention was returned to the table, Saunders asked, "Mr. Vice President, may I raise a couple of questions?"

The vice president nodded, and Saunders turned to the CNO. "Admiral, can your nuclear submarine provide us with a real-time, reliable communications link to the *Glomar?*"

"Yes, that is if she's allowed to remain near the surface to use a whip or trailing-buoy antenna."

"Fine. Let me suggest, then, that the White House simply take direct control of this operation."

"If we're using a nuclear submarine to exercise that control, then I suggest it be a White House–Defense operation," said the chairman of the Joint Chiefs, a three-star general and the junior man in the room. He suddenly found an opportunity to get into the conversation, which his aides had urgently suggested he stay out of. "The Defense Department can provide reliable and real-time communications."

"We *have* been using Defense communications—and that's been part of the problem," the director of central intelligence interjected.

The vice president, obviously tightening up, regained control of the meeting. "Okay. I have the picture. Admiral, you will get into immediate contact with the *Glomar*. You will have the submarine tell the *Glomar—in the name of the president*—that the project is ended. The Japanese ship is to be cut loose, or disengaged, or whatever, and allowed to fall down to the bottom of the sea. The *Glomar* will then hoist anchor and sail for Hawaii. Are there any questions?"

"Yes, sir. We can certainly carry out your orders. Except," the admiral said, nodding toward the director, "the agency presently has operational control of the ship. They may have to advise her that we are taking over OPCON."

"I don't know what the hell an OPCON is, Admiral, but I assume that the Navy realizes that the president is the commander-in-chief of the agency as well as the Navy. Any problems with that?" This last comment was addressed to the under secretary of defense.

"No, Mr. Vice President."

"This all sounds fine, but there's one hitch." The director had a semblance of confidence in his voice for the first time. "There's a Soviet nuclear submarine in the area. Has anybody given thought to the implications of our sending a nuclear ship into the same area as the Soviet sub?"

"I see no problems with that," Admiral Watson responded immediately. "We and they have full right of innocent passage in that area. We will certainly not take any actions that look aggressive to them."

"I hope that one submarine can tell when another one is being aggressive or innocent," the director said, almost to himself.

"Bob." It was the first acknowledgment by the vice president or anyone else in the room that one aide, Bob Martin, had been sitting along the wall with the two White House secretaries. All other aides to those around the table were in an anteroom. "I want you to prepare a private statement, with State, that the president can send to each of the involved countries advising them that the operation is halted."

The vice president looked around the table, picked up his folder, and stood up. "Enough, gentlemen. Now I have to explain to my wife why I forgot to have her and her mother picked up at National Airport this evening. Any questions? You will be notified of our next meeting, *if* one is necessary."

As the men left the room, the under secretary of defense found himself paired briefly with Keith Saunders. "He was quite impressive, wasn't he?" the under secretary commented.

"Yes. He really was. A damn good man," responded Saunders. "You're new to the administration. He's really good—except when there's blood to let. I remember my battalion CO when I was in the fifth Marines. 'You can't manage troops up a hill,' he said. 'You have to lead them.' I fear the vice president is an outstanding manager. But I hope he won't have to lead us up any hills."

26

THE RUSSIAN-DESIGNED, CHINESE-BUILT Il-28 bomber screamed skyward from the naval side of the airfield at Chaoyang and banked sharply out to sea. Inside the Il-28's cockpit, in the lefthand seat, Squadron Commander Yong Zongren looked straight ahead as he pulled back tightly on the aircraft's control yoke, oblivious to the clocklike instruments that indicated the plane was being pushed to its maximum tolerance.

His latest outburst of frustration had begun when, at Chaoyang, he had encountered some former squadron mates of the Eastern Fleet. That natural ribbing of their comrade who had recently been transferred to the South Sea Fleet's naval air arm had triggered Yong's temper. The flash point came when one of the other fliers had pointed out that he was now flying one of the twice-daily "soft runs" to take a look at the "offshore drilling ship." Few rank-and-file Chinese officers knew or cared that the *Glomar* had a reputation that was far different from that of an innocent resource-exploitation ship.

As the Il-28 passed through its assigned cruising altitude of 5,000 feet, the copilot leaned over toward Yong, exaggerated a polite tap on the shoulder, and said, "My floor. Let me off here, please."

"Fuck you. Take a parachute and get off," Yong snapped. But he had noticeably relaxed. He slightly adjusted the plane's trim tabs and made a momentary inclination of the control yoke, bringing the plane to its assigned course and altitude.

Once the plane had leveled off, heading almost due east, the flight engineer–photographer came forward into the main cockpit. In his arms were two steel food containers and three plastic bowls and three clay cups. The lunch—steamed rice with shreds of fish, and tea—was intended to be eaten halfway through the four- or five-hour flight. But all three crewmen of the Il-28 had agreed always to eat as soon as the plane reached cruising altitude. The steel container did not keep the rice and fish hot, and every moment in the container seemed to give the food more of a metallic taste.

The 150-odd sea miles from Chaoyang to the position of the *Glomar Explorer* could be covered in a half hour at the Il-28's cruise speed. Squadron Commander Yong's patrol route, however, would first take the twin-jet aircraft north, up the Formosa Strait, to look over and photograph any ships of interest or with unusual characteristics. The patrol route was the price extracted by the Eastern Fleet commander for the use of his fuel stocks at Chaoyang—"a friendly exchange," he had called it in his discussions with the commander of the hard-pressed South Sea Fleet.

The flight, straight up the center of the Strait, about fifty miles from the mainland and fifty miles from Taiwan at the narrowest point, was uneventful. Two MiG fighters flew distant escort.

Then, as the Il-28 flew southward, in the direction of the *Glomar Explorer,* Yong periodically changed course and altitude to overfly an odd ship or group of fishing craft. So far none of the ships had been of sufficient interest to awaken the dozing flight engineer–photographer.

"There's a rather large group heading south," the copilot said, pointing off to port. Some five thousand feet below were perhaps a dozen small fishing craft.

"Nothing there," responded Yong as he dipped his right wing to give himself a clear look at the junks. But out of the corner of the Plexiglas canopy, on the horizon, he caught sight of another sailing junk, three-masted and significantly larger. "Tell our friends," Yong ordered, with his thumb indicating the now unseen MiG escorts, "that we are going back to take a look at another ship."

Throttling back, Yong brought the plane lower. "Wake up our young photographer. There's something strange about that ship—no, something familiar." The copilot woke up the flight engineer–photographer, who climbed forward into the plane's glazed nose and lifted and cocked the commercial Kodak double-reflex camera.

Now down to only 200 feet, and seeming to skim the wavetops, the Il-28 made a slow, wide approach around the three-masted junk, then made a flat turn to the right to come in astern of the junk.

The copilot, on the side near the junk, raised his binoculars to read the tarnished bronze letters on the junk's stern counter. " *'Good Wind—Hong Kong.'* No flag visible. Several men and, I think, a woman—no, two—on deck, waving. The women have Western dress. . . ."

And then the II-28 was beyond the junk.

"I know that ship from somewhere," Yong declared. "I've seen her, or an almost identical ship, somewhere." He thought for a moment.

"The superstructure was different, but that stern and straight stem are unmistakable. I want to see the photographs as soon as they're developed, and I want you, Han, to look up the name as soon as we touch down. But don't say anything to anyone. I'll show those slobs from my old squadron who is making the 'soft runs.' "

"What do you think the junk is? Should we go back for another look?"

"No, Han. I don't wish to arouse suspicions more than we already have."

At that moment Yong Zongren banked the II-28 to take a closer look at the dozen fishing junks seen earlier. He hoped that the suspicious junk would see his actions and believe that it was a new pilot on the patrol run, taking the trouble for a close look at every ship or group sighted.

Two hours and fifteen minutes later, the II-28 touched down at its home base. Fifty-two minutes after that, Pilot First Class Yong stood in the red-lighted darkroom of the base's photographic laboratory, much to the annoyance of the petty officer in charge. Yong carefully examined the still-wet negatives as they hung for drying.

"Ah, this one, Han. Look, see the television antenna?"

"But just like those of any other Western-based junk," his copilot said.

"Yes, but the bend of the antenna. As if it had been moved from one deckhouse to another, larger, one and then bolted on."

"So, they moved it or transferred it from another boat. You think you have seen a suspicious junk, and now you must justify what you think you have seen."

"No. I *have* seen it. Has that clerk from headquarters called about the name?" Yong inquired of the petty officer in charge of the lab.

"No."

Yong grabbed several of the negatives and handed them to his engineer–photographer. "Prints, of these, and quickly. Especially of the deckhouse. Look at these lines," he continued to no one in particular. "There has been some change in the superstructure of the ship recently."

Just then the door to the darkroom burst open. The squadron

clerk, oblivious to the KNOCK AND WAIT TO ENTER sign on the door, entered calling, "Yong, Yong, you *have* found something!"

Yong grabbed the sheets of notes from the sailor's hands. "Here," the clerk pointed to the second sheet of notes, almost grabbing it back from Yong. "There is a *Good Wind* registered in Hong Kong, a yacht owned by a land property company. But there is a notation in our files that she was at Macao last month for major yard work. I have taken the liberty of calling a friendly source there. *Good Wind* is still in the yard!"

As soon as the five photographs of the ship identified as the *Good Wind* were printed and dried, Yong was in a Navy car driving at breakneck speed to Canton to keep his meeting, set up by telephone, with the commander of the South Sea Fleet. He wondered if the fleet commander would have the guts to let him lead an air attack against the junk.

Captain First/Rank Georgi Ivanovich Svjatov, commanding officer of the nuclear-propelled attack submarine *Petroverdets*, sat back comfortably in the cubicle that served him as both office and cabin. The coffee cup carefully placed on his folding desktop had the insignia of the Soviet submarine force—a crest showing a dolphin supporting the world on its back, with the Soviet naval ensign above the world. His submarine's name was below the crest. On the other side of the cup was inscribed: "With Admiration, Affection, and Appreciation—Your Crew."

Some things in life, he thought, like this coffee cup, were so neat and clear. It gave a reflection of himself and his relationship to his crew.

But the message that had directed him to break off exercises and to clandestinely close on the *Glomar Explorer* was obscure and confusing. In the twenty hours since the message had been received, he had seldom left the control room of his submarine. Twice he had discussed the message with his executive officer, and he had solicited views from his other officers. Always, however, he had realized fully and absolutely that once a decision had to be made it would be his and his alone. The responsibility bothered him somewhat. That, he felt, was natural. What gnawed at him much more was the vagueness of the orders from the fleet commander.

The *Petroverdets* was to carry out "close-up surveillance of the *Glomar Explorer*." Did that mean he could use his periscopes, radar, and active sonar? Or should he attempt to remain "passive"? In that state he would use his listening hydrophones and possibly the highly secretive submarine "trailing" device.

He had also been ordered to "inhibit any action by the People's Republic of China to gain possession of the American ship or impede its activities." He had been further advised that there was a Chinese destroyer in the area. Putting the destroyer out of commission could be a simple assignment—if his authority to use his weapons had been made clear. But that key indicator of authority was missing from the message. And what were the "activities" of the American ship?

Finally, he was to "avoid contact with all U.S. warships in the area" but to "take all necessary actions to assure self-protection." Still, even without a weapons-use indicator in the message, "all necessary actions" seemed to give him authority to use his weapons.

Svjatov had made an active and passive sonar search of the area around the *Glomar Explorer.* He was able to identify several ships, including the Soviet surface surveillance ship. But after detecting one particular "target," Svjatov had suddenly ceased the sonar search, gone deep, and quietly exited the area. Just over an hour later, when his submarine was twenty miles from the *Glomar,* he had come up to a shallow depth and transmitted a lengthy message to Vladivostok about the object—probably a ship or very large submarine—suspended some 400 feet beneath the *Glomar Explorer.*

Now, in the cabin of the *Petroverdets,* he waited for word from Vladivostok that would give him clear orders for future action. He had said in his message that the "target" under the *Glomar Explorer* appeared to be a surface ship. However, there was some possibility that it might be a large submarine—perhaps a stricken American Polaris missile submarine.

Svjatov drank the last of the coffee lightly laced with brandy, swung around in his chair, put his feet atop the small sink that was folded into the bulkhead of his cabin, and leaned back, hoping to catnap for a few minutes. His eyes never closed. As soon as he turned his back to the curtained doorway, there was a gentle knock.

"Come."

"I beg your pardon, sir." The assistant communications officer stood awkwardly in the doorway. He knew that his captain had entered his cabin only a few moments earlier. "A priority message from fleet headquarters."

"Decoded?"

"Yes, sir. It was in an operational, not an executive, code."

"Thank you," replied Svjatov, taking the cardboard folder from the young officer. After skimming the message, Svjatov sat up. "Get the executive officer here immediately." And then, under his breath, "We may yet see some action this day."

Despite twice having had to slow to a crawl for road construction, Pilot First Class Yong arrived at the headquarters of the South Sea Fleet in Canton a few minutes before his appointment with the fleet commander. His driving, like his flying, was considered reckless by many who knew him. But men who were themselves good drivers—or fliers—knew that Yong Zongren's skills more than compensated for his recklessness.

Fleet Commander Tan Chih-keng had looked into why the Eastern Fleet had allowed such a skilled pilot to be transferred to him. Yong had been given bad grades by the Eastern Fleet commander, but it was obvious to anyone who took the trouble to look at his records that the grades could not have been based on his professional performance. Politically, Yong was safe—an active member of the Party. But he preferred to work with the youth, to exhort the young officers, sailors, and airmen to work harder, to learn more, to improve their skills. And that came to be his downfall with the Eastern Fleet commander. For Yong's pride in the future of China led to his constant ridicule of those commanders who cherished the status quo, who resisted change, who preferred to promote and reward older men—especially long-serving colleagues—rather than the young men and women who worked harder and produced more results.

Tan, who had never met Yong, knew much about him. Yong's telephone call had been made without the approval of the fleet air commander, who had told his superior that he had attempted to dissuade Yong from bothering the admiral.

When Yong was finally admitted, he went directly to Tan's desk without any salutation. He spread out the five photographs that he had carried in his hands. "Here, Commander Tan. Look at these." Even before Tan could reach for his glasses, Yong continued, "Note these marks on the deck. The bridge structure is different than it was before. Larger, I think, but the side here has been moved inboard, I think to give more access to this hatch."

Tan did not reply but proceeded to examine the photographs.

"While looking at the deck structure, please notice the manner in which the television antenna is bent. I believe it was on a smaller structure and now put on this one. And the hatch combings. I can understand two aft. But why two forward—where the ship's sheer would not allow the ladders to go down more than one level? That would be acceptable in a ship with a large central cargo hatch forward. But there is no such hatch and, again, the sheer is too great."

Tan put the photos down and looked at the young pilot, who stood easily in the presence of a fleet commander. "I would like to ask you two questions, young man, if you will allow me to interrupt you. How do you know so much about ships? And why do you bring these photographs to my personal attention?"

"My father was a crafter of junks. He was a master builder, as was his revered father before him. I *know* what a junk should look like."

"And my other question, young man?"

"I wish to lead an air strike against this junk. It is a pirate vessel."

"And how do you know that?"

"My father told me how pirate junks change their lines and disguise themselves. He told me their tricks. This is a pirate ship, and it is on a course for the American spy ship."

"I know of one 'spy ship' in the area," Tan said, surprised that knowledge of the *Glomar* had reached the junior ranks. "Where exactly did you take these photographs?"

Yong walked behind the fleet commander's desk and picked up a chart from another table; he spread the chart over the desk, heedless of papers, pens, and inkwells. Yong leaned forward and pointed to the approximate locations of the *Glomar* and the junk.

"Please, Comrade. Let me lead an air strike against the junk. I can stop it dead in the water. The surface navy can board her."

"No, my young comrade. There will be no shooting of your weapons, much as your fingers may itch. Your camera perhaps performed an important mission. For now, that is enough. I thank you for the photographs. Sometimes it is good to run up the ladder without touching all the rungs." Tan affectionately put his right arm about Yong's shoulders. "Sometimes. Not always."

Tan dismissed Yong with kind words and then dictated a lengthy message to the Chinese destroyer that was patroling some thirty miles from the *Glomar*'s location. Immediately upon receipt of the message, the destroyer speeded up and headed northward, toward an estimated intercept position with the *Golden Moon*.

*

The Chinese destroyer *Anshan*, which had for days steamed in lazy circles around the *Glomar Explorer*, generally just over the horizon and out of sight of the American ship, usually increased distance from the *Glomar* at night. The nocturnal maneuver enabled the thirty troops crowded below to exercise and relax on deck.

So the crew and troops were surprised when in broad daylight the destroyer began to accelerate and turn north, away from the *Glomar Explorer*. There was similar surprise aboard the Soviet intelligence ship *Primorye*, which at that moment, steaming in her own lazy circles through the area, was in sight of the destroyer *Anshan*. The captain of the *Primorye*, alerted to the destroyer's sudden movement northward, immediately sent off a message to fleet headquarters at Vladivostok.

One other ship in the general area took special notice of the *Anshan*'s movement, the U.S.S. *Queenfish*. The nuclear submarine was almost fifty miles south of the *Glomar* and slightly less than that from the *Anshan*. The *Queenfish*'s passive sonar instantly detected the sudden spurt of power from the destroyer's twin steam turbines, which were soon producing their maximum 48,000 horsepower to drive the ship northward at a fraction over thirty knots.

At that moment, the *Queenfish* was beginning to copy a lengthy message that had originated in the Pentagon. The priority of that message led the commanding officer of the *Queenfish* to delay sending out a message about the sudden movement of the Chinese destroyer.

Some seventy miles north of the *Queenfish*, the Soviet submarine *Petroverdets* also detected the Chinese destroyer's engines. A short time before, the Soviet submarine had intercepted the message sent by the intelligence ship to Vladivostok announcing the sudden movement of the Chinese destroyer. That message had been purposely broadcast on a frequency and in a code that the submarine would normally monitor if she were near the surface.

Quietly, the *Petroverdets* turned northward in unseen company with the Chinese destroyer. Although the submarine could outrun the *Anshan*, the *Petroverdets* proceeded slowly, letting the destroyer pull ahead. The submarine easily followed the noise produced by the destroyer's machinery and movement through the water.

The captain of the *Petroverdets* had taken the conn. He was beginning to feel the excitement of the chase when the mate of the watch relayed a report from the sonar operator. "Captain," the officer said, "I have another ship on sonar. Probably twenty miles ahead and to the west of the Chinese destroyer. It is a slow-speed ship with diesels—moving slowly, only a few knots." The *Petroverdets* had detected the *Golden Moon* moments after the junk had been sighted by the *Anshan*'s own search radar.

A brief periscope sweep detected the *Anshan* several miles away, a heavy wake churning astern of her. Svjatov lowered the periscope and ordered his submarine ahead at high speed to close with the two ships.

27

The radar array atop the *Golden Moon*'s mainmast looked identical to that of commercial radar equipment carried by many large fishing and pleasure craft. But inside the *Golden Moon*'s visible "radar can" was a long-range, high-resolution radar that permitted Cheng to detect *Anshan* almost the moment that the destroyer had located his ship. The *Anshan* had been guided to the *Golden Moon* by the afternoon Chinese naval search aircraft, which had sighted the ship. Unlike Yong on the previous day, this pilot had not taken a close look at the ship.

Cheng had known that the close look taken the day before might have accurately identified his ship. He minutely inspected his ship during the night, and he knew there were no further preparations to be made. His crew, their weapons, and the *Golden Moon* herself were at maximum readiness. Of his forty men, half were former Marines trained both in close-in and ground combat. The other twenty-odd men were seamen who could fight and sail the ship with her twin turbo-charged diesels, which could provide a maximum speed of about fifteen knots.

"I had not expected to place you in danger, my niece," Cheng said in Chinese.

"I understand, Uncle," Chia Min said. She stood next to him on the deck, near the mainmast. She wore a wide-brimmed white straw hat, a white blouse, and skintight jeans. She was barefoot.

"A masquerade," she said in English, then repeated a word with a similar meaning in Chinese. Cheng nodded. His eyes were on the horizon. The *Anshan* was now in sight.

"You will stay here—in your costume—for a few minutes. So their sailors can see you—and be pleased by your appearance. Then, if I tell you, you must go below. You must do what I say. That is agreed?"

"I understand, Uncle," she said in Chinese.

As the *Anshan* approached the *Golden Moon*, a signal lamp on the destroyer's bridge flashed out a Morse code message: STOP AND BE SEARCHED. After a few moments, Cheng had a seaman use a flashlight to return a signal, which he made twice, with intentional errors both times: INTERNATIONAL WATERS.

Cheng surveyed his adversary. Forward and aft, the destroyer had a total of four 130-millimeter guns. There were also several lighter 20- and 37-millimeter guns. They were his major concern. The ship's four launchers for Styx missiles would be useless in a close encounter. The *Golden Moon* was outgunned by a larger, faster warship. But Cheng had a plan. And he had the luck that had been with his uncle on the deck of this junk, the luck that had been with his ancestors who had pirated in these waters for generations beyond memory.

Cheng remained on the low poop of the *Golden Moon*. Half a dozen seamen pulled in sails. Chia Min, the two crewmen disguised as women, and two men in Western dress remained on deck, leaning on the rail, looking at the approaching destroyer, pointing and chatting rapidly in Chinese. The longer that Cheng kept up the illusion of a pleasure ship from Hong Kong, the more confused would be those on the destroyer's bridge.

Some of the lighter guns on the destroyer were now trained on the *Golden Moon*, but the main 130-millimeter guns were still in the fore and aft position. Amidships, a small motor launch was being readied for lowering as soon as the two ships hove to. On the destroyer's afterdeck was a platoon of troops. From them a squad was being called out to clamber into the launch after it was lowered into the water.

Cheng told Chia Min to go below to his cabin. She started in that direction, but instead of obeying him, she stopped when out of his sight. She could see that he was concentrating on his ship, not her. She wanted to see what was going to happen. She was not afraid, and had never been afraid.

She thought of Harry. There had been so much to say, and they had not said it. She had wanted to tell him that she knew more than he, knew that they would be together again. She had the promise of her uncle, who was a resourceful man.

Cheng had no more thoughts of Chia Min. He ordered the sails pulled in and the diesels idled. With a few hundred yards of open water between the stopped ships, the launch was lowered from the *Anshan*.

The troops, burdened with rifles and small packs, climbed over the rail and onto the web net thrown over the side. Cheng waited for the right moment. It came as the officers on the destroyer bridge shouted down to the army officers to hurry the troops into the launch. The sailors at the open 20- and 37-milimeter gun mounts looked on, commenting with jokes and gestures about the difficulties the troops were having on the net.

Cheng pulled up the cover on a small electrical junction box near the ship's steering rudder and depressed a red button. Cheng's well-trained crew simultaneously undertook a score of actions.

The sailors on deck and the two "couples" instantly disappeared beneath the junk's gunwale. The two large hatch combings on the foredeck—those that Yong had thought unlikely—collapsed, each revealing a 20-millimeter Oerlikon cannon. The rig of the *Golden Moon* and her carefully maneuvered position gave both guns wide fields of fire. The guns began blasting away immediately, both concentrating on the unarmored light gun mounts of the *Anshan*. Simultaneously, the after hatch combing on the junk's starboard side fell open, as did a portion of the enlarged deckhouse, revealing a rapid-fire 40-millimeter cannon, which immediately began spraying the destroyer's bridge and the fire-control director above it.

Amidships, a small boat, upside down on the main deck, was lifted off a pair of 60-millimeter mortars bolted to steel plates on the deck. The instant they were uncovered, their crews dropped three-pound bombs into their muzzles.

Round after round—*thwang, thwang, thwang*—hurtled out of their barrels. When Cheng heard that unique sound, he knew that the last move in his plan had been swiftly carried out. Now he needed luck—the kind of luck that rewards the planner but eludes the spontaneous seeker of luck. Luck would be a mortar round or two striking the Styx missile tubes or other weapons and touching off massive secondary explosions. Luck would be his three automatic cannon eliminating the destroyer's light guns and wiping out the men on the bridge.

But he could not take time to assess his luck. *"Now!"* he screamed into the speaking tube to the *Golden Moon*'s engine room. The two turbo-charged diesels sprang to life, and the junk closed with the destroyer, but only for a couple of minutes.

The *Anshan*, built at the Soviet port of Nikolayev on the Black Sea in the late 1930s, was old but well maintained and well commanded. And she had some luck on *her* side. When ordered to intercept the *Golden Moon*, the ship fortuitously had had steam up in all three water-tube boilers, so she was able to immediately come to full power. When the destroyer had stopped to send over the boarding party, her commander had kept the ship ready for instant action.

The officer of the deck had fortunately paid more attention to the *Golden Moon* than to the boarding party. He noticed the slow swing of the junk, which was presenting a smaller and smaller target to the *Anshan*'s guns. As he was about to inform his commanding officer, the *Golden Moon*'s guns were uncovered and the firing began. The officer of the deck screamed into his speaking tube for full speed and ordered the main guns to prepare to fire. His order, though, had gone to crews who were lounging at their guns.

In those furious moments, the *Anshan*'s decks were raked with cannon fire. Mortar bombs exploded amidships.

But the order for full speed had been carried out. The sudden movement of the destroyer threw off the aim of the *Golden Moon*'s mortar crews. The *Anshan*'s captain, although seriously wounded, took the conn and ordered a turn to port, now presenting the junk with a smaller stern target. The launch, with some troops aboard, was turned over by the destroyer's acceleration. A few soldiers and sailors managed to cling to the launch, which was being pulled along by the *Anshan*.

Presented with the smaller target of the stern of the *Anshan*, Cheng's gunners concentrated their fire there, scoring hits on both after 130-millimeter guns, causing damage and killing several men in their crews. The *Golden Moon*, accelerating to fifteen knots, pulled away from the destroyer, which was now up to twenty knots and steaming in the opposite direction.

Cheng was elated. A few rounds from the *Anshan*'s smaller guns had struck his junk, but there was no significant damage, and not one of his men had been hit. In contrast, he estimated that several hundred rounds of 20-millimeter and 40-millimeter fire, as well as at least five mortar bombs, had hit the destroyer. However, he knew that the destroyer had not suffered serious damage, unless the officers and controls on the bridge had been hit.

The bridge had in fact been hit repeatedly. Four officers and two sailors were dead; all others on the bridge, the captain and watch officer among them, were wounded. Blood ran freely on the deck of the bridge, and the main steering and annunicator controls were smashed. His left arm hanging useless, shrapnel wounds in his neck and left shoulder, the captain still could speak. He called his orders to the auxiliary steering position, ordering the ship to change course and fall in behind the *Golden Moon*, matching her speed. Then, he slowed his ship. As the distance opened to twelve miles, he gave the order to prepare to commence fire.

Cheng watched the destroyer make a wide turn behind him. By the time she had completed the half turn and was steaming southward, in the same direction as the *Golden Moon,* she was twelve miles behind him. The destroyer, he now knew, had not suffered serious damage and, capable of a maximum speed of about thirty knots, could overtake his junk in perhaps three-quarters of an hour. Before that, at some ten miles or less, the ship's two forward 130-millimeter guns would take the junk under fire. That would be the most dangerous period of the whole fight.

If the junk could evade the shells until the destroyer was perhaps eight miles away, the *Golden Moon* could use her "stinger." Hidden in the stern of the junk were two torpedo tubes holding homing torpedoes. Launched into the water, they would seek out the noises of the destroyer's machinery. During the initial engagement, the angle of the *Golden Moon* to the destroyer, necessary to use the guns to maximum advantage, had prevented use of the torpedoes at that time.

Cheng raised his binoculars to look again at the destroyer, still some twelve miles astern. The larger ship's twin masts were initially in line, showing the ship was heading straight at the junk. Then suddenly they separated a little. She was no long directly astern of the *Golden Moon.* She was falling behind, to a position off the *Golden Moon*'s port quarter. A moment later, Cheng thought he detected smoke billowing forth from the destroyer. Had there been a mortar hit in a critical location, one that had now erupted into flames, causing an engineering casualty? Perhaps his luck still was running high.

The smile that had begun to form on Cheng's face faded. From out of the smoke he saw a small black pencil-shaped object rise up to a height of perhaps a hundred feet, fall to about thirty feet above the water, and then come rushing toward the *Golden Moon.* The shape grew in Cheng's binoculars.

Seconds later the modified Styx missile slammed into the port side of the *Golden Moon.* The trajectory took the missile through one wooden side and then through the other side; the 1,100-pound high-explosive warhead detonated some twenty feet from the junk. Only half of the highly volatile rocket fuel had been expended in the twelve-mile flight from the *Anshan.* The remaining fuel, ignited in the explosion, splattered onto the *Golden Moon* like napalm.

Within moments the shattered junk was aflame from bow to stern. No one below decks escaped the inferno.

Chia Min and a few crewmen were blown over the side. She bobbed to the surface, disappeared, limply rose again, and then slowly began to vanish beneath the strangely calm sea. A young man, in the tatters of a garishly yellow frock, had been swimming toward her white straw hat. He snatched at her long hair and pulled her to the surface. He managed to get both of them to a floating spar. Several other men clutched bits of wreckage.

Cheng, standing on the junk's stern, was thrown to the deck as the Styx warhead exploded. His luck had put the deckhouse between him and the direct blast. Flames were flowing like water across the junk's deck. His face seared, his hair and beard singed, his quilted black jacket afire, he tried to get on his feet, grabbing for something to help him stand. His fingers grasped the cool black muzzle of a gun that was old even when his aunt was young. The end of the barrel against which he leaned was marked with a crown and dated 1812. He had affectionately loaded it himself that morning, the powder wadded with newspaper, the charge tamped down with a wooden rammer, now smoldering at his feet. The gun was fired by applying a lighted stick to a few coarse grains of powder poured into the touchhole. The gun could fire a nine-pound ball a distance of 1,500 yards.

Cheng struggled out of his burning jacket and flung it aside. Staggering, biting his lower lip against his pain, he turned to see what was left of his ship.

The jacket, now a bundle of flame, had fallen across the breech of the gun. Below the crown and the numerals, Cheng's uncle had etched, in Chinese characters, "To the Audacious Goes Victory." The burning jacket had covered the motto, and the touchhole.

Cheng never heard the hiss of the touchhole powder. The nine-pound iron cannonball hurtled through him as it emerged from the barrel and flew into the sea.

The *Anshan* slowed when she reached the debris and the almost fully submerged *Golden Moon*. Then the ship stopped and put boarding nets over the side. Three men began to claw their way up the net. The young man in the yellow tatters pushed Chia Min toward the net. As her fingers curled around the rough hemp, a lookout on the shattered bridge shouted that he had detected a periscope. The *Anshan* was configured as a missile ship without antisubmarine weapons. The captain ordered immediate full speed.

The first of Cheng's men had reached the *Anshan*'s deck. Chia Min was near the top of the net when the ship suddenly seemed to leap from the water, tearing the net from her right hand and sending a man below her plunging into the sea. She clung for a moment with her left hand and then, buffeted by the wind, she swung back against the net and wove her right hand into the netting. She looked down. The surge of speed created a suction that pulled two men into the twin thrashing propellers at the destroyer's stern. Her hat and a flash of yellow vanished in the frothing wake. She began to slip from the net when she felt the strong arm of an *Anshan* crewman around her. As he hauled her upward, she saw her white hat bob to the surface.

Realizing that his periscope had been sighted by the *Anshan,* Captain First/Rank Svjatov ordered the *Petroverdets* deeper and southward, back toward the *Glomar Explorer*. He had sent a brief radio report of the events he had witnessed in the past hour. At the same time, the whip antenna raised above the waves had brought him news that the *Primorye,* the Soviet intelligence ship watching the *Glomar,* had detected an American nuclear submarine.

Who knows, Svjatov thought, there may be two battles in the South China Sea this day. Leaning over the plotting board, he and his navigator prepared a track that would take them close to the *Primorye,* which would place noisemakers in the water to mask the submarine's approach. While the noise would blind the Russians' sonar as well as that of the American submarine, the *Primorye* would be able to provide Svjatov with the location of the American undersea craft. He would slow to quiet running speed before entering the acoustic detection range of the American undersea craft. Svjatov knew that submarine versus submarine warfare must be a duel of tactics as well as technology. He was not certain which side had better technology, but, from reading American journals and his Navy's intelligence reports, he was convinced that his tactics were far superior to those of American submarines.

Yes, he thought, if necessary, there could be two battles in the South China Sea this day.

*

The potential target of Svjatov's thoughts, the U.S.S. *Queenfish*, had decoded the lengthy message from the Pentagon, had called the *Glomar Explorer* by ship-to-ship radio, and, in clear language, directed Dysart to cut loose the hulk of the *Osaka Maru* and let it fall to the ocean floor. The deadline for dropping the hulk was two hours off.

Dysart looked up fom the classified message board and said, "Roth."

"Aye?"

"Those assholes in Washington have apparently told the submarine *Queenfish* to 'advise' us to drop the hulk at oh-two-hundred." He handed the board to Roth.

"Captain, there must be more to the message than just that. Some 'or else' or something more."

"Yeah. Strange message. Let's query Langley on this. I don't take orders from another ship's skipper who I can't even see.

"And I'm sure as hell not dropping that thing at two o'clock in the morning. I need light. I want to be able to put the submersible or divers over the side to check the release bolts before we let go."

Then, motioning to the cipher clerk who had brought the message board, Dysart dictated a message to CIA Headquarters: Confirm message from U.S.S. *Queenfish* to release cargo. Require six additional hours to ensure ship safety before release.

"Got that Jonesy? Let's get it off right away. And let's make the U.S.S. *Queenfish* an 'info addressee' on that one."

The last part of the message from the Pentagon, which had perplexed James Pratt, the *Queenfish*'s commanding officer, had not been passed on to Dysart. That part, in a separate code held only by the submarine's commanding officer, had instructed him to prepare the ship's two outdated Mark 37 torpedoes (retained in the fleet because of the shortage of Mark 48s) for possible use.

The *Queenfish* was to fire the torpedoes into the hulk of the *Osaka Maru*, suspended four hundred feet beneath the *Glomar*, if the hulk was not cut loose by the specified deadline. The shock wave from such an attack would make the *Glomar* ride uneasy for a few minutes but probably would cause the ship no real damage. Shattered, the *Osaka Maru* would fall to the bottom of the ocean.

The specially coded message was signed, "Chief of Naval Operations for the Commander-in-Chief."

With the ship's young weapons officer, the commanding officer of the *Queenfish* entered the submarine's amidships torpedo room. There, on the two-layer "table" in the center of the compartment and on five racks on either side, were a score of Mark 48 antisubmarine torpedoes, several SUBROCs—nuclear-tipped antisubmarine rockets—and the pair of Mark 37s.

"Okay, John, I want you to pull one Mark 48 and one Harpoon missile from the tubes and load the two Mark 37s. I assume you've fired these?"

"Yes, sir. Back in submarine school. That was three, no—almost four—years ago. But no sweat, sir. You tell me the target and I'll kill her."

"She's already dead, John," said the commanding officer as he turned to exit the compartment. The torpedo officer and several enlisted men in the compartment turned and shrugged their shoulders in puzzlement.

28

THE CAR TURNED OFF THE HIGHWAY. Gunnison looked at his watch again. Five minutes past seven, Monday morning. He had been held a prisoner for a full day. From what he knew of the geography of Kaohsiung, the car was certainly not being driven to the airport, where China Air was located. They were moving more slowly now, down a two-lane paved road. Just beyond the road, to his right, Gunnison could see a high fence topped by three strands of barbed wire. Along the road there were blue signs with Chinese characters in white. He assumed they had driven onto a military reservation. On both sides of the road there were woods, but Gunnison thought he could see the shapes of buildings through the wet trees.

The car skidded to a stop before a man in a helmet and fatigues, dull with the colors of camouflage, and a web pistol belt with a .38 service revolver in the holster. He had a red armband with Chinese characters on his right arm. Yang rolled down his window and spoke briefly to the man. He pointed to his left.

The car bounded off the pavement and down a dirt road that cut through the woods to a square clearing about 150 yards to the side. The rain had stopped, but the sky was foggy and everything was wet. There was a cruel beauty to those moments, even here. He thought of Chia Min and then tried to stop thinking about her.

Gunnison left the car and walked about, stretching his legs. Yang brought him rice and tea. Gunnison counted more than thirty men, each with a weapon—rifle, submachine gun, or grenade launcher. No blue windbreakers here. Most of the soldiers sat cross-legged on ponchos at the edge of the tree line, their weapons in their laps or held upright. A few yards from the troops, Gunnison saw five men in conversation; officers, he assumed.

Another car entered the clearing, and one of the officers trotted toward it. Gunnison started walking in that direction, but his two guards from the hotel appeared on either side of him. One politely took Gunnison's bowl and cup and handed him a blue windbreaker.

Only then did he realize he was cold. He wore slacks, a white shirt now stained and faintly smelling of vomit, and a madras jacket. He wondered what had happened to his raincoat.

He took the windbreaker, which was big enough for him to put on over his jacket. He zipped it all the way up and jammed his hands into its pockets. *I'm one of them now,* he thought. And as he thought this, he thought of Jessen. *It will be that way for a long time: Let my mind wander and it will return to those blurred hours aboard the* Golden Moon.

He forced his mind to turn outward, to observation. In the steadily growing light he now could see, on the far side of the clearing, three Bell "Huey" troop-carrying helicopters. He had seen hundreds of the ubiquitous Hueys in Vietnam. These Hueys had no markings, although they wore the olive drab paint of armies around the world. Gunnison saw no crewmen near the helicopters.

The second car, which had picked up an officer and Yang, slowly passed the Hueys and stopped before a building that looked like a small hangar. It was nestled deep enough in the woods so that it would be difficult to spot from the air.

Yang and the officer got out of the car and entered the building. Then the car turned and headed toward him. One of the guards opened a rear door and motioned him inside. The car headed back to the hangar. Gunnison was taken into the building.

"Is Cheng here?" Gunnison asked Yang, who stood near the door, the officer in camouflage fatigues at his side.

"No," Yang said. "He is still aboard the *Golden Moon*. I am his representative." He smiled.

In the center of the hangar, under flickering bare bulbs, was a Bell-13 helicopter with the markings of China Sky. A pilot was slowly walking around it, checking it out.

"Jessen. I want to know what happened to Jessen," Gunnison said.

Yang began to turn away. Gunnison lunged for him. The officer stepped forward, and Gunnison felt the edge of a hand slam him on the back of his neck. He fell forward onto a crate.

The officer spun Gunnison around, flipped him over, and pinned his shoulders against the crate. Yang spoke sharply, and the officer stepped aside.

Gunnison sat up, rubbing the back of his neck. "Jessen. What happened to him?"

"He has been detained from reaching the *Glomar Explorer*. I fear an accident," Yang said.

"What kind of an accident?"

Gunnison's voice was getting louder. The Taiwanese officer edged a step closer. His right hand moved slightly toward the shoulder holster at his left armpit.

"Mr. Gunnison." Now Yang's high-pitched voice had a command authority. "Even now General Cheng is sailing the *Golden Moon* toward your *Glomar Explorer* and the ship that she is lifting from the ocean floor. You will quickly wash and gain complete control of yourself. Then, a China Sky helicopter will fly you out to the American ship. Once there, you will have the captain complete the salvage of the ship. You and the general have agreed to this."

"I have not agreed to anything. The deal is off."

Yang said something to the officer. They both laughed.

"Deal? There is first the matter of Chia Min being aboard the *Golden Moon*. Her safety depends upon your cooperation. You, of course, know that?"

Gunnison started to speak, but he knew there was nothing to say.

"You will go aboard the *Glomar*, and you will tell the captain to raise the *Osaka Maru*. At once. When the *Osaka Maru* is safely raised, you will signal with this transponder." He placed what looked like a small tape recorder in a pocket of Gunnison's windbreaker and zipped the pocket closed.

"The signal will be received by the *Golden Moon*, which will relay it here, and thirty minutes later helicopters will land General Cheng's troops on the *Glomar Explorer*. We will take the gold and load it onto the *Golden Moon*."

"What of the crew of the *Glomar Explorer?*"

"They are unarmed. They have no way of resisting a planned assault by trained troops. Indeed," Yang said soothingly, "we believe that the gold will be taken off without any casualties to either side."

"What if the signal is not sent?"

"The helicopters will still come, but the troops will not be expecting a peaceful reception. You will do no good for yourself, those on the ship, or Chia Min if you fail to send the signal."

Yang took him to a small sink and toilet at the back of the hangar. Surprisingly clean, Gunnison thought. He was provided with an electric shaver, soap, a towel, and a clean white shirt—made in mainland China, he noticed.

A few minutes later—it was now a quarter past eight—Gunnison walked from the hangar to the China Sky Bell-13, which had been pushed from the hangar to the clearing. As soon as he emerged from the building, the pilot started up the engine. Ducking under the blades, he quickly surveyed the perimeter of the clearing—the troops, helicopters, and buildings, now more visible as the fog was burning off—and climbed into the passenger's seat. He buckled the seat belt and nodded to the pilot, who immediately took off, putting the helicopter in a sharp, nose-down position to gain maximum speed during the takeoff.

As Gunnison leaned back, trying to decide his best course of action when he reached the *Glomar Explorer,* his hands held onto the seat belt. The belt had something caked on it. He pulled his hands away with the realization that it was dried blood.

29

"YES, SIR. There was a real war going on out there—a real war. Apparently, the Chinese destroyer was shot up real badly by this junk, actually a Q-ship or decoy ship, the kind we used in both world wars against German U-boats. But the destroyer sank the damn junk. Blew her apart with a Soviet Styx missile."

Admiral Watson, the chief of naval operations, was quite animated as he described the South China Sea events with the crisis committee, which had been called into session on Monday morning, Washington time, when word of the battle was received. An assistant secretary of the treasury had been added to the committee.

That word had come as a result of Navy and National Security Agency intercepts of transmissions from the *Anshan* and a passover by a "Big Bird" satellite. The battered Chinese ship had sent a long radio report in a tactical code that NSA could read on a real-time basis. The intercept, originally made by the U.S. Naval Communications Station at Yokosuka, Japan, had provided the Navy and the CIA with details of the engagement.

The chief of naval operations, now in a key role, was graphically explaining all that he knew.

"And what about the *Glomar* situation?" Saunders, the national security adviser, interrupted.

"Well, sir," the CNO replied, "*Queenfish*, our submarine on the scene, has advised the *Glomar* of the President's directive to drop the gold ship."

"Is there confirmation that the hulk has been dropped?" Saunders asked. He was more aware than the others that several nations were violently opposed to the raising of the gold. There had been an almost steady parade of foreign officials—Chinese, Japanese, British, Dutch, Swiss, South African, and even Soviet—to the State Department and the White House to inquire about or to protest the *Glomar Explorer*'s treasure hunt.

"We are awaiting absolute confirmation of the drop, sir," Watson said.

"It's about time we got some questions answered absolutely around here," Saunders said. "We've got good reasons for wanting to wind this up fast. Let me tell you why."

The Washington Post was trying to put together a story launched by Bob Martin's vague tip about gold. The *Post* rewriteman assigned to the story had recently left the *Los Angeles Times*. He told his editor that there had been a rumor in Los Angeles that the *Glomar Explorer* had recently sailed on a mission for the CIA. He wondered if there could be a connection. . . . Through Sunday night and into Monday morning, the two papers, in a rare display of cooperation, pooled what they knew, badgered sources on both coasts, and now, as the crisis committee met, rumors from a yet unpublished story about a "ship of gold" were circulating throughout Washington—and, city by city, throughout the world, from Hong Kong to Zurich. Tomorrow's newspapers would confirm the rumors and increase the gold panic. The crisis committee had a new crisis to manage.

Even though a billion or more dollars in gold would not significantly affect the market price, the possible specter of World War II contraband gold frightened the market. Gold prices plummeted as each market opened. Brokers in the New York Commodity Exchange woke up their customers in Hong Kong; Chinese speculators there accounted for about 20 percent of New York's gold futures trading. At the neon-lit gold stores along Yawarate Road in Bangkok, there was a traffic jam of cars, bicycles, scooters, and pedestrians. In London, at the Rothschild banking house, the chairman of London Gold Fixing told frantic brokers that the two price-fixing sessions would be held as usual. His soothing voice urged calm. But he knew that the sale of half a ton of gold could drop prices a dollar. . . . And the rumors were that the *Soji* bankers were after more than fifty tons. The rumors also said that the gold's ownership was in doubt and that could lead to questions about the ownership of certain other gold holdings, including the reserves of several nations—especially West Germany.

The chairman of the London gold brokers made a discreet telephone call to No. 10 Downing Street and asked that these Americans be spoken to. So the British ambassador and others in Washington had been calling and politely inquiring or mildly demanding. The bankers and the brokers had been sending their nervous feelers through the network of high government and high finance.

The smell of gold now hung heavy here, in the White House, where Saunders was recounting the gold scare. As he finished his briefing, Bob Martin quietly passed a note, and Saunders added, "As Bob has just reminded me, the damn Russians *want* the gold brought up at this stage—CIA guesses so they can show how greedy we capitalists are and to cause some more confusion on the international monetary scene. I know the president will want this thing killed if only because the Russians want the gold up."

"There's another issue," the assistant secretary of the treasury remarked. "And that is how several of our current allies received increases in *their* gold reserves after World War II."

At that, Saunders turned to the CNO and said, "So, you see, Admiral, a lot of people want to be damn sure the gold stays on the bottom of the Pacific."

"Yes, sir," the CNO said. "I . . . understand the situation better now. Let me bring you absolutely up to date. The *Queenfish* has acknowledged that she has advised the *Glomar Explorer* that the Navy has assumed OPCON—that's operations control—of the operation and that the *Osaka Maru* is to be dropped immediately.

"As a followup—as our fall-back position—the submarine has been directed to hit the *Osaka Maru* with torpedoes. Now this can be done safely with absolutely no danger to the men aboard the *Glomar*—"

"What the hell did you say, Admiral Watson?" The incredulous look on Saunders' face, not his words, caused the chief of naval operations to stop.

"I said there was no danger to the *Glomar Explorer*. The—"

"I don't give a damn about the *Glomar Explorer*. What in the hell is that Soviet submarine out there going to do when it hears torpedoes going through the water? That is, I assume that the Russians have sonar in their submarines and that a torpedo going through the water at sixty knots or whatever makes a lot of noise."

"Well, sir, the Mark 37 torpedoes that we would use go slower than that. In fact, we have discarded all but a few of them because they are too slow to catch fast Soviet—"

"Damn it." This time it was the vice president. "Admiral, give us slowly and concisely the exact order that you had sent to that submarine about using torpedoes. And when is she scheduled to use them?"

The admiral stood and leaned over the table to shuffle through his briefing book and a stack of file folders on the table in front of him. "We set a two-hour deadline, Mr. Vice President, from the

Glomar's receipt of the submarine's message, sir. But . . . but the *Glomar* has asked for an extension, as I understand it."

"As you *understand* it?" The vice president asked, speaking the words slowly and painfully.

"Yes, sir. *Glomar* has sent a message, an encrypted message, to Langley, asking for clarification. CIA has just notified us about the message."

"Let me get this straight, Admiral Watson. If the *Glomar* does not drop the *Osaka Maru* by the deadline, your submarine will fire torpedoes at it?"

"Yes, sir."

"Does the submarine know whether the *Glomar* is, in fact, going to drop the hulk?"

"We are attempting clarification ourselves, sir."

Suddenly, the room was silent. For the first time, people heard the low hum of the air-conditioning and the hiss of the electric coffee urn that rested on the long, low service counter along one wall of the Situation Room. There were no further questions forthcoming from the vice president. He seemed, people in the room would later remember, to look straight ahead, staring at the large map of the Far East mounted on the opposite wall specifically for the session. He began to nervously tap his gold mechanical pencil on the edge of the conference table.

Saunders, looking across the length of the table at the vice president, muttered, "Jesus." Then, standing up, he shifted his gaze to Watson and said, sharply, "Admiral, I want to be in direct contact with that submarine. It is in a real-time communications situation, isn't it?"

A naval aide had entered the room. He now whispered something to the CNO, who, still standing, grabbed the edge of the table. He turned toward Saunders.

"I am afraid, Mr. Saunders, that we are temporarily out of contact with the *Queenfish*. She has broken off communications and gone deep."

"Then, goddamn it, get me the *Glomar*. Who's the captain? Dysart? Get him. Now. On a secure phone in this room."

Saunders sat down and began reading another note from Bob Martin. Saunders nodded and half-whispered to Martin, "The next chief of naval operations will not be a submarine officer. He'll be an aviator. Those guys could *always* get us contact with an aircraft carrier no matter where in the world it was."

Admiral Watson had paused. Looking directly at the vice president to get eye contact and to appear resolute, he said, "We are having problems, sir. When we set up the *Queenfish-Glomar* radio link, we advised *Glomar* to accept priority messages only on that link."

"And, I suppose, that means she is out of touch with us?" the vice president asked, trying to keep his voice under control.

"On that priority channel—that's our GOLDDUST link, yes sir. We will have to try commercial radio-telephone and patch through."

"Good God! We're down to a pay phone. Okay. Try anything!"

Saunders turned to the vice president, who was still staring at the map. "May I suggest, Mr. vice president, that you inform the president that it may be necessary for him to return from the conference in Mexico if this situation deteriorates any further."

The vice president nodded his agreement. Of those at the table, only Saunders knew that the vice president had actually heard and understood what was being said. To himself Saunders added, *I guess we're about to charge up a hill.*

Saunders looked around the room rapidly; those at the table were obviously preoccupied with trying to bring some order to the statements of the last few minutes. Only Bob Martin, sitting against the wall with the two White House secretaries, returned his glance. Martin, he knew, fully understood that a charge up the hill was beginning and that he, Saunders, not the vice president, was in command until the president returned from Mexico.

"I hope the president has a way to talk to us," Saunders angrily said to Martin. "If he has to talk to Moscow from down there it will be a patch-up. Every goddamn thing is a patch-up. But we've got to tell the Soviets about those torpedoes." He paused to neatly stack the papers around him and put them in his briefcase. "Our only hope, Bob, is that they're as fucked up as we are."

30

THE MORNING SUN WAS ONLY a glow in a sky dark with the threat of storm. Dysart, leaning on the rail outside the bridge, reminded himself to have the weather advisories from Fleet Weather Central sent to him every half hour. He always felt deprived of something valuable in a dawn like this, when there was no real sunrise, no streaming of light and color along the sky and sea.

He stepped down the ladder from the bridge and walked briskly about the main deck, sidestepping the equipment and the consoles that made his ship littered but unique. He was proud of her, proud especially of her steadiness. Even in this choppy sea he could feel only the throb of her engines. No one ever got seasick on this ship when she was doing her job.

On the fantail he stopped and again looked up at the dark sky. Dysart was a gambling man, but he did not take foolhardy risks. He took risks only when he knew he controlled the situation. And weather was out of his control.

He would be glad to drop the damn thing back where it belonged. But he would do it when he, the captain, decided to do it. The *Glomar* must not be hazarded by a storm or by some damnfool orders from some invisible U.S. Navy officer.

He made his way entirely around the main deck, returned to the bridge, and talked with the officer of the watch and the helmsman before going down the ladder and aft to the wardroom. He wanted to be the first one there for breakfast, another working breakfast.

Ishiwata and Taketomo appeared from an inner companionway and were heading toward him. Kimpei dogged them, a couple of yards behind.

"The day begins badly," Ishiwata said, gesturing toward the sky.

Dysart nodded. "When the sun doesn't rise with a big, spectacular scene," he said, "I feel gypped. You know the expression? Gypped?"

"Oh, yes," Ishiwata said. "Very well."

Both men laughed.

Dysart opened the wardroom door. "Well, I hope breakfast will suit us," he said, holding the door open for Ishiwata but not Taketomo and Kimpei. Kimpei would remain outside of the wardroom.

After the steward had cleared away most of the breakfast dishes and the white tablecloth that had covered the wardroom table, Dysart put down a chart, securing the edges of it with cups and saucers. They stood around the table—Dysart, Ishiwata, Taketomo, Jack Mooney, and Roth. Kimpei was a shadow against the frosted glass port of the closed wardroom door. Dysart ordered the steward to bring Kimpei something to eat. Like a goddamn hound.

"Something is happening," Dysart began. "I have to assume at this point that it involves Jessen." He looked at the chronometer on the bulkhead. "It will be a while before those people in Washington figure out what to do. So we are on our own here now." He pointed to the chart. "Let me give you all the picture."

His pipe had gone out, and he used the straight black stem as a pointer. Some bits of charred tobacco fell on the chart as he pointed. He brushed them aside.

"We're here," he began, tapping a red mark on the chart. "Practically anchored here. Off here, of course, that's Taiwan. Jessen was supposed to leave from there yesterday. Ninety-mile trip or so. I can't raise the company that was to take him—China Sky—on the radio telephone. I have told Washington that Jessen has not shown up, and I suppose when they get around to it, they'll find out what is holding him up. Him and Gunnison.

"On the horizon we have a frigate from the Japanese Maritime Self-Defense Force. Now the captain of that ship—as I told you, Mr. Ishiwata, but maybe Taketomo here doesn't know—the captain of the ship has asked me to send you over in a launch. Or for us to accept a visit from one of their launches. Well, I told him we aren't taking any more visitors aboard my ship. Except for Jessen and Gunnison, and, of course, they aren't exactly visitors. So the frigate just keeps going back and forth. Not in circles like the Chinese ship did."

Ishiwata said something in Japanese to Taketomo. Roth thought he heard references to the *Soji* and the prime minister.

"Off here," Dysart continued, pointing to a spot near one edge of the chart, "was the Chinese ship. She stopped going in circles and took off in this directon like a bat—"

"Enough!" Ishiwata said. "No more of this nonsense, Captain. I have told you that you are to resume hoisting up the *Osaka Maru*. You will disregard that hoax order to drop the *Osaka Maru*."

"What order?" Dysart asked.

"The order you are supposed to have received from Washington," Ishiwata said. He then spoke rapidly in Japanese to Taketomo.

Dysart glared at Ishiwata. "Gold can buy anything, can't it? You bought a code clerk."

"Two," Ishiwata said. "I bought two. But, Captain, that message. It is impossible."

"I hope your man told you the authority for that message."

"A hoax. It is a hoax."

"You are the charter-holder, Mr. Ishiwata. And a captain has to listen to the charter-holder. But when the charter-holder thinks *he* is captain, then things get dangerous."

Ishiwata started to say something, but Dysart held up his hand. "Listen to me. If you can bribe a code clerk, you can do other things. You might get the idea of having your man here"—Dysart looked across the table to Taketomo—"get some of your countrymen together and try to take over this ship. My ship.

"So let me not have to say this all again. I'm here to tell you that *I* run this ship, that *I* am awaiting further orders from *my* superiors, and that if there is any trouble aboard this ship, I want to make sure it does not come from you two. I am not talking about anything more than a peaceful handling of this situation. So, when you are walking around the ship, Jack here, or I, or Roth, or some other American officer I pick will be walking along with you. And when you go into your cabins, there will be a man outside, and he won't let anyone in to see you.

"Now that may inconvenience you a bit, and that may not be the way you might do it back home. But that is the way we are going to do it on *my* ship."

Taketomo started to speak in Japanese. Ishiwata said a few words to him, then turned to Dysart. "You speak very clearly, Captain. But you are not responding to my question about that message. It is—"

The bulkhead phone interrupted Ishiwata. Dysart took the phone, listened for a moment, and then said to Roth, "That was word from the radio shack. There's a China Sky helicopter on its way."

"You get back to the communications center," Dysart ordered Roth. "And keep up with the radio traffic." He told Mooney to escort Taketomo back to his cabin. To Ishiwata he said, "You may as well stay here until Gunnison and Jessen arrive. You paid for finding out what's happening."

Fifteen minutes later, at the sound of the approaching helicopter, Dysart walked out on the deck and headed up toward the landing pad. He saw only one figure get out of the helicopter, which immediately took off. He beckoned, and Gunnison trotted toward him.

31

GUNNISON WAS STANDING ON THE ladder to the wardroom deck when Dysart had a premonition he would never see Jessen again. Without speaking, he opened the wardroom door and motioned Gunnison inside. Ishiwata stood, bowed to Gunnison, and smiled.

"The news from Washington," Dysart said, "is that the operation is scrubbed. I've been ordered to cut loose the *Osaka Maru*. What the hell's happening? And where is Jessen?"

"I don't know. There's been a fuck-up, Steve. Some kind of fuck-up. Listen. I've . . . I've got myself involved in something that's going out of control. That message could be a phony. We've got to talk privately."

"What's there to talk about?" Dysart said. "I just got a message, a high-priority message. One that tells me I'm supposed to drop that goddamn thing."

"Goddamn it," Gunnison yelled. "Listen to me!" He jabbed Dysart's chest with his right index finger. "To me, goddamn it. Not to a fucking telegram."

Dysart looked down at the chart and moved a cup away from Japan.

"The goddamn Navy doesn't run this operation," Gunnison shouted. "You do. The agency does."

"No way," Dysart said calmly. "Unless the agency tells me otherwise, I release the bolts on the claws and that thing goes back down to the bottom. That's it."

He looked over to Ishiwata, who had slumped onto a couch at the other side of the wardroom. "Besides," Dysart said, "we aren't even sure the gold is still in the ship. The hull is holed. The gold may have fallen out. For all we really know there never was any gold aboard."

Ishiwata spoke for the first time since Gunnison's arrival. "You can believe me, Captain," he said. "And Mr. Gunnison." He bobbed his head toward Gunnison. "Captain, I *saw* the gold. I was—I am—responsible for it."

"According to the court-martial testimony," Dysart said, "she was hit by four torpedoes."

"Submarine skippers always say all the fish they fire are hits," Gunnison said. His voice had calmed. He knew that anger, passion—or emotion of any kind—did not work with Dysart.

"That hulk was holed," Dysart said. "You can *see* the holes on the TV tapes. She's shaky. Trembling, right now. Like the Soviet sub did. Her back's broken, Harry. We might not even be able to get her up any more than we have—assuming we continue the operation."

"What's the rate of lift?" Gunnison asked.

Before Dysart could answer, Ishiwata did. "It averaged six meters an hour until it was stopped."

"That's the fastest rate?" Gunnison asked.

Again, Ishiwata, not Dysart, answered. "I understand that it is about half the maximum possible rate."

"Why not lift her a bit more? Keep her coming up?" Gunnison asked. "What's the difference if it's four hundred feet under us or two hundred? Or—"

The phone near Dysart's head buzzed. "Captain speaking."

"Mooney on the bridge, Skipper. Sonar is picking up a whole mess of noises. Hank is on the console. He says it sounds like the Russian intelligence ship has put noisemakers in the water. That may be what scared off the U.S. sub."

"Got it, Jack. Thanks," Dysart said. "Hold on." He put his left hand over the mouthpiece and turned to Ishiwata. "More problems, Mr. Ishiwata." Speaking into the phone again, Dysart said, "Jack, send a man here to escort Mr. Ishiwata to his cabin."

"So I am now a prisoner, Captain," Ishiwata said.

Dysart hung up the phone. "Not a prisoner, Mr. Ishiwata. I'm clearing the decks." He motioned to Gunnison. "You said you wanted to talk. Sit down and have a cup of coffee."

As soon as Ishiwata was gone, Gunnison said, "Steve. Trouble. There isn't much time to talk. There's going to be an assault on the ship."

"That son of a bitch. He's hired guns?"

"No. Not Ishiwata. Pirates—pirates with some sponsors in the Taiwanese government who think the gold should be theirs. They have two or three helicopters with troops waiting to fly on board and a junk is sitting about fifty miles away."

He gave Dysart an outline of Cheng's plans and concluded by

taking the small radio transponder from his own jacket pocket.

"This," he said, "is to give them a signal as soon as the gold is on board."

Taking the transponder from Gunnison, Dysart asked, "And what happens if you don't give them the signal?"

"They come anyway, after some amount of time. I don't know how long."

"How many of them are there?"

"I'm not certain. I saw some of them near Kaohsiung. Two or three Huey helicopters—I guess I saw about thirty men. Well armed. Several had M-16s and there were .50-calibers mounted in two of the helicopter doors. I didn't see the third bird clearly, only the rotors in the trees.

"Steve, I couldn't stop them ashore, but if they're coming anyway, maybe we can make them do it on our terms. Ambush them."

"Should I trust you, Harry?"

"Good question," Gunnison said. "I'll push the button. You arm as many men as you can. I'll stand on the helo pad and wave the first chopper down. They'll recognize me. They gave me this windbreaker.

"Just when the chopper is near the deck, I'll duck and you start firing. As long as I know where the field of fire is and don't get caught in it, I should be okay."

"Not bad. Maybe I do trust you," Dysart said. He paused and nodded toward a locked metal cabinet at the other end of the cabin. "But I can't give you a gun. Maybe you'd shoot me or try to take me hostage or something. No gun for you. You know that, Harry."

"I know that, Steve. For a betting man you've always been cautious. Should I press the button?"

"Yes. Then get out on deck. Jack and I have work to do."

The *Glomar Explorer* was not a combat ship. She did not have the ability to defend herself from enemies she might detect. And she was not able to detect enemies as well as a combat ship could. She could only stand there in the sea, straining to see and hear. Twenty-seven minutes after Gunnison pushed the button, the helicopters appeared on the *Glomar*'s radar.

"We're getting three blips, sir. I've painted them. They're choppers on a course out from Taiwan," the radarman told Dysart. He hit the button for Roth.

"Are you talking to those guys?" he asked.

"Negative, Captain. We tried them on the international frequency in English, Chinese, and Japanese. No response."

"Sure they're hearing us?"

"No reason for them not to, Captain."

"Okay. You tell them in all three languages that they are not to attempt to approach this ship without identifying themselves."

Dysart stationed Mooney and five crewmen with shotguns and handguns around the helo pad. He armed himself with a .45 and went up to the bridge.

The helicopters came in a line, low and fast—130 knots, the radarman estimated. Dysart swept his binoculars from the helicopters to the pad on the stern. Six men were crouched behind cranes and hatch covers. Two had outdated M-1 .30-caliber carbines and four had pump-action shotguns.

Gunnison stood in the middle of the helo pad. He had taken off his blue windbreaker and was waving it at the lead helicopter. A man Gunnison could not see swung around a .50-caliber machine gun mounted on the port side of the helicopter. The lead helicopter was hovering just over the pad. Three other helicopters circled tightly off the stern of the *Glomar*.

Gunnison flung down the windbreaker and dived behind a hatch combing, next to Mooney. That was the signal for the carbines and the shotguns to fire, almost at the same instant.

A body fell out of the helicopter's open side, struck the ship's rail, and tumbled into the sea. The helicopter roared upward as its machine gun sprayed the deck area around the landing pad.

On the bridge, the phone buzzed. "Roth here, Skipper. You want an under-attack flash?" This top-priority message—a preset group of digits that would be sent directly to all U.S.military forces in the region—would trigger a response from whatever help was available.

"Negative," Dysart said. "We're doing okay by ourselves. And an overreaction might worsen the situation. No flash unless I give you the word personally."

"Aye, aye, sir," Roth said for the first time since he'd retired from the Navy.

The helicopter that had been the second in line now dropped down to the top of the waves and roared in toward the *Glomar's* stern.

Dysart punched up the public-address system on the ship's phone he was holding. "Hold your fire until the bastard is about to sit down. Then blast him."

When the helicopter's twin skids were inches from the pad,

one of the shotguns barked and caught the man at the helicopter's machine gun. He fell back into the cabin, momentarily blocking the others waiting to leap out. Bullets chipped a rotor blade, which began to vibrate violently. The men poured fire into the shuddering craft. Its pilot hit, it wobbled to the edge of the pad, whirled crazily upward, and cartwheeled into the sea. In an instant it was gone—there was no oil slick, no bodies, no debris. Nothing but a slight churning of water.

The other helicopters hovered for a few moments and then turned back on a course for Taiwan.

"Good job," Dysart screamed at Mooney. "Make sure we give the guys a bonus." He punched a button. "Roth. Get ready for a long message to Washington and the sub—a priority message."

"Gunnison and Mooney to the bridge!" Dysart ordered over the public-address system.

Mooney was already sprinting toward the bridge. Gunnison caught up with him on the ladder. "Not bad, Harry," Mooney said when they had puffed their way to the bridge. "Not bad for a couple of youngsters."

Dysart, his eyes on the horizon where the helicopters had come and gone, said, "Well done." He turned toward Mooney. "What's the damage, Jack?"

"Jonesy and Lefcowitz wounded. Nothing serious. Lavery's got them in sick bay already. Superficial damage to one of the cranes. We did all right. I don't think they'll be coming back."

"Neither do I. But let's keep three or four men out there and armed through the day.

"I'm going to be sending a long one to Langley. I'll want a Navy-style battle report. Get to work on that and do what you have to about the damage. Meet me in the wardroom in ten minutes. And have Ishiwata brought there. I'll be informing Langley that we'll be dropping the hulk and heading for Hawaii. I'll want to tell Ishiwata that in person."

"Will do," Mooney said and left the bridge.

Dysart spoke to the helmsman and the officer of the deck, then directly addressed Gunnison. "Thanks for the help. You'll be mentioned in the dispatches."

"I'd like a reward," Gunnison said.

"You're a cheeky bastard," Dysart replied. He stepped toward the entrance to the bridge and motioned Gunnison to follow.

In the wardroom, Gunnison handed Dysart a cup of coffee and poured one for himself. "All I want," Gunnison said, "is to see the gold."

"It's not there," Dysart said. "That hulk is holed."

"Want to bet?"

Dysart smiled but did not respond.

"I'll bet you ten thousand dollars there is gold in that hulk. Ten thousand to your one buck."

There was a knock at the door. "Enter," Dysart said. A crewman brought Ishiwata into the wardroom and left. Dysart pointed to a chair, and Ishiwata, looking weary, sat down.

"The gunfire," he said. "Helicopters. What happened?"

Dysart quickly described the raid and Gunnison's role in thwarting it.

"I am deeply grateful," Ishiwata said.

"I was just telling Gunnison that I don't believe there is any gold there anyway," Dysart said. He told Ishiwata about the bet and, while looking at Gunnison, pointed to the chronometer near the outer wardroom door. "You've got a minute to tell me how we'd settle a bet like that."

"*Albert*," Gunnison said. "You'd trust the TV tape from the submersible, wouldn't you?"

Ishiwata looked curiously at Gunnison. And then, from his conversation with Dysart, he remembered *Albert*, the three-man submersible used to observe the hulk as it was being lifted.

Dysart watched the minute sweep by on the chronograph.

"You should take a look at those claws anyhow," Gunnison went on. "Check the explosive bolts. See how well the whole rig is holding up."

"It's my ship," Dysart said, half to himself. "And I should check the bolts before I blow them." He hesitated. "Sometimes I buy my luck by spreading it around. There's a priest in Los Angeles. Father Huong. Sacred Heart Church. He does a lot with the Vietnam refugees in L.A. Send your ten thousand to him . . . *if* you win." He punched a button on the phone panel on the bulkhead. "Pass the word for Frankel to the wardroom. And prepare *Albert* for sea."

Frankel, a short, black-haired man with the shoulders and waist of a weightlifter, was there in two minutes. He entered, stood by the door, and listened, arms folded, as Dysart told him to go below and get a videotape of the hull—"and if you know damn well it's safe, go in."

"A moment, please," Ishiwata said. "This priest. From me. Another ten thousand."

"Another bet?" Dysart asked.

"Yes. And for a journey. To see the gold."

"Won't make any difference to me, Captain," Frankel said. "In fact, it gives me a little ballast."

"There's room for *two* observers," Gunnison said.

"That church needs a new roof," Dysart said.

"It's a bet," Gunnison said.

Ishiwata took one of his cards from a slim leather wallet. He wrote something on it in Japanese and in English. Handing it to Dysart, he said, "I believe you call this my marker. It is payable through my account in Los Angeles."

Dysart pocketed the card and tore a sheet of paper from a pad on the chart table. He wrote on it and handed it to Gunnison, who signed it.

"Maybe you're owed the ride," Dysart said to Ishiwata. "And it's a *ride*. The operator"—he thumbed the air toward Frankel—"is *my* man. And I'm telling him right now, so we all hear the same thing, that you have exactly thirty minutes from the time *Albert* leaves the deck. If you aren't back by then, I'm blowing the bolts. It might be dangerous. Maybe fatal to you. But I'm blowing the bolts thirty minutes from the time *Albert* goes in the water. That is in accord with the way I understand my orders."

He walked over to pat Frankel on the shoulder. "I don't have any worries. Frankel will get you back. He doesn't take chances."

Frankel smiled and nodded.

"I shouldn't ask this," Gunnison said. "But why are you doing this?"

"Why are you two doing this?"

"The gold," Ishiwata said.

"I've never really thought it was there, Harry. I always thought this was a lot of nonsense to make some Japanese businessmen and the agency happy. Now I don't know. Maybe I want to see that gold, too," Dysart said.

When Gunnison, on his way to the *Glomar*, had frantically been planning how to prevent the helicopter assault, he had also thought of this: a chance to get the gold, a chance to invoke Dysart's curiosity and penchant for betting. Perhaps, Gunnison had thought, he could purge some of his guilt for dealing with Cheng by making one last attempt to get the gold for Ishiwata. With gold gleaming on *Albert*'s videotape, maybe Dysart would have second thoughts about blowing the bolts. Make a run to shallow water. Ground the hulk in the shallows of the Formosa Strait. Maybe Dysart would take the chance. Gold did funny things to people. Gunnison certainly knew that.

32

On the main deck, crewmen began unbuckling the rig that held *Albert* in a cradle. Gunnison and Ishiwata stood nearby. Ishiwata was strangely calm. "I have lived a *renga*," he said. "My life has been a circle in these waters. Again I go into the green darkness."

"Are you composing a *renga?*" Gunnison asked.

"I suppose," Ishiwata replied, "that it is I who am being the *renga*. I am doing nothing. All I am is what is happening to me."

"In my home—in my former home—there is a statue of a fish becoming a dragon," Gunnison said. "Things change, people change."

Frankel made a last check of the submersible, which was kept ready for quick rescue or reconnaissance missions. Frankel helped Gunnison and Ishiwata aboard, then squeezed through the hatch himself. A crewman tightened the lugs around the hatch, made fast the cable rig, leaped down to the deck, and signaled to the crane operator. *Albert* was lifted and hung like a huge orange toy above the deck before being swung over the side. The crane lowered the craft to the sea. She pitched for a moment as the rig was cast away. Then she vanished as she began her 100-feet-a-minute descent.

Albert glided through blackness for three minutes. Then Frankel switched on powerful floodlights. The three men pressed their faces against the six-inch-thick Plexiglas viewing ports. Frankel pointed to a shadow beneath them.

The shadow slowly took form. Ishiwata said something aloud in Japanese. He had tears in his eyes. Frankel aimed *Albert* toward the shadow, which had taken form. The lights played along the stern of a ship. Ishiwata saw the Japanese characters and said softly, "*Osaka Maru*."

*

An hour after the message had been radioed to the *Glomar,* the *Queenfish* began to close in preparation for unleashing the two outdated Mark 37 torpedoes against the captive *Osaka Maru.* At that moment, the submarine's sonar operator advised Commander Pratt that the noises coming from the Soviet intelligence-collector *Primorye* were increasing.

The captain had been confused by the sounds from the moment they had started an hour before. The *Primorye* had obviously placed towed noisemakers in the water and was effectively masking the *Queenfish* sonar search to the northeast quadrant. Apparently, Pratt thought, the Soviet ship was simply trying to harass the *Queenfish.* Or could there be a more sinister reason?

"Give me a rundown on whatever we have on any Soviet or Chinese activity around here," Pratt said. "I think it's getting too damn noisy."

"There's not much, sir. That Soviet sub went hotfooting after the Chinese destroyer, and neither one's been heard of since."

"Very well," Pratt said. He went to his cabin, secured the door, opened a safe, and removed his small Gyn-334. He fed the message into his private communications screen and read it for the third time:

FM CNO X FOR CO USS QUEENFISH SSN651 X GLOMAR APPEARS UNABLE RECEIVE RADIO TRANSMISSIONS X RELAY MY MESSAGE 9270532Z X BLOWING OF LIFT CLAW BOLTS ORDERED BY 0200Z X IF QUEENFISH SONAR DOES NOT DETECT EXPLOSIVE BOLTS DISPATCH MARU WITH MARK37 X AVOID DAMAGE TO GLOMAR X CNO SENDS FOR CINC UNITED STATES X END MESSAGE.

Pratt replaced the message tape and decoder in his wall safe, spun the dial, and returned to the attack center. He called his sonar officer and told him to make absolutely sure his best sonarman was on duty for the next two hours. A short while later, the submarine's executive officer and the weapons officer discussed the possible need to fire at the suspended hulk.

"It'll be like shooting a duck in a rain barrel, Jim."

"Sir?"

"Jim, I want you and Ken here"—he beckoned to another officer—"to lay out a kill plot for a merchantman about four hundred feet long."

"Distance, sir?"

"I'd say about nine thousand yards."

"Speed?"

"Zero."

"Zero speed, sir?"

"Dead *in* the water, Ken. And, at a depth of four hundred feet."

Barrett leaned over the plot and told them what they might have to do. Pratt returned to his cabin. He had decided to give the *Glomar* a reasonable amount of time, and now he believed that time had come. He checked once more with the radio room. Still no new messages from the *Glomar Explorer* and still no signs that the *Osaku Maru* was being disengaged.

"Okay. Battle stations—torpedo. Jim," the captain said, turning to the weapons officer. "It's your show. I want one Mark 37 to hit her solid. It'll be quite a surprise for the *Glomar Exporer* but should not cause her any real problems."

The submarine's general-quarters alarm was bonging as Pratt spoke, and the weapons officer was soon out of sight, climbing down the ladder to the submarine's torpedo room, one level below the control room. He made a last check on the Mark 37s, both of which were in portside torpedo tubes ready for launching. Then he returned to the control room to direct the launch. Pratt believed in letting his junior officers perform such functions whenever possible.

The sonar screen was switched to the *Queenfish*'s close-range, mine-detecting sonar. It showed an amazingly detailed silhouette of the *Osaka Maru*.

Pratt called his executive officer. They stared at the green flickering image for several seconds. "Beautiful," Pratt said, clapping the sonarman on the back. "Beautiful." The image was complete, even to the steel cables holding the ship.

"Sir."

"Yes, Max?" Pratt turned to his sonar officer.

"What about that 'sled' or towed camera that the *Glomar Explorer* has down? I'm not certain that they've recovered it. Do you want to check on it, sir?"

"No. I have my orders on this, Max. Apparently if they haven't released the ship by now, there's some problem on board and I'm supposed to cut the damn ship loose myself—with the help of what may be the last two Mark 37s in the Pacific Fleet."

The *Queenfish* drew to within 9,000 yards of the *Glomar Explorer* and the *Osaka Maru*.

To the north, the Soviet nuclear-propelled attack submarine

Petroverdets approached the intelligence-collector *Primorye.* The submarine's sonar was totally "blinded" by the noisemakers being towed by the *Primorye.* But both the skipper of the surfaced ship and Svjatov, aboard the *Petroverdets,* knew, on the basis of a prearranged tactical plan, the exact moment the intelligence ship was to cease the acoustic jamming.

At that moment, the submarine would be in the immediate vicinity of the *Glomar Explorer,* ready to make a quick active sonar search, in the hope of catching the American ship by surprise as she carried out her secret actions.

"Stand by," Svjatov ordered his senior sonar operator. But the noisemakers did not cease at the agreed-upon moment. They were not shut down until eight minutes past the specified time.

Watching the clock, Svjatov cursed softly. To the assistant commander, he muttered his usual opinion about the damn surface sailors who could never be at the right place at the right time because they could neither navigate nor tell time. "There're all Uzbeks," his assistant commander agreed.

In those eight minutes, the *Petroverdets* had traveled farther than Svjatov had planned in the direction of the *Glomar Explorer* and the as yet undetected U.S.S. *Queenfish.*

The noisemakers were shut off. Suddenly the ocean was quiet. "Now," yelled Svjatov. "Immediate active search, three hundred and sixty degrees. Two sweeps and feed any targets directly into the computer. Then only passive search. Maintain quiet ship."

"Captain! I have submarine propellers bearing almost dead ahead." It was the passive-sonar operator.

"Active sonar!" shouted Svjatov.

"I have it. I am 'painting' a large submarine. Moving on a reciprocal course."

"Battle stations," screamed Svjatov, rushing to the sonar displays in the after section of the control room of the *Petroverdets.*

"Down!" screamed Svjatov, "make depth to two hundred and fifty meters! Hard right rudder! Twenty knots! Ready torpedo tubes for immediate action! Launch noisemaker!"

A moment later, even before the *Petroverdets* could respond to her captain's orders, a small canister was ejected from a tube in the submarine's outer hull. The device was propelled several hundred feet by compressed air. A few seconds later, it began generating acoustic signals, to lure enemy torpedoes away from the submarine.

At the same moment, almost ten miles away, Lieutenant James Graham, weapons officer of the U.S.S. *Queenfish,* depressed the firing key, and a Mark 37 torpedo sped from the submarine's No. 4 torpedo tube.

The torpedo was being guided by a thin wire, simultaneously unwound from the submarine and the torpedo. A torpedoman's mate first class, watching a sonar-control console, directed the torpedo—by sending signals through the wire—toward the image of the *Osaka Maru* being painted by the submarine's active sonar.

Suddenly, the American submarine's entire crew was electrified by the words, "Captain. I have a submarine on the screen! Dead ahead! Approximately our depth." The cry was from the enlisted man at a passive sonar console. "My God, sir. They've fired a torpedo or something." It was seven seconds after the *Petroverdets* had fired her noisemaker.

Stunned for an instant, Commander James Pratt stood frozen, his hands gripping the rail around the control platform in the submarine's control room.

Then, after seconds that seemed to be hours to some standing nearby: "John—the Mark 37 in the water. Send it after him." And then, "Hard left rudder. Make depth eight hundred feet. Stand by to launch a Mark 48 from number one tube."

The Mark 37 being guided toward the hulk of the *Osaka Maru,* suspended some four hundred feet beneath the *Glomar Explorer,* changed course at a signal from the *Queenfish* and headed toward the slowly approaching Soviet submarine. As the thin guidance wire ran out from the *Queenfish* and the torpedo, the line broke. An instant before, a signal had been transmitted to the torpedo, activating its self-contained homing sonar. This device was to guide the torpedo toward the propeller noises created by the *Petroverdets.*

But as the torpedo approached the submarine, it was distracted by the sounds produced by the decoy, now several hundred feet from the submarine. When the Mark 37 reached the decoy, the torpedo's 330-pound warhead, packed with HBX-3 high explosive, detonated.

In response to the approaching Mark 37, Captain Svjatov had hastily ordered the preparations to fire two homing torpedoes at the last known position of the *Queenfish.* The decoy fired by the *Petroverdets,* however, was interfering with the submarine's sonar, as were sounds now coming from the hulk suspended beneath the *Glomar Explorer*. This interference with the Soviet submarine's sonar forced Svjatov to delay firing.

The Soviet submarine, in an accelerating downward curve, collided with the *Queenfish.*

The American submarine displaced almost 7,000 tons submerged, almost twice that of the submarine *Petroverdets*. Thus, the American submarine, which was at about the same depth and making the same slow speed as the Soviet submarine when they detected each other, went down faster than the Sovet craft. The Soviet submarine passed just over the American one. The hulls scraped. A sudden attempt by Svjatov to bring his submarine up the moment before they collided raised his submarine's bow, smashing its rudder and propellers down onto the steel hull of the *Queenfish*.

The collision dislodged the Soviet submarine's rudder from its post. Both propellers were bent and began vibrating wildly. The *Petroverdets* began to rise and then, as the vibrations of the propeller shafts loosened the packing glands that sealed the submarine's inner pressure hull—where it was pierced by the twin propeller shafts—water began pouring in. At a depth of almost 800 feet, the seawater was under a pressure of some 350 pounds per square inch. The inrush of water slowly made the *Petroverdets* stern heavy. As power was increased to the propellers in an attempt to drive the submarine upward, the vibrating shafts admitted more water.

The steep angles knocked many men off their feet, and they slid backward as the deck tilted upward. Men at critical controls attempted to hold stanchions or piping, wrapping their arms or legs around them like monkeys as they feverishly turned valves and pulled levers.

"All watertight doors secured."

"Water in number two machinery room."

Rapidly, Svjatov gave orders to blow all ballast tanks, to expel with high pressure the tons of water that had been taken into the submarine tanks to make her neutrally buoyant before submerging.

"All ballast tanks being blown except number seven and number eight—possibly damage."

"Engineer believes he can hold the power load."

Information was being passed to the control center by an intercom system. Svjatov stood on the attack platform in the control room. He listened, carefully, very carefully, especially to the depth reading.

"Keel depth two-one-five meters . . ."

"Two-two-five meters . . ."

"Two . . ."

His responses were clear, concise. He had trained himself and his crew to act carefully and deliberately in time of crisis. This discipline was the result.

"Keel depth three-six-zero meters . . ." The center of the submarine was almost 1,200 feet beneath the surface; the stern deeper by perhaps 100 feet.

"All tanks blown except number seven and eight . . . Engineer officer reports those tanks may be damaged."

"May be?" It was the first time Svjatov's voice seemed under strain. His engineer officer was too good not to immediately know the condition of the ballast tanks.

"Depth now three-seven-zero meters, Captain."

"Keel depth remains three-seven-zero. We are holding depth, Captain!"

"Silence," Svjatov ordered when several men in the control room yelled loudly.

The submarine seemed to hover, but with her bow still angled sharply upward.

"Engineer to captain." The loudspeaker in the control room carried the calm, husky voice of the ship's engineer officer, Captain Third/Rank Mikhail Zhdanov.

"I am using high-pressure air to fend off the flooding of the machinery spaces. The propulsion plant remains on line. I believe the damage to the shafts is minimal. But we have bent propeller blades, and our rudder is heavily damaged. We have two damaged ballast tanks—numbers seven and eight; I would like to expend the rest of our air to them to keep any pockets free of water."

"Continue to blow the damaged ballast tanks—blow everything," Svjatov ordered. Although the descent of the submarine had halted with the stern over 1,300 feet beneath the surface, the submarine could not hang suspended indefinitely. She would continue to sink. A few hundred feet more and the submarine would reach her theoretical collapse depth. Even at the present depth, a damaged valve or other opening to the sea might give way. It was unlikely that the shedding of water ballast alone would bring her up.

"I will try our low-power turbine," Zhdanov responded. Svjatov and the others in the control room who heard his voice knew that if anyone could handle a potential catastrophe, it would be Zhdanov.

In the control room they felt the vibration as the *Petroverdets'* twin propeller shafts began to turn slowly. The vibration semed to increase, almost imperceptibly, as the engineer officer, standing with his arms wrapped around the station master's chair in the maneuvering room, gave orders for the throttle levers to be inched forward.

Zhdanov's deep voice sounded from the loudspeakers: "We are taking some water through the shaft seals, but our pumps can handle it."

"Captain, sir, keel depth now three-six-five meters . . .

"Now three six-zero . . ."

This time Svjatov didn't try to quiet the men cheering in the control room. The Petroverdets *was slowly pushing herself upward.*

Slowly, painfully, she rose toward the surface. Svjatov did not try to change her steep angle, fearing that such an attempt might slow or halt her return to the surface.

From the submarine's signal tube popped a cylinder that rose rapidly to the surface.

Four miles away, her pressure hull badly scraped but otherwise intact, the U.S.S. *Queenfish* rose slowly toward the surface. "Come right to course one-six-zero," Pratt ordered. "We're heading for the *Glomar.*"

33

The *Albert* was level with the waterline of the *Osaka Maru*. The Japanese hulk, hanging evenly from the *Glomar Explorer* but angled over to port about thirty degrees, swayed slightly on the cables that held the huge claws grasping the ship. A school of fish appeared, followed by a shark. The shark wheeled and, curious, swept by the *Albert*'s viewing ports. The lights of the *Albert* caught the shark for a moment. Its eyes gleamed green. The lights played along the *Osaka Maru*'s hull, which was rusty and almost solidly barnacled, except for some patches of gray and the remains of white markings.

"The crosses," Gunnison said. "The white crosses for safe passage. The *Tigerfish* crew never saw those crosses. Take her up about ten feet."

The *Albert* rose and passed along the rail on the starboard side of the main deck. The lights picked up the remains of a life raft. The *Albert* hovered near it. The raft, still tethered, seemed to float on an invisible surface. In the tangle of the raft was a skull, bobbing within the rags of a life jacket and a web of boat lines.

Ishiwata spoke rapidly in Japanese, in a keening voice. A *renga* was flowing from his soul: "In the green-black silence of a forgotten sea . . ."

Albert glided slowly toward the bow, its lights rippling along the hull. Suddenly, the beam showed nothing. Only blackness.

"That's it," Gunnison said. "The videotapes showed that two torpedoes probably hit close together, tearing open the midships section. Amazing the hulk has held together. There—closer, get closer."

The *Albert* edged closer. The lights showed jagged, blackened steel. Frankel nosed the *Albert* toward the center of the opening and swung the forward lights around so that they pierced the darkness, only to reveal more darkness.

"Closer, closer," Gunnison urged.

Instead, Frankel pulled the *Albert* back from the opening.

"No deal, Gunnison," Frankel said. "You don't know *Albert* the way I do. He doesn't go inside things, especially dead ships. We're heading back up to the *Glomar*."

"Come on, you can get a little bit closer. What about the *Albert*'s claw? How far will it reach?"

"Twenty, maybe forty, feet since we rigged the extension."

"There's still the recovery basket, isn't there?"

"Yeah. We've got the basket for saving stuff off the bottom that we pick up with the claw. What do you have in mind?"

"All I'm asking, Frankel, is that we take a good look. And, if it looks okay, we can get closer and feel around with the claw. Jesus, Fankel, we're talking about gold. You'll be touching gold—lots of it."

It was Gunnison's last chance—and Ishiwata's too. Now Ishiwata spoke up, as if emerging from a trance.

"Proof," said Ishiwata softly. "Proof. One bar of gold from the *Osaka Maru*. Gold from the green dark."

"Okay," Frankel said. "A little closer. To see the gold."

Frankel maneuvered the *Albert* a few feet closer to the hole, aiming the submersible so that its powerful lights shone into the blackness of hold No. 4, ripped open by the *Tigerfish* torpedoes so long ago. Something in the hold was gleaming.

No one spoke. The only sound was the whirring of the *Albert*'s electric motors and the low hum of the air-conditioning. Gunnison, Frankel, and Ishiwata pressed their faces to the three viewing ports. Frankel eased the *Albert* closer to the jagged opening. The submersible's nose was inside the opening—a few inches inside the hulk of the *Osaka Maru*. There was another low hum as Frankel activated the controls that extended the telescoping grappling claw. It scraped across broken hull plates and into the hull. A light near the end of the claw threw a thin beam into the darkness.

Albert turned slightly. Another gleam. And another.

Frankel's right hand grasped the control lever for the claw, so that the claw seemed almost an extension of his hand. "It's going to be close. Maybe I can touch it, or get one of those—bars—*they're bars of gold!*"

Red lights flashed on the *Albert*'s control panel.

"What is it—?" Gunnison asked, a hint of suppressed panic in his voice.

"Nothing, Harry. We've damaged one of the external air bottles. Probably hit the hull. Tight squeeze here. Not to worry. We shouldn't need it. The line automatically closes off."

"There!" It was Ishiwata. Again all three men pressed their faces to the view ports. There, perhaps twenty feet from the submersible was a stack of gold bars that had tumbled down onto the deck. Nothing remained of the crates that had held them when they were loaded aboard the *Osaka Maru*.

Then, somewhere in the distance, there was a low rumble—a muffled explosion—the distant explosion of the Mark 37 torpedo. The sound was barely audible in the *Albert*. A slight underwater swell gently rocked the submersible.

Frankel activated one of the small thruster motors, first backing the *Albert* off and then nestling against the hulk, edging slowly into the opening. The long telescopic claw opened as it was about to touch the heap of golden bars.

"The first one's mine," Frankel said. Slowly, using his left hand to control the submersible and the right to control the claw, he grasped a bar of gold from the heap in the *Osaka Maru*.

"Got it!"

The bar gleamed dully in the beam of light from the claw.

Ishiwata, reciting softly, finished his *renga:* "To rise again. To touch light."

As the first bar was pulled from near the bottom of the heap of gold, two other bars fell forward. Four other bars moved slightly. Then eight. Some of the gold bars fell from the heap to the deck. Others moved. Soon the whole stack of gold was moving, alive, a heaving yellow mass.

The *Osaka Maru* swayed gently as the weight shifted in her ravaged hold. The gold began to slide. Bars tumbled, and the remains of stacks tipped forward. Then, the hulk, already turned at a thirty-degree angle, rolled another degree, at first imperceptibly . . . and then another.

For an instant, the *Albert*'s lights illuminated a wave of gold bars swirling through the darkness.

Frankel turned the throttle knobs to full power as he tried desperately to back the submersible away from the avalanche of gold. Bars of gold battered the *Albert*'s thin outer hull. The spotlights reflected the gold for one last second and then were snuffed out.

"Get us out! Get us out of here!" Gunnison shouted in the darkness.

"I'm trying. I'm trying," Frankel quietly replied. "We're moving as fast as we can."

The staccato pounding of the gold bars increased, beating against the hull, tearing away the spotlights and other external fittings—cameras, cables, and oxygen cylinders. The starboard propeller pod was ripped off, and the *Albert* spun violently, smashing against the hull of the *Osaka Maru*.

"That's it," Frankel said calmly. "No more power."

The shifting weight of the gold threatened to roll the *Osaka Maru* on her side. Still held in the grasp of the *Glomar*'s claws, the ship twisted and, in a slow, agonizing movement, broke in two. The separate sections slipped from the *Glomar Explorer*'s claws and followed the shower of gold to the floor of the Formosa Strait. The floatation bags that helped hold the hulk slipped away and caught on one of the claws.

"Hang on," Frankel said as he punched an emergency button for compressed air to blow out the water remaining in the craft's ballast tanks.

"We're going up!" Gunnison shouted. He paused as the cramped cabin filled with the sound of hissing air. "I think we're going to make it." The submersible began an uncontrolled, rolling ascent.

As the *Albert* reached the surface, waves washed over the craft. Frankel opened the hatch, pulled himself out, and reached back to help Gunnison. Balancing himself against the hatch combing with his left hand, Gunnison with his right hand groped down into the cabin for Ishiwata. Each wave hitting the *Albert* was spilling water over the hatch combing and down into the craft. Gunnison looked up at Frankel.

"Some of our ballast tanks are smashed," Frankel said. "We're lower in the water than we should be. We're going to flood and sink!"

As Frankel spoke, he looked over the side at the damage. "The gold bar! It's still in the claw. I'm going to get it. Get Ishiwata out, fast."

Frankel shed his sneakers and jacket and dove into the sea.

Gunnison frantically reached down for Ishiwata's hand. "God-damn it," he screamed, "come on up." There was no answer. Gunnison lowered himself back into the water of the cabin. He saw Ishiwata, still stoically seated, as if the voyage had not yet ended.

"This damn thing is sinking," Gunnison shouted into Ishiwata's face.

"I know. I have vowed to recover the gold or to join it. There is now no chance of recovery."

"Bullshit!" Gunnison grabbed Ishiwata's arm, pulled him erect, and pushed him up the short steel ladder and through the hatch against a cascade of water. Out of the cabin, Ishiwata instinctively grabbed a stanchion of the *Albert*'s deck, now awash.

When Gunnison emerged, he screamed, "Frankel!" Then he saw him. Frankel was a few feet below the surface, his legs entwined in the *Albert*'s smashed recovery basket, his arms still grasping the bar of gold. He had locked his legs in the basket to steady himself while he disengaged the gold bar from the recovery claw. He was trying to kick himself free as he clutched the gold bar.

Gunnison felt the *Albert* sinking from under him. The sea was pouring over the lip of the hatch combing. He grabbed Ishiwata and slipped off the slanting deck. In a moment, the *Albert*—and Frankel—disappeared.

Ishiwata had lost consciousness. Gunnison threw an arm around Ishiwata's head to keep him afloat. Bobbing between choppy waves, Gunnison could see nothing but sky and sea.

"Submarine closing!" the sonar man aboard the *Glomar Explorer* shouted into his phone. Then, a split second later: "Torpedo in water!"

On the bridge, Dysart knew that, with the hulk hanging beneath his ship, evasive maneuvers were impossible. "Just hold on, son. I'm on my way." He gave the conn to Mooney, ran down the ladder to the main deck, and sprinted to the sonar shack.

By the time he reached the shack, the sonar operator had two submarines on the screen. There was a flash on the screen, and then everyone aboard the *Glomar* felt the vibration of a nearby explosion.

The phone rang. It was Mooney. "Roth is getting a message from our sub, Captain. She was in a collision, apparently with another sub. She's surfacing and—"

"Captain!" the sonarman shouted, pointing to the screen. "One of the subs is going down . . . I lost her."

"Find her!" Dysart said. He punched a button. "Roth. Dysart here. What have we got?"

"Apparently two—repeat, two—submarines, Captain. Ours is just breaking the surface. The other one—"

"Captain," the sonarman interrupted, "I've got the Russian sub back. She's sort of hanging there. Wait. She's—"

Dysart was thrown against a bulkhead as the *Glomar* heaved to port, shuddered, then lurched to starboard. He cut off Mooney and punched Engineering: "Dysart. What the hell is going on?"

"We've lost some stabilization, sir. It's the hulk. The *Osaka Maru* is beginning to break up."

Dysart hit another button. "Mr. Mooney. Blow the bolts."

"What about *Albert?*" Mooney asked.

"I've got to assume Frankel got the hell out of there when he heard the torpedo. Right now, I've got a ship in trouble."

A few moments later, Dysart was back on the bridge, and the *Glomar* shuddered again as the last remnants of the *Osaka Maru* were released to plunge to the ocean floor.

34

IT WAS HALF PAST MIDNIGHT and the crisis committee was meeting again in the Situation Room of the White House. On a sideboard along the only wall without maps or projector screens, stewards had put sandwiches and fruit, cups and saucers, a coffee urn, and a pot of tea. In front of each place at the long table was a copy of a message sent over the Soviet-American hot-line teletype and simultaneously delivered by hand to the State Department by the Soviet ambassador.

The original hot line actually was hardly more than a telegraph line, a special cable circuit—Washington-London-Copenhagen-Stockholm-Helsinki-Moscow—backed up by a Washington-Tangier-Moscow radio telegraph circuit. But in 1978 the hot line became not a line but a faster and more reliable space communications system. The United States reserves a circuit on an Intelsat satellite for emergency Washington-Moscow communications, and the Soviets use a circuit on a Molniya II satellite.

The message being read by the crisis committee stated that a Soviet submarine on a "normal operation" in the Formosa Strait was being threatened by U.S. naval forces. Similar messages were routinely received every few days over standard U.S.-Soviet diplomatic communication channels. The messages were just as routinely ignored. But this one was ominous because of the use of the hot line and the simultaneous delivery by the ambassador.

Moments after this message was received, there had been a telephone call directly from the Soviet general secretary to the secretary of state, who was awakened by a State Department watch officer. A message had just been received, Leonid Brezhnev said through an interpreter—with some excited comments from Brezhnev himself injected in his good but halting English—that a U.S. nuclear submarine had attacked and possibly sunk a Soviet submarine. The message, the interpreter said, was still being authenticated, but because the Soviet Union had not detected any U.S.

strategic forces on alert, Brezhnev was calling the secretary of state on a personal basis "to ensure that there was no misstep that could lead to a 'crisis situation'."

The secretary of state had immediately advised the president, who was attending a Latin American defense summit conference in Acapulco, Mexico. He had reconvened the crisis committee and had begun discussing with his advisers in Mexico the public alarm that might be generated if he abruptly left the conference. The president had also approved the secretary of defense's recommendation that some U.S. military forces increase their readiness level to DEFCON-3, without public notice. Some Strategic Air Command planes carrying nuclear bombs had gone aloft. Special Forces units in Europe had reported to military airfields. General officers had begun replacing lower-ranking officers at the command post in Cheyenne Mountain, Colorado, the underground headquarters of the North American Aerospace Defense Command. The National Security Agency and the Central Intelligence Agency were ordered to seek out indicators of any step-up in Soviet military readiness.

Now, the secretary of defense was telling the crisis committee, those reports were coming in. "Even while they were telling us that the Soviets wanted to keep things cool," the secretary said, "Brezhnev was putting his own strategic forces on a higher level of alert." He paused to shuffle through his papers. "And, based on some Japanese radio intercepts that they automatically share with us, we think the Soviets' Far East air forces are really being readied for something; they seem to be going on a full alert."

Taking another sheet of paper in his hand and adjusting his gold-rimmed glasses, Secretary of Defense Michael Woolsey said, "This last item, from an extremely sensitive NSA source, says that the message that started this flap was transmitted from an emergency signal buoy released by a Soviet submarine."

Woolsey, who had been under secretary of the Navy several years before, briefly told the crisis committee that the Soviet submarine device not only transmitted a message that a submarine was down but also played back the last eight minutes of sounds in the control room, much like an aircraft flight recorder.

"Here's the rub," continued Woolsey. "Our source says that the message that the buoy transmitted claimed that the Russian submarine was under attack from a U.S. submarine. That's almost certainly the *Queenfish*."

"Oh my God, oh my God, oh my God . . ." It was the vice president, stunned and ashen-faced. Everyone else in the room was silent. Saunders stood up, walked over to the vice president's chair at the head of the table, put an arm on his shoulder, and spoke quietly to him. A moment later Saunders and the vice president walked from the room.

Woolsey took no further notice of the vice president's exit. "Gentlemen," Woolsey said, "the president will be returning to Washington in about three hours. Right about now Air Force One is picking him up. He has asked Saunders to continue to handle things here in the committee and for me to stand by to assume Natonal Command Authority should something break before he gets here. I have asked Admiral Thompson, the vice chief of naval operations, to sit in with us, as well as General Buchanan, who is acting chairman of the Joint Chiefs while the chairman is with the president."

"Is the chairman also coming back?" asked Martin, who continued to sit on the side, taking his own form of shorthand minutes for the president.

"No. We've got an F-15 fighter taking him to Albuquerque, where he will board *Looking Glass,* the airborne command post, along with Kerr, who is about to become deputy secretary of defense, plus the commander of the Strategic Air Command. That way, just in case things get out of hand here, we will have a good team in the air to run the show."

Woolsey stood quietly for a moment. Everyone in the room knew that *Looking Glass* would be aloft as insurance in case of "strategic decapitation," a Soviet nuclear attack aimed at wiping out national leadership with strikes at Washington and key command centers. Woolsey with his matter-of-fact briefing had just conjured up images of nuclear war.

Saunders returned and went back to his position at the foot of the table. The vice president's chair, at the head of the table, remained empty. "The vice president is okay," Saunders said. "Really okay. But he's going upstairs to lie down. The doc gave him a shot to help him relax."

He paused and resumed his briefing voice. The phone in front of Saunders buzzed. During a meeting, that phone buzzed only for calls from the president or for a call that the White House communications duty officer felt was of vital importance.

The call was from a member of the Intelligence Community Staff, who told Saunders that there was still no way to confirm that a Soviet submarine had indeed been sunk. Saunders turned to the director of central intelligence, who while sitting at the table had periodically held hushed telephone conversations with his office.

"Apparently there is still no confirmation of what's happened out there. Have you got anything more from your sources?"

"Nothing to add at this point. I can confirm what you've just said from a second source, from the people at Fort Meade."

Meade, about twenty miles northeast of Washington, was the site of the vast National Security Agency, which detects, decodes, and translates communications of interest to the United States. The director of central intelligence is the nominal head of the NSA and the DIA, the Defense Intelligence Agency. But, in a crisis, a man's effectiveness depended on what he could find out, not on what a table of organization said. And the director was finding out little. Bob Martin wondered if the director would, like Admiral Watson, find himself driven out into the cold by a crisis.

While the director was speaking, a White House messenger entered the Situation Room and handed a message folder to Admiral Thompson. He opened the folder and took from it several sheets of paper. "This is a message from the *Glomar Explorer*," Thompson said. "She's been under some sort of helicopter attack—from pirates, according to this.

"The *Glomar* beat them off with no casualties except two wounded. Apparently several helicopters were involved. A CIA man"—Thompson looked down the table to the director—"a man named Gunnison, came aboard and warned the *Glomar*. This report is a bit confusing. My watch officer has asked for amplifying information.

"But, first, the ship appears to be all right, and there is no further threat of attack—although damned if I know how they know that, and, second, the hulk of that gold ship was released."

"Was there anything in that message about the U.S. or Russian submarines?" Saunders asked.

"No sir, not a word."

"Thank you, Admiral. But *pirates?*" Saunders allowed himself a quick smile. "Surely that can't be right. Terrorists, maybe. But certainly not pirates."

"As a matter of fact, Mr. Saunders, we've been getting more and more reports about pirates. Just a month ago six men boarded a Military Sealift Command ship, a freighter, in the Strait of Malacca and forced the master to open the safe. They got away in a speedboat with about twenty thousand dollars. It was like a mugging. But helicopters. That's escalation!"

"Well," Saunders said, "tell your people to keep you advised of further communications with *Glomar*. Okay, let's see what we have here," Saunders continued. He placed a yellow pad directly in front of him and neatly wrote the numeral one. "One," he said, writing as he spoke, "we have an American submarine in the area. A: Status unknown. B: Not in contact.

"Two. Russian submarine in the area. A: Reportedly sunk. B: Possibly attacked by U.S. sub.

"Three. We have the *Glomar Explorer*, which seems to have survived this pirate thing, and has released the gold ship. And—"

35

THE TWO MEN BOBBED IN the choppy sea, Gunnison holding the back of Ishiwata's life jacket to keep his head above the water. Ishiwata, barely conscious, was moaning rhythmically in Japanese. Rising on a crest, Gunnison looked around the empty sea. He wondered how far the tumbling submersible, fighting to get to the surface, had carried them from the *Glomar Explorer*. Neither Frankel nor the craft could be seen.

Gunnison, struggling to keep himself and his burden afloat, was already exhausted after only a few minutes in the water. He had kicked off his sneakers, but he could feel even that effort sapping his strength. He tried to think of something that could give him and his burden a little more time. His memory reached back to basic training when the Navy swimming instructor had taught the sailors how to pull off their trousers while in the water, knot the pants legs, and capture air in them to provide floatation. Gunnison wanted to laugh, but couldn't. The chief who showed how easy it was to do this had never done it in the ocean, exhausted and trying to keep an old, partially conscious man alive.

"Damn it," Gunnison screamed. He was trying to concentrate on counting how many times he paddled with his free left arm, how many times he pedaled with his feet. As long as he could count, he knew he could stay alive. He began to imagine that he was biking up a long, gentle hill. He knew he could reach the top, but he also knew there was no top. And he was getting ready to stop. But first, before he stopped the bike, he would get rid of the package he was holding with his right arm.

He tried to remember what was in the package. And if he stopped biking he knew he could not reach the top of the hill, where Chia Min was waiting for him. He sensed she was there, waiting for him.

"Damn it," he screamed again, to clear his mind. What was in the package he was going to put down?

Package. Gunnison was startled back to reality by what he thought he saw for a moment on the crest of a wave. *A package.* It looked like a huge tin can, and it was only a few yards away. Perhaps something had broken loose from the *Albert,* something he could cling to. Using what he feared were his last reserves of strength, Gunnison threw his right arm across Ishiwata's chest, turned him on his back, and thrashed toward the pitching object.

As he rode high on the next wave, stroking his left arm, moving slowly toward the object, he could see that it was a gray cylinder. He lunged for it, and pain shot along his arm. His fingers slipped along the smooth top and then found a rim. He folded his fingers around the rim and felt himself bobbing with the cylinder, which was about three feet long and eight or nine inches in diameter. The cylinder was buoyant enough to help him remain afloat. He jammed Ishiwata's fingers into the rim and worked his hand around to cover Ishiwata's. The weight of the two men pulled the cylinder to an almost horizontal position. Protruding from the top of the cylinder was an extended, telescoping aerial. Inscribed around the top were Cyrillic letters.

Gunnison realized that he could neither hold the now-unconscious Ishiwata afloat nor remain afloat himself for much longer. He had been in the water, he reckoned, for almost half an hour, and he was getting too numb to survive. At some long moment later, he suddenly felt the sea heave around him. He heard a loud sound he could not distinguish, and then he saw it—something surging from the waves . . . The *Osaka Maru* . . . A whale . . . No . . . A great black hulk with a sharp-edged silhouette.

He seemed to slip into some kind of darkness, and then he felt hands on him, hauling him. He was on a black deck. He sensed rather than knew that he was on a submarine. He could feel energy pulsating beneath him. There were men around him, saying things he did not understand. Ishiwata lay curled up next to him on the listing deck. He seemed very small and very quiet. A man in a uniform crouched and leaned his head against Ishiwata's chest, listening.

Then arms were on him again and Gunnison was taken off the deck and into what he now knew was not an American submarine. He was coming back to full consciousness, and he now recognized the language he was hearing. He was being taken into a Soviet submarine.

The man who had listened at Ishiwata's chest handed Gunnison a white mug. He took a sip of hot coffee laced with a large dose of brandy. The man said, in heavily accented English, "Friend is dead. He has died. From the water."

The man wore the green, loose-fitting work uniform of a Soviet naval officer. "I am Karpov. Number three officer. You are prisoner on Soviet submarine."

"Wait one minute. Are you sure my friend is dead?"

"Yes," Karpov said. "When we pull you from water, you both pass out. Your friend dead. You—how do you say?—you blued out when we pull you from sea."

"Where is my friend?" Gunnison asked. He wondered now what Ishiwata had been saying. Poetry, Gunnison hoped. A *renga*.

"In sea," Karpov said. "No way here"—he swept the air with his hand—" . . . a body."

"He did join the gold."

"He? Who is he?" Karpov asked. He held up a clear plastic bag. In it Gunnison could see a billfold, a pair of glasses, a Rolex watch, currency in a gold money clip, and an iron ring.

"A Japanese business man. His name was Ishiwata."

"You? You are American sailor?"

"No. An American—businessman. Gunnison." He held up the mug. "Thank you for the coffee and the brandy. Did you surface to save us—to pull us from the sea?"

"American joke? You cannot see? You are sailor. Submarine sailor. You know this is damaged submarine."

"What happened to your submarine?" Gunnison asked.

Karpov angrily swore in Russian. "You know. You are not fool. Your American submarine tried torpedo and ram. They left us for being sunk. They hear breaking of ship noises, and they believe we sunk." He said something in Russian and then put his face close to Gunnison's. "Your submarine. Tell me about your submarine."

"I know nothing of this. See how old my friend was. No sailor. We saw your rescue buoy in the water." Gunnison made motions with his hands to indicate the cylinder. "I—we—held onto it."

"Not for . . . for . . ." Karpov said a Russian word. "Not for that. Not for saving. It is communicator. Our means for telling our fleet commander we are under attack."

"Under attack? Who attacked you?"

"Your submarine and your *Glomar Explorer* ship."

"You do not understand. There was not an attack. No attack. You—we—you and I must speak to our superiors. The *Glomar Explorer* was on a peaceful mission."

"What do you mean? Were you lifting another Soviet submarine?"

"No. No. Let me speak to your captain."

"No. The captain is very busy with submarine. In few minutes our communication ship will be here. *Primorye* officers will interrogate you."

"Damn it! You don't understand. The American submarine was not attacking you. She was involved with the *Glomar* and a sunken ship, an old Japanese ship."

Karpov, for the first time, looked more interested, more puzzled, than angry.

"This is very, very . . . difficult, Karpov. You don't understand."

"My English not good, Gunnison."

"Your English is fine. But this is very dangerous. *War,* Karpov. We may need Moscow. Washington. White House. Kremlin. Let me talk to your captain."

"He speaks no English at all. I am intelligence officer and assistant executive officer. I speak English on submarine."

"One more time, Karpov. The American submarine was *not* trying to sink you. If you told that to your fleet commander, *you* could be starting World War Three. Can you understand that?"

"The Soviet Union does not start World War Three."

"Okay. Fine. Let me talk to your captain. Then I must send a message to the American fleet commanders telling them what did happen."

"You will talk, Gunnison. You will talk to the officers of *Primorye.*"

"The *Primorye,* Karpov. Is there an admiral on board?" Gunnison drew imaginary stars on his shoulders and pointed to Karpov's shoulders. "Big shots on the *Primorye?*"

Karpov smiled. "Yes, Gunnison. Big shots."

36

By the time Gunnison had been taken by rubber raft to the *Primorye,* escorted by two armed guards to a large cabin, and placed in a chair across a table from an empty chair, the strategic forces of the United States and the Soviet Union were nearing a hair-trigger alert status. The president had arrived back in Washington and had attempted to talk to the Soviet prime minister on the hot line. But the prime minister, convinced that an American submarine had attacked and destroyed a Soviet sub, was in no mood to talk amiably. He had broken off communication and raised his defense forces' alert one notch. The crisis committee now had three crises to deal with: escalation, lack of solid information from either side about what the other side was doing, and fear that the American public would learn of the rush toward U.S.-U.S.S.R. confrontation and react with panic.

The man who entered the admiral's cabin of the *Primorye* knew much about the crisis. The intelligence ship had become the principal source of information to the Kremlin, and Admiral Emil Nikolayevich Spiridonov, commander-in-chief of the Soviet Pacific Fleet, had been flown out to the *Primorye* with three staff officers to take personal charge. Now he faced Gunnison. Two other officers had followed him in and had taken chairs at opposite ends of the table.

The one to the admiral's right introduced himself as Captain Second/Rank Lysenko. "Josef Lysenko. I am an interpreter of the *first* rank, Gunnison," he said. "My job is to"—he broke into a passable imitation of a southern accent—"give the good ol' boys here the real stuff from the words we-all pick up from American rah-dio transmissions. So, pal, you just tell me and the admiral here what the hell's been going on."

"First of all, Joe, let's make sure the good ol' boys on both sides know that what is happening is *not* Pearl Harbor. There may be people on both sides who think that, Joe."

Lysenko spoke rapidly to Spiridonov, who nodded impassively

and then began asking a series of questions that Lysenko relayed in English. The questions and answers rapidly reconstructed the events leading up to the helicopter assault on the *Glomar*. Then came a question that stunned Gunnison:

"Why did the Chinese destroyer sink the junk known as the *Golden Moon?*"

"What! The *Golden Moon* sunk?" Gunnison asked, half rising in his chair. "How do you know this? Are you sure this is true?"

"Easy, Gunnison, easy," Lysenko said. "The battle was seen through the periscope of our submarine. We also picked up the Chinese destroyer's long transmission of the battle report. Yes, it is certainly true. But, Gunnison, it was a minor event. It—"

"A woman. There was a woman I loved aboard," Gunnison said haltingly. "Were there any survivors?"

"It was a junk hit by a Styx missile, Gunnison. Damn sorry." Lysenko softly said something to the admiral, who nodded and then spoke to his aide. The young officer strode rapidly out of the room.

"The admiral has asked for the Russian text of the Chinese ship's battle report," Lysenko said. "I haven't seen it. He thought it might give you an answer. I will translate . . . whatever it may say about the woman. Your woman."

"Thanks. And thank the admiral. Tell him I appreciate it. But now, quickly, we should be doing something about this crisis between our countries. I'd like to talk to him about what we call the hot line."

Both sides agreed that the transmission from the *Primorye* would be in English first, then in Russian, and that the *Glomar Explorer,* now 500 yards off the *Primorye,* would relay the transmission to a U.S. satellite. Officially, the patch-up was not the hot line; in reality, it technically came close. Each country could hear what the other said. Gunnison talked directly to the Situation Room through the *Glomar,* and his words were simultaneously translated by Lysenko and relayed, through the *Primorye,* to the Kremlin. Spiridonov's words were also translated by Lysenko and monitored in the Situation Room by a U.S. State Department interpreter.

Gunnison augmented his report with information passed to him from the *Queenfish* and the *Glomar*. He also had been given some personal information: A line in the Chinese destroyer's battle report said: "Young Chinese woman claims American residency among survivors. Refer to U.S. Embassy, Beijing."

Gunnison concluded his report with an answer to a gruff inquiry directly from the president. "Yes, Mr. President," Gunnison said, "I can assure you the *Osaka Maru* and her gold are on the bottom. I saw the gold go past my eyes."

An hour later, Gunnison, clutching a bottle of vodka, climbed down a ladder to the *Glomar*'s launch.

"There was some back-channel chatter going on during that broadcast of yours," Dysart told Gunnison over a glass of vodka in the wardroom. "By presidential direction, the U.S. Embassy in Beijing is to see to it that Chia Min is flown to Hawaii. That's where we're going, too. You're welcome to stay aboard. I'm also supposed to tell you that the director wants you to write the report on this. He says you're the only one who knows who did what. And then the director suggests that you stay in Hawaii until he figures out what to do with a guy he fired and wants to shoot, and who the president wants to pin a medal on."

EPILOGUE

THE PRICE OF GOLD WENT PAST $300 A TROY OUNCE for the first time in history when Ishiwata suddenly decided to seek the *Osaka Maru*.

In January 1980, with the *Osaka Maru* and her gold scattered beyond recovery on the floor of the Pacific, the price of gold reached $660 an ounce.

AUTHOR'S NOTE

According to official U.S. Navy records, on April 1, 1945, a U.S. submarine torpedoed and sank a Japanese merchant ship in the Formosa Strait. The merchant ship had been given safe-passage assurances by the American government for the purpose of carrying supplies to Allied prisoners of war in southeast Asia. There was only one survivor. Immediately after the sinking, the commanding officer of the submarine was relieved of command, and subsequently court-martialed, and found guilty.

All of the events and actions ascribed to U.S. submarines and submariners in the Pacific War actually occurred. But there was no submarine named *Tigerfish* and no commanding officer named David Porter. Rather, the authors have combined events and actions of several United States submarines and naval officers in this tale of the *Tigerfish* and the *Osaka Maru* and what occurred after World War II.